DOMINION

SWORD OF JUSTICE: BOOK 2

EVA HULETT

Cover designed by: Art By Kerri

This book is a work of fiction. Names, characters, places, and incidents either are products of the author's imagination or are used fictitiously. Any resemblance to actual persons, living or dead, events, or locales is entirely coincidental.

Eva Hulett
Visit my website at www.EvaHulett.com

Printed in the United States of America

First Printing: April 2019

ISBN-978-1-7339590-0-1

Dadda,
Thank you for perpetuating the stubborn gene.
You made me strong enough to push through hurt, closed doors
and impossibility.
Without you, I would've given up at the beginning.

CHAPTER ONE

Aiden woke to a knock on his door. Rolling to his side, he grabbed his phone from the nightstand. 1:35.

"Father Aiden?" Father Joseph's voice was muffled.

"Yes?"

"I need your help, Father." Joseph's words had a strange tone, like worry was pushing them through the door.

"Just a minute." Aiden got out of bed and looked around the room for his T-shirt. He'd only been in the parish for a week. The lack of sleep kept him from gathering his clothes with ease. At Abraham's house, with Elidad, he knew right where he would've left his shirt. Rubbing the sleep out of his eyes, he caught a glimpse of it lying across the chair in the corner. When he opened the door Joseph's face was as white as the shirt he'd just pulled over his head.

"What can I do for you, Joseph?"

"I need you to come with me, quickly. Please."

An elevated pitch emanated from under the fenders of Father Joseph's car when they stopped kitty-corner to an apartment building. Parking the car on the street, the priests walked down the block towards the entrance. It was an older building, but its white paint was clean and the fire escape didn't look rickety. A green canvas, worn by weather, shaded the front doors from the streetlights. It wasn't ripped or tattered, just slightly askew in color, hinting its age.

"So, what are we doing here?" Aiden asked, hoping for an explanation.

Joseph's eyes shifted.

"Last night, I came to this apartment to visit a family from our church. Their daughter, Emily, has been ill. It was late when they called, but her parents asked if I would come over and pray with them. Emily's been sick for months. Her doctors are at a loss. None of them can figure out what's wrong with her. The mother was a disaster. I'm pretty sure they think Emily is in her final days.

"After the parents and I prayed together, they urged me to go in and see Emily. She was lying in her bed." Joseph rubbed his fingers against the palms of his hands at the memory. "She's pale and her body looks frail. Dark rings under her eyes make her look deathly. Honestly, I thought it looked like her parents have been starving her."

"Are they?" Aiden asked.

The elevator they were waiting for opened. The two men entered.

Joseph pushed the button for the eighth floor. "I don't think so. They're good people. I've known them for years."

"Sometimes good people do bad things. Just because they're good to *you*, doesn't mean they can't abuse their child," Aiden said.

"They told me she refuses to eat. There was a tray of food in her room." Joseph's hand went through his hair as if ruffling it would shake loose the answer to what was wrong with Emily. "But when I spoke to her, she hid her face from me like an abused child might. She was definitely acting strange. She wouldn't look at me. She's never been like that … she knows me, she's always talked to me."

Joseph was four years Aiden's senior, making him thirty, but the concern weighing down his brow made him look older. In the first week of his new job, Aiden had learned Joseph's age but hadn't found out where he was from. Aiden guessed Joseph was a local Italian man; his Brooklyn accent and dark features gave him away.

Joseph continued his story. "Emily got out of bed and stood in the corner when I spoke to her. I told her I was going to pray with her and that praying would help. She appeared to understand, but when I began to pray, she started screaming."

Joseph's eyes looked empty, taken hostage by memory. "Her parents came bursting through the door like I was hurting her. Thank God I was standing on the opposite side of the room."

Joseph turned, locking eyes with Aiden. "There's something *wrong* with her. Her parents are afraid to be in the same room as her. I could *feel* it. They asked me to keep praying… they insisted. They were so desperate, I couldn't say no. I began again… Emily started screaming like she did before. She ran and grabbed my arm, pleading with me to stop. She acted like I was *hurting* her." Joseph pulled his long sleeve back to reveal a distinct bruise on his forearm.

The shadow of a tiny hand on Joseph's arm made Aiden realize a cold sweat had moistened his palms. He wiped them on his pressed, black slacks. "This happened just before you came to get me?"

"Yes, just over an hour ago. I don't bruise easily," he added.

The doors of the elevator opened.

Joseph was acting like he knew something more, but wasn't offering it. Aiden couldn't put all the clues together. It didn't sound like Emily *was* being abused.

Stepping into the hall lined with apartment doors, Aiden felt a rash of goosebumps tidal wave across his skin, climb up his neck, and wash past his knees. Carpet lined the floor, muffling their footsteps. It harbored a faint hint of mildew mixed with pet dander. Sounds of TV shows and conversations were a light hum behind some of the closed doors when they passed. Aiden looked at his watch. 2:46. How were these people still up?

Joseph escorted Aiden to a door and lightly knocked on it. They could hear footsteps inside. Aiden wasn't sure why, but his heart began to pound, almost loud enough to knock on the door itself.

A man with a receding hairline, three inches shorter than Aiden, answered the door, the chain still attached.

"Hello Father," the man said, closing the door. The drag of metal on metal was amplified in the quiet hallway as he removed the chain and opened it again.

Joseph introduced him. "This is Father Aiden."

"Hello," Aiden said.

"Thank you for coming, Father." The man stretched out his hand to shake Aiden's. "My name is Seth."

"Of course," Aiden answered, not sure what else to say.

"This way." Seth led them past the living room where a woman sat over her Bible with a rosary in her hand. She didn't bother to lift her head as the priests walked to the back of the apartment.

Seth stopped in front of a door. His fingers paused on the handle. Taking a deep breath, he cracked it open slowly.

"Emily," Seth said softly. With no response, Seth moved into the room. Aiden and Joseph followed.

A white lamp with a green shade, sparkly fringe and the image of Tinkerbell lit the room. Aiden's eyes went to the bed where he expected the sick girl to be. Empty. The white furniture contrasted the purple Disney princess comforter that lay across the mattress. A stuffed unicorn sat on a nightstand next to an untouched glass of water.

A movement caught Aiden's eye. Turning his head, he saw Emily's frail body. She couldn't be much older than eight. She was standing in the corner staring at the wall. The same feeling that prickled Aiden's skin earlier made him shiver as he watched her. There was something about the way she stared into the layers of white paint, her finger tracing an imaginary line, that made his heart pound against his ribcage.

"Emily," Seth spoke softly to his daughter, "the Father is back to see you and he brought a friend."

"I don't want to meet him." The little voice came from behind her long dark hair.

Aiden wondered how she knew he was a *he* without looking in his direction.

Seth looked over his shoulder, like he needed reassurance to speak to Emily. Rubbing his hands on his pants, he tried again. "Emily, these men can help you."

Joseph was right. Seth look terrified of Emily.

"I said: I don't want . . ." her face turned toward them, her eyes were yellow and her voice became deep and animalistic, "to meet him! I don't need their help!" Her breath was raspy as she panted. Anger shook her body.

Aiden suddenly knew why they were afraid of Emily. There was no question in his mind.

She was possessed.

"Excuse me a minute," Aiden said, turning to leave the room with his extremities shaking. He rounded the corner and was by the front door when he heard Joseph behind him.

"Wait," Joseph said, grabbing Aiden's arm. "You can't leave."

Aiden frowned, "I'm not leaving." He said, withdrawing his cell phone from his pocket. Adrenaline surged through his hands as he scrolled though his recent calls.

"Are you calling *her*?" Joseph asked.

Aiden wondered how Joseph knew who *she* was as he selected Elidad's name.

CHAPTER TWO

When the elevator doors opened for Elidad, some of the pressure in Aiden's chest escaped his lips at the sight of her. Living at the new church, and a busy schedule, meant he hadn't seen her, until now. The transition from being with her every day to not at all was strange. When he received his new orders, Elidad was convinced the church leaders were trying to keep them apart, and doing so, would make it harder for them to locate the missing keys.

Aiden knew Elidad was right, it would be difficult for them to find the keys if they were separated, but the keys weren't his only problem.

Since the day he walked through Elidad's door, their strained childhood acquaintance riddled with resentment, began to morph into something else. Friendship? After all they'd been through it felt like something more, something deeper. People who'd been through battle together often grew close; perhaps it was something like that.

They *had* been in battle together—a war against a demon army.

The search for Abraham led them to bishop Blankenship, on the run with a key. They tracked him to Mt. Denali where he planned to take his key to the high demon, Ghelgath. The Bishop needed to be stopped. They couldn't allow Ghelgath to gain possession of the key.

Brought together by fear, the night before their battle, Aiden held Elidad until they both fell asleep. Every night after, he'd lay in bed, unable to sleep. Thoughts of her body next to his, would keep him awake. He remembered everything. Her steady breathing as she slumbered, the way her hair fell around her face, and her fingertips moving across his stomach.

It felt like ages ago... another lifetime—a life where he hadn't vowed to devote his life to God.

His thoughts sent him to confession... bearing his soul about his lustful thoughts, like an addict in a private N.A. meeting. He should've chosen a different church to confess in—one where no one knew him. After three confessions, the Bishop contacted him, placing him in his new home across town from Elidad.

"Are you sure?" Elidad disrupted his thoughts, searching his eyes.

"Is it that hard to tell?" He cocked an eyebrow.

"Well, she's not faking, is she?"

"If she was, I'd be impressed. Like academy award, impressed." Aiden was impatient. Elidad had already asked him a slew of questions on the phone.

"Ok, lead the way." She appeared to believe him. "Do you remember what I told you about exorcisms?"

"What part? The fear killing you?"

"Yes. You have to push the fear aside. Depend on God. Fear will only hurt you." She grabbed Aiden's arm. "Don't worry. This won't be anything like Mexico."

She was talking about her father's—Abraham's—exorcism. She didn't allow Aiden to participate in *that* exorcism. They knew going in it would be dangerous. Having no experience, she was certain Aiden wouldn't survive it. Like the rest of his whirlwind life, it seemed long ago.

It'd only been a couple of weeks.

When they came back from Mexico, Elidad described Abraham's exorcism in detail. Aiden couldn't imagine witnessing that kind of evil. Three priests, Crusaders for the church, were dead in the barn when she found her father. Even though their lifeless bodies hung from the rafters, when Elidad entered the barn, demons had possessed them, waiting for her arrival. They used the men's bodies as empty vessels, morphing into grotesque creatures like bizarre demonic puppets. They became powerful creatures, with the sole purpose of killing her or possessing her.

"This demon should be much weaker, easier to control." Elidad continued, "Now is when you have to learn to control your fear, depend on God. It's the only way."

"Okay, good to know I won't die." Aiden's sarcasm escaped him.

"Well, as long as we keep her under control. Don't give her an opportunity."

"Right," Aiden agreed.

"Try not to look her in the eye." Elidad warned.

"Why? What will happen?" Aiden asked cautiously.

"You won't sleep for months. Just take my word for it: don't look her in the eyes once the demon starts fighting to stay."

Elidad stopped in front of the apartment door. Her warning distracted Aiden enough, he'd walked passed it.

"This is it." Elidad said, as if she'd been there before.

"How did you know?" Aiden frowned, walking back to wrap on the door lightly.

She smirked, "Apparently she's not faking."

Aiden and Elidad found Joseph in the living room with the woman who'd been hovering over her Bible before. She gripped her rosary like it was a life preserver on a sinking ship.

"Are you the one who's going to help my daughter?" The woman directed her question to Elidad.

"That's what I came here to do," Elidad answered.

Tears filled her eyes. Seth put his arm around his wife. "She's a sweet girl, she's never hurt a soul. Please, you need to help her."

"I will do everything in my power to help her." Elidad said honestly. "I need you and your husband to stay out here and pray. Pray hard for her safety. Pray for her release."

The couple nodded their heads.

"No matter what you hear from the other room, under no circumstances are you allowed to enter the room." Elidad was stern. "It will sound terrible. It will be scary, but you can't come into the room. It's too dangerous. Do you understand?"

"Yes," they said in unison.

Aiden knew they were terrified to go into that room, anyway.

Elidad looked at Aiden, "Will you show me to her then?"

Aiden stood. It took more strength than he anticipated to steer himself in the direction of Emily's room. Any sane person would be headed for the front door. Like so many other times lately, he found strength in Elidad's presence. She pushed him to fight harder and lean on his faith.

His imagination went back to the stories Elidad told him of her past exorcisms. Aiden's palms began to perspire.

Pictures of Emily hung on the wall, portraits of sunny days and laughing faces. Aiden wanted to send Emily back to those days, teleport her *into* the images, to escape the hell she was living now.

"Elidad." Joseph called after them in a whisper.

Elidad turned.

"May I please attend?" Joseph asked, not lifting his eyes to meet hers.

"This is not an exorcism condoned by the church, Father. None of the proper channels have been followed."

Joseph shook his head to signify he understood. "I've been Emily's priest since she was born. I baptized her. I would like to be there for her. It would be an experience of a lifetime, to see you work."

Elidad stared at him for what felt like an eternity. "Ok. Stay out of the way. Do *not* look her in the eyes and, no matter what she says, do *not* try to help her."

"Ok," Joseph agreed.

"Joseph. Look at me."

He obeyed.

"Don't try to help her. The demon has control of her. If you need to leave the room, do it, but don't interfere in any way."

"I can do that." He assured her.

CHAPTER THREE

"Emily, this is..." Father Joseph's voice trailed off.

Joseph, Elidad and Aiden froze, mid-step, as they entered Emily's room. Emily was in the corner where Joseph and Aiden left her, tracing lines with her finger. What was an invisible line before was now apparent. A cut on her arm produced a steady flow that spattered the floor beneath her bare feet. Her finger would dip into her blood like a quill dipping in ink before returning to the wall to define her image.

Her body stiffened, unnaturally, at the sound of their entrance. Not turning toward them, her pause was momentary.

She continued drawing.

Elidad's mouth began to water. She felt like someone had just punched her in the stomach. That awful feeling of getting the wind knocked out of her burned in her chest.

In Emily's blood, a replica of the triangle that surrounded Abraham's body, when he died, screamed at her like a caution sign on a winding road. The image, crimson against Emily's stark white wall, was too neat for her little hands to have do alone, just like the triangle around Abraham's body. The triangle in Mexico was cut into dirt, too perfect for human hands to have drawn it. When Elidad walked across *that* image, it woke up the demons in the barn, bringing forth a force stronger than any other she'd seen. The strongest demons she'd ever encountered.

What was this symbol? What did it mean? Over the last couple of weeks, Elidad had sketched it, researched it, and burnt it into her memory. She couldn't find the answer to what it was, just like she couldn't locate the remaining keys. Elidad kept a picture of the triangle on her phone but couldn't find anyone that knew what it meant. It kept her up at all hours of the night with relentless research. The triangle was part of the mystery surrounding Abraham's disappearance; it contributed to his death. It was yet another piece to the puzzle of her life that she couldn't place.

Joseph walked toward Emily, apparently to stop her. Elidad grabbed his arm. Elidad sternly pointed to a different corner. "You may stand over there."

"We need to help her." Joseph said as the color in his face began to fade.

"I will help her. After you stand over there, or leave."

Reluctantly Joseph moved out of the way, but not too far.

"Emily," Elidad said her name like a schoolteacher. "Emily, are you there? I would like to talk to you."

The girl stopped drawing again, never taking her eyes off the wall.

"Yes." Her small voice answered.

"Emily, I'm here to help you."

The girl began giggling, her voice changed into a deep cackle as her head slightly turned to look over her shoulder. Her eyes began to glow yellow. "I don't need your help, *Elidad*."

Aiden and Joseph looked at each other. Emily hadn't been told Elidad's name.

Emily's breath became heavy and raspy, "I don't *need* you."

"That's because you're not Emily," Elidad said.

A grotesque noise began in Emily's belly, moving up her throat and sped toward Elidad, "Who am I *Elidad*?" The beast asked.

"That's what I came here to find out." Elidad said, "Who *are* you?"

"Not so easily will I let her go, *Elidad*." The beast lunged toward Elidad, hissing.

The two priests jumped backward, Elidad didn't move.

Aiden knew Elidad was doing exactly what she told him to do: refusing to show any fear. He wondered how she didn't feel any fear now.

Elidad pulled a vial from her pocket and opened it. She threw its contents toward Emily; it landed on the floor in front of her. The beast retreated into the corner hissing at the liquid as it fell around her. One drop hit Emily's bare foot. Her skin sizzled and smoked, bubbling into an open wound. Aiden could smell Emily's flesh as it burned.

Emily whimpered.

"What did you throw on her?" Joseph demanded.

"Acid, she burned me with acid," Emily shrieked, the beast apparently gone. Only a terrified, helpless girl remained.

"Holy water," Elidad answered. "The *demon* was burned by holy water, not Emily."

"How could you burn her like that?" Joseph demanded. His anger swelled as he moved closer to Emily.

"Don't." Elidad held up her hand. "I warned you, don't help her. You can't help her. It's holy water, I threw it on the floor in front of the demon to contain it; it can't cross over to our side. It's the only thing that will keep you safe from her."

Joseph moved between Elidad and Emily in a protective stance. His feet inched backward over the moist line on the carpet.

"Shit." Elidad stuffed the container back in her pocket, "Joseph, you're making a mistake."

Joseph knelt in front of Emily, his arms wrapped around her as if to protect her from Elidad and Aiden. Emily allowed Joseph to hold her.

"Joseph, *get* away from her." Elidad's voice was stern.

"The only one that needs to get away is you!" He yelled. "You're evil. You hurt her. I thought you were a warrior of Christ. You are a monster! How could you hurt a defenseless child?" Joseph brushed the hair off Emily's face. "Emily, are you ok?"

Emily's tears streamed from her eyes, "Please, Father Joseph, don't let them hurt me anymore. I didn't do anything wrong."

"Of course, you didn't," the priest hugged her. "You didn't do anything wrong," he assured.

Feeling helpless, Aiden looked at Elidad, he knew the look on her face. This was not a good situation.

"Father, you need to get out of there. Come away from her," Elidad said again.

"So you can continue torturing her?" He demanded.

"Joseph, I know Elidad," Aiden tried to assure him, "she'd never hurt Emily. She came to help. You need to trust her."

"She *did* hurt Emily, look at her," Joseph argued.

Emily wrapped her little arms around Joseph's neck. "Please don't let them hurt me again, Father," she cooed, her face rested on his shoulder. Her brown eyes fixated on Elidad and Aiden.

Like a match being ignited, Emily's eyes turned yellow again.

"Joseph—" was the only word Aiden got out.

Emily smiled with a heavily fanged mouth. She turned into the priest and attacked. Joseph's screams filled the room as the little creature bit and scratched the priest. Blood spilled from Joseph's face and neck.

"Aiden," Elidad yelled, "lock the door before the parents try to come in! The last things we need are more victims."

Aiden obeyed. He knew better than to ask questions. When he turned, Elidad stood on the other side of the wet line on the floor. When Joseph's arm flailed, Elidad grabbed it and pulled. The demon girl pulled in the opposite direction.

"Aiden, help me!"

Aiden ran to throw his arms around Elidad and pulled. They fell backward, dragging Joseph across the wet line on the floor. When Emily's body encountered the invisible barrier, she looked like she was hit by a shock wave. Her body was thrown back into the corner.

"Apply pressure," Elidad threw a blanket at Aiden, "and call an ambulance."

Aiden withdrew his cellphone from his pocket and realized he had no idea where they were.

"Is everything okay in there?" Seth shouted, banging on the door.

"Joseph's been hurt. Call an ambulance!" Aiden yelled back. He was relieved to hear Seth's footsteps headed back down the hall.

Pacing the confined corner like a rabid cat, Emily screamed, blood dripping off her chin. The metallic smell of blood wafted in the air as Emily frantically moved around the space.

"Who are you?" Elidad demanded.

"I am one who seeks *you*, Elidad," the beast spat.

"Release Emily, go back to Hell, I command you."

The demon slid down the wall to crouch in the corner, looking at Elidad with its golden eyes, "I will go, *you* will come with me, Elidad."

"Get thee behind me Satan: for it is written, Thou shalt worship the Lord thy God, and Him only shalt thou serve!" Elidad responded.

"Who do *you* serve, Elidad?" The demon asked.

Elidad withdrew her Bible and another vile of holy water. "In the name of the Father, the Son, and the Holy Spirit, I command you to tell me your name!" She threw the water on the little girl. Her skin bubbled and burned. A wisp of black smoke plumed toward Elidad and with it the rank smell of flesh, stifling the smell of blood.

Aiden understood why Joseph had been so scared for Emily. The sound and the smell were horrendous. The image of Emily's flesh boiling off her body was terrifying, but Aiden believed in Elidad.

"I am Keirum!" The demon shrieked. Lose flesh hung off Emily's face. "Elidad..." She purred, "You shall come with me. Come with me to Hell."

"Keirum," Elidad said, "I condemn you to Hell."

Seth was back at the other side of the door pounding on it. "Open this door."

Aiden looked from Elidad to Joseph then back to Emily. Emily began screaming again, her voice changing from its evil pitch to that of a little girl's. In Emily's eyes, the yellow began to glow brighter with a vibrant blue light behind them, her skin radiating light.

Seth splintered the doorframe with his shoulder. The door burst inward, hurling Seth forward, just in time to see light take over his daughter. The yellow eyes of the demon disappeared. Emily's skin began to clear; the burns from the holy water lifted away like raindrops falling upward. Her flesh became whole again as the demon inside her dissipated into a black mist.

Elidad turned to Seth, "Stay outside the room. Go now." Seth obeyed without a word. He stood outside the door wrapping his arm around Emily's mom, who just appeared in the doorway.

Elidad turned to Emily. "Emily, are you okay?"

Emily nodded looking like she just awoke from a deep sleep.

"Aiden, get away from Joseph." Elidad said.

"He'll bleed to death, I have to keep pressure on it. He's already lost so much blood." Aiden protested.

"Aiden, get away from him now! Grab the girl! Cover her eyes!"

The franticness in Elidad's voice made Aiden look down at Joseph. The grisly wounds that laced his chest and face were hard to look at. Under Aiden's hands, Joseph's eyes opened, burning bright yellow. Aiden pushed himself off the floor and, running to the corner, he scooped Emily up into his arms. He put her over his shoulder and turned so she would be facing the corner and he could see what happened to Elidad.

Emily was sobbing. "Everything is going to be fine, Emily. We're just going to wait for Joseph to get some help. Close your eyes, okay?" Aiden pressed his hand over Emily's dark hair, holding her head, so she couldn't peek. Emily's warm breath pressed into his neck. Her sniffles were as loud in his ear as his heartbeat.

Joseph's body quickly rose into a standing position and covered the ground towards Aiden and Emily, his arms outstretched. When his hands attempted to pass over the line of holy water, the creature jolted backward, howling in pain. The corner that kept the demon in Emily confined to the small space was now protecting her and Aiden. Aiden avoided Joseph's eyes, looking instead at the gashes on his neck and chest. It was difficult to look away from the flesh hanging in ribbons.

Joseph turned to Elidad. "I came for *you* Elidad. They can watch you die." The demon sprang on her.

Aiden felt like his heart leapt forward with Joseph. He stood helpless, as he watched Joseph attack.

Elidad had her Bible in her hand. Aiden hadn't noticed her pick it up off the floor during the commotion but when the demon jumped at her, she pressed it on his face. He screamed. His flesh and hands caught fire as he tried to tear it away.

"Keirum, in the name of the Lord thy God I command you, go back to Hell!" Elidad demanded.

The blue light that was within Joseph began to glow and emanate from his eyes until the yellow faded away altogether and Joseph's body fell to the floor. The burns lifted from his face, disappearing like Emily's.

Aiden was as still as Seth and Emily's mother. Emily's faint whimper was the only sound in the room.

"What happened?" Joseph asked weakly.

"You've been hurt," Elidad told him. "You'll be fine."

"Emily?" Joseph managed to ask.

"She's fine," Elidad answered, looking up. "Aiden, we need to get Joseph out to the living room before the paramedics get here."

Aiden felt an urge to stay in the corner where he and Emily were protected. Reluctantly, he stepped over the line, giving Emily to her father.

Elidad looked at Emily's mother, "What's your name?"

"Sarah."

"Sarah, you need to take Emily into your room. Clean her up and get her fresh clothes. Be quiet. Don't let the paramedics know you're here. Go now."

Emily's mother nodded and turned into the room across the hall, shutting the door.

Elidad looked at Aiden. "We can't be seen here. When the paramedics get here, we'll stay in Emily's room until they leave." She addressed Seth. "Don't say anything about us. Don't say anything about demons, and nothing about your wife and your daughter. Not a word."

"Okay," Seth agreed like he was sleepwalking through a nightmare.

Aiden and Elidad grabbed Joseph under the arms and drug him to the living room. They placed him in the middle of the floor.

Elidad stood, looking around the room. She grabbed a mirror that hung on the wall and pulled it down hard. It hit the floor, shattering.

"Why did you do that?" Seth asked.

"How are you going to explain his injuries to the medics?" Elidad said as she began staging the mirror to look like it fell on Joseph.

Elidad kneeled next to Joseph and sprinkled some broken shards of glass across his wounds before lightly patting his cheek. "Joseph, you need to tell the paramedics that a mirror fell on you. Can you hear me? Say it."

"A mirror fell on me," Joseph muttered softly.

Elidad stood.

"That needs to be your story too," she told Seth.

Seth looked at Joseph on the floor.

"They won't ask too many questions here tonight. Tell them the mirror fell on him and they will go. You can't tell them anyone else is here in your home."

"I understand," Seth said.

There was a knock at the door.

CHAPTER FOUR

"Paramedics. We received a call from this address," the man speaking attempted to open the door, the chain kept them from coming in.

"I'll be right there," Seth yelled as Elidad and Aiden hurried toward Emily's room.

Emily's door wouldn't latch closed, the wood splintered from Seth busting his way through. From behind the door, Elidad and Aiden heard Seth open the front door.

"Is there someone injured in here?" One of the paramedics asked.

"Yes, right in here," Seth said. "The mirror fell on him, it's just awful."

Aiden moved closer to Elidad so she could hear him whisper.

"Why are we hiding in here?"

"Because if you're always around when someone is tragically hurt, eventually someone will ask questions. Trust me, it's better they don't know we're here, and better for us if they don't write our names down."

Aiden was satisfied with her response but wondered how many times, exactly, she'd been present when someone was tragically hurt. Aiden moved back to listen to what was going on in the living room. He could hear the men count together; he assumed they were moving Joseph onto the stretcher. The sooner they got Joseph out of here, the better. Aiden couldn't shake the image of his throat and chest where Emily had so brutally slashed his skin.

Aiden looked back at Elidad, she sat in a tiny chair at a table made for a person a quarter of her size. On top, crayons were scattered around blank white papers. Primary-colored pictures of unicorns were hanging on the wall. Elidad's face was the exact opposite of the drawings, identical to the blank pages, a pale white.

"What's wrong?" Aiden asked, moving back across the room to Elidad.

Silently, Elidad turned a paper on Emily's table toward Aiden. Emily had dozens of drawings on the table. Each image looked like the next. A man, shadowed with no detail, and green eyes. Aiden knew what Elidad thought. This was Elidad's Shadow Man—the same one that almost killed Elidad in her dream, the one that had been following her for weeks.

"It can't be," Aiden's words were so soft, they barely made it past his lips.

"Can't it?" Elidad said.

Elidad stood with the drawing in her hand.

"Look," she pointed at the triangle on the wall. "Is this a coincidence?"

"It has to be," Aiden's arms broke out in goosebumps.

Elidad pulled her phone from her pocket.

"Look," she shoved the picture in his face. The triangle that surrounded Abraham's body mirrored the one written in blood on Emily's wall.

Elidad headed toward the door, shoving her phone back in her pocket.

"Elidad, where are you going? We can't go out there now. It will look suspicious!" Aiden pleaded.

Elidad peered down the hall. The paramedics were still there; she couldn't see anyone, but their voices lingered in the front room. Before she was seen, she dashed out the door across the hall into the room where Emily and her mother went. Before she shut the door behind her, Aiden was right on her heels.

Emily and her mother looked up at Aiden and Elidad as they blew through the door.

"Sorry," Elidad said quietly, "I didn't mean to scare you two. I'd like to talk to Emily, if I could?" Elidad looked at Sarah for permission.

"Of course," her mother agreed. "Is everything ok? Is she going to be alright?"

"She's fine," Elidad smiled at Emily when she spoke. "Hello Emily."

"Hi," she answered.

"Do you remember me?" Elidad asked.

The girl nodded her head to signify she did.

"Do you remember what happened here tonight?" Elidad questioned.

Emily looked at the ground, seemingly shy.

"It's okay, Emily, if you don't remember," Elidad reassured.

"I remember..." her little voice trailed off. "I remember he wouldn't let me go. I wanted him to leave, I did," she said, almost apologetically.

"I know you did, sweetie, it's okay," Elidad consoled her. "How's your arm?" Elidad's eyes moved to a bandage that covered most of her skin.

"She'll probably need stitches," Sarah said. "We can take her in when the paramedics leave."

"That's going to be tricky," Elidad cringed, worried someone might put Joseph and Emily's injuries together.

"My sister is a nurse. I think we can make it work," Sarah replied.

"You saved me," Emily gazed at Elidad, "You came to make him leave. He wouldn't go, I wanted him to." Emily's eyes looked painful as she clutched a brightly colored blanket in her lap.

"Is this Ariel?" Elidad touched Emily's blanket.

"Yes," Emily agreed.

"Ariel had to be brave, do you remember? She had to fight Ursula. Can you be brave like Ariel, and help me, Emily?"

Emily nodded.

"You're already brave like Ariel." Elidad pulled the picture she found in Emily's room from behind her back. "Is this who wouldn't go away? Is this who you wanted to go?"

Emily cringed at the picture, burying her head in her mom's lap.

"She's been drawing that man for weeks," Emily's Mom said. "She would wake up from nightmares and draw him. Her father and I thought it was a stage. We thought maybe she'd watched a scary movie at a friend's house. We'd recently talked to her about what can happen if you talk to strangers, so we thought maybe that was what started her night terrors. We never thought these drawings, or her dreams, would lead to this."

"It's not your fault," Elidad grabbed Sarah's arm to enforce her sincerity. "No one can see this coming. Believe me, I've been doing this a long time."

Emily's mother began stroking her daughter's head as tears streamed down her face. "Thank you."

Elidad reached out to touch Emily's hair too. "You've helped me so much, Emily. I want you to remember that the Shadow Man, the one who wouldn't leave, won't come back. You don't have to be afraid anymore, okay?"

Emily peeked one eye out. "Are you sure?"

"I'm sure. I've done this for a long time. I make them go away, and when I do, they never come back." A soft smile bought up the edges of Elidad's lips. "You just need to remember to say your prayers, listen to your parents and don't be afraid anymore."

Aiden wasn't sure how Emily could accomplish not being scared after an ordeal like this. He wasn't sure how *he* would accomplish it.

"The one who wouldn't go away, the one inside me, that isn't him." Emily pointed at the drawing of the Shadow Man. "The one inside me was afraid of him."

"Then who is this?" Elidad looked down at the dark figure with burning green eyes.

"I don't know. The one who wouldn't go away thought about him. He was afraid of him. He never said his name."

"What about the drawing on your wall?" Elidad asked.

"He showed it to him." Emily pointed to the Shadow Man. "He showed it to the one who wouldn't leave."

"Did he say what it meant?"

"No. The Shadow Man said *it* was coming. But they needed the keys."

Elidad and Aiden exchanged looks.

"He is coming," Emily finished.

"Who is coming?" Elidad asked.

"The Shadow Man."

A shiver set Elidad's skin alive.

"Don't worry about him. He's not coming anymore," Elidad lied.

Seth walked through the bedroom door. "They're gone."

"Good," Elidad said. "Emily you've remembered so much." She clasped Emily's hand in hers. "You're so brave. Can you remember anything else?"

"No. Are you sure he's not coming?" Emily's eyes were desperate.

"He's not. I promise. They're all gone. Forever. If you think of anything else, can your parents call me?" Elidad looked at Seth and Sarah.

They nodded. "Anything you want," Seth said. "Thank you for saving our daughter," Seth's eyes began to shine with gratitude.

"Make sure to go see father Joseph, he'll be happy to see you when he's better." Elidad withdrew a business card from her pocket and handed it to Seth. "If the police come and ask you questions in the next few days, tell them you don't have time and you'll go into the precinct to make a statement. Before you go, call this man and tell him I gave you his number and you need to give a statement. He's a detective. He'll make sure he's assigned to your case and he'll take care of everything."

"Okay," Seth agreed.

"Are you ready?" Elidad asked Aiden.

"Yes."

"Be brave, Emily, say your prayers," Elidad reminded.

Aiden noticed Elidad's lingering look. Perhaps Elidad felt the way he did; wondering how Emily could live past this event and wished there was something more she could do.

Elidad and Aiden made their way to the elevator and took it to the ground floor. When they got there, the paramedics were loading Joseph into the ambulance in front of the building. Walking past, Elidad and Aiden could hear them talking to each other.

As one of them climbed inside the brightly lit rig, he said, "These wounds aren't consistent with something falling on him."

"I don't think so either," the other paramedic responded, pushing Joseph into the ambulance. "What does it look like to you?"

The man in the vehicle guided the stretcher inside and locked it into place. "It looks like he was attacked by some kind of animal. Like a dog."

Aiden and Elidad exchanged glances as they walked by.

CHAPTER FIVE

"Elidad, did you hear what I said?" Aiden's voice had a ring of excitement on the other end of the phone.

"I'm sorry, Aiden, I heard you." She answered, silently wiping away tears.

"Isaac's been found! Isn't that amazing? They aren't sure if he is well enough to travel home yet, but they know where he is."

"He was in Jerusalem?"

"Yes, he's in a small hospital now."

It'd been three months since Isaac left. Isaac had once traveled to the Holy City when he was a young man and had always dreamt of seeing it again. He'd wanted to make the pilgrimage before he got too old. Abraham and Isaac often spoke of going together, but there was no one Isaac trusted more to watch his antique shop. Abraham insisted Isaac go without him, leaving the store in Abraham's care. When Abraham went missing seven months ago, Isaac decided not to postpone his flight. He asked Lucian to watch over *Isaac's Import Books & Treasures* until Abraham returned.

Elidad suddenly felt anxiety closing in around her. How could she keep the shop open and operating if Isaac wasn't able to work? Lucian had already stayed longer than anticipated. How could she ask him to continue to stay?

"I'm coming over." Aiden announced.

"No, don't. I was about to leave. I'll be fine," Elidad quickly lied. She didn't want to admit how badly she wanted to see Aiden. He'd stayed with her at Abraham's for a couple weeks after Abraham's exorcism. After that, the Bishop insisted Aiden move into a local church to help a parish that was shorthanded. Elidad suspected they were trying to keep distance between her and Aiden. They wouldn't want her extremist ways to rub off on their prized possession. She was surprised they hadn't found him a job at the Vatican, to get him as far away from her as possible.

The doorbell rang. Not expecting anyone, Elidad dried her face with the sleeve of her sweater before opening the door. Aiden stood in the doorway with his phone pressed against his ear.

He dared to throw a boastful smirk at her as he hung up his phone.

"Leaving, huh?" He asked, closing the door behind him.

Elidad put her own phone in her pocket. "I, uh …" She couldn't think of a believable lie.

Aiden wrapped his arms around her, her body melted into his. He was the strength she needed, the only thing that had gotten her through the past few weeks. She hated feeling so dependent on him.

He pulled away to look at her, "*Are* you okay?"

She nodded. "I'm fine. I'm just so… relieved." Tears began to trail down her face. She didn't feel obligated to hide them from Aiden. "When we got back from Mexico and I went looking for him, no one had heard from him…" her voice trailed off.

She didn't have to tell Aiden what she thought happened to Isaac. She also didn't need to tell Aiden how severe the pain would be with the loss of another person close to her.

Abraham's death was enough. Aiden had recently spent many nights pacing the hall between his and Elidad's rooms to shake her from nightmares. Elidad's screams would tear him from sleep. Waking her to the reality that her father was dead, and the grief that accompanied that fact, tested his strength. Leaning on God was his only guide through grief.

Aiden pulled her towards him again.

"You don't have to think about that," He said. "Isaac was found. He left his hotel to have dinner, left his ID in his room and had a stroke on the street. He'd just gotten to town so no one recognized him. That's why we couldn't find him. When he was taken to the hospital, they treated him as a John Doe. He's going to be okay and he'll be back home soon."

Aiden led Elidad into Abraham's study. Elidad plopped into one of the twin leather chairs in front of the fireplace. The force of her body pushed the smell of warm leather into the air, a smell that made her heart ache for Abraham.

"As soon as he is well enough, I'll bring him home," She said.

"Elidad, what are you going to do with him? He'll need constant home care."

"What am I supposed to do, Aiden? Leave him in Jerusalem because it's more convenient?"

"No, of course not. But, I want you to think this through." His eyes were heavy with concern. "Taking care of him will be a full-time job. How will you find the other keys if you have to take care of him?"

Over the last month, Elidad and Aiden had been focused on finding the lost keys. Before Abraham went missing, he'd hidden one in this study. Elidad found the key in a crucifix, which she'd been led to by Abraham's riddle, delivered in a dream. The keys were the reason Abraham went missing. There were four all together, all identical, each made of a different metal. If placed together, they would become one key with the power to open a book. The book and the keys needed to be protected and hidden from evil forces hard at work to find them.

Elidad still had the key they'd found in Abraham's home. She'd placed it in a hidden room under Isaac's shop. The room was guarded by magic, keeping any intruder from being able to find it.

When Elidad and Aiden tried to retrieve a second key from the high demon, Ghelgath, a winged lizard stole it before *they* could take it. The creature had vanished into the ice; even Ghelgath was unable to stop him. Elidad and Aiden hadn't been able to determine who owned the sneaky thief, but Elidad was determined to find out. Weeks of research left them unable to find information on the remaining two keys, or the book they opened, but that didn't keep Elidad from looking. She was relentless in her search. In the two weeks Aiden stayed at Abraham's house with her, they'd spent every minute looking through books in Abraham's study or in Isaac's store, both above and below the ground.

"I have to find a way," Elidad said, staring defiantly into the fireplace. The first time she'd seen the Shadow Man, he'd appeared out of it. Though it was a dream, he'd nearly killed her with his tight fingers wrapped around her throat. She shuddered, remembered her searing flesh, how her hands burned when she touched his skin while attempting to fight him off. Aiden saved her life by waking her up.

Through their travels, the Shadow Man followed Elidad. Even when she couldn't see him, she could *feel* him watching her. She thought, possibly, it was her imagination, but Leucosia confirmed her fear. He was following her. Who was he? Even Leucosia couldn't see. A seer who could see the future and the past, but she couldn't see who *he* was. What did he want? The keys? Was he responsible for Abraham's death?

"Elidad, I know you love Isaac," Aiden knew he was on thin ice with Elidad when her emotions were in such a fragile state. "Do you think this is what Isaac would want you to do? Take care of him? Because I think, Isaac would want us to find the keys and the book before someone else finds them. If they fall into the wrong hands …"

He shook his head at a loss for words. "Do you remember what Leucosia told us?"

How could she forget? Leucosia made it clear how important the book was. *"The world will unite as one, the evils of the world will reign, and people will blame God. They will declare war on the Creator of all, and the world will lose."*

Elidad looked away from the empty fireplace to meet Aiden's eyes, "The book will reunite the world as one race and if the book is opened before the world is ready, man will wage war on God. God will be forced to destroy us."

Aiden and Elidad sat back at the severity of her words.

"Don't you find it curious that after Abraham went missing, Isaac still left for Jerusalem?" Aiden asked.

"What do you mean? His trip was planned for a long time." Elidad defended Isaac.

"If you went missing, I think I'd postpone my vacation."

Elidad felt the intensity of his words when they locked eyes. He would fight to find her.

The depth of his eyes made her heart race.

"I just can't help but think maybe he was going for more reasons than we know," Aiden suggested.

Aiden was right. She was ashamed she hadn't questioned it before. Why *would* he leave after Abraham disappeared? Her mind spun with possibilities. She was proud of Aiden for realizing it didn't fit. He'd learned so much in a few short months. It felt like it'd been forever since he helped himself into her apartment. In that brief time, he'd gone from someone she despised to the only person she trusted.

"Well Aiden, we won't know anything until we can get Isaac home and ask him."

Aiden looked trim in all black; she was glad he wore a clerical shirt and not a Cassock. While priests wore their Cassocks to special events, Elidad couldn't imagine Aiden in one although she was used to seeing Abraham in his. Aiden hoped to be a Bishop, making his Cassock a frequent attire, especially if he transferred to the Vatican. The traditional dark gown with thirty-three buttons down the front only seemed to fit much older priests.

Now that Aiden was back in a parish, he hadn't been shaving. She'd gotten the impression that letting his facial hair grow made him feel like he would be more accepted. She could imagine it was hard to be so young in an ancient field where men valued aged wisdom.

Then again, it was even harder to be a woman in their men-only club.

Aiden's black clothes made his eyes stand out, like a blue sky against a dark raincloud. The white tab in his collar was a barrier between them, a dam holding back her feelings. Aiden must have recently cut his blonde hair; the sides were shorter than the last time she'd seen him. The top was always longer and looked careless, though it was deliberately styled.

Elidad wondered how many women in his parish wished he hadn't taken vows.

CHAPTER SIX

The door to Isaac's *Import Books & Treasures* squeaked under the chime of a bell, announcing Elidad's arrival. Being in Isaac's store brought her a taste of comfort amidst her anxiety. Her stomach had been twisted in knots since she'd left Abraham's house. How could she ask Lucian to stay? She barely knew him. Maybe he'd do it for Isaac.

Elidad spent almost as much time in this store, growing up, as she did her own home. Abraham and Isaac spent most days discussing theology, archeology, art and the antique trade.

Sandalwood wafted into the air as Elidad walked past a buffet covered in delicate tea sets and silver cutlery. The peppery smell of eucalyptus and leather slowly interlaced as she passed a stack of wood chests adorned with leather straps.

How much longer would Lucian stay and operate the store? He'd already been here months longer than originally planned. Elidad didn't know enough about antiques to keep the store operating by herself. She was relieved that Isaac was found but now she had so many things to deal with. How could she take care of Isaac *and* the store? It would be easier if Abraham were here.

Her life was about to change, significantly.

The sound of the bell summoned Lucian from behind a curtain to the cash register. It was a beautiful cash register; gold in hue and embellished with filigree, it was a work of art all on its own. When she was little, Isaac would let her press the numbers. They were heavy and clicked hard into place. When the numbers were depressed, you pulled a handle, completing your math and printing a receipt.

"Elidad, how are you?" Lucian's voice was smoky with the right touch of gravel that made her skin come alive. Was it his voice or the way his green eyes reflected light against his olive skin? His features were chiseled, a fallen angel kind of look. She had to force her eyes to focus on his face so she wouldn't ravage his body with them.

"I'm fine," She said, trying to sound casual.

"You sounded upset on the phone," his dark brow creased slightly. "What do you need to talk to me about?"

"They found Isaac," she blurted.

"That's great," Lucian's lips pressed upward in a smile.

"Well, not totally great." The weight of the truth hung heavy in Elidad's stomach.

"What's wrong? Is he ... ok?"

"Yeah, he's alive, if that's what you mean." Elidad looked over her shoulder, making sure she didn't miss any customers when she walked in. "Let's go to the back."

"Of course." Lucian held back the curtain, allowing Elidad to lead him to the private library hidden behind the red velvet.

Elidad felt calmer, being in this room. She had so many memories with Abraham and Isaac here; it felt like they were with her now.

Elidad ran her fingers down the table in the center of the room where their makeshift family shared many meals. She continued across the room and plopped onto the sofa that lined one wall.

"Isaac is alive, but he's not well. We won't know how bad it is until he comes home. We're getting all our information from the church right now, and they aren't giving us much."

"What *do* you know?" Lucian asked.

Elidad kept her eyes locked on the floor as tears began to swell in her eyes. "He had a stroke, that's why we couldn't find him. He can't remember anything. He couldn't remember where he lived or where he was from. I guess, he recently asked them to call Abraham at the Vatican. Abraham hasn't been at the Vatican for almost thirty years."

"Well, I'm glad he remembered something, that's a start." Lucian said.

"Yeah, it's something," Elidad agreed.

"So, what will you do? Bring him home?"

This time, Elidad look up at Lucian.

"I don't know. I'd like to bring him home. Aiden thinks I will be overwhelmed. He's right, taking care of him will be a full-time job. I don't even know if I'll be able to do it by myself," Elidad took a breath at that reality. "And, I'll have to find someone to run the store."

Lucian sat next to Elidad placing a hand on her knee. "I'll stay as long as you need."

Her body responded to his touch.

Elidad shook her head. "I can't ask you to stay. I've already taken advantage of your kindness."

"You didn't ask. I offered and you *can* take advantage of me, anytime."

Heat flared in Elidad's cheeks. *Was he flirting?* "You've stayed way longer than you were supposed to. You have a life to live, you can't keep it on hold."

Lucian pulled his hand away from her knee.

"Seriously, it's not that big of a deal. I'm getting the better end of the arrangement, really. If I weren't working here, I'd be somewhere, doing the same thing I'm doing now. This job includes housing and I'm in the heart of New York. Who can afford an apartment in New York? When the store's slow, I have time to work on my freelance projects. I'm really not pressed to leave," he assured. "I live in New York, working in one of the best antique stores in the country, it's really no loss to me."

Elidad smirked. "Well, since you put it that way…"

"But full disclosure," Lucian interrupted.

"What?"

Lucian leaned back resting his arm on the back of the couch. "If I stay here, it's under the condition that I may add general manager to my resume."

Elidad laughed. "If you stay and help me, you can put whatever you want on your resume."

"Well then, I'll have to think of something good." Lucian's face became hard to read, his eyes refusing to let go of hers. "I have one additional condition."

"Okay… do you have a list?" Elidad teased.

"No. Just one more thing."

"Spit it out. What do you want, a raise?" Elidad smiled.

"Let me take you to dinner."

Elidad's smile fell from her lips. "Dinner?" She wanted to say yes, but her heart was screaming no. *What would Aiden think?*

"Yes, it's a meal most Americans enjoy in the evening."

Elidad rolled her eyes. "Smartass."

"I've been accused of this… smartassery before," Lucian chuckled.

"Somehow, that doesn't surprise me," Elidad recanted.

His eyes went serious. "Does Saturday at six work for you?"

Elidad swallowed hard. "Yes."

Lucian's eyes creased at the edges as a smile flashed across his lips. "You might want to wear a dress, assuming you own one?"

That smile. Elidad picked up a decorative pillow off the couch and threw it at him. "You really know how to talk to the ladies, don't you?"

Lucian caught it, laughing in his baritone voice. "Nothing personal, you're just more of a leather jacket and jeans kina' girl. There's nothing wrong with that. I just wanted to make sure you knew what you were in for." His eyes softened. "You've had a tough time lately, I thought it might be a nice treat for you to have a night off."

The way he switched from fun to serious made her heart stumble, the beat struggling to slow with his fluid transition. He'd been working pretty much every day, in the shop. Maybe he was just lonely. Perhaps in his loneliness, he recognized hers. Elidad always felt isolated here. In a city of nine million people. She wasn't sure how it was possible, but it was, especially since Aiden moved to his new Church.

"A lot *has* happened in my life," Elidad agreed. "but that's not your problem. Are you sure you want to stay?" Elidad tried to give him a way out. "You don't have anywhere better to be?"

"Elidad, there's no place I'd rather be."

The sincerity in his voice heated her blood. "I appreciate you staying. I think I'm going to need all the help I can get."

"I'm sure Aiden will help you, as much as he can," Lucian's words were hinting at something deeper.

Elidad couldn't suppress her laugh. "Until he can't."

"What would stop him?"

"The Church." Elidad could hear the resentment in her tone.

"Why would he *let* them stop him?" Lucian asked.

"He did devote his life to the Church, so I guess that could give them some weight."

"Oh, that's right… celibacy, and all…" Sarcasm dripped from Lucian's words.

Elidad smirked. "To each his own."

"Better him than me," Lucian's lips twisted. "Does he ever think of breaking those vows?"

"How would I know?" Elidad fidgeted in her seat.

"I would think if anyone knew, it'd be you," Lucian leaned back into the couch like interrogation was his natural state.

Elidad crossed her arms. "Why's that?"

She already knew.

"You're always together. I've seen the way he looks at you."

"He doesn't look at me any way." *Does he?* "We're just friends."

"Friends," Lucian repeated.

"We've been through a lot together," Elidad added. "Anyway, the Church leaders hate me. That's why they moved him across town. I'm sure they'll move him further, when they get a chance. If anyone else were in need, they'd let him help. They just don't like me."

"Didn't they love your father?" Lucian seemed hesitant to mention Abraham.

"Yes. They loved him." Elidad sat back, flailing her hands. "But I'm a wild card. I can't be controlled, so I can't be trusted. And besides, I'm not his biological daughter, so their loyalty ended when he died."

"I see."

"At least they are taking care of Isaac. They're flying him home."

"I wasn't aware Isaac worked for the church," Lucian said thoughtfully.

"He didn't, not really," Elidad thought of the right words. "I'd say he worked *with* the church. He has books that they frequently need to reference. He's like a consultant."

"In the room?" Lucian gestured to the hidden door in the floor that led to a library. Not like the library they were in, but a spellbinding library, with ladders reaching into an abyss of books—important ones whose information wasn't fit for the general public. Lavish furniture served as a sitting area in front of a fireplace that was wider than Elidad's arm span and burned with an eternal flame. As many times as Elidad had come and gone from the library, the fire was always burning, the air was always warm. The first time Elidad met Lucian, she'd come to the library looking for information on the keys, but she never found any.

As far as she knew, Isaac had never given access to the library to anyone, other than she and Abraham. Few knew of the library's existence, but part of the responsibility of watching over the store would be protecting it. Isaac must have trusted Lucian.

In reality, trust didn't matter too much when a spell was guarding the library. Even with the key, if Lucian didn't have good intentions, he'd never be able to enter the room.

It was strange that she'd never heard of Lucian before meeting him. Of course, if she'd visited Isaac more over the past couple of years, maybe she would've heard about him.

"So, your uncle and Isaac were friends?" Elidad turned the questions back on Lucian.

"Yes, they met when they were in college. They wrote back and forth, keeping in touch over the years. It's priceless, having contacts in the antique trade. Especially before the computer era."

"I'm sure." Elidad agreed. "What did we ever do without computers and phones?"

"Connect with people."

Elidad shot him a smirk. "You're one of *those*, huh?"

"One of what?" Lucian caulked an eyebrow.

"You know, the *technology is the downfall of humanity*, kind."

Lucian's lips spread wider. "Technology *is* the downfall of humanity."

Elidad laughed. "Do you *have* a cell phone?" Elidad teased. "Or do I have to send smoke signals to get ahold of you?"

Lucian removed a cell phone from his pocket. "I have a brand-new phone, thank you. I don't live in the Stone Age. I'm just saying, technology keeps us a little disconnected, that's all. But, speaking of being connected, I should probably get your number."

Elidad could feel her cheeks heating up. Hopefully it was subtle enough he wouldn't notice. "Yeah, if you're staying, it would be nice not to have to call the store to get ahold of you."

Lucian shrugged. "Even if I weren't staying, I think you should have my number."

He would most definitely notice the color of her face now.

CHAPTER SEVEN

The bell rang, startling Aiden. He was at Abraham's house while Elidad was at Isaac's prepping the living spaces in anticipation of his return. Isaac would need a wheelchair and a walker to get around his house; furniture would need to be moved to make space for him. Aiden was thankful for the distraction. Finding Isaac would change Elidad's focus from the loss of Abraham to something more positive.

Walking to the front door, Aiden wondered how Elidad had been sleeping. Since moving to his new church, there was no one here to wake her from her nightmares.

Aiden invited in a gust of wind when he swung the door open. The breeze surrounded him with a familiar smell of flowers. Green eyes radiated back from the other side of the threshold.

"Aren't you going to invite me in?" Her soft smile came across rosy lips.

"Sophia." Aiden stated. The shock of seeing her resonated through him. If she were anyone else, he wouldn't be able to remember her name. They'd only met once, months ago, and only for a few minutes. How could he forget her face and the burning touch she held on him? She was the first siren he'd met on the way to meet Leucosia. She was the first *thing* he encountered, in a long string of others, that took his knowledge of this world, threw it in a blender with no top, and turned it on high.

Though he'd been given 'the antidote' to the *siren's song*, her beauty was still persuasive. "Of course, please," Aiden said, extending his arm. "Elidad isn't here," he said as he closed the door.

She smiled, "I know."

"Right," Aiden remembered. "The powers of premonition."

Sophia removed her jacket and handed it to Aiden before walking into Abraham's study. Aiden hung it up, watching as she moved around the room inspecting Abraham's shelves. She paused in front of a metronome that wasn't active. She pushed the metal with her finger, the movement sending a ticking noise through the stale quiet. Sophia gestured to the chairs in front of the hearth.

Aiden sat across from her. "So, if you aren't here to see Elidad," he frowned, "then why *are* you here?"

"Mother said you'd need an invitation."

Her mother was Leucosia, she and her sisters were the three sirens from the Odysseus tale in Greek mythology. The sisters, being the origins of the siren power, were exceptionally stronger in their supernatural abilities. When the power was passed to their children, it varied in strength and consistency.

Sophia, being second-generation, wasn't as persuasive as her mother, but certainly strong enough. The first time they'd met, Sophia could provoke Aiden do anything, but only through touch. After placing her hand on his chest, desire would've driven him to immeasurable distances. That physical contact was like nothing he'd ever experienced. Fortunately, Aiden wasn't sure of the extent Leucosia's power because she'd given him the antidote, that's what she called it. Whatever it was, made Aiden immune to any and all of the siren's powers. Aiden had heard legends of sirens coercing men with their voices. He hadn't thought such a thing was possible until he'd heard Leucosia speak. The sound of her voice enveloped his soul… until the antidote set in. If he was forced to explain the ordeal in words, he wasn't sure he would be able to convey it.

Of the three sisters, only two ancient sirens remained: Leucosia and Ignacia. The third, Calandra, had been killed.

Overtaken with a lust for power, Calandra had been determined to use her gifts for evil. Leucosia refused to stand with her. Calandra attempted to kill Leucosia for her betrayal, but was stopped by Ghelgath, the high demon.

Leucosia and Ignacia's power wasn't limited to influencing men. They were seers, with the ability to see the future or the past. By touching the water in a birdbath, they were able to share their visions with anyone.

"So, I'm being *summoned* by Leucosia?" Aiden clarified.

"You could call it that," Sophia agreed. "But, you still owe me a dance," she said playfully. "You could come by to pay up and just pop in to see mother while you were there. Of course, it would be much different … now."

"You mean you wouldn't have total control of me?" Aiden felt affronted.

The first time they met, she intended to victimize him in some way. Laying a hand on him, she'd asked him to dance, her powers making the nightclub and the throbbing music dissipate. He would've stayed with her until the world ended, but Elidad saved him.

"Now, that's not fair. You hardly know me," she pretended to be insulted. "I was only having some fun. You are so sweet, how could I just let you walk by?"

The last time they met, she described him with the same words. "What's so sweet about me?"

"I can feel how pure you are, Aiden. My powers are not the same as my Mother's but I can *feel*. When you walked by in that crowd, the truth of your heart radiated from you.

In all that darkness, you shone through the crowd like a lighthouse on a stormy night. And when I touched you…" Her eyes sparkled.

"When you touched me, what?"

She leaned forward. "It's difficult to describe what I see in my premonitions. I don't look into birdbaths, like Mother. My visions are primitive compared to hers but I *know* you, Aiden. I know your heart. And I know that you are too innocent for Elidad."

Aiden's eyebrows creased together. "What's that supposed to mean? *For* her?"

Sophia leaned back into her chair. "You know what I mean. You shouldn't play coy with a seer, it makes you sound like a child."

"I'm not being *coy*. Who says coy?"

"I'm older than you, remember?" *Over two hundred years.* Sophia leaned across the space separating the two chairs and grabbed Aiden's hand. Aiden was surprised there was no burning sensation from her touch this time. Though he'd been given the antidote, her presence made him feel like her touch might over take him.

She held his hand delicately. "You're not, are you?"

"Not what?" He forgot what they were talking about.

"Being coy. You really have yourself fooled." She released his hand.

"Have myself fooled about what?"

"You love Elidad." Her tone was flat.

"I—" he shook his head no but couldn't find the words. "I—" Realizing he didn't *want* to say no, he pressed his lips together.

Sophia held up her hand, waving her fingers. "Never lie."

Her premonitions came through touch; she could read his thoughts. Apparently, the antidote made him immune to her power, but she was still able to look into his feelings. Would she know what he thought about her?

"Well, I didn't come here to discuss your love life, I came to offer an invitation. Mother said without one, you might never use that match."

Aiden was reminded of the blue matches. One for him, and one for Elidad, from when they visited Leucosia last. Before they'd left Leucosia, the matches had appeared in his pocket. At that point, he couldn't imagine ever returning to the club, for any reason, especially alone. Now, the pull of curiosity and his acceptance of magic in the world changed his perspective. What did Leucosia want from him and why did she think it necessary for him to go alone?

"Naturally, you won't tell Elidad I was here," Sophia suggested.

"Why?" Aiden's brows pushed together.

A mischievous grin adorned her lips.

"Elidad isn't fond of me. It would probably be in *our* best interest if you didn't bother her concerning my visit." Her fingernails rapped on the leather of the chair. "Besides, if Mother wanted to see the two of you, I'm sure she would've asked. And if Elidad was ready, she would've come to see her already."

Sophia was right, Elidad would've gone alone. When Elidad found him, Abraham was too weak to explain why he'd killed her parents, but he encouraged Elidad to go to Leucosia for answers. Aiden was surprised when Elidad didn't rush to see her as soon as they came back from Mexico. He wouldn't have put it off this long. The truth was eating at Aiden. How could Elidad live without knowing? He knew Elidad felt betrayed. Aiden tried to imagine what that would feel like. He wasn't sure he'd want to see Leucosia either, if he were in Elidad's shoes. Perhaps he was meant to be the messenger between Leucosia and Elidad.

"Okay, I won't tell Elidad." Aiden agreed. "When does Leucosia want me to visit her?"

Sophia stood. "That love, is entirely up to you."

Aiden followed Sophia to the entry. Sophia picked up her coat as Aiden moved to open the door for her. She smiled at him and lightly touched his face. "Until we meet again, Aiden."

"Goodbye," he said, closing the door as she walked down the stairs leading to the sidewalk.

Aiden stood in the foyer, thinking back to the last time he and Elidad went to the club. In the floor-length mirror, he caught the reflection of his blue eyes, the same way he had just before seeing Elidad's tattoo for the first time. Elidad had pirouetted as Aiden held open her jacket, a low sweeping back on her dress revealed the work of art covering her skin. A demon slain between her hips, grasping at a sword that protruded from his chest. The sword's hilt, between her shoulder blades, looked like a cross, unwavering in its authority. How sad a life it depicted.

Elidad used a sword to slay demons and simultaneously created some of her own. He wondered where the Sword of Justice was now. He'd never asked Elidad what she'd done with it when they returned from Mexico. Like her tattoo, it would be a gruesome reminder of the reality that was her life.

After finding Abraham, Elidad didn't have any time to mourn. The church leaders sent a cleanup crew to ensure a fire incinerated all evidence of human remains. They couldn't afford for anyone to find a barn in Mexico with four dead priests inside. When the cleaners arrived, Elidad was composed as she made her statement, reliving the hours after her father's death. Aiden admired her strength.

Once the cleaners were gone, Aiden had been left with the responsibility of escorting the half-sane Elidad back to her father's house. As they left Mexico, she'd begun to unravel as the miles flew behind them.

Aiden's phone began to ring in his pocket. He slipped his hand inside to retrieve it, Elidad's name flashed on the screen.

"Hello?"

"Aiden," he could hear noise in the background as Elidad spoke, "I don't think I am going to make it back tonight, not early enough to have dinner with you, anyway. I have a lot of things to get done here and I told Lucian I'd help him with inventory."

"He can't do it by himself?" Aiden frowned.

"He probably could, but it would take a long time. It's much faster with two people. I'll call you tomorrow."

The stress in her voice kept Aiden from pushing further. "Okay, I'll lock up here. I'll talk to you later." He hung up the phone.

It wasn't an accident that Sophia showed up today. Leucosia knew Aiden's plans would change. Aiden's hand went to his pocket again.

This time he retrieved a single blue match.

CHAPTER EIGHT

As Aiden's cab swished down the back streets, his heart began to beat against the inside of his ribcage. He pulled at his tie to relieve the tension. How could he do this? The last time he'd been in the club, he'd thought he wouldn't survive the night. He smirked at the memory of Sophia and her touch. He'd thought she'd slipped him a drug. If only it'd been that simple. Fear of being drugged almost drove him off the cliff of sanity. Little did he know, insanity wasn't a cliff but an all-encompassing black hole. A void of which he'd already walked into, unknowingly, and was unable to find an escape from.

If he'd been drugged, the past few months wouldn't have been true, and magic wouldn't be the explanation.

He could live a life without exorcisms, demons, yeti and all the death and destruction that went with it. Before he started this journey, Elidad had warned him: '*No one is ready, ever.*' She was right, knowing *was* harder. He thought of Emily and father Joseph. He wondered what terrors that little girl would live with after being possessed. He prayed for her, every day.

Aiden's cab came to a stop in front of a large building in a commercial area. It could be a cannery, from the look of it. The only thing that set it apart from other buildings on the block was the line of people dressed in heels and suits, valeting Porches, Mercedes, and Aiden was pretty sure, a Bentley. He only caught the corner of the front grill, but they were unmistakable, even from this distance.

Aiden took a deep breath and adjusted his coat. He looked down at the clothes Elidad bought him. The last time they'd come here, he hadn't known they were going to a high-profile nightclub. All he'd known was they were headed to meet a friend of Elidad's in hopes of finding out more about the key. When she'd handed over the outfit, he'd protested the change, informing her he had his own clothes. She'd laughed and said he could wear whatever, if he wanted to get his ass kicked.

Aiden got out of the car and tipped the cab driver. As his feet found the sidewalk, a neon sign hummed just loud enough to be heard above the commotion of impatient patrons awaiting entry, catching his attention.

"Genus." Aiden said quietly to himself, smirking. When he and Elidad pulled up before, there was an Aston Martin being valeted. That would keep any man from noticing the sign.

Ignoring the line that trailed away from the front door, hugging the building and wrapping around the corner, Aiden approached the bouncer.

"Name." The man with the clipboard demanded. His arms were larger than Aiden's thighs. A clear, spiral tube ran out of his collar up the side of his throat and into his ear.

"Mr. Taber." A voice was clear over the shoulder of the bouncer. The bouncer glanced back at Dedrick.

Dedrick stood long and lean in a tailored suit, the black fabric trimmed with red. He waved his hand at the velvet rope. The bouncer immediately pulled it open for Aiden. Aiden stepped through reaching his hand forward to clasp Dedrick's in a firm shake. Dedrick's hand was as cold as his steel grey eyes.

Dedrick looked to be around seventy, but Aiden wasn't sure. Sophia appeared to be twenty-four, but she was a hundred and seventy-five.

"Mr. Taber, so nice to see you again. I was told you would be joining us this evening," Dedrick's voice was steady.

"Thank you," Aiden said as he released Dedrick's hand.

"Shall we?" Dedrick gestured toward the front door, the men moved away from the crowd. "I find it interesting, Mr. Taber, the first time you joined us here you were paralyzed with fear and dare I say... wonderment. This time your calm state speaks volumes on your behalf. It compels me to wonder, sir, what have you seen in the little time since we last met?"

Aiden paused a moment just inside the doorway. "Please, Dedrick, call me Aiden."

"Of course, Aiden."

"What makes you believe I was fearful the last time we met? I didn't speak a word to you," Aiden said.

Dedrick smiled. "Your heart was racing like a rabbit's does the second it realizes a predator has it in its grip... No matter," Dedrick brushed off his comment before Aiden had a chance to digest it. "I shall take you to her."

"To Leucosia? You don't have to take me all the way down there. I remember how to get there."

Dedrick looked amused. "Not Leucosia."

The elevator pinged and the doors opened as Aiden and Dedrick approached. Aiden could see Sophia's silhouette against the back wall. The single bulb inside lit the ends of her thick red hair as it cascaded over her ivory shoulder. Green eyes glistened back at the two men.

"Sophia," Aiden's surprise was apparent.

She pouted her lips. "Oh Aiden, don't sound so happy to see me."

"Just surprised, that's all. You didn't tell me you'd meet me here," Aiden reached out his had to shake Dedrick's again. "Thank you."

"A pleasure, sir."

When the elevator began to lower, Sophia put her arm through Aiden's. "You don't seem as nervous, this time."

Aiden laughed. "Dedrick said last time my heart was racing like a rabbit's does when a predator has it in its grip."

"He's such a poet," Sophia laughed.

Even without the influence of the siren's song, Aiden found Sophia's demeanor enchanting.

"How does he know what my heart was doing?" Aiden wondered aloud.

"Because," the smile on her lips implied Aiden should know the answer, "he can hear it."

The doors of the elevator opened.

Aiden felt an electric shock race through the floor. The percussion began in the souls of his feet and surged thorough his body. Arm and arm with Sophia, they stepped into the crowd.

Aiden felt like he'd entered a different place. The club, once overwhelmingly crude and intimidating, seemed like a blip in the reality that his life had become. He'd thought Elidad cruel to bring him here; now, he knew the truth. The evil and temptation that Elidad knew was much more consuming than this place could ever be.

Looking through the crowd as they walked, the majority of people's eyes glowed in the black light. When he was with Elidad, he thought it was some strange trend. He knew now, they weren't wearing lenses; they were different *species*.

Aiden smiled to himself.

Genus, the name of the club was a Latin word; its literal translation was *species*.

What were they? If not sirens, then what? It didn't matter; none would scare him as much as Ghelgath. Aiden would never forget the fear in his body as they marched into battle against a demonic ice army, backed by a ruthless dragon. Elidad said this club was a safe place, where good and evil existed under one roof. The only venue of its kind. A peace treaty between opposing sides made it possible. Elidad said a lot of good came out of the club and, at the time, it had been hard to believe. Now, Aiden could understand its importance and why the Catholic Church would fund such a place.

Aiden looked up to see women cascading down silk sheets that hung from the ceiling. The imagery they projected didn't seem as intimidating as it had before. Their ability to pull themselves to the ceiling was commendable. He envied their strength, dangling above danger, climbing up and away to safety. Aiden wondered if he would be able to pull himself out of the chaos he was surrounded in now. If only he had their strength.

"Are you okay, love?" Sophia's tug pulled him out of his thoughts.

Aiden looked at her. Sharing this moment made him feel close to her. "It's just strange. When I was here last, I thought they were a sign of evil and temptation. Now, they make me feel like there's hope. Hope to pull myself out of any evil pit I might find myself in."

Her laugh rang over the music. "Such an optimist."

Aiden barely heard her last word as she turned into the crowd, the club consuming her on all sides.

CHAPTER NINE

Aiden recognized one of the bartenders as he and Sophia pushed their way to the bar. The tattoo enveloping his body made him impossible to miss. The thick black ink began on his clean-shaven head, following his wide frame down the back of his neck and peeking out of his shirt everywhere that skin showed. His back was turned to Aiden and Sophia, with two other bartenders between. Without looking their way, he grabbed under the counter, retrieving a bottle that Aiden also recognized. The bartender turned, making his way through the chaos that three bodies caused, while serving the hordes of people on the other side of the bar.

The bartender's hand fished underneath the counter to produce two glasses and set them on the counter. The bar was transparent, a blue light shining from the inside. In minute details all over the club, Aiden could see Leucosia's signature; hints of light and water. If you knew her, you knew she was responsible. You could see her in the glowing blue light, all around.

Aiden watched as the man, who could've been carved out of stone, silently worked.

Holding the bottle of liquid high above each glass, Aiden watched as the transparent liquid cascaded out of the bottle, sparkling like gold when it hit the air. As it fell into each glass, it shimmered purple like a thunder egg. *Amethyst, perhaps?* Churning at the bottom, it plumed into a dark black liquid, just before sparking into flames.

Aiden watched it burn for a second before covering his glass with his hand to extinguish the fire. Sophia did the same as her red hair drifted softly, a light wave hanging around her breast. With her hand over her glass, she shrugged her hair behind her shoulder to face Aiden. She smiled when she realized Aiden was staring at her. She removed her hand from her glass, Aiden mirroring her movement. Black smoke swelled over the rim of their glasses carrying a smell that was seared into Aiden's mind: the smell of flowers. Aiden inhaled the smoke as if it were meant to be a snifter. His taste buds welcomed the teasing aroma, fragrant and sweet.

Sophia held up her glass, "To what's to come."

"Cheers." Aiden replied, the soft glasses clinking under his fingertips, though he was unable to hear it over the music. Aiden swallowed, still unsure what he was drinking. He'd thought about it, many times after his first visit. The way the liquid transformed in the air and in the glass, lighting itself on fire. *Magic.* The first time he came to *Genus*, he hadn't believed in magic. He hadn't believed in sirens then either, yet here he was, sharing a drink with one.

Every sip pleasantly seared Aiden's throat with a warmth that traced to his belly, lifting the weight of his thoughts. "Ready?"

"Of course," Sophia deposited her glass on the bar to take his arm.

A hall leading to private rooms loomed in the shadows at the back of the club. Aiden smiled to himself. The last time he was here, the drink at the bar was the only thing that kept him moving after Elidad, his numb mind, unable to stop his forward progression. The first time, he'd thought the rooms were full of movie stars in exquisite costumes. Now, he knew the truth; different creatures and varying races gathered here, able to show their true selves in these dark rooms.

Sophia and Aiden approached the blue room, where the doorway leading to Leucosia's lair was hidden.

When he was with Elidad, she'd stopped Aiden outside the door. Leaning her body against his, she whispered in his ear, preparing him for the difficult walk through the room. Her action had shocked him. She was playing into a cover, attempting to be inconspicuous as she gave him directions.

Trying to play along, his hands moved to the small of her back, pulling her into his body. Her frame was small but not petite; Aiden stood at six-two and she was a good five inches shorter than him. That night, she was the same height in her black stiletto heels. Her hard muscle was soft against him as she ran her fingers through his hair. That was the first time he'd felt *something.* The drink at the bar numbed all his senses except for the way *she'd* made him feel.

"Careful, Priest, I might think you are enjoying yourself." She'd teased as her breath wisped past his ear, sending a shockwave through his body.

Sophia walked into the room, washed in blue light. "Come on."

Her words pulled Aiden out of his memory. People were scattered around the sofas, their faces dull and lifeless, frozen in a trance. The siren in the center of the room was put there to protect the doorway to Leucosia's hiding place. She trapped anyone who entered with her gaze. Aiden remembered when he could feel the pull of that siren, before he'd been given 'the antidote.'

Elidad had warned Aiden, if he'd been caught in the room, she would've left him, stuck for days. That night, panic almost overtook him. He'd felt the siren staring at him; he needed to look at her. He'd known he shouldn't, but how badly he wanted to lay eyes on her.

Now he could.

Standing shoulder to shoulder with Sophia, Aiden gazed upon her flawless body. She danced, or rather, floated rhythmically to the music. Her hair and clothing moved around her, like Leucosia's did in the air. The tube of water was stretched from floor to ceiling, like an aquarium, and appeared to be the source of light for the room. Periodically, bubbles ascended from the bottom of the tank, floating around her body as she moved.

"She's in water," Aiden said.

Sophia giggled. "I forgot. The last time you came through you hadn't had the antidote. You didn't see her, last time?"

"No, it took everything in me to get through the room. I almost didn't," Aiden admitted.

Sophia smiled. "Don't feel bad. She has that effect on everyone, even women."

Aiden frowned looking around the room. "Even women? Has Elidad had the antidote, then?"

"No. Somehow, she's immune to the siren song."

"Is that common?" Aiden assumed.

"Women naturally have a higher tolerance, but if a siren wants to sway you, she will. Most of us can control our persuasion. I have to concentrate to use my power. This one," Sophia pointed to the buoyant woman, "she has a look that can get you. My mother doesn't even have to try, but she's an origin. However, if any of us sing, there's no escaping our draw. No human has ever been known to be immune before Elidad. It's a quandary, really."

"One more mystery surrounding Elidad's life." Aiden said, more to himself than to Sophia. "How can she breathe in there?" Aiden gestured to the woman submerged in water.

"We are daughters of the river," Sophia answered. "Naturally, we can breathe under water."

"Elidad mentioned that. What does it mean, to be the daughters of the river?"

"Certainly, you've heard of Achelous?"

"Wasn't he the one that fought Heracles?" It'd been a long time since Aiden studied Greek Mythology.

Sophia smiled. "The god of the river."

"God?" Aiden's brow furrowed.

Sophia laughed. "He wasn't really. Before this century, when our kind was still allowed to live in the open, humans thought of us as gods. Their fascination with our power skewed the truth."

"What changed? Why don't you still live in the open." Aiden had wanted to know the answer to this question for a long time.

"We were killed off, mostly. When humans became powerful, they removed the majority of the monsters that remained. It was easier to hide our power and pretend we were a myth."

"You aren't monsters." Aiden said.

"Humans are strange," Sophia analyzed, "if you're not like them, they assume you're a monster. They try to destroy anything that isn't like them." She looked at Aiden, "You even try to destroy each other when you're not alike.

"That's a fair assessment," Aiden agreed.

"Humans are especially dangerous to species that have something they covet. It's better for us to not exist, at all."

The siren in the tank stretched her hand toward Aiden. The night he was with Elidad, his imagination ran wild with the possibility of what she might look like. When he'd walked through the room, his skin burned where Sophia touched him, invoking a deeper yearning to see her. His curiosity had nearly taken him captive. If he hadn't been shocked to see Elidad melt into the mirror, he wouldn't have been able to continue without looking back at her.

She was extraordinary. Her skin glowed in the light that illuminated the tank. The only resemblance to Sophia was her green eyes, he noticed as she winked at him. Aiden stretch his hand forward in response to her action. Their hands, separated by glass pressed together, as if a formal introduction. The surface of the tank was warm to the touch.

"Ready?" Sophia asked over his shoulder.

"She doesn't look that much like you," Aiden observed.

"She's my half-sister," Sophia said as Aiden removed his hand from the glass. "She's a little older than me."

"How much is a little?" Aiden turned to follow her to the mirror. He could see Sophia's smile in the refection.

"Two hundred years."

"Wow." Aiden realized he'd made an awful attempt at hiding his shock. "Two hundred years older than you? Do you have any other siblings?"

"A few that are still alive," She answered, looking at herself in the mirror, leaning in to check her makeup.

Aiden recalled the swirl of emotions he felt when he saw Elidad melt into that mirror. It looked like she was being absorbed into mercury as she moved through it. He hadn't known what was happening to her and he'd been afraid of what was going to happen to him. The pressure of the Siren had been too much for him to bear without Elidad's presence.

Standing next to Sophia, Aiden held up his hand and stretched it forward to reach into the passageway. The cool pressure around his hand felt familiar, the eerie feeling of being in the depths of water without being wet. Aiden glanced into the reflection one last time to see the Siren and the people she held captive, before stepping through to the darkness on the other side. He could hear Sophia by his side as he reached into his pocket for the match that would light their way.

He pulled his phone from his pocket, the same way Elidad did. The light made it easy to locate the rock wall where he would strike the blue match. When the flame lit, a small plume of smoke billowed toward Aiden's face, bringing the smell of flowers that sparked his memory of Sophia. Sophia's petite figure was flawless in the low light.

She was flawless anytime, really.

The flame grew more intense as he held the match and it became increasingly difficult to look in its direction. He squinted at the tiny flair as it began to drip with sparks to the ground.

Aiden tossed the match out over the water. They stood and watched as it slowly floated in the air, delicately drifting like a down feather, before reaching the water's surface. When it lightly touched down, it paused on the surface for a moment before continuing its descent through the water. Steadily, it drifted the same way as it had above the water. The crystal-clear water made it easy to watch the downward motion. When it touched the bottom, it ignited the water like a light switch being flipped, the light revealing the vastness of their surroundings.

The pair stood on a tiny rock ledge.

The once glass-like body of water became turbulent before them. It bubbled and churned as stones began to rise to the surface, forming a path that seemed infinite across the raging water.

"Ladies first," Aiden extended his hand forward.

"Such a gentleman," Sophia giggled, walking out across the rocks. "Does she know?" Sophia asked.

"Does who know what?"

Sophia pivoted on the stone she was standing on to look him in the eye. "Does Elidad know you're in love with her?"

"I'm not …" Aiden said.

Sophia rolled her eyes. "You're *still* going to try and deny it? I thought we talked about this already. You sound ridiculous."

Aiden considered her words. She was right. In all the time spent with Elidad, his feelings had become something more. In his new parish, he'd laid in bed unable to sleep, thinking of the night they'd spent together in the bath caves in the Crystal City, where a dream of Aiden's death inspired Elidad to let her guard down and ask Aiden to stay with her.

After that night, his mind often wandered to those caves, where the air was thick and warm and the rushing sound of water was soothing. The place where, if he closed his eyes, he could remember the way Elidad felt against him. Those memories frequently sent pulses through his body, an electric connection to a life that he'd never known before her.

"Why are you so concerned about my feelings for Elidad?" Aiden asked.

Sophia shrugged. "Can't a girl be jealous?" She winked at him. Even though she was teasing, Aiden knew there was truth behind her words.

Aiden continued to follow Sophia across the pathway, not sure what to say. His mind drifted back to Elidad. He wondered how she would cope with Isaac coming home. It was difficult for her to imagine Isaac helpless. The doctors were confident he would gain some of his memory back, but Aiden wasn't so sure. Aiden hoped they were right. Elidad had already lost so much in the last year; her heart desperately needed some relief.

"Are you ready?" Sophia asked, breaking Aiden's train of thought.

Aiden realized Sophia was standing on the seventy-seventh stone.

"I'm ready."

Sophia stepped off the stone into the glowing blue water below. Aiden watched her disappear just before hopping onto the stone to step off the hard surface after her.

CHAPTER TEN

Every part of *Genus*—from the velvet rope to here—felt like a different place. Aiden realized his outlook on life was different, too. Perhaps he was a new man.

As his body slowly moved through the magical void of water, he couldn't help but wonder again why Leucosia wanted to see him without Elidad.

Elidad should've come here before now. He couldn't understand why Elidad refused to see Leucosia. Leucosia was the one that could give Elidad answers. She alone knew what happened to Elidad's parents and why Abraham had killed them.

Aiden understood the betrayal. Leucosia kept Abraham's secret. He could see why Elidad felt hurt, but his curiosity would drive him to see Leucosia and demand answers, rather than do what Elidad was doing.

As Aiden's feet hit the ground, he became aware of standing in Leucosia's lair.

Statues of men were gathered below a massive tree trunk. The tall, ebony tree was just as Aiden remembered. The bark, a deep black like coal; its branches reaching high above the ground, twisting and smooth as if shaped by the water. No foliage garnished the tree, seemingly in an ever-sleeping state, forlorn yet homely. If Aiden weren't standing in front of the tree, he might think it was dead but for its strange essence. It was as if he could *feel* the life within it, like he could feel it breathing.

The men made of stone were in heaping, gruesome piles. Aiden had learned that the semblance of tortured souls was a monument. It was built as a reminder of Calandra, Leucosia's sister, whose insanity led to the torture and dismemberment of many men.

"Aiden, it's so nice to see you." Leucosia's voice was as soft as Aiden remembered.

Aiden watched as Sophia embraced her mother. Leucosia's hand delicately touched Sophia's face. "My beauty, it's even better to see *you*."

"Why did you want me to come without Elidad?" Aiden asked. "Hasn't she been deceived enough?"

"Did someone imply that you should be deceiving?" Leucosia asked, turning her eyes from Sophia to Aiden.

Sophia shrugged. "I don't believe I did."

"You told me to keep it from her," Aiden reminded Sophia.

"She didn't need to know that you were planning on coming. You can tell her whatever you want now," Sophia said.

"I've never deceived Elidad," Leucosia said.

Aiden laughed. "Really?"

"I held, in confidence, a piece of her past. A piece that would impede her ability to grow as a healthy young woman. There was no need to burden her with the tragic truth of her parents' deaths. Most would agree that her childhood was difficult enough," Leucosia raised an eyebrow. "Wouldn't *you* agree, Aiden?"

The heat under Aiden's collar rose to his cheeks as memories of his schooldays came flooding back. The man standing before Leucosia now was ashamed of the boy he'd once been. Leucosia knew what he'd done. As a seer, she had the ability to look into his past, and she was using it against him now.

Leucosia made a gesture for Aiden to follow her through the tall fragrant flowers that were scattered below the ebony tree. They stood thigh-high with centers that spiked in iridescent colors, the pedals fell open and away from the middle. They reminded Aiden of a magical variation of Echinacea.

"What are they called?" Aiden paused.

Leucosia glanced over her shoulder to see what he was talking about. "Ekhinos."

"They're beautiful."

"They are." Leucosia agreed.

"Where do they come from?"

"Where all plants on this earth come from." Leucosia smiled.

"They don't look like they're from this earth. I've never seen anything like them, before."

"You have." Leucosia disagreed. "You've seen the Echinacea flower."

"I thought they looked similar, but they're so different." Aiden analyzed.

"Over time this species changed into what you know. These," Leucosia touched a flower bud in the middle causing it to shut around her finger, "have remained untouched by evolution."

The aroma of the flowers was burned into Aiden's memory, but somehow, their uniqueness had escaped him. Jagged leaves were striped with dark and light lime green. The petals were an assortment of purple, pink and teal. The flowers, at the top of long stems, bobbled behind him and Leucosia as they began to pushed through the waist-high field again. As they brushed past the greenery, the leaves would gently fold in on themselves and gracefully reopen once they passed, like the flower had when Leucosia touched it.

Aiden recognized Leucosia's birdbath. He'd never forget it. The first time he'd seen it operate, he'd thought the images it'd shown were 3-D, projected from an unknown source. It wasn't until Leucosia plucked the silver canister and the hilt of the Sword of Justice from its mist that he'd realized it was something *more*.

Aiden peered over the edge of the birdbath. Leucosia watched him silently, allowing his investigation of the shallow water.

"May I touch it?" Aiden asked.

Leucosia smiled. "You may. It is only water, after all."

Aiden looked down, seeing his reflection on the surface. He remembered his face as a boy. He wondered if the change in him from that time until now was merely superficial. Was the man he'd grown into really different? Was that sad, scared boy, who'd tried so hard to win the affection of his father, looming somewhere in the depths?

Aiden reached down and ran his fingers across the image of his face, sending ripples out across the water. Remembering he wasn't alone with his thoughts, he looked up to see Leucosia's blue eyes radiating back at him. Her long, white hair fell down her shoulders, framing her long face. Broad wings protruded from her back, dwarfing her thin body.

Aiden looked over his shoulder to see Sophia sitting on the shore, close to the river's edge, far enough that she wouldn't be able to hear them speak.

"Your worry is what proves you're not him." Leucosia said.

Aiden furrowed his brow. "Proves I'm not who?"

"Your father."

"If you're a seer that sees the past and future, how do you know what I was thinking?" Aiden asked.

"Am I a seer?"

"That's what Elidad calls you," Aiden said.

"That's the easiest explanation, I suppose."

"Easier than what?" Aiden asked.

"Prophet."

Aiden stared at her. "Like a prophet of God?"

"We feel things. We don't just get images of memories or things to come. We *feel* emotion. Our senses are heightened. A strand inside of us is linked to everyone. The older I became, the more I was able to develop this link. Think of it as being an extraordinary empath." Leucosia's eyes found Sophia on the riverbank. "That's why she is so taken by you. Her powers are not as strong as mine, but she reads people well. She can feel your emotions. She knows you're a good man."

Aiden's eyes followed Leucosia's to where Sophia was sitting on the bank. Sophia's red hair radiated off the white sand. Aiden looked back at Leucosia.

"Don't worry, Aiden," Leucosia smiled, "I know that's not where your heart belongs and Sophia knows it as well." Leucosia looked down into the birdbath, "Sophia's path is much different than yours, but she will enjoy your company while you are here."

"While I'm here?" Aiden echoed.

"You will be called to Vatican City," Leucosia said.

Aidan shook his head. "I can't. I need to stay here, with Elidad. She needs me."

"Does she? Or do *you* need *her*?"

"She needs me. She can't be alone," Aiden said.

"You took vows, Aiden. The more time spent with her, the more difficult it will be for you to uphold those vows."

Aiden wanted to deny what she was saying but knew there was no point.

Aidan shook his head, "How can she make it through this alone? She's lost so much."

"She won't be alone."

"Isaac needs to be taken care of, he's not company. He can't remember where he's been. He doesn't even remember if he made it to Jerusalem. How can he help her through this when he can't help himself? Who will take care of Elidad if I leave?"

"His presence will be a distraction from her pain," Leucosia said. "She'll be focused on making him well, and she will find healing in that."

"I don't see how my leaving could help her. I can't leave her."

"You must. This is why I asked you to come. If you don't go, you won't find the next key." Leucosia reached out and lightly touched the surface of the water.

Aiden watched the ripple she sent across the water with her finger. It began to rise on the surface as a mist. The mist swirled becoming thicker, taking shape until he saw figures in it. He saw himself, dressed in priest's robes in a room he didn't recognize.

"Elidad needs to spend time with Isaac, her faith is becoming difficult for her to bear. As you said, she's lost so much. She needs to find hope before she can continue her path to find the keys. But you: your faith is strong and now that you have completed the task with Elidad, the leaders of the Church will put their trust in you. They will have a new job for you and will request your presence at the Vatican. This job will help you move forward in the search." Leucosia's eyes turned back to the images floating above the water's surface, now showing Aiden turning pages in a book. "Her feelings for you, Aiden, are very real."

Aiden's eyes darted to meet Leucosia's.

"You know it's true." Leucosia leaned forward to lightly touch his hand. "Aiden, her heart cannot bear any more heartbreak. You have given yourself to God and the Church. You can't stay here. Don't build her up any more than you already have, only to break her heart."

Leucosia's words tore into his chest like a dagger. Her radiant blue eyes remained soft as she cut out his heart. Unable to process what she was saying, he shook his head.

"She doesn't— She's not in lo—"

Leucosia's eyebrows rose, daring him to complete his sentence. Without looking at the water, her hand moved across the surface and lightly touched it. The images changed to memories of him and Elidad.

Elidad stood in the bathroom, white towel wrapped around her body, causing Aiden to pause. He was drawn in by the image of her silhouette's profile as revealed by the open door, steam rolling out around her. He couldn't help but trace the image of her body with his eyes.

The mist morphed into an image of them in the entryway of Abraham's home, Aiden standing in front of the mirror. Watching Elidad walk down the stairs in her black dress, his eyes focusing on her striking red lips, leaving him to wonder what they would feel like. Then, came the hallway of the club, before entering the blue room. This was the first time she'd been close enough to smell her perfume and feel her body in his arms. The first time he'd held her. Her breath had sent shivers through his body that were easily relived.

The mist changed to the night she was almost lost on the mountain. His heart ached, reliving the emotions of helplessness as Elidad was swallowed by the winter storm. When he and Jed found her, the relief was short lived; Elidad's body had been ravaged by hypothermia. She'd lost the majority of her gear in the storm, leaving them with only one sleeping bag. They'd been forced to share it. Aiden held her that night as he slept next to her. He recalled the way her body shivered next to his, until his life-giving heat was drawn into her, enough to calm the savage quaking. Afraid to lose her again, he'd wrapped his arms around her, as if they could keep her close.

The next memory moved something inside of him. It was an image of the night they'd spent in the Crystal City baths. This was the same night his mind often wandered to, lately. It was the same image that sent him to confession and ultimately had taken him away from her. The thought of her fingertips on his skin made a chill race down his arms. He wished there was a way to live in that evening without sending him to confession.

Then finally, the image of Elidad and him standing in front of the barn where they'd found Abraham. The look he and Elidad shared reminded him how much passion was in that moment, before she'd walked into a fate unknown. He'd wanted to tell her so much before she went in, for fear he'd never see her again. Somehow… he felt, she knew. When he'd tried to stop Elidad from going, he'd pleaded with her, firmly pulling her to him. They'd stood, face to face, inches apart.

He should have kissed her.

The images fell away, gathering as mist, falling into the water like raindrops.

Aiden didn't want to look at Leucosia; he wanted to be in those memories. He could continue denying his feelings to Leucosia and Sophia but couldn't deny them to himself. Their bond grew quickly, it snuck up on him before he'd realized. Leucosia was right, he'd taken vows, and he was in danger of breaking them. He *would* have to leave.

His eyes met Leucosia's. "I understand. I'll go when I get the call."

"I know it'll be difficult, Aiden, but it's the best scenario for you. This way, Isaac and Elidad will heal together and you will refocus on your responsibilities. It's the only way you'll continue in the search for the keys while Elidad is unable. Elidad will be angry with you when you leave, but it's the only way, Aiden."

"How angry?" Aiden asked.

"You *must* take the job at the Vatican, and Elidad can never know how you feel." Leucosia stood and motioned toward Sophia. "Now, I would like to have a word with my daughter, if you don't mind."

Sophia was walking toward them, bringing the scent of the sirens with her as she passed through the flowers.

"Of course," Aiden answered. He knew Leucosia was done giving information. He had no desire to speak about Elidad in front of Sophia. He left the two sirens.

Following Sophia's path to the sandy shore, Aiden walked to the water's edge. The only place he'd seen white sand was in Florida, by the ocean. It was strange seeing it here, in this underground cave on an island in the middle of a river, if that's what it was. It certainly flowed like a river, but he couldn't imagine where it began or where it ended. Aiden raked his fingers through the silky pebbles. Grabbing a handful, he let the sand slip through his fingers, the same way he must let Elidad go. He shook his head at the thought. He *was* in love with her. Leucosia was right. He needed to leave. But could he let her slip away?

Aiden momentarily considered tying a rock to his ankles and throwing himself into the river. Too bad suicide was just as forbidden as his feelings for Elidad.

"Will he leave?" Sophia asked her mother, when she was confident that Aiden couldn't hear them.

"He says he will." Leucosia answered. "When the time comes, he will not want to go." Leucosia stopped walking and turned toward Sophia. "You need to make sure he leaves. They cannot be together."

"I understand, Mother."

Leucosia reached out for Sophia's hands, clasping them in hers. "You also need to keep your distance. He needs to stay on task; he cannot be distracted. He needs to find the next key."

Sophia pulled her hands away. "I know, Mother. I'll make sure he leaves."

"You need to remember, his heart belongs to Elidad," Leucosia said cautiously.

Sophia considered her mother's eyes. "What do you know?"

"I know I am like all mothers. I do not wish to see my daughter hurt." She said, lifting her hand to touch Sophia's face.

Sophia pulled away. "I'm not a child. I'll be fine."

Leucosia smiled affectionately. "Of course, dear."

CHAPTER ELEVEN

Standing on the porch, Aiden's mind lingered in memory before he committed to pressing the bell. Memories of his childhood, visiting Abraham, bringing Elidad home after learning Abraham was missing, saving Elidad from the Shadow Man. *That* was just the beginning. Everything they'd been through... did he have the strength to leave?

Last night, through a restless sleep, he decided not.

Leucosia didn't have all the answers. What if he stayed? What if he chose to leave the Church? Maybe God had a different plan for him. Maybe his life and Elidad's were meant to be intertwined. Maybe they were meant to be together.

He came here to put his life in *Elidad's* hands. The decision would be hers.

Staring at the doorbell, he wasn't sure he had the strength to push it. He lifted his finger, nerves pulsating in the tip. Flexing his fingers, he pressed the button. As the seconds ticked by, he had the urge to ding-dong-ditch.

Elidad pulled the door open. "Hey."

"Hey," he answered. He definitely wouldn't have had enough time to run.

"You okay?" She asked.

"Yeah, I was just thinking of... Abraham." *Half true.*

Elidad's expression changed.

"I wanted to ask you something." His nerves caused him to waver. "I came to check on you. How's the packing going?" Aiden stepped through the door.

"It's going. Abraham has a lot of stuff crammed in this house." She admitted. "And to be honest, I'm stressed about Isaac, that's a whole different project. I'm not sure I'm going to get everything done here."

"There's no rush. You don't have to sell this place." Aiden reminded her.

"I *want* to sell this place."

"I think you're just angry right now." Aiden observed. "I'd hate for you to regret it, later."

Elidad's face grew dark. "I'm not going to regret it."

"You can't know that," he argued. "Besides, it'll be good for you, to have a place to stay, away from Isaac's—" *away from Lucian,* "so you can have a break."

"I have my own home." Elidad reminded him. "What am I going to do with three houses to take care of?"

"You might have a tough time getting to your place, at first. It's different, coming to Abraham's. This place is close enough; you can get here for the night. Your house is too far, you might not see it for a few months." Aiden reasoned.

"Well, if you can stay with Isaac for a couple days, every once in a while, I could run home and get some stuff done. That'd give me a break." Elidad said.

Aiden tried to control the expression on his face. "Yeah, that'd give you a break."

"What's wrong?" Elidad's brows creased together.

"Nothing, just trying to picture how it'll all go," Aiden lied. "Hopefully I'll be here long enough to help."

"Why? Did you hear something?" Anger flared in Elidad's eyes.

"Not from the Church. I think they're happy with where I'm at, for now." *That wasn't an outright lie.*

Elidad's face softened. "Good." She seemed pacified. "Come on, I was just finishing lunch." She led Aiden into the kitchen. White subway tile gleamed off the backsplash, contrasting with the grey counters and off-white cabinets. The modern design had a sterile feel to it. Elidad put her plate in the dishwasher and refilled her water glass.

"Do you want something?" Elidad offered, spinning a bag of chips toward him.

"No, thanks." With his nerves in this state, he couldn't eat, even if he were hungry. He wasn't even sure he could discuss what he wanted.

"When did Abraham update the kitchen?" It looked different than when they were kids, he hadn't thought to ask before.

Elidad face looked grim. "When he and I weren't speaking."

"Oh." Aiden was sorry he asked. "It's beautiful."

"Yes." Elidad agreed. "Did you just come to ask about the kitchen?"

Aiden's heart took off like a greyhound after its starting gate opened. He wanted to tell her how he felt. She needed to know, but here? Like this? It needed to be different. His eyes locked with hers. "I wanted to know what you're doing Saturday."

"Tomorrow?" She defined.

The shock on her face made him regret his question. "Yes, tomorrow." He tried to cover. "I mean, it's just— you've been working hard and you're stressed. I thought we could... take a break. Talk."

"Apparently everyone thinks I need a break," her voice was flat.

"What?" Aiden pulled out a barstool from under the island and sat.

"Lucian said almost the same thing, that *I needed a break*. He offered to take me out tomorrow." Elidad watched Aiden carefully.

"Like a date?" He couldn't help ask, internally cringing at his tone.

"Does it matter?" Her voice was sharp.

Aiden felt like there was a volcano rumbling under the surface of his skin. "You think it's a good idea to start dating him? You need him to run the store and help you with Isaac. When things go sideways, it'll get messy."

"*When* things go sideways?" Elidad's eyes narrowed.

"I don't think he's the kind of guy that's in it for the long haul," Aiden spat.

Elidad crossed her arms. "If I need dating advice, I'll ask someone with experience, thanks."

"I've got plenty of experience," Aiden glared.

His statement took Elidad's words away. She stared at him for a soundless second.

"What? Do you think I've never been on a date?" Aiden snorted.

"You went out on plenty of dates in High School." Elidad's right eyebrow arched with the memory.

Aiden could feel the color draining from his face.

"You're one to talk about people *not* in it for the long haul," Elidad accused.

"I was a different person. The important thing is, I changed. I wanted to be different," Aiden hated defending himself.

"And why did you?" Elidad demanded. "You were such a dick. What on earth could cause you to change? Did something tragic happen?"

Aiden stared at her in disbelief. The heat in his body was unbearable, threatening to escape. "My mother died." His words shot out like steam from a teapot.

"Oh." Elidad was deflated by his honesty.

"I *let* her die," he corrected.

"I didn't know your mom … passed away." Elidad's voice softened. "It can't be your fault."

"I didn't do anything to help her." He shook his head.

Silence replaced the tension between them.

Aiden took a deep breath and harshly exhaled. "My father was impossible to live with. If I had been different, I could've stood up for my mother. I could have helped her… But I didn't."

Elidad stood motionless on the other side of the island.

"My father was a hard man. He demanded perfection. Money and power were the only things that mattered. Everyone, and everything else, was insignificant."

"I don't have a single memory of my father that's happy. He'd tolerate me when I was younger, as long as I stayed out of his way. In front of people, he'd act the part of a respectable family man. But in our house, emotions were thought of as weak. I remember, when I was eight, one of my favorite toys broke. I was just a kid, so I cried. He stormed over to me, shaking me, telling me to straighten up. When he couldn't stop my crying, he slapped me. My mother tried to stop him, so he hit her too."

"I'm sorry, Aiden," Elidad's voice was a whisper.

"He'd say *I don't raise pussies in my house. We're a house of winners not whiners.*" The smile that crested Aiden's lips was broken. "If you weren't the winner, you were the first loser. There was no second place."

Elidad remembered Aiden saying those words during recess when he'd play games with the other kids. *We're winners not whiners.* Then, she'd thought Aiden was insufferable. Now, she recognized his brokenness.

Aiden continued. "My mother was expected to be perfect too, and when she wasn't, there were consequences." Aiden could hear darkness invade his tone. "I think, when she broke her leg from taking a bad fall down the stairs, it was the first time the doctor gave her prescription pain killers. She didn't stop taking them after that. At first, they dulled her physical pain, but in the end, she used them to drown *all* her pain." Aiden shook his head, unable to look at Elidad.

"Craving adoration from my father, which was the closest I could get to affection, I treated women the same way he did. Including my mother… and the girls at school." Aiden's eyes flashed from the counter to Elidad.

"Imagine what it must have been like for my mother, raising a son that treated her so terribly. Imagine raising a monster, identical to the one you married. Her life was hell. I never laid a hand on her," Aiden said quickly. "But mental abuse is sometimes far worse than physical."

Elidad's heart was an empty hole, emotions pouring out of the gaping wound. She felt sorry for the boy who'd tormented her and wanted to rush to the man that was spilling his guts to her now. "Aiden, it's not your fault. Your mother let him raise you. She didn't take you out of that horrible situation. It's a miracle you changed at all."

Aiden folded his hands on the grey counter. "Some women tolerate being treated like dirt, better than others. Most of them get smart, in the end, so… naturally, I dated a lot. Even if I did like someone, and wanted to keep them around, my father would find fault in them and I was on to the next."

"When you moved to our grade, you were twelve?" Aiden verified.

"Yes." Elidad agreed.

"That made me fifteen. I hated the way we lived. I hated how angry my father was and how wasted my mother was. I hated the fights, the fear—I hated everything. I started standing up to him; I pushed back on everything, no matter the consequences." His eyes drifted to the back wall of the kitchen, unfocused in the present. "Do you remember when I was seventeen, I came to school with a broken arm?"

Elidad nodded, "I was sick of hearing your stupid story about how you broke it snowboarding. You told it a million times."

Aiden's eyes were still far away. "My father broke it in a door. He was hurting my mother; he threw her on the floor and kicked her." Aiden's hands tightened until his knuckles were white. "I was so angry. I hit him and gave him a bloody nose. He stopped kicking her, laughing. I'm not sure if he was angry or surprised. I pulled my mom off the floor and tried to get out of there, but he followed us. I pushed my mother out the door but when I went through, he grabbed ahold of my wrist, pulled my arm back and slammed the door shut on it."

Elidad felt tears stinging her eyes as she stared at him. "But you told the story about your accident, over and over again."

"I kept telling everyone the story, trying to believe it. It's easier, if you believe your own lie." Aiden explained. "After that, I spent as much time away from home as possible. I spent a lot of time in confession."

"What did you have to confess after that?" Elidad whispered.

"I wanted to kill him. I wanted my father to die a painful death, at my hands." Aiden voice was low. "Abraham saved me."

Elidad couldn't help but let tears slip from her eyes. She brushed them away.

"Abraham was the priest I confessed to. After that, he made it his mission to be a part of my life, giving me constructive things to do, things to live for. I found God, a loving father to replace my broken worldly one. And slowly, I decided I wanted to be like God, and the closest thing I could mimic was Abraham. The kindest, loving, most devoted man I've ever known."

Elidad's tears streamed down her face.

"I left home. I left my mother with that monster. I hated both of them. I blamed my mother, even though she was a victim too, I see that now. I left her to continue to self-medicate her life away." Aiden's fingers ruffled his shaggy golden hair. "When you were gone on your first mission, when you were missing, my mother swallowed a whole bottle of pain pills and washed it down with my father's most prized bottle of scotch." The corners of Aiden's mouth pulled upward in a phantom smile. "She stuck it to him, in the end."

A clock on the wall, unnoticeable earlier, pounded Aiden's story into Elidad's subconscious. The ticking, mimicking the pounding of coffin nails.

"Anyway," Aiden stood from the chair, a strange look in his eyes. "I'm not sure why I told you all that. I didn't mean to ruin your day."

Elidad moved to his side of the counter. "I'm glad you did. I understand why you were the way you were… and why you're the way you are, now."

She was close enough, Aiden reached forward and brushed away her tears. The movement seemed to surprise Elidad as much as it did himself. "Don't feel sorry for me, Elidad." His voice was stern. "I don't deserve your sympathy." He tried to translate regret through his fingertips. "I'm sorry for what I did to you."

The hurt in his eyes pierced Elidad.

"I don't deserve your forgiveness," he confessed.

Elidad moved closer, embracing him.

He wrapped his arms around her, closing his eyes. The scent of jasmine moved off her hair. All he knew in relationships was how to hurt. The risk of becoming his father was too great. What if he hurt *her*? Maybe that's what Leucosia was trying to protect Elidad from. Him. Maybe that's why he had to leave. Maybe she was better off with Lucian.

"I have to get back to work," he lied.

"Ok." Elidad was reluctant to let him go.

Aiden stepped away from her. "I'll see you later."

"Wait," she stopped him.

"What?" Aiden's feet paused.

"You were going to ask me something," Elidad reminded him.

"Oh," he thought of a million questions. *Would she have him? Would she spend the rest of her life with him, if he gave up his vows for her? Did she feel the same way he did?* "I did ask you."

"You did?"

"Yeah," he shook his head. "You're going out with Lucian."

"Oh, yeah," her eyes were pressing. "Are you sure that's all you wanted to talk about?" *How did she know?*

"I'll meet you over at Isaac's tomorrow. Are you still trying to clear out a spot for his bed?"

"Yeah, I'll be there by ten," Elidad said.

"Ok, I'll come help you for a little while." Aiden turned and left Elidad, red-eyed, in the kitchen.

CHAPTER TWELVE

Elidad glanced at Aiden; silence had slowly filled the room, like an inflatable wedge between them as they worked side by side. She wasn't sure if the blame lay with herself, driven by guilt for agreeing to go out with Lucian, or the truth of Aiden's past. He was angry she was going out with Lucian, that much was clear yesterday. She couldn't understand their disdain for each other. When Aiden offered to help get Isaac's room ready for the arrival of a hospital bed and eventually, Isaac, Elidad was happy for the help. Now, she wasn't sure it was such a good idea.

The tightness in Aiden's brows gave away the intensity of his thoughts. He wasn't fooling anyone. He needed to tell her something, and he must know she wouldn't be happy about it.

Maybe he wasn't happy about it, either.

He'd been strange over the past week, almost avoiding her. He obviously wanted to tell her something, he'd told her that much, when he stopped by unannounced. He was derailed when she informed him about going out with Lucian.

Understanding tightened Elidad's jaw. She folded her arms across her chest, as if they could protect her from what was about to happen. "Are you going to get on with it or what?

Aiden stopped working, looking confused. "Get on with what?"

Heat rumbled in Elidad's stomach, a broiler on high, singeing her cheeks with radiant heat. "Get on with telling me you're leaving."

"How—" Aiden's voice caught in the back of his throat, "did you know?"

"You've been sulking around for days," she rolled her eyes, "You're so obvious." The thought of him knowing, and not telling her, swam in her mind. "So, you're going to let them take you away that easily?"

Aiden took a deep breath. "Elidad, you know it's not that simple. I have to go."

"Do you?"

"Yes. I have to." Aiden's mind drifted back to Leucosia.

"You probably didn't even try to stay." Elidad accused.

"This is a great opportunity for me." He avoided her question. "I've worked hard for this. You should be happy for me."

"Where are you moving to?" Elidad asked.

"They are interviewing other candidates. I haven't received my instructions yet, I just know I will be moving. I won't know where until the decision is made, maybe in a week or two," Aiden's reluctance was apparent.

"I am happy for you." Elidad lied, too quickly. "You're right back on track. I'm sure you're pleased with yourself."

Her words stung. Aiden reminded himself of Leucosia's warning. He was in danger of breaking his vows, and she was better off not to get involved with him. He did have to leave. "Elidad, you know I'd stay if I could." He stepped closer to her, but she moved away.

Aiden watched her pretend to realign the photographs on top of Isaac's dresser. "Think about it, maybe this job will help us find the keys." Aiden spoke to her back. "We haven't had any new leads since we left Mexico."

"Whatever makes you feel better," she said.

"You're not making this easy for me. This is why I didn't want to tell you." The sincerity in his voice made Elidad's heart miss a beat.

She turned and saw the same emotion in his eyes, sincerity with a dash of longing. The look gave her the sudden urge to move closer to him and touch his face.

What would he do if she kissed him? Would it make him want to stay?

Elidad felt like she was on a rollercoaster of impending doom. Her gut, swirling as she climbed a track that would descend into fear and loss, splashing into emotions, now threatened to leak from her eyes. She wouldn't let him have the satisfaction of knowing she'd miss him. She'd never let him know how much she needed him.

Apparently, he didn't need her.

"You know what. Don't worry about it. It's not a big deal. I knew they'd move you away. I don't really care," she scowled through her long lashes.

"Elidad, I'm sorry. You do care. I care. You know I'd stay if I could," Aiden felt desperate as she began to shut down.

If her eyes were daggers, the pain of this situation would've been over a long time ago.

"Don't worry about it," she shrugged. "Lucian said he'd stay as long as I need him."

Aiden picked up a box, his fingers pressed into the cardboard.

"I'm sure he did," he said as he moved the box across the room, setting it down harder than he intended.

"What's that supposed to mean?" Elidad demanded.

Aiden's eyes shot toward Elidad, they were gray when he was angry. "I think he's looking for a little more than money for services rendered, that's all."

"Are you jealous?"

"Of what? *Lucian*? There's nothing to be jealous of. If I wanted to be like *that*, I could. *I* chose to be different, thanks."

There was an emotion in his eyes that Elidad had never seen before.

"Like what? What's he *like*?" Elidad demanded.

Aiden wasn't sure why his heart was racing. The thought of Lucian made his skin crawl. Elidad thought he was jealous of Lucian? Pft…

"Like he is. If you don't see him for who he is, you won't. And no one will convince you otherwise."

"You don't even know him." Elidad clenched her fingers into fists until her nails cut the palms of her hand. "How did I end up defending Lucian? You're the one leaving. He's staying to help. You're supposed to be my—" Fury made it difficult to find the right word. "Friend. *You're* supposed to help me. You can say whatever you want, but I'll make judgments based on actions, not your opinion."

Aiden pursed his lips together, trying to slow his breath. She couldn't know the sacrifice he was making.

"Elidad, you don't know him. You just met him. It's great that he wants to help, but you need to be careful. You have enough going on in your life. Losing Abraham, Isaac coming home, you don't need any more drama in your life. That's all I'm saying."

Elidad mouth curved into a line of mockery. "I didn't take vows to be celibate, Aiden. That's your problem. Not mine."

She was trying to hurt him. There'd be no getting through to her, now.

"I'll do my best to help you from where I'm at."

"What are you going to do from the other side of the world?"

"I told you, I don't know where I'm going."

"We both know where you're going to end up, Aiden. I'm surprised you haven't left for the Vatican, already. You and I both know that's where they're going to place you."

She was right. There was no sense in arguing.

Aiden took a breath. "We need new information. We're at a standstill in our search. I'm hoping this new job will bring new contacts and new information that will help us find the other keys. If it happens to be at the Vatican, it might be a blessing. We need to finish what Abraham started. Otherwise, he died for nothing."

"He did die for nothing." She glared.

Apparently, her anger wasn't only reserved for Aiden. There was plenty to go around.

"He died to protect you, Elidad."

"From who? Himself?"

Aiden stared at her in disbelief.

"He killed my parents. Remember? He tried to keep me from finding the keys; he hid the truth from me. There's a prophecy about… my life. He knew about it and he kept it from me. Who was he really protecting?"

Aiden shook his head. "You knew him. You loved him— love—you love him. I understand that it doesn't make sense. I get that it doesn't look good, but you know Abraham. There has to be an explanation."

The conviction in Aiden's voice cut at the edges of Elidad's anger. She walked to the dresser where she'd already straightened the photos. She moved them around, again. It was a good excuse to turn her back to Aiden. She picked up her favorite picture of her and Abraham; they were sitting on the front steps of their home. She carried the same photo in her Bible. Abraham was younger in the picture, but his hair and beard were still silver. His smile was the same, but there were less lines crinkling around the edges of his eyes.

"If there was an explanation, he didn't tell me." Elidad couldn't deny it, she still loved Abraham. She couldn't understand how the nurturing man she loved could be a ruthless killer.

"He told you to go to Leucosia and you haven't. He told you she would explain. Why haven't you gone?"

Elidad closed her eyes to hold back the tears, "How can I?"

"I don't understand why you wouldn't." Aiden was standing right behind her now. The depth and tenderness in his voice made it harder to keep her tears at bay.

"I'm afraid to know who he really was. I don't want to distort his image," she whispered.

"It's already been distorted, but it's Abraham. There has to be some explanation."

Elidad shook her head, replacing the picture.

Aiden's hand softly touched her shoulder. The heat from his palm radiated through her shirt, warming her to her fingertips. Elidad turned toward him. They were standing so close; her chest was nearly touching his.

He reached up and softly pushed a stray lock of hair behind her ear, sending a chill down her spine. The stark contrast between hot and cold made her body react with a shiver.

"Don't let your anger dominate your life," Aiden warned.

His eyes softened back to the shade of blue that reminded her of cloudless, summer days. She wanted to remember him, like this. His handsome face, so full of emotion, it was almost heartbreaking. It was maddening how perfect his skin was. Elidad couldn't take her eyes off his lips as his hand rested on her shoulder, his thumb brushing the base of her neck.

Suddenly, she felt like she was on a rollercoaster, again.

Aiden's eyes were as hungry as hers. His hand slightly tightened, subtly pulling her toward him. She allowed her fingers to grasp the soft shirt at his sides. Her hands moved around him, tracing his spine, moving from his waist, running up the small of his back. The rise and fall of his abdomen drew to a stop, a reaction to her touch. Elidad's heart pounded with anticipation as she clung to him, bracing herself against the centripetal force.

In response, Aiden lowered his lips, inches from hers. She could feel his breath.

"Elidad." Lucian's voice called from the hall.

Elidad and Aiden jumped apart.

"Yeah?" Elidad's voice waivered.

Lucian stepped through the door.

"Oh, I didn't realize you had company. Aiden." He nodded a stiff greeting toward Aiden.

"Yeah, we were just moving things out so there's room for the bed," Elidad said quickly.

Lucian looked from Elidad to Aiden.

Aiden rubbed the back of his neck. "I've uh… got to get back. Are you going to be okay, finishing up without me?"

"Yeah, thanks for the help," Elidad avoided his eyes.

"Call me if you need anything, I'll see you later." Aiden made eye contact with Lucian as he moved across the room.

"Lucian," Aiden mimicked Lucian's greeting for an equally stuffy exit.

When Aiden was gone, Lucian folded his arms and leaned against the door jam. "Did I interrupt something?"

Elidad's heart was a racehorse.

"No," she shrugged.

"Funny, it felt like I was."

"Well, I guess… maybe?" Elidad confessed.

"Oh?" Lucian raised an eyebrow.

"He was telling me he's leaving," the words rushed out. "Aiden's leaving."

"Leaving where?" Lucian's face changed, but Elidad was unable to decipher its meaning.

"The… Vatican." It was harder to say than she anticipated.

"Kind of poor timing," Lucian observed.

"It was only a matter of time. I'm surprised they didn't move him sooner."

"Whether it was expected or not, I'm sure it's not easy for you. I'm sorry," Lucian's green eyes were consoling.

Lucian and Aiden couldn't be more different. Lucian was forward, relaxed and confident to the point where he wasn't afraid to say what was on his mind. It was no wonder he and Aiden didn't get along. Aiden was controlled, methodical; his life was devoted to practicing patience and restraint.

Elidad faked a smile, "It's fine."

"It's really not fine. I don't even know him, and *I* expected him to stay," Lucian said.

"You did, why?"

"I've seen the way he looks at you," he shrugged. "I thought he'd do anything in his power to stay close to you." Lucian's insinuation was clear.

"He vowed to devote his life to God, and the Church." Elidad said with more resentment than she meant to allow.

Lucian's full lips pulled upward on the edges. "Isn't that a pity."

CHAPTER THIRTEEN

After finishing her look with lipstick, Elidad stood back from the floor-length mirror. Her hair was a waterfall of braids and curls, pulled back on her left side in a tight, intricate design freely falling over her right shoulder. The look mimicked Lagertha, a ruthless warrior, someone who Elidad could easily identify with. Elidad smirked; her smoky eyes went along with the theme.

Elidad pressed her lips together; the matte, nude color looked perfect against the dark shade of purple she wore. The amethyst colored dress reminded her of royalty, not Viking-inspired in any way. It was modest in the front, dipping not much lower than her collarbone. She complimented it with a long rose gold necklace and large earrings. Short sleeves exposed her shoulders and a lacy open-back showed a good portion of her tattoo. Only the sword depicted in her tattoo was perfectly visible.

Elidad's lips curved upward, thinking back to Aiden and the first time he'd seen her tattoo. At first glance, she'd thought he hadn't liked it. His shock had been apparent as he stood gaping, but then he'd seemed awed by the meticulous piece. Eventually his face morphed into something different, almost sad. The memory played over in her mind, many times, but she never quite understood.

She loved her tattoo. The artist's interpretation of her work was exquisite; intuitive, perhaps even foreboding.

She moved side to side, checking all angles of her dress. It was light, perfect for the night air that waited on the other side of the door. It didn't pull too tightly around her body. She loved the way it flared, stopping just below her thigh. She wasn't one to wear something so short on a first date, if that's what this was.

She remembered the first time she took Aiden to *Genus*. That night, her dress *was* way too short, and way too tight. She smiled. She didn't do that on purpose…

Thinking of Aiden made her heart feel like a fifty-pound weight was strapped to her chest. The compression made it hard to breathe. She'd carried his truth with her all night. The unbearable stress kept her tossing and turning, she had to hide it with extra concealer this morning.

What a cross Aiden had to bear, almost as sad as her own. How could she have never known? Looking back on who he was in school, she was ashamed for not being able to see the signs. Bullies are built in broken homes. Distracted by her own pain, it had taken her this long to recognize his.

Reality threatened to escape from her eyes.

She blinked her dark lashes to remove the extra liquid, refusing to mess up her makeup. Rarely did she put this much effort into herself; she wasn't going to ruin it now, no matter how sad Aiden's life was.

She wasn't even sure how the conversation had turned to his childhood. He'd never spoken of it before now. What inspired it? Come to think of it, it wasn't like him to stop by without calling. It wasn't like him to ring the doorbell and wait for her to answer the door, either. She couldn't help but feel there was something else he wanted to talk about. She knew him well enough, he had something important on his mind. Something had changed when their conversation lead to his parents.

The doorbell rang. The daunting, heavy weight that refused to leave her all night was fleeting, replaced with butterflies. She swallowed, nervous that she might be overdressed.

Elidad picked up her clutch and walked into the study, rather than answering the door. She opened the top drawer to Abraham's desk. The Sword of Justice, just a hilt, lay on top of a stack of papers. She eyed it. I'd never fit in her purse. Closing the drawer, she told herself she didn't need it. It was only dinner. Besides, she could probably take Lucian, if need be. She chuckled to herself. He was an archeologist with a law degree…

Elidad was surprised the bell didn't ring again as she walked into the foyer. Opening the door allowed the heat of the evening to flow in, churning with the controlled temperature of the house.

As expected, Lucian stood in the doorway. The butterflies that afflicted her earlier became a pulsating swarm.

He wore a navy-blue suit. Under his jacket, the shirt, though the same color, was so heavily polka doted in minute dots, it appeared one shade lighter. Under his chin, cresting his broad chest, was a floral bow tie with white and purple roses that picked up tones in Elidad's dress perfectly.

His typically careless hair was combed and mostly contained in a wave. The cool color of his outfit enhanced the golden tone of his skin. He belonged on the cover of a magazine.

In this moment, she began to appreciate a man in a suit.

"*You* look stunning," his eyes smoldered with the compliment.

As if the way he looked wasn't enough, he had to compliment her too. Blood rushed to her cheeks. "Thanks. You clean up pretty good, yourself."

He smiled. "This old thing?" He held his arms out. "I found it in the back of my closet."

Elidad laughed. "I'm sure." She agreed. "Aren't you dying in your jacket? It's hot out there."

"As a matter of fact, I am," he confessed. "I was fine in the air conditioning, until someone made me wait," he flashed perfect teeth with a smile that sparkled in his eyes.

"Well, you can't rush perfection," Elidad teased.

"And for that, I would wait an eternity," his tone was teasing, but his words contained an air of sincerity.

Elidad stepped through the door. "We don't want you to melt. Should we go?" She turned to lock it behind her.

Lucian was standing on the steps when she turned around, another pose for whatever cover he was meant for. It was unbelievable how effortlessly perfect he was, almost unnatural.

Elidad noticed a car parked right out front, a sporty Audi. Chrome glistened behind the door; the stripe of metal was striking against the matte black of the exterior. The body sat inches off the ground. Rapacious headlights made the car look like it could devour any obstacle in its way. The scoop, meant to divide, would have little memory of any space it slashed its way through.

"Tell me that's not your car," Elidad demanded.

He beamed. "Okay, who shall I tell you it belongs to?"

She rolled her eyes. "Way to roll incognito."

His smile broadened. "Are we hiding?"

"I will be, now. That's for sure."

Lucian, appearing amused, opened the door for her with a fluid motion. The bucket seats were diamond-patterned with red stitching. When she climbed inside Lucian swung the door closed.

Elidad looked around in the slowly fading, ambient lighting. Without the glow, it was difficult to inspect the interior with the dwindling evening sunlight blocked by dark tinted windows. The interior smelled fresh, a leathery new car scent mixed with Lucian's fragrance. She hadn't considered it before, his fragrance. But she knew it—a spicy aromatic. Elidad considered the complexity. Rose? Teak, blended into a vanilla musk and a hint of rum. Or was it whiskey? She watched Lucian walk around to the driver side.

"This is ridiculous." She said when he got in.

"I'm glad you like it," he mused.

"I didn't even know you had a car."

"Did you think I got to New York by bus?" He suggested.

"No, you're an archeologist. I figured you hitchhiked."

"Come on," he pleaded, "I'm more resourceful than that."

"Apparently," she agreed, dramatically looking around. "But I don't think this is what your fundraised dollars are supposed to buy."

Lucian's laugh was a rich sound in the confined space.

"Why not? I'll have you know this thing is a machine." His sarcasm was bright. "I use it at all my archeological sites. It is excellent for moving artifacts."

"I hope you tell the government that." Elidad considered. "I think you need every write off you can get."

Lucian pushed a red button on the steering wheel. The engine raged to life, growling behind Elidad's seat. The power inspired her heart to pick up speed... almost as much as the company sitting beside her.

They came to a thundering stop in front of a tall building. Before Elidad could place her hand on the door handle, a man pulled it open and offered a hand. Recognizing his attire as a valet, Elidad allowed him to help her out of the low-profile car. It was hard to get out of Lucian's car wearing a short dress and tall heels. Elidad threw the long strap of her clutch over her shoulder.

"Sir, nice to see you again," the valet said.

Elidad noticed Lucian slip him a tip as their hands embraced.

"Thank you." Lucian said turning toward Elidad. "Shall we?"

Another man held a door open for them, leading into the skyscraper.

"You come here often?" Elidad guessed.

Lucian smirked. "They don't recognize me. They recognize my car."

Lucian escorted Elidad onto an elevator.

"Where are we going?" Elidad inquired.

"I told you, you need a night off. We're going to have fun." He said pressing a button for the thirty-fifth floor.

"That sounds ominous." Elidad observed.

Lucian flashed a crooked smile at her. "Trust me."

With a face like that, she wanted to.

The elevator was new, moving double time, fluidly racing upward, passing floors with ease. The movement was so smooth, Elidad barely felt it come to a stop. They stepped out in front of two massive, red-stained, mahogany doors. The handles of the doors were coiled cobras, cast in black iron, their heads hooded wide, poised in a venomous hiss. The snakes' eyes, though carved, looked as if they followed Elidad's movement.

Guards stood on either side of the doors. Lucian spoke a word Elidad didn't understand, but she wasn't paying attention, distracted by the décor. He could have said an English word, and she would've missed it, but it was different. Latin? The thick men standing on either side placed a hand atop a snake's head and pulled the doors open.

Laughter rolled out of the open space behind the mahogany, relieving Elidad's tension. She wasn't sure why the foyer made her so tense. Maybe Aiden and Lucian were right. Maybe she *did* need a break.

People clustered around game tables talking loud enough to be heard over the band on the far side of the room. Elidad could see the singer, a stunning woman, in an elegant dress standing in front of a retro microphone. She sang a Metallica song, in a key of Vintage New Orleans Dirge, a kind of Postmodern Jukebox flair. Elidad instantly liked the rendition.

Weaving through the tables after Lucian, they made their way to a podium where a hostess stood. As Lucian approached, the hostess rolled her shoulders back to stand a little taller, her eyes examining him from his face to his feet.

"Hello, do you have a reservation?" Her voice was whimsical.

"Lucian," he said his own name in confirmation.

The girl's eyes flickered from Lucian to Elidad before looking down at the podium.

"Yes, for two." She sounded annoyed as she picked up two menus. "Adrianne will take you to your table."

Taking the menus from her, Adrian's eyes held on Lucian's face, "This way." She directed.

Lucian held his arm out as an invitation for Elidad. "Ladies' first."

Elidad walked after the young woman. She moved effortlessly in her form-fitting, black dress. Elidad noticed all the employees wore black. She was glad she decided to wear purple, otherwise, next to Lucian, she might be mistaken for a server.

Tables were covered in light linens with beautifully folded napkins atop white plates. Silverware glistened in the light of the dining area. Crystal glasses tinkled against plates as they continued through the room. People turned to look as they passed by. Curious eyes followed them through the crowd.

Some of those eyes, catching the light of the room, glowed the way a wild animal's would at night. Just like *Genus*, Leucosia's club, this was a gathering place for a variety of species. That explained the strange guarded entrance and a password…

The woman stopped at a table in the corner of the room, it was slightly more secluded than the others. Lucian pulled out a chair for Elidad. She sat, looking through solid glass walls. The view was only inhibited in the corner where the walls of the building met. Other braces were staggered down the large opening, but the lack of solid matter made the restaurant feel like it was on a terrace. This table had the best view. Elidad realized the planning that must have been involved to reserve it.

Being thirty-five floors up, the city looked like a microscopic doll house. The elevation made Elidad's heart pick up, similar to the way Lucian's car did. She wasn't afraid of heights; this was just a typical reaction, her body's instincts kicking in.

"Elidad." A booming voice called her name.

Elidad turned to see a masculine man with glowing red eyes and beautiful obsidian skin approaching their table. He wore a black suit with a black undershirt that gave the look a casual feel. A clear tube peeked out of his shirt and spiraled to his right ear. He was most defiantly some kind of security, not a waiter. Elidad couldn't place his race. Orc? He smelled too nice. Maybe Gog?

"Yes?" Elidad answered, her eyes flitting to Lucian who looked as confused as she was.

"You need to come with me." He wasn't asking.

"Why?" Lucian demanded.

The security guard's jaw flexed. Someone else would read the guard's action as anger; however, Elidad realized he was nervous. "Mr. Tabor would like to have a word with you." He didn't pull his eyes off Elidad when he spoke.

Elidad's mouth ran dry. "Mr. Tabor?" *Why would Aiden want to talk to her now? How on earth could he be here, in a place like this? How did he know where to find her?*

"Yes, miss. It will only take a minute of your time." He held out his hand in invitation though Elidad knew it was a demand. *Aiden wouldn't consort with anyone like this.*

She grabbed her purse and stood. "Of course." She flashed a smile.

Lucian stood.

The guard's body tensed. "Just the girl."

Lucian's brow tightened. "I'm going with her."

The hulking man towered over Lucian and was easily double his width.

"No, you will not. You will sit. I've ordered you your drink. Dalmore, eighteen-year-old Highland Single Malt, no ice."

Lucian was unable to hide the look of surprise on his face.

"She'll be back before your finish it," the guard assured.

As if on cue, a server appeared with a crystal tumbler full of a honey colored liquid. Elidad got the feeling she needed that drink more than Lucian did.

The guard's eyes hadn't left Elidad. He was more on edge with her, than Lucian. He was cordial with Lucian, yet firm, he wasn't afraid of Lucian. With her, it was like he was expecting a fight.

Elidad gave Lucian a reassuring smile. "I'll be right back."

Lucian begrudgingly sat, his eyes inflamed in a way she hadn't seen before.

Elidad turned to follow the bouncer. Despite the strange circumstances, she couldn't help but smile.

It was whiskey. Vanilla musk and whiskey.

CHAPTER FOURTEEN

Elidad followed the man resembling a mountain through the club. The band was now playing a swing tune that dozens of couples danced to. Elidad watched them float in circles, hands flying, pulling one direction, then the other, like a carnival ride.

The bouncer stopped in front of a different elevator tucked away at the back of the club. Four other equally intimidating bouncers stood guard around it. They all had the same burning, red eyes and dark skin.

The man Elidad initially followed placed his hand on a dark piece of glass to the right of the elevator. The glass surface glowed red and the elevator doors opened. Elidad followed his lead, stepping inside. She clung to her purse. Aiden wouldn't know anyone here. How would they know to use his name as a ruse? Out of the corner of her eye, she evaluated the guard. He'd be hard to take down, especially since he looked like he was expecting a fight, but it could be done. Why did she leave the Sword of Justice at Abraham's house? She should have brought a bigger purse, rather than leave it behind. She was supposed to be having fun, not working.

The elevator opened into another foyer, where guards stood on either side of doors identical to those in the entrance to the casino.

The doors were pulled open for them as they approached. Elidad followed her chaperone into an office. The view was identical to the casino below. Pressed against the wall of glass, a mahogany desk glistened in the low light. In the center of the massive room, black leather sofas made a seating area around a modern coffee table. The décor, though tastefully arranged, had a sterile feel to it. The chair behind the desk was turned toward the windows. The high-backed, leather hid whoever was sitting in it.

The chair slowly turned with the sound of their entrance.

"Mr. Tabor," Elidad's guide said in a voice, low enough to be a growl.

Elidad stared at Mr. Tabor. When his face came into view, she recognized his blue eyes. Although she knew them as soft and compassionate, these eyes were hard and fierce. Mr. Tabor rose to his feet behind the desk. Not one strand of his silver hair was out of place. It was meticulous, like the suit he wore. This is what Aiden would look like, thirty years from now. There was no question in Elidad's mind: she was face to face with Aiden's father.

"Elidad." He stated.

"Yes." She agreed.

"I am Donald Tabor." His smooth voice was similar to Aiden's but harder in some way.

"What do you want?" Elidad demanded. She already hated him. She pictured Aiden's face when he spoke of his father for the first time, yesterday.

His lips twisted into a smirk. Elidad wanted to slap that smug grin off his face.

"Straight and to the point. A woman after my own heart."

"My heart is nothing like yours. I assure you." Elidad was curt.

His eyes narrowed. "Did I wrong you in another life, Elidad? Do we know each other?"

"I know your son," she kept her tone even.

Elidad saw something flash in his eyes. Was it pain? The look was gone as fast as it appeared.

"I don't have a son," his lips pressed into a flat line.

She didn't see that coming.

"That's funny. He looks just like you, only younger. His name is Aiden Tabor. No one you know, huh?" Elidad dramatically overplayed her words.

The large guard at her side shifted his weight. It was a tell. He stood solid, like a statue chiseled out of ebony but the subtle movement was enough of a signal that *he* knew of Aiden.

"Aiden, is no son of mine." Donald's tone was infinite.

"That's fine," Elidad shrugged. "I'm surprised you're alive. The way Aiden talks about you, I assumed you were dead. He talks about you in the past tense. Imagine my surprise, meeting you here this evening."

That curious look flashed in his eyes again, his face remaining lifeless. Owning a casino had strengthened his poker face.

"I summoned you, Elidad, because I wanted to speak to you."

"Why?" She wondered aloud. He clearly didn't know she knew Aiden, before now.

He gestured to the wall behind her., "We have one of the most sophisticated security systems on the planet. It recognized you as soon as you walked in," he said.

"Maybe you should get your money back." Elidad's condescending tone reached her eyes. "I don't gamble. Why would your system recognize me?"

"I said it was the *greatest* security system. It doesn't just recognize gamblers and cheats. It recognizes … violent offenders," he searched her face. "Whether they've been here before, or not."

Elidad laughed. "Violent offenders? I don't have a record."

"You do in the Underworld."

That explained the unease of the security guard.

"I came here with a friend and it was his choice, I had no idea where we were going. I'm not working," Elidad ensured.

"That is encouraging," Mr. Tabor's face grew dark, "because if you were to interfere with my business, in any way, I'd hate for Aiden to lose a friend… the way he lost his mother."

Hatred twitched the tips of Elidad's fingers. "If I were you, I'd watch who you're threatening," Elidad warned.

Donald's lips curled in a sneer, "I have no need to make threats." He looked through her, as if she already didn't exist.

"I came here for fun," Elidad asserted. "Don't make me to come back, for work."

Mr. Tabor sat back into the sofa adjacent to where she stood. "And if you do, will I disappear? Like Pythious?"

Elidad froze at the mention of Pythious' name.

Donald's mouth widened into a ravenous grin. "It's strange, isn't it, Elidad, how it all happened? A promising young man, an untouchable, last seen being threatened by you, and he was never heard from again. He just disappeared, off the earth, no body, no witnesses."

Elidad didn't respond.

Donald brought his hand up flicking his finger in the air. "Poof. Just disappeared. No trace."

"I wasn't found guilty," Elidad worked at keeping her voice from trembling.

Mr. Tabor smirked, "Yes, no body and no witnesses does complicate things, doesn't it? But the Church still terminated you, didn't they?"

A chill ran down Elidad's arms. Where did he get his information? He knew way too much. It had been kept a secret. Even Aiden hadn't heard about the charges. "I don't know what you're talking about. The one has nothing to do with the other. I wasn't shocked to hear about Pythious' disappearance, anyone who knew him, knew he was living wrong. It was only a matter of time. I'm sorry I wasn't the one who finished him off," Elidad's honesty rang through.

"The reason the Church fired me is because I'm a woman. I'm not allowed to do a priest's job. Performing exorcisms— especially unsanctioned exorcisms—is unforgivable." Elidad's eyes shifted to the security guard who shifted his weight, again. "I'll send any demon back to Hell. I don't wait for their approval. I don't care what they think," She added.

"I can see how that'd be annoying." Donald agreed. "No one likes a renegade vigilante."

"Especially if all your security guards are demons." Elidad laughed. "I see how you'd be threatened by my presence. I didn't' come to hunt your security. If they are working here and obeying the laws, they aren't technically breaking any rules, I have no grounds to send them back."

"You just testified you don't follow the rules," Donald observed.

"I said I didn't follow the Church's rules. I follow the rules of engagement. If I hunted down every demon who was following the outline, eventually, they'd all be hunting *me*. Besides, how motivated do you think I am?" Elidad looked down at herself. "Do I look like I'm ready for a fight? Not much else is going to fit into this dress, certainly not a weapon."

Donald considered her appearance. "You look lovely." His words felt more like an assault than a compliment. "I hope you enjoy your time in my establishment, Elidad." He flicked his finger and the guard moved to escort Elidad back.

Elidad turned to follow. She paused to look back at Mr. Tabor, "Should I tell Aiden hello for you?"

His eyes narrowed, "I told you. I have no son."

CHAPTER FIFTEEN

Lucian was leaning back in his plush chair overlooking the city, now dazzling with millions of lights. He clutched his glass in a way that told Elidad he still wasn't happy about being ordered to stay put while she was taken away.

Lucian saw Elidad approaching with her escort and stood.

"Are you alright?" His eyes flickered over the guard and back to her.

Elidad faked a smile. "Oh, yeah. I'm fine. Some company I am."

"Or I." Annoyance was present in Lucian's tone. "What was *that* about?"

Elidad looked up at the guard, he remained close when she sat.

The guard stepped in, towering over Elidad and Lucian. "Mr. Tabor apologizes for inconveniencing your evening."

"He must have forgotten to apologize to me in person," Elidad said.

Two more security guards showed up, each carrying a stack of chips. They each placed a stack in front of Elidad and Lucian.

"What's this?" Elidad frowned.

"Compliments of the house. For your time." Elidad's escort bowed without taking his eyes off her, "Good evening." With his polite closing, he and the others turned and disbursed into the room.

Lucian's eyes had a hint of skepticism. "What did they want?"

Elidad shrugged. "Nothing, really."

"Nothing?" His eyes were doubtful.

"Someone wanted to chat with me," she shrugged.

"Elidad, there's ten thousand dollars in chips here." Lucian's kept his voice low.

"It's not a big deal." She insisted.

"Usually a casino doesn't give out money, unless they have to."

"Think of it as a consultation fee." Elidad offered.

Lucian's eyebrow arched with curiosity. "What, exactly, were you consulting on?"

Elidad's smirk arched into a smug grin. "How to live a long life."

"Who is Mr. Tabor?" Lucian continued to pry.

"Apparently, he's the owner of this casino."

"You know the owner of this place?" Lucian seemed confused.

He wasn't the only one.

"No." She answered honestly. "But I do now."

His dark brows pulled together. "Then, how does he know you?"

Arrogance pulled at the edges of her mouth. "I have a… *reputation.*"

Amusement played across Lucian's face. "And I assume it's not for going on too many dates."

Elidad laughed aloud. "No, it's not."

Lucian's eyes brightened beneath his dark lashes as his lips formed a mischievous line. "Maybe we can change that."

Elidad's heart raced at the honesty behind his teasing. She hoped he didn't notice the blush that was reacting to his words.

"It's obvious. You have no intention on disclosing the topic of your… *consultation,*" he used her word. "But, you know what this means, don't you?" Lucian's eyes were alight, again.

"What?"

"You're going to have to go out with me again."

Elidad pretended to be annoyed. "Why?"

"I told you *I* was taking you out. Clearly, you are paying, tonight."

Elidad's laugh was genuine, even though the evening had turned into something strange.

"How did you find this place?" Elidad was curious. "Is this a normal hang out for you?"

Lucian sipped his whiskey, leaning back into his chair. "A client wanted to meet me here, once. I'd found him an artifact and we met here to discuss a price. Why? Would it be undesirable if this was my normal hang out?"

Elidad shrugged. "It's run by demons." She watched him for his expression. She still wasn't sure how much he knew, or believed. This conversation could get interesting, real quick.

He didn't flinch. "Really? I hadn't noticed. I guess it would explain the red eyes. I'm not really good at spotting them, unless they're out in the open."

Elidad considered that. "I guess most people don't notice."

"Is that why they wanted to see you?" Lucian guessed. "You *are* a Crusader. That would explain the pay off." He gestured to the chips on the table.

"Retired," Elidad said casually.

A waitress came to the table and set a drink in front of Elidad. It was in a long-stemmed martini glass that glowed purple with a blue sugared rim.

"I ordered you a drink," Lucian said. "I didn't know what you'd like so I thought I'd order something purple." His lips widened.

Elidad laughed. "Thank you," she said looking up at the waitress.

The waitress didn't look back; her eyes were glued on Lucian. "Did you need anything else?" She asked, still ignoring Elidad's thanks.

"Not right now, thank you." He answered, not taking his eyes off Elidad.

The waitress went off in a hurry.

Elidad took a sip. It was tangy, not too sweet.

"How is it?" Lucian watched intently.

"It's good, and it matches my dress."

Lucian laughed. "Is there a better reason to order a drink?"

Elidad scrunched her face. "I can't think of anything right this second."

Chuckling, Lucian inquired. "What *do* you drink? Maybe next time I'll get it right."

"Extra dirty martini."

"*Extra dirty*, hmm?" His eyes sparkled with amusement. "Sounds like we're on the right path to change that reputation."

This time, Elidad laughed.

Taking a sip of her drink, she hoped the alcohol was a good excuse for the color in her cheeks. She really needed to get control of herself.

"Lucian." A masculine voice behind Elidad spoke.

Elidad looked over her shoulder. A couple seated a few tables away were looking in their direction. The woman waved. The man wore a black suit with a white shirt and a black bow tie, a new spin on an old look, reminding Elidad of a thirty's gangster. He appeared to be the kind of man that would ride on the running board of a Plymouth with a Tommy Gun. The woman who waved wore an evening gown adorned with crystals and a fur. A black hat sat crooked on her head, allowing pin curls to wave down the side of her face, stopping above her shoulder. Her outfit complimented her partner's and the music.

They weren't demons. Elidad thought, but they weren't human, either. She couldn't put her finger on their race, not that it mattered.

"Elidad, will you excuse me for a moment?"

When Elidad turned to face Lucian, his eyes were apologetic.

"Of course."

"They are clients of mine. I'll just be a minute," he said.

"Take your time," Elidad smiled. "Apparently, neither of us are good at leaving work behind."

He looked relieved as he swept her hand in his.

"Thank you," his voice was low as he bowed to lightly touch his lips to the crown of her knuckle. "I'll be right back."

Heat radiated through her body.

She would need the time he was away to pull herself together.

The first time they'd met, he'd kissed her hand. At the time, she hadn't known how to read him. It was a strange gesture. It made her suspicious of him. Now that she'd gotten to know him, she found his timeless charm unforgettable. Well, that, and his amazing green eyes.

Or was it his beautiful full lips, chiseled body, and russet skin?

His persona didn't fit with his sports car or this Casino that he obviously frequented. He was an anomaly.

Aiden didn't like Lucian, he actually compared him to his father. Elidad sipped her drink, her brows pressed together like the liquid had affronted her in some way. She'd just met Donald Tabor, and Lucian was nothing like him.

Maybe Aiden was jealous of Lucian, but why? Aiden didn't want to be with her. *Did he?*

What happened this morning at Isaac's? If felt like *something* was happening. She'd replayed the conversation over again in her head. It was an unavoidable pull, like gravity was centered between them, pulling them together. It felt like he was going to kiss her. She *wanted* to kiss him. Was she just trying to convince herself he wanted the same thing, or was it really going to happen?

Elidad shook her head. How did this happen? She was here, with Lucian, and somehow Aiden showed up, not physically, but in every other way. She tried to push him from her thoughts. She didn't want to think about him… She *couldn't* think about him leaving and what almost happened. She wanted to push all those thoughts as far away from her mind as she could, but meeting his father brought him to the forefront.

Poor Aiden. His father was a monster. She saw only a glimpse of the man that Aiden lived with, and she already hated Donald. Elidad's hand tightly gripped the stem of her glass. Mr. Tabor had so carelessly thrown around threats, including Aiden's mother. If Aiden hadn't told her yesterday about his family, she might not have understood the severity of his words. Thankfully, she knew, and it was perfectly clear. Donald was ruthless and worse, he hung out with demons. She counted fifteen in the Casino. There was sure to be more. None of them seemed to be breaking any rules, but they were demons. If they hadn't already, they were sure to. Nothing good could come of this many undesirables under one roof.

If demons came to the earth and kept to themselves, not tipping the scales of good and evil in anyway, the Church would ignore their existence. The Church referred to this as: sticking to the outline. They were expected to outline society, not interfere with it.

Embodied demons were different than the spirits. Fallen angel was the correct terminology for them. They still had the ability to become good, like Ghelgath. It wasn't likely, but it did happen. It'd been this way since the beginning of time. The ebb and flow of good and evil was always monitored and always changing. Demons weren't allowed to show their 'real selves' to people, they had to be able to pass for a human. If they wreaked havoc on society, Crusaders would be sent to send them back to Hell. On occasion, one would slip through the cracks. Jack the Ripper, Charles Manson, Osama bin Laden; they were more powerful demons, harder to get ahold of. Most demons were destroyed by Crusaders before they could make a name for themselves. Some, the justice system would take care of. A study done by the Church hypothesized that seventy percent of inmates in jail were demons. Elidad could never understand why they would stay in prison, but supposed it was better than being sent back to Hell.

"Elidad?" Lucian broke her from her thoughts.

"Yes." She smiled up at him.

"Would you like to play a few games?" Lucian gestured to the card tables.

"I'm not really a gambler." She said.

"Just with your life?" Lucian flashed a sly smile that made her forget Aiden and demons for a second.

CHAPTER SIXTEEN

Elidad took a breath. "I don't know if I really want to gamble."

There was a bemused look on Lucian's face. "We can dance, if you prefer."

Elidad glanced at the dance floor, trying to control her reaction. Everyone out there looked like professional swing dancers.

"I don't like the man who gave me these chips. It doesn't feel right, taking his money," Elidad admitted.

Lucian smiled. "So, what are you going to do? Throw them away?"

"Tempting," Elidad agreed.

One of Lucian's eyebrows rose. "Isn't gambling about the same as throwing it into a dumpster?"

Elidad's lips twisted. "I walked right into that one, didn't I?"

Lucian's face was smooth, his eyes widened with innocence. "Walked into what?"

Elidad couldn't help but let a laugh slip. "You're incorrigible."

"You say that as if it's a bad thing," he stood offering his hand. "Shall we?"

They moved across the crowded floor of people mixed with other beings. A few Leprechauns gathered in one area, they were hard to miss, and not at all surprising to find in a casino. Some sort of Goblin descendants and, from the look of the men at the roulette table getting worked over by two beautiful women, sirens as well. But the most visible species in the room were the Delphi. They were a serpent race. Their attendance probably explained the snake motif that defined the entry décor and that was littered around the casino. Elidad wondered why the casino catered to them. Maybe Aiden's dad was fascinated by them? Maybe they spent enough money to theme the club?

Delphi were easy to spot, their eyes were their tell. Narrow slits glistened with unique colors and they always looked like they were ready to strike. The subtler cues were their small ears and forked tongues. You'd never recognize their tongues, you had to look for it; most were disciplined enough to keep them hidden in their mouths. If you got them angry enough, however, it'd come darting out.

Other than the demons, no one seemed to recognize Elidad. It became easier for her to let her guard down.

"What client brought you to this place?" Elidad couldn't help but to ask.

Lucian carried the chips. "I wondered when you'd ask," he admitted. "My uncle always dealt with *all kinds*. Through his years in business, he found that many of the ancient families valued artifacts more than most. Being around for so long, they tend to appreciate their value, and are willing to pay their worth," he added. "I carried on with his business plan."

That explained the car, Elidad thought.

Lucian continued. "When I began searching for stolen artifacts, my connections proved to be priceless," he smirked, "pun intended. But it helps to know wealthy, powerful creatures. They may not always be the people I want to be associated with, but they get the job done. This is a nice place, and I've never seen anything here that was against the rules." He stopped at the edge of the craps table. "Many of my clients come here, it's nice to interface with them, I never expected my company to be harassed."

Elidad got the feeling he knew more about her, than she knew about him.

She looked away from his eyes. "Craps? All I know about this game is what you see in movies."

"If you can roll dice, you'll be fine," he said placing the chips on the rail.

"Ok, what do I do?" Elidad looked around at the faces of the players.

"You can put your chips anywhere on the table. Why don't you start with the pass line," he suggested. "Also, the six and the eight are more likely to win."

"I won't bet on six." Elidad said picking up a hundred-dollar chip. "How much should I put down?"

"I thought you were trying to throw it away?" Lucian mused, picking up three thousand dollars' worth of chips. "Why don't you start with this?"

"Really?" Elidad couldn't control the shock in her tone.

"You're going to try gambling, with something other than your life, remember?" He kept his voice low.

"I feel comfortable betting on myself," she answered.

"Well you roll next, so you kind of are," he offered.

"Bet?" The man with the long stick in his hands said.

Elidad put the chips on the pass line, her heart drumming out a precession. The dealer, or whatever he was called waited for the others at the table to place their bets before pushing the dice in Elidad's direction. She scooped them up.

"They have to hit the other side of the table," Lucian warned. It was a detail she'd also learned from movies.

Elidad gave the dice a timid shake and threw them against the short wall. They thudded against the rich, green velvet.

"Eleven," the man with the stick said over the hum of the room.

Elidad's heart leapt, simultaneously realizing her hands were clammy. The group of people around the table murmured their approval. The dealer pushed a stack of chips next to Elidad's. "Now what?" She asked Lucian.

"You can pick them up or place them around the table," he said.

"Aren't you going to play?" She wondered aloud.

"I haven't changed any money for chips, and you're doing good."

"Come on, play," Elidad pleaded handing him one of the containers holding half of the tokens. "I don't know if I can take this pressure. I might prefer dumping the chips into a dumpster."

"I can go get my own chips," Lucian insisted, looking embarrassed.

Elidad flashed him a smile. "This way, I won't have to find a dumpster."

"I'll try not to take that personally."

Elidad laughed.

Lucian leaned over the table, placing chips on the pass bar and on the twelve. He rolled. People smiled as the dealer took away his stack on the pass line. He only let a slight smile escape when the dealer slid a stack of chips his way.

"You have to have money on the pass line but rolling a twelve means I essentially was betting against myself." Lucian explained, deciphering her confusion at his loss and win.

He placed his bet. Elidad's stomach tightened as he threw the dice again. People clapped and shouted sounds of joy. Elidad tried to keep up as chips were pushed next to hers and the other players. Lucian rolled again and again, winning over and over, his stack increasing.

After five minutes the intensity at the table increased threefold She found herself laughing and cheering, when she knew what to be excited about.

Lucian pulled a stack of his chips off the table. He leaned into Elidad, making her heart pick up pace. "You might want to pick up some of your chips." He said.

Elidad did as he said. "Why?"

He grinned. "No one wins forever."

"You don't seem to know how to lose," Elidad observed, pulling some of her chips back.

When the table was set, Lucian threw the dice again. People around the table shouted and laughed with excitement.

Elidad shot a sideways glance at Lucian.

"I'm not a fortune teller," he pointed out. He rolled again.

"Seven." The dealer shouted. The people around the table booed and hissed at the roll.

"Do you want to keep playing?" Lucian asked.

"Not a fortune teller, huh?" Skepticism was thick in Elidad's voice. "I'm ready to get something to eat, if you are."

Lucian piled his chips, the dealer handing him another tray to stack them in. After filling one he handed it to Elidad.

"What's this?" She asked.

"I borrowed from you to get my game going. It's what I owe you."

She shook her head. "I told you, I didn't want them in the first place."

"Well, these are technically from me," he offered, "and I hope you like me well enough that you won't throw money in the dumpster."

Elidad felt a familiar smile widen her lips. It seemed to show up more often with Lucian around.

CHAPTER SEVENTEEN

Lucian's car roared with a low growl as they pulled in front of Abraham's house. Lucian quickly jumped out of the car, coming around to Elidad's door and pulling it open, offering her a hand. He pulled her to her feet so quickly that she was suddenly inches from him. Vanilla musk and whiskey alighted her senses. She took a small step toward the door, enough to hide her pink cheeks, but not enough to make the moment awkward.

"Thanks, for tonight," she said.

"Thank *you*, for coming with me. It was way more fun than being alone."

"Yes," Elidad agreed. "It was, wasn't it?" He must be alone as much as she was. He had the store's customers for company and she had Aiden. She turned to walk up the stairs. Aiden. She wouldn't have him for much longer.

Lucian followed Elidad to the top of the steps. "You'd think the city would do something about the street lights," he said.

Elidad's eyes gazed up and down the street. "Yeah, they've been out for a while." In fact, they'd been out since they'd started looking for Abraham. She'd called the city about it a few times. "There's some problem with the wiring. It's going to take some time to fix them."

Across the street, a dark figure stood, staring at them. Elidad's heart picked up. It was exactly like the night she'd stood here with Aiden. *That* person who'd been watching them had disappeared when a car's lights hit the spot where he'd been standing. The Shadow Man. Elidad was convinced it had to be him, tonight. He'd followed her, terrorized her, and almost killed her. There'd been no sign of him for a while, and recently, she didn't feel like she was being followed. But Emily confirmed he was still around. Elidad's heart felt like a base drum.

"Are you okay?" Lucian sounded concerned.

"Fine," Elidad tried to control her breathing, watching the dark figure across the street.

A car came down the road.

"What's wrong?" Lucian didn't appear to believe her lie.

"There's someone across the street, I was trying to see who it was." The car's headlights passed over the person. A kid. Maybe sixteen years old.

Elidad's heart skipped with relief. *Not* the Shadow Man.

The kid lit a cigarette and walked down the street, the cherry bobbling as he went.

"Who smokes, anymore?" Elidad scoffed, trying to hide the quiver in her voice.

"Rebels," he offered.

"Sorry," Elidad apologized. "Paranoid, I guess."

"At least you pay attention."

"Thanks," Elidad appreciated his effort to make her feel better.

Elidad turned to walk up the steps. Lucian was beside her, their feet in unison. Elidad's heart began to drum out the march. He was walking her to the door, after a date. She suppressed a groan. She should have realized sooner. The look in his eye as he helped her out of the car...

He was going to try *something*. Not that it was a bad thing. He was hot... like smokin'... not only that, he was fun, and smart... and nice. But this evening had been crazy. Meeting Aiden's dad and Aiden leaving. Aiden. It all went back to Aiden.

They reached the top of the stairs.

"Thanks again," Elidad took the key for the door out of her clutch.

"I think I should be thanking you." In the light that shown down the street she could make out his smile. "What are you going to do with your winnings?" Lucian asked.

"I think there's a dumpster around back," Elidad teased.

"You just give me a call, if you get that desperate."

Elidad laughed. "Deal."

"You know, you can call me, even if you're not desperate." Lucian's voice was a touch deeper. Heated.

"I'll keep that in mind."

"You can come see me, too," he suggested. "Someone should make sure I don't die of boredom in the shop."

"I think you'll get sick of me soon enough. When Isaac gets back, I'll be there all the time."

"You say that as if it's a bad thing," his laugh was gravelly. "It will be nice to have the company."

"Careful what you wish for," Elidad warned.

Lucian reached out in the dark and grasped Elidad's hand. He brought it to his face, kissing it lightly, the way he usually did. In unison, goosebumps raced down Elidad's arm, electrifying her senses. He continued to hold her hand in his while the other traced her arm to her elbow, the goose bump infection spread across her body. The sound of the city was drowned out by the pace of her heart. Lucian took a half step closer, draping her arm on his shoulder, he wrapped his arm around her waist.

The teak and rose smell that intertwined with his whiskey and vanilla was as intoxicating as her last drink at the bar. His hand went to her face, soft and firm. He pulled her forward, his chest hard against hers. Elidad's fingertips held the curve of his back, feeling the deeply carved muscle hidden under the shape of his shirt.

Leaning forward, his eyes locked with hers, in the low light. The energy that transmitted from them sent Elidad's heart into a frenzy.

Closing the distance between them, Lucian pressed his lips against hers. They felt like silk, smooth and assured.

She could taste the whisky on his tongue.

Her mind flurried and everything else fell away. The City disappeared, the Shadow Man was nowhere to be found. In this moment, nothing else mattered.

For one second, she was unable to think of anything. Even Aiden.

CHAPTER EIGHTEEN

Elidad was running. From what, she didn't know. But death was surely stalking her as her feet thudded down the corridor.

Breath wheezed through her lips and screamed through her lungs. Her shoulder and arm hurt, she looked down at the sword in her hand. The Sword of Justice. It was in full form and ready to fight. Frantically, she turned a corner, daring to cast a glance over her shoulder. Nothing was there, and yet she knew *it* was.

Her legs burned as she ran faster. Someone was lying in her path, her steps slowed. He turned to look up at her. Aiden. She raced to his side. "Aiden, you have to get up! We have to go."

Fear radiated from his eyes. "I can't go with you," his voice was a whisper.

"What? Why not?" Elidad demanded. She heard footsteps down the alley. She looked back, again. The Shadow Man stood, eyes burning green, at the end of the corridor. "Aiden, get up," She pleaded.

"I can't Elidad," Aiden's voice was dejected.

The Shadow Man was soundless under his cloak; an intensity *so* dark needed no sound, after all. In all the times she had come into contact with him, once face to face, inches apart, she'd only seen nothingness. His face, shapeless liquid, gave the impression of reality, yet remained elusive... An illusion with the power to kill.

His hooded form could easily be mistaken for the grim reaper, but for the lack of a scythe. His hands were gnarled—not like a skeleton— but strong, wicked hands. When he tried to kill Elidad, she'd dug at his face, trying to poke out his brilliant green eyes. Her fingers passed through them, her hands caught on fire when she touched his black flesh.

Cocking his head to the side, as if to consider her, the movement sent Elidad's heart spiraling. The Shadow Man took a step toward her and Aiden.

Elidad's breath pierced her chest, bearing the burden of Aiden's life. She looked at the sword in her hand, still ready. It wouldn't let her down. Elidad looked at Aiden, helpless, at her feet. Aiden reached a hand forward, she enveloped it in hers.

"Don't leave me," he begged.

"I won't." Elidad's voice was a whisper.

Elidad looked back at the Shadow Man, he wasn't alone. There were two figures standing at the end of the corridor. Was it another demon? Elidad strained to see.

"Elidad," she recognized Lucian's voice before her eyes registered his face.

"Lucian!" Elidad's scream echoed between the brick walls.

Lucian crumpled to his knees under the Shadow Man's grip. Lucian's skin bursting into flames at the demon's touch.

"No!" Elidad's voice echoed in her ears. She looked back to Aiden.

"Don't go," he begged. "Don't leave me."

"I'm sorry." Her words slipped over her shoulder as she turned to walk away.

The phone rang, startling Elidad awake.

"Hello?" Her voice was horse.

"You're not up yet?" Aiden demanded.

"No."

"Long night, huh?" Aiden's voice was an accusation.

"What do you want, Aiden?"

"Are you alone?" Aiden asked.

Elidad glanced at the face of her phone, it was just after nine a.m. "Wow. You must think pretty highly of me," Elidad frowned at the phone.

"Sorry," Aiden sounded like he regretted what he said. "I wanted to know when it would be a good time for Beth to come over and talk to you about Isaac's care. He'll be home within the week and we need to have a plan."

Elidad could hear his sincerity about the meeting, but it was obvious he was checking in on her after her date with Lucian.

"We?" Elidad repeated. "I thought you were leaving."

There was a strained silence on the other side of the phone.

Aiden sighed, "Elidad."

"I know… I know… you don't have a choice." She rolled her eyes, "I can meet her whenever I need to." Elidad wanted to get Aiden off the phone.

"She can meet tomorrow around one."

"Ok. I'll be there," Elidad agreed.

Aiden was silent again. He wanted her to say something, but she wouldn't give him the satisfaction. He deserved to wonder.

"Anything else?" Elidad asked.

"No," Aiden agreed. "I guess I'll see you tomorrow."

CHAPTER NINETEEN

Beth's face looked like she'd spent her younger years in a tanning bed. Loose skin sagged around her jowls and at the base of her neck. She couldn't be much older than fifty and looked to be in relatively decent shape. She was strong, anyway. Red, spiky hair faded to a short buzz on the sides, probably a necessity of caretaking. She must've been a caregiver for years. She was the heartless kind; the kind of person that had probably started this career to help people, but watched so many pass away, it eventually hardened her heart.

She was straight and to the point, apparently tolerating little bullshit. Maybe she'd been jerked around by too many family members, over the years. As soon as she'd walked through the door, she'd made it perfectly clear that she was the boss. Elidad liked her.

"I'll be here three days a week. Monday, Wednesday, Friday. If you need me more, you can ask. It'll cost you, but I'm available. When I'm working, I'm here to do a job, not to be your psychiatrist. They have specialist to get the family through these times. If you need one, I'm sure you could find a nice shoulder to cry on." Beth said.

"Thank you, Beth. That won't be necessary," Elidad told her.

"Strokes can be difficult. He might get scared, or emotional. From what I hear, he probably won't recognize you. Patients can get scared and want to fight or run. It's all normal," she warned.

"I did the research. I know what we can be up against." Elidad responded.

Beth gazed back at her, doubtful.

Elidad appreciated Beth's concern, but if she could fight demons for a living, she could deal with Isaac.

Elidad sat on Isaac's sofa in his cluttered living room. It wasn't cluttered so much as it was crowded with antiques. Nothing in the room matched, an eclectic harmony of old collectibles and heirlooms. It was too bad that there wasn't the same harmony amongst the humans in the room. Without Beth's presence to neutralize the area, tension was steadily rising.

Aiden felt like a rod had been stuffed down his spine. Elidad glanced at him, she was probably wondering why he was so tense. Aiden rolled his shoulder back, attempted to loosen his posture.

Lucian, sitting in the arm chair across from Elidad and Aiden, was much more relaxed, in a smug kind of way. Aiden didn't want to imagine why. Apparently, their date went well.

"I suppose I should tell you both, since you're here," Aiden broke the thick silence.

Elidad cautiously turned her body toward him.

"I have my new orders. I'll be leaving the week after Isaac gets here. That should allow me to assist you for the first week, get Isaac settled, and then I'll begin my new job."

Aiden understood the tension in Elidad's face and regretted not telling her, alone. But he wasn't sure he could've handled that interaction.

"Where?" Her voice was unnaturally even.

"The Vatican." Aiden eyes held hers. It wouldn't be a surprise; they both knew that's where he was heading.

"The Vatican?" Elidad's words were slow. "You're leaving in less than two weeks?"

The pain in her eyes motivated Aiden to stretch his hand out, to reach for hers. He thought better of it and pulled his hand back. Maybe Lucian would notice, maybe not. He didn't care.

"You've been working toward this your whole life and now you made it." Elidad's words didn't sound like a compliment, or a congratulations.

"And that's the reason I'm taking the job, even though the timing is terrible," Aiden knew it was a lost cause, trying to explain away the betrayal she must be feeling.

"Well, that's great news. Congratulations," Lucian interjected.

Elidad shot him a look.

"Thank you," Aiden accepted, graciously. Though he was sure Lucian was just happy to have him out of the way.

"I'm sure it will be a great adventure for you," Lucian added.

"I'm sure it will be," Aiden muttered.

The look Elidad gave Lucian was full of contempt.

"What?" Lucian shrugged. "I thought you knew he was leaving."

"I did," Elidad's tone was sharp. "I'm not surprised. It's just not great timing."

"I assume, it'd be difficult to find the right time," Lucian maintained his calm state.

"Okay," Aiden stood, "I wanted you to know when I knew. I'll keep you informed when I get more details. Elidad, call me if you need anything."

Elidad didn't take her eyes off the coffee table when she nodded a solemn goodbye.

CHAPTER TWENTY

Elidad hadn't been able to eat, all morning. The wisps of steam that wafted out of the top of her mug had lost its thickness as time pressed forward. The liquid inside was barely sipped. She tried to make herself quit pacing the room by sitting on the sofa. Isaac's living room was eerily quiet as her knees bounced up and down. She rubbed her hands over her jeans so vigorously, she was afraid her hands would turn blue.

The door clicked open. Elidad stopped her bouncing as Aiden stepped through the door. For a second the weight in her chest grew lighter. She rose to her feet, meeting Aiden in the center of the room. Without a word, she threw her arms around his waist. Before she buried her face in his chest, she caught the shock in his blue eyes. Without hesitation, his arms wrapped around her.

"How are you?" Aiden's voice was deeper this morning, full of meaning. Elidad was too nervous to read into it.

"I'm— I don't know," Elidad's voice broke off.

"There's a lot to be feeling, right now," Aiden said.

Elidad's arms tightened around him in response.

Aiden took a deep breath, "Elidad... I—"

The door opened again, pulling Elidad and Aiden apart.

Lucian closed the door behind him. The look on his face indicated his discomfort at interrupting their embrace, but it quickly vanished. Elidad appreciatively smiled. She found it attractive that he didn't act like a jealous idiot. She liked a confident man. Of course, if Aiden weren't a priest, Lucian might act differently, and he would have cause to. If Aiden weren't a priest, she probably never would've gone out with Lucian. The kiss that took place between them might not have ever happened. But, it was an amazing kiss.

Elidad's cheeks grew hot at the thought. Would it have never happened? What did that say about her and Lucian? What did that say about her feelings for him? Was he a fall back? Did she go out with him to make herself feel better? Or worse, to hurt Aiden? Her eyes moved over Lucian's face. No, she was certainly attracted to him and his mystique.

"When do they get here?" Aiden's question broke Elidad out of her thoughts.

"Beth will be here any time and Isaac's transport will be here within the hour," Elidad answered.

As if on cue, there was a knock at the door.

"Come in," Elidad said.

The door opened and Beth walked in. "Morning," she glanced around the room to greet everyone. "Looks like the transport is a little early."

Elidad's heart rose to the back of her throat, choking back her words. "Early?"

"Yes, they pulled up in the alley just as I was walking in," Beth said.

Elidad swallowed.

Aiden's warm hand embraced hers, giving a reassuring squeeze. "We're ready for this. I'll go talk to them, why don't you wait for them to bring him in."

Elidad nodded in agreement.

When Aiden swung the door open, the rumbling of the ambulance transport was audible in the alley. The gust of wind that billowed through the door brought the smell of diesel gusting through the living room.

Elidad's feet began to trace the outline of the decorative rug in the center of the living space. She followed it behind the sofa, past the coffee table and around the sitting chairs. The carpet was a middle-eastern inspired design, maroon with gold and blue detail. The edges were a luxurious gold fringe hiding most of the taupe Berber carpet beneath it.

The sound of the transport rumbled again as the door pushed open, snapping Elidad out of her inspection of the carpet.

Aiden's smile felt reassuring. "They'll be in with him in a few minutes. He'll be a little groggy from the medication they gave him to help him travel."

Elidad nodded and began her inspection of the rug again.

"He can't remember anyone or anything." Beth said, as if to remind everyone in the room. "It's difficult to have someone we love not recognize us, but remember, he's not doing it on purpose. He's sick."

Elidad knew Beth's words were mostly pointed at her. Elidad knew it wasn't going to be easy, but she didn't need anyone to spell it out for her. To avoid telling Beth that, Elidad kept her eyes on the fringe, which was unraveling at the edges, mirroring her life. This would be easier if Abraham were here, he'd know what to do. He would've been a perfect caretaker. His patience was infinite, she could never be as loving and caring as he was. That thought drew Elidad's attention to Aiden. She could see a glimmer of Abraham in him.

Lucian was also kind, but different from her father and Aiden. She was sure Abraham would appreciate Lucian's love of the past and his drive to protect it. Isaac must've appreciated it, he'd left the store under his care. Elidad's eyes slid to where Lucian sat in one of the chairs. Confidence exuded from him, reminding her of a king sitting on his throne.

A light rapping on the door drew her attention away, the knock echoing in her chest. Aiden pulled the door open and a man in a blue uniform stood on the other side, a yellow stretcher behind him. He smiled at Aiden and stepped through the door, carefully guiding the bed, keeping it from bumping the door casing. Another man, on the other side of the threshold guided the back end of the stretcher.

The two men guided the waist-high, yellow contraption into the living room. It moved effortlessly over the blue and red rug that Elidad had committed to memory in the last fifteen minutes.

Elidad tried to hold back any expectation. She reminded herself, Isaac hadn't recognized anyone. He couldn't remember his name or where he lived. He couldn't remember anything about his life to help the hospital locate anyone that knew him.

Isaac's frail body was tethered to the stretcher with blue straps that crossed over his legs, waist and chest. His face was an unnatural color, ashen. When they bumped the last wheels over the threshold, Isaac's eyes snapped open and moved around the space, unfocused. An awareness sparked in his face, clearing the confusion in his look. His gray eyes moved over the people in the room, before resting on Elidad.

Elidad smiled at him as the bed came to a stop inside the door. He didn't smile back, he just stared at her.

Isaac's shoulder began pulling upward, tugging and jerking. Elidad looked from Aiden to the men standing at either side of the bed. The way they exchanged looks, she was sure this wasn't normal behavior.

Isaac's body began thrashing against the restraints.

"Elidad!" He shouted. Everyone's eyes went to her.

"I'm here, Isaac," Elidad said.

His body movement quieted at the sound of her voice.

"Elidad," his eyes found her face, "where's Abraham?"

A pain tugged at her heart. "He couldn't be here, Isaac, but he sends his love." She couldn't give him the news, not like this.

Isaac's eyes turned to understanding. "Your father is a busy man, always working."

"Yes," she agreed.

Isaac looked around the room. "I don't like this place, Elidad. I don't want to stay here."

"This is your home, Isaac," her words were soft.

"No! This isn't my home!" He insisted. "No one should live here. This place is evil."

Elidad's eyes flashed to Beth, maybe she'd had some experience with this. Beth looked as shocked as the rest of them. Beth's face smoothed over, as she moved to Isaac's other side. "Isaac, my name is Beth. I'm here to help you. Elidad is right, this is your home. You're going to feel much better, being here."

"This isn't my home!" Isaac shouted. He pulled hard against the restraints. "Elidad, don't make me stay here. They're going to get me if I stay."

"Who's going to get you, Isaac?" Elidad's heart ached at the fear in his eyes. He was legitimately afraid.

Isaac's eyes darted around the room searching the ceiling corner to corner. "The demons. They'll get me."

Elidad cringed at the words. The transport men and Beth would just think he was delusional.

Isaac began thrashing against his restraints, again. His face contorted as he pulled harder, this time. "We have to go, Elidad. We can't stay here," he insisted.

Elidad moved forward and placed her hand on Isaac's chest. "You're going to hurt yourself, will you please stop?"

His body calmed as if her hand were the antidote to his convulsions.

"Elidad, I don't want to stay here," he pleaded.

"Okay," Elidad looked desperately at Aiden, "we'll figure something out."

Elidad looked at the two men dressed in blue. "Gentlemen, will you please load Isaac back into the transport? Apparently, he won't be staying here."

"Where are we going to take him?" The man closest to Elidad asked.

"I'll have to figure that out," Elidad's hand found Isaac's, "and quickly."

The men exchanged glances.

"Okay." One of them shrugged. "It's on your dime. We'll load him up and wait for instructions."

"Thank you." Elidad said. She turned back to Isaac, "Isaac, these men are going to take you back to the transport. We're going to find you a place to go so you don't have to stay here."

Isaac's looked like he'd just received the best news of his life. The emotion welled up behind his eyelids and threatened to spill over the edges. "Will you come with me? You can't stay here."

"I will, as soon as I can. I promise," she assured.

"And your father," Isaac added.

Elidad nodded. "He won't stay here either."

"Good. This place is evil," he looked around the room. If Elidad didn't know better, the look on his face could have convinced her there were demons in every corner.

"Ok, Isaac, I'll just finish up here, and I'll be right out," Elidad assured.

Elidad nodded to the paramedics and they slowly made the way back to the door and over the threshold.

"What the hell was that?" Elidad demanded.

No one answered, as if it were rhetorical.

"Have you ever seen anything like that before?" Elidad directed her question to Beth.

Beth looked hesitant to answer.

"What?" Elidad glared.

"I have seen it before. In Alzheimer patients."

Alzheimer. The word took Elidad's breath from her. "Do you think that's what it is?"

Beth shook her head. "I don't know. Elidad, this was the first time he's remembered anything. He remembered you and your father, that's a good thing. For some reason, he doesn't recognize his house, but there's no rhyme or reason to the brain when it gets damaged. It's going to take time."

"It's not that he didn't recognize his own home," Elidad's voice was low. "It's the fact that he's terrified of it. He thinks it's *evil*. What are we going to do with him?"

"I can make some phone calls," Aiden offered. "I can pull some strings at St. Joseph's."

"I wanted him to come home," Elidad protested. "I didn't want him to be in a home."

"Elidad," Lucian interjected, "If you force him, he might end up in an insane asylum. We all appreciate what you've tried to do, but none of us could see this coming."

Elidad looked around the room, desperate to see what was haunting Isaac. Nothing. "Make your calls, Aiden. I don't think we have any other option, right now. He can't stay in the transport all day."

Aiden nodded. Without a word he slipped into the other room, pulling his cellphone out of his pocket.

"We can only do what we can do," Elidad's voice was flat. "We'll get him home soon, but in the meantime, we'll have to make do."

CHAPTER TWENTY-ONE

Aiden made good on his word. Isaac was placed at St. Josephs, a place which typically had a six-month waiting list. Elidad had no idea what it took to get Isaac admitted in an afternoon, but she guessed it was more about protecting the Church's welfare, than Isaac's. Isaac was a keeper and the store he owned housed many secrets in its depths. Secrets the Church would want to gain control of, if something were to happen to Isaac.

Beth helped move Isaac into the home and reassured Elidad, when the time was right, they'd move Isaac home. Over the week, Isaac vastly improved, remembering bits about his travel to Jerusalem and being in the hospital. He remembered being taken to his house, but still insisted it wasn't his home, though he couldn't remember his home, or where it was located. He asked about the store and wanted to go back to work, until he was informed it was in the same building they'd tried to take him to. He wanted nothing to do with it.

Elidad lifted her hand to knock on 110 B. There was no response, so she pushed the door open into the little studio. Isaac sat in a recliner facing a garden window that looked over a manicured courtyard filled with flowers and bright green grass.

"Good morning, Isaac," Elidad greeted.

His head turned toward her.

"Elidad," he smiled, "It's so nice to see you, again. How long are you staying in town?"

They'd been over this for the past few days. "I'll be in town a while. I'm going to get you better, so you can go home."

Isaac frowned. "You want to take me back to that, place."

Elidad sighed, plopping into a chair that faced him. "That place is your home."

"It wasn't my home," he shook his head. "My home is somewhere else."

"Isaac, your home is in the same place it's always been. It hasn't changed a bit in the last thirty years." This was the same argument they'd had over the past few days.

"Ask your father what he thinks," Isaac said. "If he says it's my home, then I'll believe him. But I want to hear him say it."

Elidad stood, moving two steps forward to look out the window. She still hadn't told Isaac about Abraham. The time hadn't been right. Now, it was starting to feel like she was deceiving him. She'd have to come clean.

"Isaac…" her voice broke.

"He's gone, isn't he?" Isaac's words were low, like he was afraid the roses on the other side of the glass would hear him.

Elidad closed her eyes. "Yes."

"How?"

Elidad's mind became a tornado of images, sounds and smell. All the memories she'd tried to forget. "He was possessed."

"And you couldn't save him?" Isaac's words weren't accusing, more a statement of fact.

"No." She agreed as a tear escaped her eye. She turned to Isaac, kneeling at his feet. "I tried. I tried so hard."

Isaac's brown eyes were soft as his hand reached out for her face. "Of course, you did. Your father knows, he was so proud of you."

More tears. Elidad couldn't hold them back, now. "But I couldn't save him."

"You did. You saved him from the moment you appeared in his life. There is no escaping the prophecy. Your fates were intertwined from the beginning. He knew it would be the end of him."

Elidad's brows creased. "What do you mean, he knew it would be the end of him? Do you know what the prophecy is?"

Isaac shook his head. "I can't remember," his brows hardened. "I know it's there, I know it's important."

"What do you know about my parents, and how I came to live with Abraham?"

Isaac brushed away Elidad's tears with his thumb. "I know it was a tragedy, that's all I can remember, Elidad. Perhaps, this would be an excellent question for Leucosia."

"I'm not speaking to her." Elidad wanted him to give her the answers now.

"That's a shame. She's done so much to protect you. It's sad you would punish her, this way."

"Protect me?" Elidad demanded. "By letting me stay with my parent's killer?" Elidad pushed herself to her feet and away from Isaac.

"*Parents*?" Isaac's words sounded like they had some hidden inflection. "Maybe a visit with Leucosia will make things clear for you?"

"There's nothing to clear up! They're all dead! My parents, Abraham… all of them. And for what? For nothing." Elidad could feel the heat under her collar.

"Not for nothing. To protect you." Isaac corrected.

"To protect me from what?" Elidad demanded.

"My mind isn't what it used to be, Elidad. That's why I'm here." Isaac gestured around the room. "I think your best bet, is to ask Leucosia. She has the answers."

"I don't want to see her," Elidad spat.

Isaac's eyes deepened. "You've always been strong willed. Just like your father. But I wonder, who are you hurting most?"

Elidad looked away from his eyes.

"I can see how you would feel betrayed, but does this circumstance deserve this amount of anger?"

Choking back the tears that threatened to start pouring again, Elidad stood at the glass to inspect the roses. By now, she could probably sketch them from memory.

"I wonder," Isaac continued, "Is your anger from being betrayed or is it rooted in regret? It sounds to me like you have more questions than answers. Remember, it's difficult to make accurate judgments before having all the information, and yet, it sounds like you are not willing to gather that information, but jump directly to judgment. I would assume you feel some regret for not speaking to your father for the last year. The hurt of time lost, that you can't get back, *is* regrettable. It's not your fault, Elidad. He knew his fate when he took you in."

"What does that mean? He knew he'd die when he adopted me? How could he know that?"

"He knew it could cost him his life, to protect you. Just like your Mother."

"And my Father," Elidad added.

There was a knock at the door just before it cracked open.

"Isaac. It's time for your physical therapy." A feminine voice called. A middle-aged woman in scrubs with cartoon owls printed across the fabric walked in. "Oh, you have a visitor." Her ID hung from her neck with her picture squarely set in the center. Just like her photo, her dark hair was pulled back into a tightly wrapped bun. Under her left eye were three faded dots in the shape of a triangle. More tattoos poked out from under the sleeves of her work clothes. "I'll get your chair, I'll be right back." She said, and she disappeared out the door.

When she was gone, Isaac looked up at Elidad. "Were there markings?"

Elidad stared at him, "Markings?"

"When Abraham was taken, where he died, were there markings on the wall or the floor?"

The triangle flashed in Elidad's mind.

"Yes."

Isaac nodded his head, as if he could see it, himself. "There was no way you could have saved him. He fought a greater battle than you were prepared for."

"What battle?"

"The rise of the Inferno," Isaac's voice was ominous. "They are preparing to rise."

The knock at the door made Elidad jump. The woman came in with a wheelchair for Isaac.

"I can come back after your P.T. and you can tell me about it." Elidad said as the nurse locked the wheelchair into place next to Isaac.

"I think it best if you speak with Leucosia. You need to make amends with her. I'm sure she's heartbroken you've waited this long. Go see her." Isaac's eyes were pleading.

"I'll think about it."

CHAPTER TWENTY-TWO

Aiden's alarm went off. He'd been lying awake for the past two hours, dreading today. He'd imagined, if he'd stayed in bed and refused to put his feet on the ground, the day wouldn't start. Remaining under the covers would keep today in the future and wouldn't become the day that would take him away from Elidad.

He was already drifting away and Lucian was replacing him. This job, across the city, made room for Lucian, and Lucian was all too willing to capitalize on the opportunity. Aiden couldn't help but remember Leucosia's warning. *"Aiden, her heart cannot bear any more heartbreak. You have given yourself to God, and the church. You can't stay here. Don't build her up any more than you already have, only to break her heart."* The truth was, it was breaking his own heart. He couldn't bear to see her with Lucian. She was in a bad place, emotionally, and it was causing her to make bad decisions. But on the flip side, did that mean Lucian *wouldn't* break her heart? Otherwise, Leucosia would try to keep them apart, too. Right?

Aiden's alarm chimed again, startling him out of his thoughts. He pressed the screen on his phone to turn it off. His bags were packed in the corner of his sterile room; it looked the same as the day he'd moved in. He hadn't bothered with personal effects because he'd known from the beginning, his stay would be brief.

The Vatican, he thought. He'd worked hard for this, and now that it was here, you'd think he'd misplaced his most valuable possession. He certainly wasn't acting like he was blessed with the opportunity of a lifetime.

The Lord works in mysterious ways, Aiden reminded himself. He'd been looking to crack that mystery for weeks with relentless hours of prayer. What *mysterious way* was He working? God wasn't offering any answers, this time. It would come. The answers always came when he kept his focus in the right direction. Up.

Today was his last day in New York, his ticket was for six a.m. out of J.F.K. International Airport. He'd have to call it an early night. His alarm was set for three a.m. to make sure he would miss the rush-hour on the train.

Elidad whipped through the door, she smiled when she saw Aiden sitting in the corner. He watched her move through the crowded space of tables, mismatched sofas and people sipping hot coffee. It was a modestly temperate August day for New York and Elidad wore her trademark dark denim jeans accompanied by a T-shirt. She looked a little dressier than usual. Instead of boots, she wore oxfords and her T-shirt sat low on her collarbone, exposing one shoulder. Aiden was sure, if he had been standing behind her, he'd be able to see her tattoo peeking out from behind the fabric.

The hiss of steamed milk in metal cups and the Indi mix playing on the speakers, periodically placed across the ceiling, silenced her approach.

"Hey," Elidad said when she got close.

Aiden stood to give her a hug. "Hey." When they embraced, he breathed in her perfume: floral fragrance with a woody undertone.

"Sorry I'm late." She said as she sat in the chair next to him. "I got hung up with Isaac. He's really starting to remember things. I might be able to get him to tell me about my parents soon. He says he can't remember, but he's remembering so much."

"That's great, Elidad. I'm glad to hear it. You deserve to know," he said.

Elidad stared at him with no response.

"What?" He frowned at her interrogating eyes.

Her right eyebrow hiked upward. "You're not going to get all mushy on me, are you?"

"I wouldn't dare," he teased.

"Good," she smirked.

"We wouldn't want you to get a reputation," he offered.

"A reputation?"

"We wouldn't want anyone to know you're… human," Aiden sipped his coffee.

"Soy chai," the barista called out over the clattering room.

"That's you," Aiden said.

Elidad's lips widened. "Thanks."

She got up to fight the crowd hovering around the counter. She came back, large glass mug in hand, with a perfect dollop of foam. She took a sip.

"Yum, best chai in the city."

"You've tried them all?" Aiden doubted.

"I don't have to. I stopped when I found this place. The chai's good, the atmosphere is great, even their music is perfect and… it's not Starbucks."

"It's nothing like Starbucks," Aiden observed.

"And that," Elidad smiled, "is why we're here."

"I thought you were here for the company," Aiden reminded.

Elidad exhaled audibly through her nose. "The company is so-so."

"Well, in that case, you should be happy I'm leaving," Aiden suggested with a grin that pulled up the edges of his mouth.

Elidad's playful banter fizzled from her eyes. "I'm not happy. I'm going to miss you, Aiden. I don't know what I'm going to do without you."

"You'll do what you've always done."

"And what's that?" She asked, looking into the bottom of her cup like it held the answer.

"Kick ass."

Her smile moved her lips, but didn't touch her eyes. It made Aiden feel guilty. He *was* hurting her. Leucosia was right, he needed to get out of town.

After stretching out the time as long as possible, they were forced to face the inevitable: it was time to go. Aiden drank enough coffee to keep a college kid trucking though finals. Elidad wasn't sure how he kept himself from bouncing off the walls.

They'd made their way out of the coffee shop and onto the street without a word between them. Instead of words, Elidad locked arms with Aiden. She wanted to keep him close, as long as she could. They turned down another street, quieter than the one before. People weren't as compact here—more intermittent—as they strolled.

Aiden broke the silence. "You never did say how your date went, the other night."

"That…" Elidad shrugged, trying to think of what to say while keeping Lucian as far from her mind as she could. "I wouldn't call it a date, we're friends. It was nice."

"That's not the way he looks at you," Flashes of Elidad and Lucian in the same room came to Aiden's mind. He gave his head a slight shake in an attempt to get rid of them.

"How does he look at me?" Elidad asked.

"Like he wants you. Or wants something from you."

"Oh, come on Aiden, we've been through this. He's a nice guy, and he's helping me out. Stop trying to give him a bad rap," Elidad pleaded.

Aiden noticed the streetlights coming on around them. It was later than he'd thought. "Alright, I'll try to give him a break," he agreed, "But that doesn't mean I have to like him."

Elidad's laugh was light and genuine. He liked to hear her laugh like that. They followed the sidewalk across the block and down another street to a city park.

Across the greenscape, a cluster of swing sets emerged. A jungle gym sprung out of the ground. Bright reds and blues towered over a padded, grey mat, visible under all the surfaces, for a more forgiving place to land. Squeals of joy rang out as they continued, arm-in-arm. In the distance, Elidad could see children chasing each other in and around what little shrubbery was in the area.

"I'm going to have to catch a cab home. I have to get up early," Aiden was reluctant to go.

Elidad squeezed his arm. "Okay."

"I'll come back to see you… and you can always come see me," he suggested.

"I'm sure that would do wonders for your career," Elidad rolled her eyes at the thought.

Aiden stopped walking, breaking their arm lock to face her. "I don't care what it does to my career. I want you in my life."

The sincerity in his voice moved her brows with the weight of sentiment.

Why was he so good at saying things that had double meanings? *Did* he want her in his life? How could he? He was leaving.

In the pale light of the smoldering summer sky, there was heat in his eyes. She could feel his emotions, and knew he could feel hers, though she wanted to hide them. Maybe he knew how she felt, maybe that's why he was leaving.

"I'll miss you, Elidad." Pain was at the edge of his words.

She saw an emotion, so deep and pure in his radiant blue eyes, she was tempted to look away; the sincerity frightened her.

"I wish I didn't have to go." He took a thoughtful breath. "I wish I could stay here, with you."

There it was again.

Did he want to be with her, or *with* her? Was she just clinging to some hopeless fantasy that someone like Aiden could want her. Not like him. Actually him.

Her eyes traced his face. As painful as it was, she wanted to remember him, like this: his lips, quivering with the lack of words, sentiment pouring out of him. She wanted to remember the way his careless hair fell perfectly to one side, and his impossible fashion sense that made it hard for him to pass as a straight man, let alone a priest.

"I wish you didn't have to go," she admitted.

He reached forward, pushing her hair off her shoulder. The movement set her skin ablaze as he clasped the back of her neck. The intensity of his grip reminded her of their embrace before she'd entered the barn to save Abraham. It was simpler then, when she thought her death was inevitable. It was easier to take her feelings to the grave when she thought the grave was seconds away. Could she keep them contained, now? She was dangerously close to telling him how she felt.

Aiden looked at her with the same needy eyes. It was the kind of look that ignited desire, turning her soul into an inferno, threating to incinerate them both.

Elidad's mind raced, taking her back to the other day, in Isaac's room. Before Lucian showed up, it felt like Aiden was going to kiss her. He *was* going to kiss her. Perhaps being friends with her was too difficult. He could be leaving because being in close proximity to her was making it hard to keep his vows; that could be why he kept saying he *needed* to leave. Was she driving him away?

"Remember to stay strong, Aiden, you will do good, where ever you go—" her voice broke. That's all she could say. She pressed her lips together to keep from pouring out her feelings before him.

Holding back was what she was best at.

In that moment, their feelings pulled them together for an intimate embrace, a hug goodbye. Aiden's arms wrapped tightly around her. She pressed into his chest to inhale his woody scent. Her arms tightened around him, and she imagined never letting go.

As the energy swelled between their bodies, she had to fight back the urge to whisper she loved him.

Her instinct was to release him, to permit for a seemingly shallow embrace that signified friendship. The slack in her arms didn't trigger a response. Relieved he wasn't ready to let go, she tightened her grip, again. Elidad's fingers pressed upward between his shoulder blades, digging into the fabric of his shirt.

Aiden's hands followed Elidad's spine to the small of her back. His breath caught in her hair, pushing her floral smell into the atmosphere.

Unlike in Mexico, Elidad knew she'd see him again. And yet, this time, was harder. After every moment they'd shared, this one moment felt infinite. It didn't feel absolute like when she'd left him in front of the barn as she walked away to die, but absolute, nonetheless.

She should have kissed him then… on a day when she'd had nothing left to lose.

"Stay strong, Elidad. Things will get easier for you. Call me anytime. I don't care what time it is. I'll always be here for you." Aiden's whisper sent a reaction down her arms. He slowly pulled away, dragging his cheek across hers. Aiden hesitated, their faces lightly touching, his breath resounding in her ear, pushing Elidad's blood pressure past its boiling point.

Aiden pulled away. "I'll call you, when I land."

"Okay," she nodded, looking at her hands, suddenly fighting back tears.

"I'll see you," he said, turning to walk away.

Elidad turned, her hands shaking, she stuffed them into her pockets. She took a second, trying to get her bearings, before taking a step.

"Elidad," Aiden called after her.

She turned. He was already ten yards away.

"I love you." He said it the same way you'd tell a friend before doing something dangerous, to make sure they knew, just in case.

Her heart stopped, for one breath… or a rotation of the planet… she couldn't be sure.

"Yeah, you too," she managed to make it sound casual.

CHAPTER TWENTY-THREE

Elidad walked back across the park, alone. Streetlights glowing around the edges of the open space were barely able to illuminate her path. She couldn't bear to sleep, tonight. Afraid of her dreams, she decided to search the street, on foot, for clarity. She couldn't help but come back to the last place she saw Aiden.

She was ridiculous.

It was pathetic to come back, to believe he might have left some piece of himself here. The playground was desolate… abandoned, like her.

From the dark shadows, she heard a child's laughter, an echo from her childhood. It was a reminder of the laughter she wasn't allowed to participate in. Elidad looked at the face of her phone, 3 a.m. Her eyes searched the grass for children.

An empty swing squeaked back and forth in the wind.

Elidad's eye caught movement and snapped to a little boy in a cloak. Something about the way he stood made Elidad's heart pound. The boy stepped closer, his chin lifted she could see his face, his skin was pale white and his eyes black. Black veins webbed across his face. Two more children stepped out of the dark, cloaked. Then another… and another.

Elidad's palms perspired, she could feel the cool clammy sheen race across her skin as she spun in a circle. The dark hooded children encompassed her on every side.

Hushed giggles rippled from one to the other.

"Who are you?" Elidad called out.

The rest of the children remained undefined, under their cloaks, like the Shadow Man. At the thought of his name, as if summoned, the Shadow Man appeared behind the army of shadow children. The cloaks pressed in on all sides of her, their approach was slow and gruesome, like zombies in a horror film.

Elidad's hand went to her pocket to find the Sword of Justice. It was empty. Giggles rippled through the crowd, again. Hopelessly, Elidad looked at the ground for something she could use to defend herself: a rock, stick, anything.

Cut into the ground, beneath her feet, was the symbol Emily drew on the wall in her blood, the same symbol that was cut under Abraham's body: a triangle with an intricate design. Elidad's feet were at the base of the triangle as Isaac's words came back to her.

"There was no way you could have saved him. He fought a greater battle than you were prepared for."

"What battle?"

"The rise of the Inferno," Isaac's voice was ominous. "They are preparing to rise."

The Shadow Man began laughing. Could he hear Isaac in her mind? They were so close now, only steps away.

Elidad looked up to heaven. At least Aiden was safe on the other side of the world. Tears swelled at the thought of him and his face, the way he'd stood here, just yesterday, as he'd said his goodbye. If she would've known it would be the last time she saw him, she would have kissed him, then. Maybe that's why their goodbye felt infinite. Somehow, she knew she wouldn't live long.

She'd find solace in the fact that she'd see Abraham, soon. If they were lucky enough to end up in the same place. Did she belong in Heaven? Did Abraham? That thought began the flow of tears. There was no sense in holding them back, now.

The children's laughter echoed at her feet. One of the children in the first row reached forward, grabbing her arm.

Elidad screamed in pain. Her flesh caught fire under the cloaked minion's touch, the same way it did when the Shadow Man grabbed her in a dream.

Her dream… was this a dream? Last time, she couldn't wake herself, she thought it was real. She believed it was real. Aiden had to wake her, he saved her.

More arms grabbed at her body. Her eyes, wide with pain, took in every aspect of her burning flesh. Chunks of meat rolled off her bone, the smoke that plumed off her body was thick and black, suffocating her lungs. She coughed, repulsed by the smell of her own charred skin.

She had to wake up. Aiden wasn't here to save her. Wake up. Wake—

"Aiden!" Elidad screamed into her empty room. Her chest was heaving with the weight of her breath. Unable to wick away all the sweat, she was laying in saturated covers. Elidad half-jumped out of bed, ready to defend herself from anyone in the room.

There was nothing but a dresser and her belongings scattered around. She brushed the tears away, catching her breath before sitting on the bed. Elidad rubbed her hands together to get a grip on reality.

It was okay. It was just a dream… but Aiden was still gone.

She cradled her head in her hands and continued to cry.

CHAPTER TWENTY-FOUR

Elidad answered her phone on the first ring.

"Either you are awake, or you were sleeping on your phone," she heard Lucian say on the other end.

"I was awake," Elidad said.

"Sorry, I called so early," he began. "I have an early meeting with clients. I found them a god-awful painting they've been looking for, and they can't wait to get their hands on it."

"I suppose it's never too early for art," Elidad pondered.

Lucian laughed. "You should see this thing. I guarantee, it's too early for it. It's a painting of a girl, and she looks possessed. I have no idea where they would hang this, unless they own a haunted house."

His description took her mind back to her dream. Elidad held out her arm to make sure she wasn't burned. "Well, some people like creepy."

"I suppose they do. I wanted to check on you, before I got busy," he was direct.

Elidad pondered his words. "Consider me checked."

She could hear an exhale of amused air pass his lips. "Are you okay?"

"Sure."

"I know you care a great deal for him, Elidad. You don't have to pretend otherwise. I understand," he assured. "You've lost a lot in the past year, losing a friend to the other side of the world is hard."

Tears began boiling over her lashes before she could stop them.

"I'm fine," she assured. "I knew this was coming. It's not a big surprise." She wanted to change the subject. "I'm going to go see Isaac today. He's been remembering a lot, he even talked about my parents, a little. I'm hoping he'll be able to tell me more, today."

"That's great," Lucian agreed.

Elidad didn't tell Lucian exactly what happened to her parents, not that *she* really knew. She told him they'd died in a car crash, the same thing she'd been led to believe for the majority of her life. It was easy to keep up the same charade she'd been living for the past twenty-four years.

"Do you want me to go with you?" He offered.

"No, you're busy. How about I come over, after? I'll tell you if he remembers anything."

"Okay, sounds good. I'll make dinner. You can tell me over a meal." Lucian suggested.

Despite the tears, she smiled into the phone. He was good.

"Okay," she agreed, "I'll see you around six."

"Good morning Isaac," Elidad said as she walked into his studio. "How was breakfast?"

He frowned up at her from one of the recliners. "How do you think?"

"Well, I don't know. That's why I asked."

"The closest thing to food that they serve in the morning is oatmeal. And Elidad, it's hard to get oatmeal wrong, and they still accomplish this feat. I want to go home."

"I want you to go home," she agreed. "Did you decide, you're ready to come home, then?"

A confused look glossed over Isaac's eyes. "I just told you, I want to go home."

"Remember, we tried to bring you home last week, you didn't like it. You wanted to leave."

Understanding lit his eyes. "It was scary."

"You were frightened," Elidad agreed.

"That wasn't my home. I don't want to go there."

"The problem is, it *is* your home. It's in the same place it's always been. It's a part of the store. There's no moving it, Isaac. If you want to go home, you have to go there."

Isaac shook his head with doubt. "It's not the same…"

Elidad remembered the look in his eyes as he inspected the living room. It was frightening to see him fight so violently against his restraints. It had looked like he was seeing demons in the empty corners of the room. She could relate to haunted rooms.

"What if I bring some holy water home and bless the house?" Elidad suggested.

Isaac looked hopeful. "Will your father do it?"

Elidad stared at him. "Did you forget?"

"Forget what?" His eyes were innocent.

"Abraham is gone," Elidad answered.

"Where did he go, this time?" He asked, smiling up at her. "That father of yours is always traveling."

Elidad bit her bottom lip. "Isaac, can you tell me about my parents?"

He looked thoughtful. "A tragedy, really. Are you sure you want to talk about it?"

"Yes, please."

"It's a sad story, Elidad," he warned.

"I know. I can handle it," her heart raced.

Isaac looked out the window. "They died in a terrible car accident, both of them, together. It was a sad day, indeed."

Despair shot through Elidad's veins. "They didn't die in a car accident."

Isaac looked at her confused. "Yes, they did, Elidad. I'm sorry."

The pain in his eyes was almost too much for her to bear. "You're right, they did. I'm sorry too."

CHAPTER TWENTY-FIVE

The dinner Lucian made was exquisite: savory ravioli stuffed with a cheesy mushroom mix he'd made from scratch, smothered in a red sauce that tasted like tomatoes and basil, fresh from the garden. Elidad couldn't think of a better meal she'd had recently.

"That was amazing. Thank you," she picked up Lucian's plate.

"You're welcome. I'm glad you liked it. It's been a while since I've been able to cook for someone. I'm glad I've still got it."

"Any time you'd like to practice on me, let me know," Elidad cringed at the way her words came out.

Lucian laughed. "I will."

She put the dishes in the sink to avoid looking at him, rolling her eyes at herself.

"Leave them," he meant the dishes. "I'll get to them later."

"You cooked, the least I can do is dishes," Elidad answered.

"If I thought you were going to fight me over the dishes, I would've taken you to dinner," he teased.

"Okay…okay… I'll let you do the dishes," she conceded.

"Thank you."

Elidad picked up her wine glass, finishing off what was left.

"It's late." Lucian observed. "If you'd like to skip the train ride, you can stay in the guest room," he offered.

Elidad locked eyes with Lucian. She wasn't sure staying under the same roof with him was a good idea. Besides, she wasn't planning to go home to sleep, anyway. After the failed visit with Isaac this afternoon, she'd made up her mind to go see Leucosia. She was ready for answers.

"No, that's okay," Elidad said. "I haven't been sleeping well these days. I'll go back to Abraham's house and pace around there all night. Thanks."

"I promise, I won't let you kiss me."

Elidad smiled. "Who said I need anyone to keep me from kissing you?"

"I thought that might be the reason you're leery about staying, especially after a glass of wine," Lucian took another sip, beaming.

"No, that's not the problem. I can handle myself, thank you."

"Well… that's too bad, isn't it?"

Elidad smirked at his comment. His honesty sent her heart sprinting, but after Aiden leaving yesterday, it didn't feel right, thinking of kissing Lucian right now. He was sweet, handsome, smart and sophisticated, but her heart was with Aiden.

Lucian held up the bottle of wine. "One more glass before you go?"

Elidad picked up her glass. "Why not?"

Lucian split the remaining wine between their two glasses and set the empty bottle on the counter. Elidad followed Lucian into the adjacent living room and sat on the small, golden sofa crowning the living area. In another room, the antique sofa might look like great-grandma's furniture, but with Isaac's eye for detail, and love of antiques, it looked royal. It was paired with a coffee table, adorned with beautiful filigree and sturdy brass accents. Not the kind of coffee table you kicked your feet on.

Elidad eyed the corners of the room, looking for Isaac's mysterious haunting. Why was he so afraid of his home? What a strange manifestation of his stroke.

"How are you, really?" Lucian said, turning his body so his knee touched her thigh.

Just his touch was enough to make her waiver on her morals. Elidad shrugged. "I'm fine."

"I asked how are you, *really*? I didn't ask what you tell everyone."

Taking a sip, she could feel the wine's tannin on the edge of her tongue. She hesitated to swallow, knowing she would have to give him an answer. As the wine cascaded down the side of her glass from where her lips had been, she decided to answer honestly.

"Overwhelmed," she exhaled. Aiden was the only one she was used to sharing her feelings with; this was difficult. "To be perfectly honest, I am overwhelmed."

"And rightfully so," Lucian agreed. "You lost your father, you're responsible for Isaac and you thought Aiden would help you through it, but he's leaving. There's a lot going on in a small amount of time."

When Elidad told Lucian she found Abraham dead, she left out the part where he had to be rescued from demon possession. She certainly didn't tell Lucian that she'd performed the exorcism herself. Lucian had an idea of Crusaders and what they did, but Elidad wasn't sure of his full knowledge. Hearing and *knowing* what she did were two different things.

She wanted to take the focus off herself. "You said your uncle raised you. How did that come about? Are your parents… around?"

"I never had a mother."

"It's a little difficult to be born without a mother." Elidad teased. "Even Jesus had an earthly mother."

Lucian smirked. "Mine was a junkie."

Elidad's eyes widened. "Wow, sorry. I'll just shut up."

Lucian chuckled. "It's fine. I've accepted it. She died when I was eight, I never really met her, so it wasn't as hard as you would think. My father wasn't much better. He had a tough time raising me on his own." Lucian spun his wineglass between his index finger and thumb. "Apparently, the stress of having to support a child drove him to find ways to make *easy* money."

Elidad felt guilty for bringing it up, but a little part of her was fascinated. "He was into drugs too?" She assumed.

This was the first time she'd witnessed Lucian uncomfortable.

"Among other things. He was a little smarter than a lowly drug dealer. He found himself in organized crime."

"Wow." Elidad couldn't think of anything else to say.

"Eventually, the police tied him to some executions. Some snitch pointed the finger, the snitch got three years in prison, my father was given three life sentences. The state sent me to live with my uncle."

"Do you talk to your father?"

"I did speak to him for a while, but as I got older, we didn't see eye to eye and I stopped communicating with him. It seems like centuries since we last spoke."

"I guess that's normal, isn't it?" Elidad continued to stare into her glass. "We don't understand them, and they don't understand us."

Elidad looked up into Lucian's green eyes, she liked the way his dark hair curled defiantly at the ends. Their lives were similar. As a result of a tragic history, she didn't know her parents, either.

Lucian checked his watch. "If you aren't tired enough to skip the train ride, do you want to go out and get a drink?"

As she took the last sip of wine, she contemplated the cab ride to *Genus*. It was a lot further than Abraham's house from here.

"No, thanks. I'll take a rain check. I've had a long day. I'd like to get back to my place." Elidad said.

Lucian smiled.

"What?" Elidad asked.

Lucian was stoic, sitting sideways on the sofa. His olive skin contrasted with the gold of the sofa as his arm draped over the back. His fingertips lightly touched her shoulder.

That easily, he sent her heart rate barreling. She was thankful, since their date, it was a little easier to keep her face from burning red. That made it a little easier to hide her attraction to him. But since their date, she wasn't sure where they stood, either. He was playing it pretty cool, considering.

"I know you're having a hard…" Lucian searched for a word, "year?" He inflicted.

Elidad laughed. "Yeah, it's certainly been a year."

"I'm sensing some hesitation around me."

"It's not…" Elidad's mind swam.

Lucian interrupted. "Let me finish, please."

"Okay," she agreed.

"I can't imagine, what you've been through. The loss of your father, Isaac, and now Aiden."

Elidad stared at her hands. "Aiden was bound to leave."

"I'm surprised he did," Lucian admitted.

Elidad looked up to meet his gaze. There was something in his eyes she couldn't decipher.

Lucian smiled, "I'm not a complete idiot, I told you before, I see the way he looks at you. And the way you looked at him."

Elidad couldn't keep the flush from reaching her cheeks, this time. "I don't look at him any way."

"I see how you are, together." Lucian clarified, "You two are close, there's no denying it. There's nothing wrong with having close friends."

Elidad nodded. "He's my best friend, we've been through a lot together."

"Clearly," Lucian agreed. "And there's nothing wrong with that."

Elidad couldn't help but smile at his candidness.

He sighed, "I like you, Elidad, that's obvious, and I know you like me, too. As usual, I have impeccable timing." He laughed. "I know your life is complicated. I don't want to complicate it further. I'm not pushing for anything, you don't need any more pressure in your life. I just want to be here for you. I'll help you as long as I am able."

Emotion swelled inside Elidad. His words were precisely what she needed to hear. How could he know, exactly what she needed?

She allowed her fingertips to touch his knee, "Thank you, for understanding."

Lucian's eyes were as warm as his words. Her prior hesitation began to fade, leaving her with the desire to lean in and kiss him. If she ran her fingers through his curly dark locks and allowed him to pull her against his broad chest, maybe the current state of her life would melt away.

Elidad stood abruptly before allowing her mind to go the direction it was taking her. "I have to go, it's later than I thought."

"You're sure?" There was a hint of hopefulness in Lucian's tone.

"Yes," she said a little more forcefully than she meant. It sounded like she couldn't wait to get away from him, rather than she had to *keep* herself away. She was okay with the miscommunication for now.

"I'll walk you out," Lucian offered.

"Please don't." Walking her to the door might mean a goodbye kiss. "I'm not your guest. I owe *you* for helping me. Thanks, though. I'll see you tomorrow." She grabbed her coat in a flurry and made her way out the door.

Stepping into the alley, Elidad was relieved when the door closed behind her.

Tightening her coat around her waist, she shook her head at how exceptional she'd become at looking like an idiot in front of Lucian.

As Elidad's feet moved her toward the street, she hoped there'd be a cab close by. She was ready to confront Leucosia. Her past needed to get behind her and she had a right to know the prophecy. She deserved to know what the people in her life died for and what her future held.

A chill ran down Elidad's back, sending a shiver to her knees. An overwhelming feeling of emptiness caused her to stop mid-step.

She wasn't alone.

Slowly, she looked over her shoulder, but she found only darkness there...

CHAPTER TWENTY-SIX

Did the Shadow Man finally come to confront her? Had he transitioned from stalker to terror? She couldn't see anything in the back of the alley. Her nerves pulsed as she remembered her dream with Aiden and Lucian. She looked up and down the alley for children popping out of the darkness.

Her hand went to her coat pocket. She withdrew the Sword of Justice. The weight of the hilt was heavy in her hand. She was surprised it didn't automatically materialize into a weapon. At Abraham's home, it didn't appear when she unsheathed it either, but there wasn't any impending danger then. Did that mean there was no danger now? In Mexico, the sword appeared before she stepped toward the barn. Could the sword sense impending danger? Leucosia said it would appear for her when she was in need.

The hairs on Elidad's flesh stood on end, picking up energy waves from her surroundings.

She was in need now, she wasn't alone in the alley. The sword needed to work. The cool metal did nothing. *Please Lord, let it work*, she thought, giving it a little shake.

Nothing.

Her hand began to tremor, adrenaline intertwining with fear. Why? Why wasn't it working? *"Only with purity and justice in your heart will it come to you."* Leucosia's words rang in Elidad's mind. Was there purity in her heart right now? There might not be room for justice along with all the anger.

What use was this damn sword? The magic only helped her once, against Ghelgath's army. The second time, it forced her to take her father's life.

It left her with nothing.

The only thing she had left was Isaac. Everyone else deserted her: Abraham, her parents, Aiden. They left her with this impossible task of finding these keys, and the responsibility of a prophecy threatening to control her life, but none of them stayed to help her.

The feeling of abandonment changed the shaking of her hand to a throbbing heartbeat as she glared down at the sword, refusing to come to her aid. It was a cruel reminder of all the people in her life.

She threw it to the ground.

The metal clanged on the pavement, echoing down the alley. She needed a new plan. That worthless scrap of metal wasn't going to help her. She couldn't hear any movement in the alley over a siren that echoed down the brick walls, but her body told her she was in danger. A police car sped past, lights flashing. If only *they* could help her… She knew she needed them. *Someone* was here, with her.

Now what? The decision to run back to the door from which she just exited, or to run for the end of the alley and out to the open street, could be her last.

Elidad took one cautious step. Her eye caught a flash behind her. Deciding not to put Lucian in danger, she sprinted for the end of the alley. As her legs burned with the sudden exertion, she could hear the whooshing of wings behind her. This wasn't the Shadow Man and it certainly wasn't a mugger.

She almost made it out into the street light when she felt a muscular embrace tear at her shoulder. Something strong cut deep into her flesh, causing her to cry out in pain. The creature pulled her back toward the darkness. Elidad kicked her legs trying to free herself, her struggle pulling at her shoulder where the resistance was fierce.

She thought of Aiden, across the ocean. There was no one who could save her. She was on her own. The creature's wings struggled with her weight, the ground leaving her feet only for a second or two. The flesh in her shoulder tore when she struggled. When thrust upward again, Elidad lifted her leg high enough to grab the knife that was tucked in her boot. Pulling it from its sheath, she swung it fiercely at her attacker's grasp. She felt her knife connect with muscle, her blade penetrated down to the handle. She pulled hard downward. His screech pierced her ears like a banshee's cry. She winced at the tone as he dropped her to the ground. Elidad, hoping she would be dropped, landed on her feet and quickly turned, anticipating another attack.

Elidad could see the outline of the monster as he landed at the end of the alley. He stood tall, like a man. Gruesome wings reached out from his back, but he wasn't a man, nor was he an angel. The monster's skin was charcoal, a sleek scaly armor, reminding her of medieval chainmail. Atop a massive head, an array of horns jetted out from his skull. Two of those horns reached forward from his jaw to frame his face, the other eight formed a crown around his head. His brow line, chiseled hard like his jaw, accentuated his eyes, which glowed yellow in the choked light. She was sure he could see her better than she could see him. The monster stood on large hind legs with massive feet that protruded sharp talons. Elidad could feel the sting of those talons in her shoulder, the blood from their wound trickling down her side, soaking her shirt. The sticky warmth of her own blood made her stomach turn. It was too much. She knew her ability to defend herself was limited, slowly diminishing by the second.

The monster's blood fell from the wound on his leg, hissing as it hit the pavement. The glowing red pools moved together, boiling on the ground before absorbing into the asphalt. The trail of blood, simulating lava, left a lingering smell like rotting flesh, even though it was absorbed into the ground. The aroma, mixing with the smell rising from the sewer, burned through Elidad's lungs as she struggled to catch her breath.

Gripping her knife, Elidad walked straight toward the demon. He crouched forward in response. His jagged hands were just as dangerous as the feet that pierced her shoulder. He didn't need a weapon with claws on every extremity. Elidad held tight to the knife as the monster dove at her. She stabbed him hard in the side and used her momentum to throw him away from her body. He screeched. She could feel his anger as he slashed back in response, his claws barely scratching her chest. Quickly turning, she was ready, she knew he would advance again.

He was angry now.

He ran, full force, every muscle poised to kill. She tried to stab him again. He was ready this time, diving out of the way; he knocked her off balance with his wing. Whipping her in the chest with his tail, he knocked the wind out of her before she hit the ground. She lost her grip on the knife, it fell away in the dark. The monster came to stand over her, his tail moving like a snake beneath her body, lifting her off the ground as she stared into his narrow eyes.

Without a word, he pounded her into the concrete. Her head began to sing. A high-pitched ringing filled her mind as numbness took over her body; shock consumed her. She could barely see anything but knew what would come next. Her mind was light, unfocused. She tried to get her feet under her body, but they wouldn't work. The best she could do was drag herself with one arm toward the closed door of Isaac's shop. An unnerving rattle came from the monster; Elidad imagined it to be a morbid laugh at her lame attempt to save herself. The monster's tail wrapped around her ankle, dragging her back to the recessed part of the alley.

Elidad saw another flash out of the corner of her eye. The grip on her leg released its hold. She didn't have any fight left in her. She lay against the cool pavement, awaiting her fate.

She imagined the stars, high above the bright city-lit sky. She loved looking at the stars and now, she wished she'd taken more time to admire them.

She wondered what inspired the demon to give her the reprieve from his assault. She took a deep breath and rolled to her side in a last attempt to drag herself to the door.

The door, so close, may as well have been ages away with the pain that was surging through her body. Only moving a few feet, she rested her face on the ground. The soreness in her chest from the demon's tail brutalizing her, made it hard to breath. She rolled onto her back again to look up at the heavens, relieving the pressure. She choked on the rank smell of the demon's blood, coughing up her own. She swiped her mouth with her wrist. Bright crimson streaked her arm from the split that stung her lips.

The shadows began to take over the ringing in her brain, washing away the sounds of the city at the end of the alley.

Lucian appeared, bending down to scoop her off the pavement. She didn't have the strength to ask where the monster was; she was just relieved to see Lucan's face as her body gave in to the darkness.

CHAPTER TWENTY-SEVEN

Being back at the Vatican was strange, like coming home to your room on holiday after being at college for four years. A visit like that reminded you of the person you were, so distant from the person whom you'd become. He was so different, he barely recognized himself. What he was like, without Elidad, was a fading memory, difficult to recall.

On his first day at the Vatican, he'd sat before a board of Bishops and relived the story of what he and Elidad went through to find Abraham. Now, he was being summoned to Bishop Aberdeen's office. Aberdeen was Aiden's immediate supervisor. Aidan wasn't sure what this meeting would be about, especially so soon after the other one.

Aiden gave them a truthful, detailed account of his and Elidad's trip across North America, including Yeti, Sirens and Ghelgath. With some of the looks he got during his recapping, he wasn't sure if they would fire him or have him committed, it was all an option at this point. He couldn't help but feel that one of the Bishops *had* to be involved with the Crusaders, one of them might've *been* one. Many of these men knew Abraham and admired him, someone had to know what he'd been up to, someone had to have given Abraham orders.

Elidad was certain that all the Bishops in the Vatican knew about the Crusaders. According to her, they were the ones who funded them. It was hard to believe the conspiracy came this far. The Church had kept many traditions alive, but Crusaders? Being so new to this world, it was still difficult to accept the Church playing such a large roll in this hidden world.

Aiden knocked on a large wooden door.

"You may enter." Aiden heard a voice from within.

"Father, you wanted to see me?" Aiden asked as he crossed the room to take the Bishop's hand and kiss it lightly.

"Have a seat, my son." The Bishop gestured to two large chairs.

Aiden obediently sat. The office was ornamented with tall, leaded, glass windows that towered over the bookshelves. A fireplace was on the wall directly across from where Aberdeen sat behind a walnut desk. Two leather chairs sat in front of the fireplace. When

Aiden sat in one, he couldn't help but think of sitting in the chairs in Abraham's study. He couldn't keep his mind from drifting back to the many nights he'd sat across from Elidad in those leather chairs. How he longed to be back there now, studying her face as they spoke. The way the light in her eyes changed when she was excited about a topic, or the way she bit her bottom lip when she was keeping something to herself.

"That was quite the tale you told us, the other day, Aiden." The Bishop began.

"Sir, I understand that my story may be hard to believe." Aiden felt compelled to defend his story.

"Do not fret, my son," the Bishop smiled, "We believe you. You have seen many things in the past few months. What is unbelievable is how well you have adapted in such a short period. You have handled it better than anticipated. We are very proud of you."

"Thank you, father." Aiden wasn't sure if that was really a compliment.

"In the light of things, we have found a job that will be more suitable for you." The Bishop appeared to be searching Aiden's face for a reaction.

"Of course, Father, anything the Holy Fathers ask of me, if I am able, I will do." Aiden could hear the person Elidad despised so greatly, forming his words. Over the months he'd spent with Elidad, that person had almost disappeared. Now, here he was again. How quickly the person he'd once been, came back. Elidad would be ashamed.

The Bishop stood to move to the same side of the desk as Aiden. "We knew we could count on you." The Bishop said, sitting in the chair next to Aiden. "We have decided you will take over the responsibilities of the Bishop of Records."

"Bishop?" Aiden repeated the word, stunned, knowing he was too young for the title.

"If it is a good position for you, the Fathers will discuss whether or not you shall be ordained. I have faith in you, Aiden. This is what you've worked for."

"In Records?" Aiden thought of sitting in a room surrounded by files. It wasn't what he thought of as an ideal job.

The Bishop appeared to decipher Aiden's tone. "The Bishop of Records does not remain in Records. He is in charge of Gatherers and ensures the information that they obtain stays confidential. There would be a great deal of travel involved."

Aiden shook his head, "Of course." This is what Leucosia spoke about. This was the opportunity he'd have to look for the keys.

"Do you know Daniel Song?" He asked.

"Yes, Father. I've met him a couple times. Quiet man." Aiden also remembered Daniel had illegally slipped Elidad information.

"You will be Daniels supervisor. He also works in records." Aberdeen said.

"Oh, I didn't know that Daniel worked in Records," Aiden lied.

"Tell me more about the key Ghelgath lost to the dragon, in the cave." Aberdeen locked eyes with Aiden.

Aiden swallowed, feeling like he was being interrogated. Remembering the tiny creature made him remember how furious Ghelgath was when he thought they might've been involved. That memory led to the image of Ghelgath scooping Elidad up by the throat. Aiden shuddered at the feeling, thinking she'd been killed in front of him.

"He disappeared through a small hole in the wall," Aiden answered. "Ghelgath tried to get him, and the key, by blasting the wall apart, but he was not successful. He blamed us, and almost killed us."

"Do you know anything of the creature?" The Bishop asked.

Aberdeen's body language told Aiden he knew something of the creature, himself. Aiden knew a test when he saw it.

"No Sir, if Elidad or I had known, it might have given us a destination to continue looking for the key." Aiden caught a look in the Bishop's eyes. "Of course, our number one priority was to find Abraham, the search for the keys would have only continued with a blessing from the Holy Fathers." Aiden added.

"I'm sure you would have looked for direction from us, Aiden. That is why you were sent in the first place. However, *Elidad* would be another story."

Aiden opened his mouth in an attempt to argue on Elidad's behalf, but the Bishop held up his hand. "Otherwise, you would have never ended up on Mt. Denali."

Aiden shook his head. "You may be right, Father, but we were trying to follow Abraham's path, and if we hadn't taken it, we still might not know what had happened to Bishop Blankenship, God rest his soul." Both men made the sign of the cross at the mention of his name.

"I pray, Aiden, you did not learn too many unhealthy habits from that *woman*," he spoke of Elidad as if she were poison. "It doesn't matter if her tactics are successful, she is careless. She is a renegade. That is why she is no longer an associate of ours."

"Yes, Father. She certainly has an… abrasive way about her. But if it wasn't for her, we would've never found Abraham." Aiden dared to add his opinion, in a small attempt to defend Elidad.

The Bishop didn't appear to be satisfied with his answer. "No matter, you are here now, and there will be no reason for us to continue our contact with her." His eyes were stern, clearly communicating what he meant.

Aiden knew he was being given a direct order to desist any association with Elidad. "Yes, Father."

"We have severed all communication with her, Aiden. The only reason we allowed her to help you find Abraham was for your benefit. We felt she would be able to assist you in your search, better than anyone else, being his daughter, of course."

Aiden knew he was lying. They knew Elidad was the best Crusader, and Exorcist, the church employed. The problem was, she was a woman, one they couldn't control.

Elidad didn't *help* Aiden find Abraham, she found Abraham herself. She never needed Aiden's help. Aiden couldn't comprehend why the Holy Fathers were so determined to belittle her role in finding Abraham or her ability to fight demons. Something happened between her and the Church. Something big. Whatever it was, it had happened a year or so ago and it was the same reason she and Abraham stopped talking.

"During your travels with Elidad, did you hear the name Ignacia?" The Bishop asked.

"After we met Leucosia, Elidad mentioned that her sister, Ignacia, was hunted by the Crusaders." Aiden lied. It was one of the parts of his and Elidad's trip he left out. "Why do you ask?"

"The little draconic lizard you described, that stole the key from Ghelgath…" the Bishop seemed like he was choosing his words.

"Yes…" Aiden confirmed he was following.

"Dragons are rare, most in captivity. All are appointed a gatherer, to ensure they stay out of sight, hidden from humanity."

"Of course," Aiden agreed, realizing in the following days, he might be responsible for keeping dragons hidden.

"They live in cages, similar to a zoo. The only pet that we are aware of, allowed to run around—against our rules, of course—is the one that belongs to Ignacia." The Bishop watched Aiden.

Aiden's mind began to swirl, what did that mean? Ignacia stole the key before they went to her for help? Did she have the key while they spoke to her? She must have. If that were true, he was surprised she didn't offer it up, for a price; unless she had another buyer. Elidad had said Ignacia didn't have a side; she was neither good nor evil. Instead, she picked the side that could pay the most.

"Do you know where to find Ignacia?" The Bishop studied him carefully.

"I can ask Elidad, Father, if you wish." Aiden didn't want to lie.

"I don't think that will be necessary, I doubt she would tell you, if she knew."

Of course, she would. Not only had Elidad already told him, but she had taken him there. Aiden felt like a double agent. He loved the Church and believed in their mission, but he also admired Elidad, and believed in her as well. A few short months ago, he followed the Church blindly, and now, his feelings only caused him confusion. He would have to gather his thoughts and pray about his path. He was walking a thin line.

"You would probably like to consider the offer for this new position." Aberdeen suggested.

"No, Father, it is a generous offer, I will take the position." Aiden knew Leucosia wanted him to take the job.

"Very well, I will let the Holy Fathers know," he beamed. "You are the right person for this job," he leaned forward and patted Aiden's knee. "Make us proud."

"I will do my best, Father."

"Now then, would you like to go see the Records Room?" The Bishop asked.

"Yes, I would love to," Aiden said, honestly. When Elidad had described the Records Room, his mind conjured up a million images. He'd never imagined he'd actually see it for himself.

The Bishop stood. "Very, well. Shall we?

CHAPTER TWENTY-EIGHT

Elidad had no sense of time or space when she woke. Memories of what happened flashed in her mind: throwing the sword to the ground when it refused to appear, the demon, his talons cutting through her shoulder.

When she tried to sit up, every part of her body disapproved. She settled on rolling over onto her good arm, which faced her toward the wall. She stayed there for a moment, unsure if she had the strength to do anything else. She knew she was in Isaac's home, over the store. Even before she opened her eyes, she smelled the leather and eucalyptus.

The door opened behind her. "Elidad, are you awake?" She recognized Lucian's voice.

"I guess." She croaked. She could feel his hand on her back as he pushed pillows behind her and helped her roll onto them. Elidad grimaced as her shoulder pressed against the pillows.

"I cleaned your wounds, but they haven't stopped weeping."

"Poison." Elidad said. She could feel the fever in her body. It burned in her bones and radiated though her skin.

Lucian nodded. "Not like anything I've seen." He pulled back the bandage on her shoulder so she could see puss oozing from the torn flesh. The smell made her nauseous.

"That's attractive." Elidad said through clenched teeth, realizing her camisole strap was cut off and her bra was missing. Why did Lucian have to be the one to find her in the alley?

Lucian smiled. "Well, your allure has never abandoned you, but if you're worried about it, perhaps we should keep you away from a mirror for a few days."

His words sent her good hand to her face. Her eye and cheek were so swollen there was nothing to distinguish the difference between them. Her lips on the same side were fat and dry, feeling their roughness made her realize how thirsty she was.

"I guess I'm a sight." She said as she reached toward the glass of water Lucian was offering. She was relieved when he helped her drink.

Lucian smiled. "I'm just glad you're alive. I wanted to take you to the hospital, but they would've asked …"

She considered his open-ended statement as the cool water stung her parched lips. "Yeah, no hospital. How long have I been here?" She asked looking around the room for some indication.

"Two days."

"Really? Two days? What did you see?" She asked.

Lucian smiled. "I saw you getting your ass handed to you by a demon."

Elidad smiled, as much as her lips would allow. "That's a poetic way to put it."

Lucian stomach quivered as he suppressed a laugh. "You asked."

"How are you? Are you okay?" Elidad looked him over, wondering how he'd survived without a scratch. The demon should have killed her and, by the pain in her arm, he still might. "Why didn't he attack you?"

"I'm not sure," he admitted. "I heard a noise outside the door when I went to lock up after you left. I opened the door and saw him. His was dragging you to the back of the alley. He let go of you when he saw me. We stood there, staring at each other for a moment. I think he was trying to decide what he would do; I was doing the same. You rolled to your side and began to crawl to me, I could see how badly you'd been beaten. He never took his eyes off me, not even when you tried to move away from him. I saw your knife on the ground, so I ran for it, and just like that he flexed his wings and was gone."

"Gone? He left you alone, just like that?"

"Straight up in the air, like a rocket," Lucian pointed.

"Wow, you must be scary when you're determined." The pain in Elidad's brows reminded her to limit facial expressions when being a smart ass. Images of the demon rolled over in her mind. He was strong, and clearly came for her. He was so close, why didn't he finish her off? Lucian wouldn't have been much of a threat to him.

"I found this, too. I don't know what it is," Lucian picked up the hilt of the Sword of Justice that was lying on the bedside table.

"I know what it is," Elidad offered.

"You do?"

"Yep. It's a piece of shit," Elidad scowled as much as her face allowed.

"Okay, good to know." Lucian set it back on the nightstand. "A piece of shit paperweight." He didn't press any further, as if he understood Elidad's resentment. "I haven't called Aiden," he said cautiously.

"No, don't," Elidad said quickly. "We don't need the Church to find out." Elidad's heart felt heavy. Aiden would want to know... but he left, that was his choice. If he hadn't left, she would have been able to tell him.

Lucian nodded. "That's why I waited. I thought you might not want me to. He's called a few times, I didn't want to answer, if I didn't have to, but he's going to start to wonder."

"Yeah, we're going to have to tell him something," Elidad agreed. "I don't know if I can lie to him. You might have to answer, one of these times."

"We can worry about that later," Lucian said, "the real problem is, the poison in your wound. It's the main reason I didn't take you to the hospital. They would've asked how you got hurt. I couldn't come up with a good story. How do you explain those big gaping holes?"

Elidad's fingers touched her chest, just below the wounds. "You can't."

He shook his head. "I don't think they'll heal easily, even with medicine. After two days, they still haven't closed and I'm not sure they will. That would be hard to explain, too, your wounds not healing. I didn't want to stitch them up, to give the poison an opportunity to bleed out. You barely moved while you slept, so you weren't losing too much blood. Even if I did sew them, I don't think they would heal, so I thought I'd spare you the pain."

He was right. The holes in her shoulder should've tried to scab over, by now. Even without stitches. She was in trouble. She needed a hospital, but like Lucian, doubted they could help. Hospitals meant questions… questions they couldn't answer.

It wasn't worth trying.

"How's Isaac?" Elidad asked, realizing she'd neglected him for two days.

"He's fine. He's been asking about you. I think mostly because he still doesn't remember me. He gets a little nervous, still. I told him you are sick and that seems to satisfy him, so far."

"I'm so sorry, Lucian. You've helped me so much. I hoped you could leave soon. I'm sorry I'm such a burden to you," she said, trying to blink away tears.

She wasn't usually so emotional. It must be the fever.

Lucian reached out to squeeze her hand. "Elidad, I don't mind helping you. I told you I would stay as long as you need me. I'm not in a hurry to go. The only burden is the one you put on yourself. You're so strong and independent, you know, it's ok to need help."

"I have to sleep Lucian." Elidad lay her head back on the pillow, shutting her eyes. Her eyelashes were the only thing holding back the tears. "I'm tired."

"Okay," he released her hand. "Get some rest," he urged.

CHAPTER TWENTY-NINE

A iden followed the Bishop down a corridor that lay beyond a restricted area. At the end of the long hall, hand-painted with cherubim dancing across every open space, was a row of doors. The Bishop stood in front of the third to last door on the left. The doors and casings were made of wood, polished to a high sheen, and reflective enough that Aiden could see their silhouettes in them. Like everywhere else, the door casings and moldings were intricately carved with immaculate detail.

The Bishop withdrew a keychain that had a handful of keys dangling from it. "This will be yours, Aiden. You cannot afford to lose these keys, they cannot be replaced."

"I understand," Aiden answered.

The Bishop held up the first key, it was a typical door key. "This will open the office door." He said, sliding it into the lock.

Aiden noticed the placard on the wall, *Records.*

When the Bishop pushed the door open, Aiden felt uneasy. He wasn't sure why, but his stomach fluttered, like a swarm of bees. When the door swung wide, it revealed a small office stacked with white cardboard boxes marked with bold, black sharpie on the sides.

It wasn't quite what Aiden had envisioned.

Aberdeen strode to the back of the office. Hidden behind the towers of white, office boxes, was another door. The Bishop led Aiden to it, pulling another key from the keychain. He held it out for Aiden to see.

"This key will open this door." The Bishop said as he pushed the key into the lock, opening the door to reveal another room similar to the first. In this room, boxes were stacked higher than their heads. Aiden was beginning to see a pattern. He began imagining himself in these rooms for the rest of his life, surrounded by white, musty mountains of cardboard.

The Bishop led Aiden to the back corner of the room. Hidden behind more boxes, was an old elevator, the kind that had a gate behind another gate. The Bishop pulled the gates open, then pulled the safety guard open, climbing into the confined space. Aiden stepped forward, turning to face the door, standing shoulder to shoulder with the Bishop whose shoulder was a few inches shorter than Aiden's.

Aberdeen closed the doors.

The Bishop selected the button indicating the basement. The elevator moved with ease, much quicker than an elevator of its apparent age. The metal box plummeted downward, fast enough to make Aiden's stomach rise to the bottom of his chin. As quickly as it began, the descent began to slow, coming to an elegant halt.

Removing a round key from the keychain, the Bishop held it up for Aiden to see. This key looked far older than the rest and it appeared hollow with two sets of teeth hanging off opposite sides. There was also ridging around the key shaft. Aiden knew enough about locks; this key was designed for a complex lock, not your average house door.

Aberdeen pushed a series of buttons. 1...2...1...9...6...2. When the series was complete, a hole in the center of the panel opened. It was a modern addition, much too technologically advanced for the age of the elevator. The Bishop looked at Aiden.

"October 12th, 1962. Do you know the significance of this date?"

"Yes, Father. The year Second Vatican Council began," Aiden said.

"Very good, my son," he said. "You saw how it worked?"

"Yes, Father." Aiden replied.

"You must remember to enter the code after the elevator stops, or you will remain on the basement level."

"Okay." Aiden said as he watched the Bishop press and hold the basement button.

The elevator began to descend even further. How many stories lay beneath the Vatican? Perhaps they weren't passing floors, as much as empty space. It made Aiden's mind drift to *Genus*, and another elevator that changed his life.

"I am sure I don't need to tell you, Aiden, that the Records Room is strictly protected. Under no circumstance are you to bring anyone to the Records Room, ever."

"Yes, Father."

"The world does not need to be burdened with our work, or the fears of what evils really exist. There is enough terror to keep them up at night."

"Yes, Father." Aiden replied.

The elevator began to slow, coming to a fluid stop. The Bishop took the key from the panel. Aiden reached forward and pushed up on the security gate, pulling back the metal doors like an accordion. They stepped into a small room that was nearly identical to the last one. Sterile, white paint housed stacks of boxes. On the far wall was a single door.

The Bishop handed the key ring to Aiden. "The keys can get you to this point. Take care of them, don't lose them: as far as we're concerned, they are priceless." Aberdeen walked across the small space and stood with his toes nearly touching the wall. He was facing black glass panels next to the door. The glass came to life, chirping and humming as it scanned his face.

"Bishop Aberdeen, welcome," a robotic female voice said. "Please insert your hands."

Aberdeen placed his hands on top of two glass plates directly under the one reading his face. His hands rested at waist height. Aiden had seen this before, in the movies: face recognition and palm or fingerprint scanners.

"Thank you." The robot said as the door clicked open. "You may enter."

The Bishop smiled at Aiden, "Daniel can get your biometric scans imputed into the computer. He will also set up an emergency code for you. The glass panels where I placed my hands is touch sensitive. I have my own process that informs the computer I have opened this door. If I stray from my code by one digit, the room will fill with gas." He looked at the vent above their heads to point it out.

"What kind of gas?" Aiden felt like he already knew the answer.

"Poison." The Bishop answered.

Why would the Records Room be so heavily guarded?

Aberdeen held out the keys for Aiden. Aiden slowly reached forward to take them. His heart moved at a pace that told him taking the keys was a larger commitment than he'd originally anticipated.

The Bishop pushed open the oversized door. Despite how large it was, the Bishop moved it with little effort. The room behind the door made Aiden think of the Vatican Library, somewhere above them. The ceilings were tall and the arches were just as beautifully decorated, detailed with countless brushstrokes. The shelves appeared to continue as far as his eyes would allow. At a desk, staring at Aiden and the Bishop over the rim of his glasses, sat Daniel Song, who hovered over an open book, displaying perfectly aligned molars.

Daniel's grin broadened as he stood. "Aiden, so nice to see you. Welcome."

"Hello, Daniel. It's nice to see you, again," Aiden replied.

There wasn't much of Daniel, his head barely reached Aiden's shoulder. What he lacked in height, he made up for in warmth. His eyes, made narrow from the strain of smiling, peered back from behind thinly rimmed glasses. His lips also formed a minute line on his round face. Daniel had dark hair that he styled spikily on top, and good genetics made him appear young, but Aiden guessed he was at least eight years older than Aiden.

"You must be excited to start your new job," Daniel guessed.

"I am," Aide agreed. "Maybe a little overwhelmed."

"Don't be, it's an easy job. It's nothing compared to your quest with Elidad." Daniel sounded enchanted. Catching the Bishops glance, he stifled his smile.

"I'm sure there is much more to learn, here." Aiden attempted to divert the conversation.

"Of course. There's much to learn. I'll show you around, with the Bishop's blessing." Daniel looked at Aberdeen for approval.

"Yes, that is why I brought him." The Bishop held his arms out, "There is a vast amount of information here, Aiden. You are the Record Keepers. It is your duty to keep the information in this room safe." He lowered his arms. "Daniel, I trust you can get Aiden set up in the computer?"

"Yes, Father." Daniel assured.

"Aiden, spend the afternoon with Daniel, get familiar with the Records Room, and tomorrow, come see me. We will discuss your duties inside and outside the Vatican. I will supply you with your list of Gatherers. It will be a challenging month for you, there is much for you to learn."

"Yes, Father, and thank you for the opportunity. I pray I will be the man the Holy Fathers expect me to be." Aiden said hopeful.

"I trust, Aiden, you will not let us down." His words sounded more like a warning, than a vote of confidence.

"Thank you, Father." Aiden said.

Aberdeen walked out the way they came in. Aiden and Daniel silently watched the door shut behind him.

Aiden turned to Daniel who was snickering behind the desk. "I'm good at saying the wrong thing. That's why they keep me down here."

"If you say anything nice about Elidad, it's the wrong thing." Aiden observed.

Daniel's smile widened further. "She scares them. The whole mess scares them."

"What mess?" Aiden frowned.

Daniel's smile fell from his eyes. "You know," he shrugged, "Abraham, and the keys."

"That is a bit of a mess, isn't it?" Aiden agreed, wondering how much Daniel knew.

"Some of them think the prophecy is about her, others refuse to accept it." Daniel added.

"Do you know what the prophecy is, Daniel?" Aiden's heart skipped at the possibility.

Daniel's smile returned. "That's another reason they keep me down here."

"Because you know the prophecy?" Aiden clarified.

"Because I know entirely too much." Daniel's face changed. "Tell me, what is was like to work with her."

"That could take a while." Aiden wasn't sure he was ready to talk about Elidad. All he could think about was the hole in him, since he left, and the hurt he'd caused her by leaving. He couldn't get her eyes out of his mind. Her green eyes usually burned with fire, but that day, there was nothing in them. The only thing that got him on the plane and into Vatican City was Leucosia's warning. He would've come up with a thousand excuses to stay and help Elidad, but in reality, it would've been for himself.

Aiden looked over the rows of shelves, filled with books and containers, "Tell me how all of this works."

Daniel moved a chair behind his desk, sitting in one he gestured to Aiden to take the other. "All of the items are catalogued in this computer." He touched the screen to wake it up; the screen displayed a black hand in the middle. Daniel placed his palm over it.

"Hello, Daniel." The computer said in a woman's voice.

"This is Vici," Daniel pointed at the desk. "She is the only one I get to talk to, most days. I call her my girlfriend, when the Bishop isn't around. She can tell you where everything is."

"I don't really know what is kept here." Aiden admitted. "I have a pretty good idea, but not really."

"Oh, that's easy. We have everything." Daniel faced the screen. "Vici, find me Elidad Sameer's file."

There was a brief pause. "Elidad Sameer, located in section J, level three, cross section twenty-five."

"Thank you, Vici," Daniel answered.

"Sameer?" Aiden repeated. "Her last name is Waller."

Daniel looked amused. "Waller is Abraham's last name."

"Her name was changed when Abraham adopted her." Aiden realized.

"Shall we?" Daniel gestured.

Aiden allowed Daniel to lead the way as his mind raced in circles. Did Elidad know her real last name? She had to know it had been different, at one time.

As they pressed further into the Records Room, the mass of it became overwhelming.

"Are we the only ones who come down here?" Aiden guessed.

"Usually. A few of the Bishops have access, but they try to keep the traffic to a minimum. Some of the information is highly classified."

Aiden tried to imagine all the information that was kept in this room. The size of it was less like a room, and more like a stadium. Books and boxes lined every shelf, numerically and alphabetically aligned. Each row had ladders that would enable you to retrieve, or place information on the shelves. Each shelf was marked with a placard from A and continued on past J, though they turned down J.

Aiden had a feeling Daniel knew exactly where they were going. Aiden could see the cross sections labeled starting at one and continuing to grow in numbers as they walked.

The entire room was designed like a grid and labeled accordingly. Daniel stopped at the section labeled twenty-five. On a shelf above them, a spot was glowing.

Daniel pointed up to the glowing area. "You see?"

"Yes." Aiden answered.

Daniel went and grabbed the closest ladder, moving it to the wall with the glowing space. "Go ahead," he said, stepping back to allow space for Aiden to climb the ladder.

Aiden climbed, one step after the other toward the light. When he reached the spot, he investigated the glowing nook. There were two boxes, both labeled Elidad Sameer. Aiden looked down at Daniel.

"Bring down box two."

Aiden put his hand into the open tab of the white cardboard with #2 written on it. Aiden gave it a tug to remove it from the shelf; it was heavier than he anticipated.

At the bottom of the ladder, Daniel pushed a button on the shelf. Aiden hadn't noticed the identical buttons up and down both sides of the isle. When he pushed the button a piece of metal, like a table, slid out of the shelf into the isle.

"Put the box here." Daniel pointed.

Obediently, Aiden rested the heavy box on the flat surface. It fit nicely on the horizontal slab, leaving work space next to it.

"Go ahead, open it." Daniel's eyes were filled with light, like a child waiting to open a present.

"What's in it?" Aiden imagined Elidad telling him about the Records Room and how she joked about her file being large, holding up both hands. Little did she know, she was way off with her estimate.

"Information." Daniel seemed confused at Aiden's hesitation.

Aiden removed the lid and peered inside. On top was a picture of a burning barn in the hot Mexican dessert. The image didn't do the flames justice. Aiden's mind drifted to that moment, standing next to Elidad as they watched the flames engulf the structure, taking Abraham with them. Another picture was of Elidad and Aiden in the Mt. Denali basecamp and another in front of Isaac's shop. Aiden looked up at Daniel.

Daniel's eyes were filled with wonderment, "You went with her when she found Abraham, right?"

"Yes."

"Was it… *so* cool?" His words were dreamy.

"Most of the time it was terrifying," Aiden admitted.

Daniel laughed. "It would've been a little easier for you if someone would've prepped you for the trip! But how *awesome* was it all?"

Aiden thought back. "I was with my best friend when she found, and couldn't save, her father. I held her as we watched his body burn after she was forced to decapitate him, to release the demons that possessed his body. I escorted her back to her father's home where she finally broke down, dealing with her father's death."

Daniel stared at Aiden, wordless for a moment. "When you put it that way, it sounds terrible… You must think I'm terrible."

"I don't think you're terrible, you just didn't think about the whole story. I can see how you glorify her job. It's exciting, dangerous. She *is* amazing, and it's a blessing to have worked with her, but the trip to find Abraham ended in tragedy."

Daniel looked down at the box. "But you got to work with *Elidad!*"

"I did. We certainly saw a lot together," Aiden agreed.

"You will be remembered for that, Aiden. Maybe not among normal people, but to the Gatherers, you will be remembered." Daniel's words had an air of pride.

Aiden realized there was a lot he still didn't know about the Church. The Bishops didn't appear impressed, at all, with Elidad. Daniel sounded like he was talking about a legend, speaking of Elidad and the Gatherers as though Elidad had her own groupies.

"Daniel, how many Gatherers are there?" Aiden asked.

Daniel shrugged. "Probably thousands, but they are all over the world and not all of them are managed by one Bishop. They don't just open up and tell me everything, even if they trust me with all the information. 'Course who's to say we have all the information, here?"

"Do you think there is more information somewhere else?" Aiden asked as he took in their surroundings.

"They like to have control," Daniel pointed upward. "I imagine many small rooms like this, hidden, with more sensitive information."

Aiden remembered the room beneath the Trinity church and Elidad telling him about the one under Isaac's shop. "That is an interesting theory," Aiden agreed.

Aiden told the panel of Bishops that he and Elidad had found Bishop Blankenship's coat in a church and told them that he and Elidad knew Blankenship had been headed for the Yeti. He left out the part about the hidden room under the church that looked out over the ocean floor. Did they know the significance of Trinity? Abraham had been there before, as well.

"You can keep going through her file, if you want." Daniel offered.

Aiden replaced the lid. "I think I'll pass."

Daniel looked disappointed.

"I feel like I'm intruding," Aiden explained. "If she wants me to know about her life, she'll tell me."

"I understand. That is kind of you, I don't know her, so it's a little different for me," Daniel said.

CHAPTER THIRTY

Flashes of Abraham's disfigured body appeared real as Elidad struggled against the memory. Abraham held her by the throat, high enough that her feet dangled in the air, crushing her air way with his gnarled hand. Oceans of demons under his skin were writhing like a pulsing wave as she looked in his eyes. The man she loved was absent from within them.

A green glowing light began to shine from his mouth. Elidad closed her eyes at the piercing brightness, as her heart raced. Opening them again, she found herself in the barn where she last saw Abraham. The barn was saturated in light from fire that was now engulfing the structure. Flames dripped from the ceiling, embers swirled in the wind. The barn door behind her, rocked back and forth in an eerie squeak. From the flames, emerged the demon that attacked her in the alley. His arms were long and powerful and his tail whipped erratically behind him, his narrow eyes pierced her subconscious. She could *feel* him looking into her as fear began to swarm inside her soul. She knew she couldn't defeat him. She'd never met a demon that she couldn't beat. Until now.

What changed?

Elidad's breath was labored at the thought of death becoming real. There was no escape. The fire grew, closing in on all sides around her.

The click of the door startled Elidad awake. The fever had clearly taken over her dreams.

Lucian set a bowl of water next to her on the nightstand. He withdrew a washcloth, wringing it out before placing it on Elidad's forehead. The cool water sent chills down her arms. He didn't say anything, he didn't need to; his face was riddled with concern.

"I need you to go to Abraham's house." Elidad managed to say through chattering teeth.

"Okay, what am I going for?"

"I need you to find my room, and in my pack, there's a silver canister. I need it."

"A silver canister, I can do that."

"I think you should hurry." Elidad couldn't hold her eyes open any longer. She heard the door close behind Lucian. She suspected he already knew her life was in danger. The canister had been a gift from Leucosia. It contained a liquid with the ability to heal. Why hadn't she thought of it before?

Elidad wasn't sure how much time had passed when Lucian reentered the room. Horrifying dreams mixed with agonizing memories haunted her while he'd been away. She was relieved to be awakened from them.

"Is this what I was looking for?" Lucian asked as he pulled the canister from her pack.

"Yes." Elidad's voice was weak.

"Good, I thought so. I brought your whole pack, just in case."

Elidad took the canister from Lucian, remembering when Leucosia had given it to her. Elidad used it to save Kade's life from the bite of the white wolf. Elidad had remembered Kade's face and the sadness in his eyes as he held his arm after being bitten. Even with the intimidating size of the Yeti, his eyes encouraged Elidad to help the beast. Could Leucosia have known it would heal Elidad now? Elidad spun the canister in a lazy circle, she wasn't sure there was enough left. She unscrewed the cap, tipping her head back to swallow what was left. A single drop healed the burning cracks in her lips as it passed, but that was it.

Only a drop.

As the minutes ticked past, her fever showed no sign of breaking. Any hope of the serum working, began to dissipate. Elidad, too tired to care shivered in a hot sweat.

"Elidad are you going to be alright?" The look on Lucian's face spoke volumes.

She smiled to herself. What was his definition of alright? If she weren't dying, she would've been mortified to be laying here, like this, in front of him. Her hair a mess, in the same clothes for three days, her body exuding fever from every pore. The stench from her wound was the worst of it all and he still changed her bandages every day.

"Well, on the up side, if I die, you can remember me like this." Elidad's sarcasm was accentuated with a flare of her hand.

Lucian smiled, though his worry refused to leave his eyes.

"I just need to sleep," Elidad said, hoping she was right.

"Is there anyone who can help you?"

Elidad only shook her head in response as she rolled away from him, pulling the covers up over her head.

The night brought more terrifying dreams. Visions of Abraham with demons, pushing and biting from within, trying to scratch their way free, swirled around in her mind. Pain from her hand, cut open from flying debris in the barn, was agony spreading up her arm as blood dripped from her palm onto her open Bible at her feet.

Elidad awoke, her shoulder and arm on fire. She pushed the covers off herself. Her pain, masquerading in her dream, was a clear reminder of Abraham's death. Elidad turned her palm toward her face. So much had happened in the time since it'd healed, and yet, her heart had not followed.

She lowered her hand, unable to hold it up any longer. Saving Abraham would have to be enough. The keys would have to be Aiden's task, should he choose to continue. She looked at the phone on the nightstand and considered calling him, she could hear his voice one last time. She knew Aiden would rush to be by her side if he knew… but it would be too late. By the time he arrived, she'd be just a memory. She felt a glimmer of satisfaction at that thought. It would hurt him, knowing she didn't reach out to him in her last hours.

That's what he got for leaving.

She considered praying, but guilt held her back. She knew she shouldn't be angry with God, but he brought her here and for what? What did she do to deserve this? He took Abraham away, and Abraham took away her parents. He didn't just take them away, he'd *killed* them.

God took Aiden away. She began to realize she resented God for the feelings she had for Aiden. If Abraham hadn't gone missing, she never would've traveled with Aiden, she never would have known who he really was. She could've spent the rest of her life despising him. If she didn't know him, she wouldn't long to hear his voice, now. The hole through her soul wouldn't be hurting more than her mortal wounds.

God must hate her. He'd turned his back on her. He didn't even help her in the alley when she was being attacked. And he wasn't helping her now.

Her mind replayed that night in the alley. She'd thought it was the Shadow Man, like in her dreams. It might've been better if it was. The Shadow Man would've killed her. She would've combusted, diminished into ashes, and the whole thing would be over.

The Sword of Justice didn't work for her anymore. She swallowed. She could see it in her mind's eye. Angry, she'd thrown it on the ground, like garbage. It *was* garbage. It didn't work. *"Only with purity and justice in your heart will it come to you."* Elidad could hear Leucosia's words, again. It didn't come to her. What did that mean? She did her best to defend herself.

Looking down at her shoulder, her best wasn't good enough. She should've died. God *must* hate her. Demons didn't win in a fight against her. She defeated them. All of them. The fire in her shoulder burned hotter.

Arrogance. A voice in the back of her mind whispered. Did *she* defeat demons, or did God? What was different this time? The fight replayed in her mind, again.

She hadn't *prayed.*

Every other exorcism, every other fight, she counted on God to defeat her demons. With this riff between them, she tried to do it on her own.

She'd failed.

CHAPTER THIRTY-ONE

A iden found himself wandering the streets of Vatican City to clear his head. He couldn't decide if it helped him think less—or more—of Elidad. He spent most of his walk praying for strength to keep *her* off his mind, to stay committed to his vows… committed to the Lord.

The dark streets were soothing, the beauty of the architecture truly inspiring. He'd worked his whole life to get here, and now that he was, his mind was elsewhere. The irony didn't escape him. Relentless thoughts drove him out of the Vatican and into Rome.

Footsteps behind him caught his attention, heightening his awareness. In his walk, he'd wandered to a remote area in the city. The street doors and windows were in shambles. Trash lined the alleyways; he hadn't seen anyone for blocks. His gut told him it was a mistake to be caught on these streets alone, whether in priest's clothing or not. The footsteps continued. There was someone following him, not just someone strolling the streets.

Aiden began to take in his surroundings more carefully, considering how they could help him, or hurt him, in an attack. A fountain in an open courtyard was ahead, the noise could give him an advantage. He picked up the pace, his feet pounding out a quick beat. The footsteps behind him echoed the change.

Aiden rounded the corner, he pressed his back against a brick wall and steadied his breath to enable him to better hear the approaching footsteps. Aiden's heart began to pulse frantically as the steps grew nearer. Before rounding the corner, they slowed to half the time. A dark hood was the first thing Aiden saw as he leapt forward, grabbing an arm and aggressively pulling the person to the wall by way of their throat.

An alarmed scream came from under the hood of his follower, obviously a woman. With his hands still on her throat, Aiden threw back her hood to reveal beautiful locks of auburn hair, ivory skin and dark green eyes.

"Sophia?" The surprise was evident in Aiden's voice.

She smiled mischievously. "Hello, love. I thought you might miss me. Not exactly the warm welcome I'd envisioned."

Aiden released his hand. "Sorry. You caught me off guard."

"I like a man who can protect himself." She straightened her clothes. "I certainly don't mind a man getting a little rough."

Her candidness made Aiden uncomfortable.

"Sophia, what are you doing here?" Aiden demanded.

"Mother sent me."

"Why? She told me to come here, she said it would be the best thing for Elidad." Aiden wished Leucosia would be clearer with her wishes.

"She *did* want you to leave New York, but she didn't know what she knows now." Sophia looked side to side over Aiden's shoulder.

"What does she know *now*?" Aiden was leery.

"Let's go somewhere cozy, shall we?" Sophia grabbed Aiden by the arm dragging him down the street.

Aiden and Sophia found a dark corner in a café. He watched as Sophia took a sip of red wine from a tall, stemmed glass, her eyes sparkling like emeralds.

"Mother is worried about you."

"Why?" His feelings for Leucosia had always leaned towards suspicion.

"She had a premonition about you," she sipped again before continuing. "You were in trouble and you needed help."

"Why would I need help?"

Sophia shrugged. "You know Mother, she won't tell me anything I don't need to know."

"Why would you come all this way, not knowing? You could've called, sent a text, emailed."

"And pass up a chance to see you again?" Sophia teased.

"Sophia." Aiden was stern.

Her eyes were steady as her smile twisted slightly. "Elidad cares for you, and you'll help to keep her grounded through… some rough times."

"You might be worse at this than your Mother." Aiden offered. "What rough times?"

"Aiden," Sophia sighed, setting her glass on the table. "You and Elidad just found this path, following Abraham, finding the keys. It's been less than two months."

"Yes." Aiden agreed.

"My mother knew this would happen. She's known for a long time."

"She's a seer. She can see the future. She probably knew when Elidad and I went to see her." Aiden said. He'd thought about it after they'd found Abraham. Did Leucosia know that Elidad would have to kill Abraham? Did she know the weight Elidad would have to bear?

Sophia shook her head. "No. My mother knew *before*. She knew hundreds of years ago."

Aiden stared at her. "She had a premonition about Elidad, hundreds of years ago?"

"She had premonitions about *you*, also," she took a heavy sip as if attempting to lighten the sting for Aiden.

Aiden took a drink from his glass for the first time. "About me?"

"You are important to Elidad's story." Sophia said, sounding resentful of that fact.

"What does that mean?" Aiden asked.

"I don't really know. I just know you will help Elidad complete her quest and because of that, you are now a target." Sophia told him.

Aiden pushed air through his nose in response. "Quest? It sounds like we should be saddling up with swords at hand. It sounds ridiculous."

Sophia smiled over her glass. "Like The Sword of Justice?"

Aiden's face fell. The Sword of Justice, how soon he'd forgotten. He'd found himself in the midst of a contemporary quest.

"Aiden, you need to be careful." Sophia warned. "You need to be prepared for anything."

"Like what?"

"Something is trying to kill you." Sophia blurted out.

"*Something?*" Aiden repeated the word slowly as he digested the fact that she hadn't said *someone.*

"I'm sure I am telling you too much. Mother would have a fit." Sophia laughed as she took another drink.

Aiden took a big gulp of his wine in response to her news, not finding it so easy to laugh.

"You'll be fine," she assured.

"You tell me *something* is trying to kill me, and now you tell me I'll be fine. You need to make up your mind."

"I will be staying just outside the city." Sophia informed him.

"You'll be staying?"

"I'm not like my mother," Sophia reminded him. "I have to catch a plane. I've never been to Vatican City. It's really fascinating, isn't it?"

"I have always thought so. That's why I decided to devote my life to trying to get here."

Sophia smiled. "And what would inspire such a handsome, passionate man to commit to being celibate for his entire life?"

Aiden looked into his glass, as if to find an answer in the burgundy liquid. "It's not an easy response. It's *complicated*."

Sophia stretched her hand across the table. "I could make it less complicated for you."

She had the ability to read his mind when she touched his skin. He wasn't sure of the extent of her power; she wasn't as strong as Leucosia, but she was powerful enough. Could she pull any of his memories? He held tightly to his wine glass as his eyes met hers, he had no intention on sharing his thoughts.

A grim smile crossed Sophia's lips. "It was worth a try," she said with a shrug.

"I'll walk you to where you're staying." Sophia told Aiden.

Aiden frowned. "Shouldn't *I* be walking *you* to where you're staying?"

"You're the one who's in danger, not me," She reminded him.

"No offence, Sophia, but what exactly are you going to do to help me if I am attacked?" Aiden said, sizing her up.

"You have to remember, I've been around a lot longer than you. I might look helpless, but I can kick some ass."

"*You* can kick ass?" Aiden said, doubtful.

"Mother insisted I learn to defend myself, so I've spent centuries training. I can fight and I can to protect you. Don't get all proud on me, love, there is no shame in it."

Aiden decided not to argue. She'd certainly been alive long enough to learn how to fight and study many self-defense techniques.

Aiden wondered how he could have become so important in Elidad's life, to the point where someone would want to hurt him? *Something.* Sophia had said *something* would be hunting him. How could he be so significant from so far away? Maybe it wasn't his place in Elidad's life that put him in danger, but his role in finding the keys. His new job put him in the right position to find the keys; that could be why he was being hunted. If that were true, he needed to focus and find them.

CHAPTER THIRTY-TWO

Elidad hated New York, the city that refused to sleep. The street light, that would deny being extinguished until morning, illuminated the floor next to her bed—her deathbed. She'd never leave this wretched city. The thought made her mouth water. What a tragedy, to die in this place.

The luminescent glow began to move like fog across the floor. Believing her eyesight was failing, she closed her eyes. Death had to be close. Feeling a chill, she couldn't help but open her eyes, again. The room *was* filling with fog. With her body exhausted and defeated, she refused to be alarmed. What could anything do to her now? Her fate was already sealed.

She watched as the mist began to form into a figure next to her bed. A flawless body morphed out of thin air. Elidad recognized Leucosia as her wings came into focus.

Leucosia's eyes darted over Elidad's body. "Elidad, why didn't you come see me after you found Abraham?"

Lying in bed over the past week, Elidad had often wondered the same thing. She could've gone to Leucosia to get the answers she was looking for. Abraham's dying wish was for her to go to Leucosia and learn his story. If she had gone, she'd know about her parents and the prophecy.

She couldn't bear it. How could she hear about the awful things that Abraham did? The man she loved, the man she admired, how could she bear to see him as a ruthless killer? How could she find it in herself to forgive his betrayal? How could she forgive Leucosia's betrayal?

"It wouldn't have made a difference, coming to see you," Elidad said. "Everything would be the same. Knowing the past wouldn't change anything."

"Is that so?" Leucosia stepped closer to the bed and sat next to Elidad, opening her hand. In it, a tiny glass vial topped with a crystal stopper trapped a murky liquid inside. "You never gave me a chance. You never gave Abraham a chance."

Elidad found strength in her anger. "He killed my parents, you hid it from me, and now you're telling me I didn't give *you* a chance?"

Leucosia held up the small cylinder. "Drink this, you can come see me when you are well again," she hovered her hand over Elidad's bandage. "*If* you are well again."

"*If* I'm well again?"

"You've let this sickness go too far. The poison in your body is growing stronger. You should've come to see me before now or sent Lucian." She withdrew the stopper and held out the vial.

"I drank the rest of that. It didn't work," Elidad nodded at the silver canister on the bedside table.

"This is not like what you gave Kade, in the cave. That serum wouldn't do anything against this," Leucosia's finger lightly touched the soft bandage. "The poison is too strong."

This poison was stronger than Ghelgath's poison? Ghelgath was a high demon. What did that make the demon in the alley?

"This will be the most likely option to heal you." Leucosia offered the glass vial.

Elidad took it from her hand. She knew better than to sniff it. Holding her breath, she swallowed. It was as bitter as her feelings for Leucosia and burned past her esophagus. Despite her feelings, Elidad couldn't help but feel relieved in Leucosia's presence. Leucosia was the first being Elidad had ever met who made her feel *normal*. With Abraham dead, and Isaac's memory not working right, Leucosia was the closest thing Elidad had to family.

Being a siren, Leucosia was hauntingly beautiful. She was thousands of years old, but could pass as Elidad's older sister, if her sister were blonde and fair-skinned. Leucosia's skin wasn't just fair, it was the essence of radiance, literally glowing. Elidad loved how her wings contoured around her body, the same way a birds would. Through the years, Leucosia helped Elidad through an extensive list of challenging times; if she survived the demon's poison, this would be one more to add to the list.

"I cannot see your future, Elidad," Leucosia's words were solemn.

"Then why did you bother making me drink this awful stuff?" Elidad asked, handing the empty vial back.

"Not seeing your future doesn't mean you don't have one, it just means it is undecided. To know one's future, it is necessary to know one's past."

"I know my past." Elidad said dismissively. "Abraham killed my parents and raised me to do a job I wasn't supposed to do."

Elidad hated the look of understanding and patience Leucosia displayed as she sat an arm's length away. Maybe in a life of immortality, Elidad could learn to be as patient as Leucosia. Maybe over time, she would learn to accept the loss of her parents, too.

"He didn't kill your parents."

"I saw him. Your sister showed me in her birdbath. You told me the waters always tell the truth, and that's where I saw him do it."

"You also remember, the Church wants Ignacia *removed* for creating issues with her visions. She abuses her power. The waters cannot lie, but like any other truth, it can be manipulated. Abraham killed your father, this is true. You did see his face in the memory. Did you see his face in the memory of your mother's death?"

Elidad thought back to the images portrayed in Ignacia's fountain. After seeing Abraham kill her father, she'd seen a cloaked figure kill her mother; it could've been anyone. A tear escaped Elidad's eye.

"I didn't see his face," she realized aloud.

"That's because he didn't kill her." Leucosia reached out for Elidad's hand. Leucosia's was cool and small around Elidad's. "There is so much to your story, Elidad. If you had come to see me, you would have spared yourself an immense amount of pain."

How was it possible? "If Abraham didn't kill my mother, who did?"

Leucosia's lips pursed together in a brief thought. "The fact that it wasn't Abraham should ease some of your distress, until you are able to come see me."

"You're not going to tell me?" Anger began to swell in Elidad's chest. "What if I die? You're going to let me die without knowing the truth?"

Leucosia smiled, squeezing Elidad's hand. "I know you. You won't let that happen." Leucosia's hand moved to Elidad's forehead. "You need to rest, you can hardly keep your eyes open. We don't have time for a history lesson right now."

Elidad knew she was right but refused to admit it. She was fighting to keep her eyelids open. "I'll do my best, but I don't really feel better and you can't see my future. I don't think that adds up to anything good," Elidad analyzed.

Leucosia's eyes narrowed. "Elidad, do you know what kind of demon attacked you?"

"No. Nothing I've ever seen before."

"I would be surprised if you had, he was a Houdoch demon. Houdoch demons are not commonly sent to this world. They are guards."

"Guards? Why would a guard come to earth to attack me?"

"They guard items coveted by the ruler of demons."

"You mean the Devil?" Elidad said slowly. "They are guardians for the Devil's most prized possessions?"

"That is correct," Leucosia confirmed.

"What does that mean?"

"It means you are lucky to be alive. The poison in his talons is strong enough to kill every other demon in existence. That is why the Houdochs are chosen to be guards: they are the only demon that has the ability to kill *all* demons. Their venom is quick to work, it feeds off fear and anger, destroying their victims from the inside out. I assume that is why it has not consumed you, completely. You love God and have his goodness in you. My hope is that and the serum, together, is enough to rid your blood of the poison."

"Why would the Houdoch come after me? If they don't come to earth, why would this one come now?"

"There will be time for questions later. For now, you need to rest," Leucosia reminded.

The aching in Elidad's bones pulsed through her body. "Okay, but take that with you." Elidad pointed to the sword on the nightstand. "I don't want it."

"You were meant to wield it. It was made for you," Leucosia protested.

"Get it out of here. I don't want to look at it." Elidad sneered.

Leucosia picked it up, examining it in her palm. "Are you sure you won't keep it?"

Elidad shook her head.

With her other hand, Leucosia wrapped her delicate fingers around a pendant that hung from a chain around her neck. The side of Elidad's bed began to fill with mist.

"Is this a new thing? Appearing and disappearing in fog?" Elidad asked.

"It's an old thing," Leucosia held up her necklace. On the end of a sturdy chain was a slender metal pendant encasing a sliver of crystal that glowed blue. It pulsated, as if it had its own heartbeat. "It was my mother's. A gift from my father. A way to manipulate water. I thought it was lost, but it found its way back to me.

"You know where to find me, Elidad. Be well my friend," Leucosia's voice fell away as her figure vanished in the mist.

CHAPTER THIRTY-THREE

"All this information is useless," Daniel said, scrolling through pages of procedures on the computer.

"I thought the Bishop wanted me to learn all of it?" Aiden liked Daniel's honesty.

"They aren't going to test you on it," Daniel shrugged.

A pleasant chime dinged, drawing Aiden and Daniel's attention to the direction of the noise.

"You're first drop. This is exciting." The excitement glistened from behind Daniel's thin, rimmed glasses.

"Drop?"

"Come on," Daniel sprang out of his office chair.

On the exit door wall was a smaller door. Aiden had noticed it earlier, but hadn't asked what it was for. A rectangular window was in the center of the upper half of the steel. Aiden could see movement behind the glass as they approached. When the movement stopped, another chime rang through the open space around them. Daniel pushed a button next to the door and a loud click, like a lock opening, sounded in the metal. Daniel pulled on the small door; Aiden could tell it was heavy by the way Daniel strained against it.

The space inside was reminiscent of a dumbwaiter because that's exactly what it was: a small elevator for items to be transported to their floor. The elevator was large enough that Aiden could squeeze inside; it would be an uncomfortable ride, but he'd fit. There wasn't a person inside the confined space, though; it was full of random items.

Daniel pulled on a handle removing a tray.

"This is a drop," he announced.

"It's our job... well mostly *my* job... to catalogue everything and place it in records." Daniel turned back to Vici, placing the tray on a flat work surface next to the computer. He picked up an item. It was a glass container with a stopper in the opening. Daniel then picked up something that looked like a cellphone; it came to life when his fingers touched the screen. Tapping a series of numbers, the black box shot out a green scanner. Daniel pointed it toward the glass vial.

"What's that?" Aiden asked.

"That's what I'm trying to find out." Daniel answered.

"Not what's in the vial, what's in your hand?" Aiden clarified.

Daniel looked up. "Oh, I'm sorry. This is a scanner. A portable piece of Vici, really. This little thing has millions of items in its memory. It can scan size, shapes and liquid. It guesses weight, it can read fumes, it analyzes stability. It can do pretty much anything."

On cue, the scanner beeped. Vici's voice sounded from Daniel's hand, "Sleep serum. Derived from the Coma plant. Level Four violation of Dark Arts restrictions."

"Thank you, Vici," Daniel answered.

"What's a Level Four violation?" Aiden asked.

Daniel placed the vial on the tray, hitting another button. A label printed from the main computer. He removed it and placed it over the top of the stopper. "A Level Four isn't a good thing. Level four, they'll bring you in for a trial, if you don't resist. If you fight too much, or refuse to give up the contraband, they'll annihilate you in an attempt to control the item."

"They'll kill anyone that has a level four," Aiden repeated to commit it to memory. "How many levels are there?"

"There's five levels, no one should be caught with a level five."

"Good to know," Aiden rubbed the back of his neck. "What's a level five item?"

Daniel's smile turned grim. "The keys you were looking for, they're a level five."

"Would they have killed us if we found one?" Aiden's heart began to race, thinking of Elidad who was in possession of one of the keys.

"I don't know a single Crusader that would fight Elidad," Daniel moved closer to Aiden, dropping his voice. "That doesn't mean they wouldn't try to employ someone else to do it."

"Who else would they employ to kill her?"

"A demon, maybe," Daniel suggested.

The hair on Aiden's arms tingled with the idea. "They wouldn't do that, would they?"

"If they did, could we prove it?"

Daniel sounded like a conspiracy theorist, but being down here, he had a lot more information than most people.

"*You* can be in possession of level four and level five items," Daniel said.

"I can?" Aiden wasn't sure that was a good thing.

"Yes, you will be collecting items from Gatherers. You can have any restricted item. It's your job to drop the drop," Daniel smiled, "Pun intended."

"So, I'm a transporter?" Aiden formed the thought as he spoke the words.

"Essentially, among other things," Daniel agreed.

"Sounds dangerous," Aiden analyzed.

Daniel's face widened. "Not compared to working with *Elidad*. You've got the experience, that's why you're qualified for the job. It's no surprise they picked you." Daniel turned back to the sleep serum. "Now that the label is placed on the item, Vici assigns a spot for it in the Records Room. Think of it as a huge evidence room. Sometimes the items are used in court against the accused, but most of the time, they stay down here and collect dust."

"Would you like to do the next one?" Daniel held out the scanner for Aiden.

The phone rang and Daniel moved to pick it up.

"Records." Daniel smiled into the phone as the person on the other end spoke. "Yes, sir. I'll send him right away." He hung up. "Bishop Aberdeen would like to see you in his office. You've only been here a day and you're already requested in the principal's office."

"Nothing different from my school years," Aiden joked. "He told me, yesterday, we would be going over my job duties."

"That will be a treat." Daniel teased.

Aiden rapped his knuckles on the door.

"Come in," came the Bishop's reply.

The Bishop was sitting behind his desk when Aiden entered.

"Hello, Aiden. How is the Records Room?" Aberdeen asked, standing.

"It's quite large," Aiden analyzed.

A low chuckle came from the Bishop. "I realize, Aiden, this new position will be overwhelming, at first. Please, sit," he gestured to two chairs in front of his desk as he moved around to sit with Aiden. "I fear the pressure will not lighten for you, in the near future."

"I understand, Father," Aiden assured, "I'm ready for the challenge."

"We believe you are, Aiden, that's why we chose you."

"Thank you for your confidence in me, Father."

"You will begin this new position with only a handful of Gatherers to oversee. We don't wish to smother you with this new set of responsibilities. The Records Room has its own responsibilities, and of course, managing people adds a whole different aspect to the job, one you haven't had much experience in. As you become accustomed to your job, we will assign additional Gatherers to you."

"I understand," Aiden said.

"Other priests are taking on the additional work load, until you get up to speed. So, we implore you to learn as quickly as possible."

"I will, Father."

"Has Daniel educated you on restricted items?"

"A little, we were discussing them when you called me up here. I understand the concept."

"He needs to give you every detail; you need to understand them completely. You've had plenty of things to learn, of that, I'm certain. However, you need to know the difference between each of the restrictions and their consequential punishments. In the field, you will be executioner, whenever necessary."

Aiden felt like the Bishop was analyzing Aiden's response.

"Of course," Aiden agreed, keeping the nauseous feeling in his stomach from rising to his face.

"Very well," Aberdeen stood, pulling a stack of files off his desk, handing them to Aiden. "These are your first assigned Gatherers. You are responsible for all communication with them and assisting in analyzing threats. Daniel will help you with your contacts and supply you with any information you need while you are training. I expect you to ask as many questions as needed, Aiden. There is no question too small, there is no room for error in this occupation."

"I understand."

"You will check the Gatherers' reports and bring to me any concerning items. You are the Gatherers' designated contact for drops. You are the only collector for your Gatherers. They have a dangerous job and you have a dangerous job. You all will operate with extreme caution."

"Yes, sir."

"Study these subjects. Their identities are strictly classified."

"Of course."

"Now, other Gatherers may know the identity of your subjects, they may have been their Gatherers before. Discussing between Gatherers is allowed. However, under no circumstances are you to discuss items that are being taken in. The items are highly coveted and there are creatures that would kill to get their hands on these items. We need to keep you and your Gatherers safe."

"Yes, Father."

"Of course, Daniel knows all the Gatherers and all the subjects that are watched. He typically knows the items that are being taken in. He will be the only person with whom you will be able to discuss your files, Gatherers and confiscated items. He will be a tremendous help to you throughout this process."

"I'm sure he'll be extremely helpful," Aiden's appreciation for Daniel grew deeper.

"Now, I'll give you a week to go through that material," he pointed at the stack of files, "and learn the various Restrictions and the consequences for each violation. In between your other duties, you will train with Father Guerrero three days a week."

"Father Guerrero? I don't believe I've met him."

"He specializes in defense."

"What kind of defense?" Aiden asked.

"Self," Aberdeen looked amused.

"I see," Aiden was just beginning to understand how dangerous this new job was. This could be the real reason his life was in danger, not his association with Elidad.

Aiden didn't mind being underground, but at the end of the day it was nice to finally be outside. His apartment was just outside the Vatican walls, a ten-minute walk to work. He enjoyed walking back and forth; it allowed him to take in the architecture of the surrounding city of Rome.

"Beautiful evening," Sophia called after him.

She wore an emerald green dress that emphasized her eyes and stopped short above her knee.

"Sophia, what are you wearing?"

"I thought I looked ravishing, thank you," she pretended to be hurt.

"Women aren't supposed to have dresses shorter than their knees, here." Aiden glanced around.

Sophia giggle, "Well, I am fabulous at breaking the rules," she turned to take Aiden by the arm, "besides, I'm a tourist, no one will notice."

"Oh, they'll notice," Aiden disagreed.

As they passed the Vatican gate, Sophia waved at the guards in blue, yellow and red stripes manning the entrance. Their faces were beaming when she passed. Aiden smiled to himself; he'd forgotten the power of the siren song. The tension in Aiden's shoulders began to release as the distance between their backs and the Vatican grew. He wouldn't have to worry about the guards turning him in; they'd never betray Sophia.

He and Sophia meandered along the streets, exploring. Aiden was surprised at how much he enjoyed her company; it was easy to be friends with her. Spending time with Sophia wasn't like being with Elidad. She wasn't guarded, she allowed herself to enjoy the small things. Aiden found her charming; he liked that she laughed a lot.

"Have you started looking for the other keys?" Sophia asked.

"I don't know where to begin," Aiden admitted.

"There has to be some information in the Vatican," she frowned.

"I suppose you're right," Aiden agreed. "One of the keys was at the Vatican and was passed down from Bishop to Bishop. It was a privilege to carry it. It was important enough to Bishop Blankenship that he sacrificed his life to protect it. There has to be more information on them. I'm sure Daniel will know something. Why doesn't your mother tell us where they are?"

Sophia sighed, "Mother plays by the rules."

Aiden snorted. "Whose rules? Her own?"

"God's." Sophia's tone was flat.

"Are you telling me that God doesn't want these keys found? Or he doesn't want them found by us?" Aiden's tone turned condescending.

"I'm saying that mother is a prophet. When she receives premonitions, it's a message from God. She tries to direct people when she can, when it's necessary, but she does her best to keep her desires in line with God's. If she follows her heart, she's in danger of changing the outcome. I'd be willing to bet Mother has seen a possible ending to the quest for these keys and that's why she's so set against revealing too much."

"Is she really a prophet?" Aiden refused to believe this idea.

"She is, Aiden. I know you have a difficult time trusting her. The antidote affected the way you see her, but my whole life, all one hundred and seventy-five years of my life, she's done nothing but God's work."

"I guess I'll just have to take your word for it," Aiden said.

"You know, something that's always bothered me is why Abraham had a key. Did you know he had one hidden in his home?"

"Yeah, Mother told me," Sophia confirmed.

"Why was it in his house? It was dangerous to keep it, and Abraham was a loyal follower of the rules. Wouldn't he turn it into the Holy Fathers? Didn't it belong around the neck of a Bishop or in the Records Room? Why would he choose to keep it to himself?"

Sophia shrugged. "He wanted to protect Elidad. That was always his goal. Besides, why would he want to bring the keys together? The whole point is to keep them apart."

Aiden stared at her.

"What?" Sophia asked, sheepishly.

"That's the point, isn't it? We're supposed to keep them apart."

"I thought so," Sophia answered, confusion pressed her brow.

"We keep trying to gather them up, to keep them from whoever else wants them. We really need to keep them apart." Aiden's thoughts formed as he spoke. "How are we going to keep them apart?"

"They've been kept apart this long," Sophia was hopeful.

"True, but isn't Elidad supposed to find them? Isn't that what the prophecy is about?" Aiden hoped she knew.

"Mother never told me the prophecy. She and Abraham kept it a secret, to keep Elidad from finding out."

Some of Aiden's hope dwindled. "This would be a whole lot easier if we knew what we were up against." Aiden's shoulder bumped Sophia's as they walked down uneven, cobbled streets. "We need to find the book." Aiden realized. "Maybe if we find it, we can destroy it. Then the keys won't matter anymore."

"I don't know if it's that easy," Sophia shook her head.

"Why not?" Aiden liked his plan.

"If it was that easy, Mother would've sent us in that direction or she and Abraham would've done it, already. That'd be the easiest fix, if it were possible."

"We need to find the book or a key. We need to be doing something. Your mom thought this was the right job for me, she said it would lead me to the next key." Aiden said.

"If Mother said it would lead you to the next key, then it will. What is it that you do exactly?"

"I'm a record keeper," he said.

"You told me that. What records do you keep? Taxes, expenses?"

"I keep the records of Gatherers."

Sophia rolled her eyes, "Oh, them."

"Do they follow you?" Aiden realized for the first time that it could be a possibility.

"Not anymore. They used to, when I was young. At first, they watched me all the time. As I got older, they'd check on me every few months. Once they decided I didn't have my mother's powers, they stopped stalking me. I'm sure they have their hands full with all the *others*."

"Did they ever talk to you?" Aiden was curious.

"Not usually. Some of them did, thinking they were inconspicuous. After a while, you knew who they were. You could see right through them."

Aiden thought of Jed, the only Gatherer he'd met, and wondered if they were all like the rough mountain man. Aiden smiled to himself imagining Jed, a cigarette hanging from his lips, watching Sophia. She could undoubtedly pick him out of a crowd.

Aiden found comfort in Sophia's company; she was a good distraction to his usual evenings of endless Elidad torment. She always teased him, pushed him to explore and laughed. They were always laughing. He liked the sound of her voice. Aiden could see why men flocked to her; even without the spell charming him, she was enchanting.

Since the first day they met, Sophia was forward in her feelings for him. At first, he thought it was the way she was; but after seeing her with other men, he found that to be untrue. The more obsessive they were with her, the shorter her patience became. It must be hurtful, to have men throwing themselves at you, not because they had a valid interest, but because they had to. They had no choice. How could she know if their feelings were legitimate?

This left Aiden to conclude that part of Sophia's attraction to him was the fact he'd been given the antidote. Some of it may have been inspired by his choice of employment. It wasn't uncommon for women to try to seduce a preacher into breaking their vows, as if it were a challenge. It was alluring, the taunting seduction of what you couldn't have. Aiden understood that sensation perfectly.

Some of her attraction to him could be his relationship with Elidad. Sophia and Elidad had had some kind of rift, resulting in a strange competitive drive between them.

"You're thinking about her, aren't you?" Sophia asked.

"I'm sorry. What did you say?"

"You're thinking about *her*, aren't you?" She repeated.

"Not that, before?" Aiden ignored her question on purpose.

"It doesn't matter, just making conversation. How long has it been since you last spoke to her?" She asked.

"A few weeks," Aiden answered, thinking of all his unanswered calls.

"I'm sure she is busy doing whatever she does," Sophia said.

Aiden was surprised Sophia wasn't taking the opportunity to say something mean about Elidad. "She has a lot going on with Isaac. Her life will settle down." Aiden hoped.

"It's Elidad, she will always have a lot going on. I think she is trying to avoid you."

There was, the real Sophia.

"That makes me feel better, thanks," Aiden considered the architecture of a building as they ambled past.

"Oh, Aiden, don't feel bad. Take it as a compliment. She cares about you."

"What makes you so sure?" He felt silly asking. He knew it was true.

"You hurt her when you left. That's why she's keeping her distance from you now. She's the type of person to push people away if she thinks she's too vulnerable. She'll come around."

"I only left because your mother told me to," Aiden defended himself.

"I know that, but Elidad doesn't. Trust me Aiden, Mother would never have you do anything unless she feels it's in the best interest of the greater good," Sophia assured.

"That's what I am afraid of. In the best interest of the greater good doesn't mean in the best interest of Elidad."

"Are you going to give up your vows for her?" Sophia asked blatantly.

Aiden thought of how many times he prayed for the strength to be Elidad's friend, to resist his attraction to her. She cared for him, that much was obvious, but was she interested in being more than friends? He doubted it. "No, of course not. We're friends, that's all."

"That's all?" Sophia's tone, doubting.

Aiden usually found it amusing when her eyebrows darted up in a playful, condescending manner; but now, it was just annoying. "Yes, friends."

"Oh good," she beamed, "Then there's still hope for me."

CHAPTER THIRTY-FOUR

"You look better."

Elidad could hear the relief in Lucian's voice when he spoke.

"Yeah, I guess that stuff worked, after all." Elidad nodded her head toward the canister on the nightstand. It was easier to let Lucian believe her recovery was due to the canister he'd retrieved than to tell him about the siren visitor who'd vaporized into the room and saved her life.

"*That* doesn't look much better, though." His eyes were on her shoulder.

Elidad looked down to the torn flesh that was radiating heat. The wounds were closing over, finally, but the flesh that wasn't red and inflamed around the opening was gray, and lifeless. Small, black veins fanned out under the skin and around the injury. They reminded Elidad of something she'd seen on TV, on a zombie.

"It's healing. It just needs time," Elidad hoped she was right.

Lucian sat on the edge of the bed. "Well, the important thing is, you lived through the night," he said, picking her hand up. The confident man she'd went to dinner with was gone. Fear radiated from him.

"The last time I checked on you, I wasn't sure…" he shook the thought away.

"I know," Elidad assured. "I didn't think I was going to make it, either," she shrugged with her one good shoulder. "Sorry about your luck."

A smile cracked across his face. He brought her hand up and pressed his warm lips to the apex of her ring finger. It sent a much different chill through her body than she'd been living with over the past few days. "I think my luck is starting to turn around."

"Oh good. Maybe mine will, too." Elidad snorted.

"Elidad, you being alive today is pretty lucky." Lucian said.

"Yeah, I'm not so sure if it's luck, or God prolonging my torture."

Lucian's smile turned wicked. "He can prolong your torture in the afterlife, as much as he can on the earth."

"Touché." Elidad adjusted herself, pulling her hand out of Lucian's grip. "As long as I'm forced to stay here, I may as well try to be presentable."

"Would you like to get dressed?" Lucan offered.

"I'd like to take a shower."

Lucian grinned.

"Don't get any ideas," she said, countering his smile. The pain in her cheeks reminded her that was a mistake.

Elidad reached her hand forward into the cascading water. Its warmth radiated through her fingertips, sending a shiver to her core. Carefully choosing her footing, she maneuvered her body into the steaming downpour to shield her hurt shoulder from the water. The specks of warmth were a mixture of pleasure and pain depending on the placement across her skin. She felt as if the days of fever slid off her and ran down the drain. She wished her troubles would follow.

Feeling human again, Elidad wiped the fog off the mirror. Her hazy image stared back, face still swollen, the deep shades of purple and green refusing to fade. Leaning in, she inspected her lips. The cuts had been healed with the canister's serum. They'd vanished in a second but the serum hadn't touched the rest of her wounds. It was strange, considering how quickly it had healed Kade. Why couldn't it heal her?

The thought drove her eyes down to her shoulder. The skin still looked necrotic around the three puncture marks. The black veins distended under her flesh looked larger. Were they? With the mirror, it was easier to see them; maybe they looked more pronounced from this angle. She turned to look over her shoulder to inspect the damage. One puncture wound pierced the very tip of her tattoo on her shoulder. Not bad, considering.

Thinking back, she realized her tattoo was six years old. How could that much time pass so quickly? How had her life turned into this? If only she could go back and start over. Would six years do it? If she could turn back time, would she go back to the Prophet and decide against getting her tattoo? Did her tattoo define her future, or was her path written long before then? She closed her eyes, allowing her mind to recall when everything hadn't gone to Hell...

CHAPTER THIRTY-FIVE

"**A**re you going?" Elise's eyes narrowed. She pulled her brown hair into a messy bun on top of her head.

"Why wouldn't I?" Elidad asked.

Elise shrugged. "Doesn't seem like your style."

"I think it's her style. She just might not get anything done; she wouldn't want to disappoint *daddy*," Sophia's tone was snide, like usual.

Elidad shot her a look. "I wouldn't disappoint him, no matter what I do."

Sophia laughed. "You don't have to *tell* him you're getting a tattoo. Do you even know how to keep secrets from him?"

"He probably won't give her one, anyway," Elise said.

"Who might not give me one?" Elidad asked.

"The Prophet," Sophia answered. "Don't you know anything about him?"

"I know he's a tattoo artist and a lot of people have gotten their tattoos done by him," Elidad said.

"He's not just a tattoo artist. He's *the* tattoo artist. You don't go there and pick out a stupid tattoo, you don't even go there with an idea. He decides what you get. He chooses the perfect tattoo for you. They say he knows you're coming before you do, no appointment necessary. When you walk in, he's ready for you. Not just ready, *waiting*. If he's not waiting for you, no tattoo." Elise said.

"Who's the *they* that say this?" Elidad was skeptical.

"Everyone." Sophia answered.

"Maybe none of us will get a tattoo." Elise suggested.

"Oh, I think he'll be waiting for *me*." Sophia seemed confident.

When the girls entered the front room of the tattoo parlor, a digital bell dinged upon their entry. The shop had a strange chemical, plastic-like smell. The wood floor creaked under their feet as the three girls huddled together. The black walls were soothing in a way. Photographs of tattoos were framed on the walls. Each image was illuminated by individual lights, like an art gallery. A hard, contemporary sofa sat beneath the images. In front of the sofa was a white coffee table, littered with tattoo collection books. Elidad sat in a chair with purple fur that was three inches long. It looked like a more comfortable option than the sofa where Sophia and Elise sat.

"Ladies." A young woman greeted them, stepping out of a hallway.

The three girls turned to look at her.

"Hey," Sophia answered. "We're here to see if he's expecting us."

"I know why you're here," she responded, looking annoyed. "I'm Avalon." Avalon looked to be about Elise's age, nineteen or twenty. Elidad was eighteen at the time and Sophia, much older.

Avalon's hair was a deep, rich, blue that faded into a soft purple on the ends. The sides of her head were shaved in a tight design, intricately shaved into the short hair. Perfectly swept bangs covered her left eye, the visible one was a grey blue. Her ears displayed large ear gauges that shimmered like glitter along with a dozen other piercings, not including the two rings in her nostril, a septum piercing and the marline on her right upper lip.

"I'm Sophia."

Avalon made eye contact with her. "I know who you are."

"Good. Then he's waiting for me?" Sophia's voice rang with entitlement.

"No, he's not."

Sophia's face scrunched with annoyance. "Are you sure?"

Ignoring the question, Avalon's eyes moved to Elidad. "He's waiting for you."

"*Her?*" Sophia demanded.

"Me?" Elidad echoed.

"She didn't even want to come," Sophia said.

Elidad scowled at Sophia for making it sound like she was afraid. "She's the one who wanted to come here. She wants the tattoo," Elidad pointed at Sophia.

"Look, I don't make the rules, I don't call the subjects. We're very busy, so if you didn't come here to get a tattoo, then leave. I've got shit to do." Avalon crossed her arms. "You've got five seconds to make up your mind."

Elidad stared at Avalon, she could feel Sophia and Elise staring at her. If she didn't do it, she'd never hear the end of it. The sound of her heart began to rise, she was afraid it would echo in the cold décor. Maybe she could ask for a small tattoo, it wouldn't be a big deal.

"Okay," Elidad stood before she lost her courage.

The corner of Avalon's mouth pulled upward. "Good."

Avalon led Elidad into an intimate room in the back. Just like the waiting room, the walls in this room were lined with art.

"Do you have any tattoos?" Avalon asked.

"No."

Avalon smiled. "A virgin. And for your first time, you choose The Prophet. This'll be fun."

"Is he that different than other tattoo artists? I mean, other than not letting you chose your tattoo?"

"You really *didn't* want to come here, did you?" Avalon's brow had a hint of condescension.

"What does that have to do with my question? Or should I assume, since you're answering my question with a question, he *isn't* much different. He's just got it a little easier, not giving his customers what they want. It can't be difficult to tattoo the first thing that comes to mind."

Avalon handed a clipboard to Elidad. "Initial where it's highlighted, sign and date at the bottom."

"Will I have an idea of what it is, or how big it is before we start?" Elidad asked.

"No."

Elidad's eyebrows rose dramatically. "Good to know."

A light thud on the ground made Elidad turn her head to the door to see a man standing in the opening. He appeared to be in his thirties. A magenta tie contrasted with the grey shirt he wore under a black vest. The arms of his shirt were rolled up to his elbows, revealing tattoos on almost every available piece of skin above his wrist. The ink and his skin were so similar in color it was difficult to distinguish what the tattoos were in the low light. The only thing Elidad could make out was a cross on the top of his right arm. It was made apparent in the light as he gripped a cane. When he walked across the room, he didn't appear to limp, making Elidad wonder what the cane was for.

His tie matched the magenta socks that peeked out from under his fit slacks as he moved across the room. The fedora hat on his head was the same gray as his shirt and a black band displayed a cluster of feathers, mostly black with a pop of magenta, to tie his outfit together. His dark hair was shaved short, and his beard was trimmed thin with clean lines.

"Welcome, Elidad." His voice was deep and rich.

"Thanks," Elidad answered, handing the clipboard back to Avalon. "Are you the Prophet?"

"I am."

The Prophet walked to the corner and put his cane down, pulling a chair forward to sit across from Elidad. It was hard for Elidad to get a read on him through his horn-rimmed sunglasses. Apparently, the room they were in, with its black walls and no windows, was too much for him. The Prophet reached his hand forward to clasp Elidad's between his manicured fingers. The ebony of his skin contrasted the lighter pink of his palm.

"You know my mother," he said in his robust voice.

Elidad knew instantly, by the way he held her hands, who his mother was. She pulled her hand away.

"You're Leucosia's son? I... didn't know that was possible. Sirens are women."

A smile came across his full lips. "I'm her only son. It shouldn't be possible, yet, here I am."

Elidad's mind wondered. In a lifetime of two thousand years, how many children had Leucosia had? Ten? A hundred? How ever many she'd had, she'd only had *one* son.

"Sophia is your sister? No wonder why she was so pissed you didn't choose her."

The Prophet smiled. "I don't choose my visions, my visions choose my subjects. I can't control them any more than she can. She'll get over it."

"She might forgive you, but I doubt she'll forgive me." Elidad said. "Do you have visions, like your mother?"

"We are all different, especially compared to my mother, but I have the sight. Being male, my powers are much different. I don't influence men, or women, for that matter. My premonitions are strictly about the future and they manifest as art. I'm able to draw important images that have some connection to people's lives. The premonition begins with the subject and then turns into the tattoo. When my subject arrives, I'm ready. Are *you* ready, Elidad."

"With something as profound as that... I don't know how I couldn't be." Elidad said. Now she understood why he was known as the Prophet.

"Avalon, will you please tell Elidad's friends that we will be a few hours?"

"*Hours?*" Elidad couldn't contain her surprise.

"Oh yes," The Prophet pulled a rolling cart to the center of the room that displayed various tools. "What I have planned for you is going to take a long time."

Elidad stared at herself in the floor-length mirror that hung on the opposite wall. Its black frame had fingers that twisted outward, reminding her of the tree that stood in Leucosia's lair. Elidad had been straddling the same chair for hours. With her shirt off, she'd pressed her body into the back to keep her shirt around her chest and expose every inch of skin on her back. The buzz of the tattoo machine hummed as the stinging on her skin grew. It was only painful in certain spots. Periodically, it felt like the Prophet was trying to dig through her skin, rubbing the needle over the same spot. He said he was shading, but Elidad thought it felt like he was sanding her skin off.

"I think you've had enough for one day," he'd said, leaning back.

The heat from the fresh ink told Elidad he was right. It also told her that he had an outline of his image, but the shading wasn't done.

"I'll have to finish up the shading on your next visit."

Elidad stood and stretched her back. "Can I look at it now?"

"You may."

Elidad turned her back to the mirror as the Prophet handed her a silver backed hand mirror. It was heavy in her grip. The black ink that scathed her back was outlined in red skin; her body's protest of the last three and a half hours of torture. Her breath caught in her lips when she saw the large cross on her back—but it wasn't a cross, it was a sword. The handle reached up her neck, the hilt across her shoulder blades. A demon lay in the small of her back, the sword driven through his chest. The demon gripped the sword as he lay dying. Elidad thought of the demons she'd fought in her life and of the ones likely to come. She loved the way the sword represented justice and the cross for which she fought. The sword stood over the evil being, proud and unmoved, the way she knew she must be. The beauty and significance were so much, it inspired a tear to escape her eye.

The Prophet removed his glasses to rub where they sat on his nose, "What do you think?"

With them missing, it was easy to see a cluster of freckles on the bridge of his nose and his grey eyes. The lamp in the room reflected in the mirror and onto his face. His eyes moved strangely, one staring forward, the other wondering a bit, not connecting with Elidad's as she looked at him.

"Are you… blind?" Elidad asked carefully.

The Prophet laughed. "You didn't know?"

CHAPTER THIRTY-SIX

Aiden picked up his phone. No missed calls.

What was Elidad doing? He thought they'd left on good terms. She was angry, but was she angry enough to stop talking to him?

Sophia had been in town for a few weeks now. He needed to tell Elidad. She didn't need to know that Sophia came to warn him something was trying to kill him, but she'd be angry if he didn't tell her she was here.

Aiden could feel perspiration on the back of his phone as he held it to his ear. He'd only spoke once—briefly—with Elidad and that was right after he got to Rome. When they did speak, he could sense the tension on the other end of the line. She was still angry. How would she react to Sophia coming to Vatican City? Being so close to him? It shouldn't matter, but Elidad didn't like anything Sophia did.

Aiden thought back to the first time he'd met Sophia in the nightclub, his memory of the interaction was blurry. The spell of the siren left his mind foggy, but he remembered Elidad holding Sophia's arm. He could picture Sophia struggling to free herself from Elidad's grip, like a child struggling against the grasp of an adult. Elidad loved Leucosia, apparently that affection didn't extend to her daughter. What could've caused that kind of tension between them?

The phone rang again, Aiden moved his finger to hang up before Elidad's voicemail could pick up. Lately, it was the only way he could hear her voice. He couldn't bear to listen to her message today.

The phone was answered. Aiden could hear fumbling on the other end.

"Hello?" The male voice on the other end surprised Aiden.

"Hello." Aiden answered, deciding it wasn't Isaac. "Is Elidad there?"

Brief pause. "She's busy, Aiden. I can let her know you called."

"Is this Lucian?" Heat radiated off the back of Aiden's neck. Why would Lucian be answering Elidad's phone?

"This is."

"What is she busy with?" Aiden demanded.

Pause. "She's in the shower."

Anger choked Aiden's words.

"I know you've been trying to get ahold of her, I just thought I'd let you know, she's busy… Trying to get into the swing of things, with Isaac and all."

"Will you have her call me when she has time?" Aiden strained to sound polite.

"Of course. If she feels up to it." Lucian responded.

"What's that supposed to mean?" Aiden spat into the phone.

"Aiden, we both know she's been avoiding you. Who could blame her? You left her here to deal with Isaac and the loss of her father to go chase your dreams. Who wouldn't be hurt by that?"

"How's that any of your business?" The hand holding the phone began to shake.

"You made it my business when you left. It became my business when *I* stayed to pick up the pieces."

Aiden bit the inside of his cheek to hold back what he really wanted to say. Of course, Lucian was trying to pick up the pieces while Elidad was vulnerable. That's usually when guys like him made their move.

"Have Elidad call me." Aiden hung up the phone, throwing it across the room. He regretted it when it hit the ground.

"Rhahhhhhh!" Aiden growled. Why did he let that ass incite him enough to break his phone?

It rang from the corner. A leap of hope shot through him. Was Elidad calling him back? Aiden sprinted to it. He picked it up, turning it over in his hand he could see through the newly shattered glass, Sophia's name.

"Hello?"

"Hello, love. What's wrong?"

"I just dropped my phone. I'm going to need a new one," he lied.

CHAPTER THIRTY-SEVEN

Feeling stronger after her shower, Elidad made her way down to the store to look for Lucian.

Lucian smiled when she walked into the room. "I found something of yours."

"You did?"

"I'm pretty sure it's yours," he said pulling a box from under the counter.

When she saw what was in his hands her stomach felt like she'd just stepped up to an open door on an airplane before an unavoidable plummet to the ground.

The wood of the box was highly polished, reflecting the light of the store. Her name was hand painted in beautiful calligraphy in the center of the lid, adorned by filigree. She knew what it would smell like when she lifted the lid.

"Are you ok?" Lucian looked puzzled. "You look like you're going to be sick."

"Um… Yeah. I'm fine. This is the most energy I've used all week, I feel a little light-headed. I'm ready to go back to bed."

Lucian set the box on the counter. "This *is* yours, isn't it? It has your name on it."

"Yeah. I gave it to Isaac for safekeeping. Where did you find it?"

"Before I took his mattress to the dumpster, I found it."

"In the mattress?"

"In the box spring, I thought it might be smart to check. That's where my uncle used to hide money. It's an old school thing."

Elidad leaned against the counter, eyeing the box. She lightly placed her hand on its lid. The cool exterior was smooth under her fingertips. She rolled the brass latch up and opened it. The peppery smell of eucalyptus exhaled from the confined space like a genie being released from its prison.

Inside, the flat black metal of her custom-made handgun was cold against the warm velvet that lined the box. Rose gold filigree, mimicking the art on the lid, shone against the dull metal, eloquently decorating the barrel. The trigger, hammer, safety and clip release were also rose gold. A cross, intricately detailed in silver, was inlayed in mother of pearl on the handgrip.

Cautiously pressing her fingers against the steel, a flood of memories came rushing back.

"You seem… agitated, Elidad. Is everything alright?" Dedrick's stone eyes interrogated her.

"I'm fine, Dedrick." She stood on the other side of the velvet rope.

Dedrick waved his hand and a bouncer removed the barrier from her path.

"Thank you." She flashed a smile.

"Always my pleasure," he said, turning to escort her to the elevator, the way he always did. He paused, mid-step, "Are you sure there is nothing I can help you with, my dear?"

"I'm fine, really."

"Very well. If you change your mind," he asserted, resting his hand on her shoulder, "Call for me right, away."

"I will, thank you," Elidad said, stepping out from the weight of his hand and into the elevator. When the door closed, she was relived to be out of his company. Nerves were pushing her heart at an unnatural pace. Dedrick had heard it, that's probably why he was so persistent with his questions. Elidad knew it wouldn't take her heartbeat to notify Dedrick there was a problem; he'd known her since she was a child.

Elidad grew up in *Genus*, during the day when the employees were the only ones around. Elidad had loved it. Dedrick would turn on the spotlight and microphone so she could sing for an invisible crowd. It was the only time she was popular. With a group of imaginary friends, and doting grownups, it was the only time she was cool.

The muffled throbbing in the floor of the elevator raced through the soles of Elidad's combat boots before the doors slid open. The hammering base was the only thing with the ability to make her heartbeat less noticeable. She elbowed her way through the crowd. People, demons and other creatures danced under the beams of light pulsing to the music.

Elidad knew her destination. She plowed her way to the bar on the back wall. When she approached it, the bartender put the bottle in his hand under the counter, signaling to Elidad with a slight twitch of the head. Elidad followed him to a hallway in the depths of the club. Pulling an access card from his pocket, he swiped it through a reader to open the door. Holding the door open, Elidad slid past him.

"Is it true, Mike?" Elidad demanded before the door closed all the way.

"I don't know," he shook his head. "I can't imagine her being that stupid, Elidad. I thought I raised her better."

"Mike, kids make their own decisions. Sometimes, outside influences have more impact on people than how they were raised. This isn't your fault," she added.

"I just don't know what to do." Mike rubbed his tattooed hands together. The tribal pattern that crawled up his forearm, went up the side of his neck and ended on top of his bald head. Anger began to grow beneath the look of worry. "If it is true, I'll kill him."

"Something should've been done about him a long time ago, he's been a menace for as long as I can remember, but you can't kill him. He's off limits," Elidad warned. "Believe me, I've asked, many times."

"It's his father," the words spat from Mike's lips. "If it wasn't for his father, they wouldn't let him get away with all the shit he does."

Elidad nodded her head in agreement. "How long has it been since she's been home?"

"Couple weeks." The hurt resonated in Mike's eyes. "She's here now."

"She's here? With him?" Elidad tightened her fist.

"She's here almost every night. But I can't *do* anything. She's an adult and I can't afford to lose my job."

"I understand," Elidad agreed, "but, she's your daughter."

"I know, and that's why I called you." Mike said. "Can't you do *something*? Can't you talk to the Church? Your father? Can't they make him stop?"

"I'll try, again, but you shouldn't get your hopes up. They haven't done anything about him for years, why would they start now?" A thought crept into Elidad's mind. "What about Sophia?" She was afraid to ask.

Mike's face turned from worry to disdain. "She's the one who got her into this. When things got hard, she left Elise. She left her with *him*."

"Maybe she tried to help her and couldn't," Elidad suggested.

"Elise never would've met Pythious if it weren't for Sophia. You know her, Elidad. Elise wouldn't try drugs. She was never that way. This is all Sophia's fault."

Elidad did know, but she didn't want to confirm. "Mike, I'll go talk to him, I'll try to talk to Elise, but like you said, she's an adult. I don't know what good it'll do."

His eyes were misty. "Anything you can do, Elidad. I'll appreciate you trying. I need my little girl back." His heavy sigh signified the end of the conversation. Desperation was its own communication between them.

Elidad followed Mike out of the back room that was lined with boxes. Mike took a left out to the club to continue his shift and Elidad took a right, heading down the hall lined with VIP rooms. Elidad loved how each room represented its own world. The varied species that laced the dance floor together now separated, segregating themselves down this corridor.

The sound in her chest, no longer muffled by the music, raged like her heart might leap out and lead her down the hall. She could feel the clammy perspiration on her palms that indicated she was about to do something stupid.

Elidad turned into the room where she knew Pythious would be. As soon as Elidad entered the room, two men stopped her. One grabbed her arm, the other put his hand on her chest, just inside her shoulder. She looked down at their hands.

"Get your damn hands off me." It wasn't a suggestion.

One of them removed his hand quickly. He must have recognized her. She locked eyes with the one still touching her. "I said, get your hand off me."

"You better do what she tells you. It would be embarrassing—for all of us—if she kicks your ass," Pythious hissed from the middle of the room.

Pythious was sitting on a sofa, women piled around him.

The bodyguard removed his hand from Elidad's arm at Pythious' suggestion. Elidad searched each of the girl's faces, counting ten all together. Some of them looked too young to be in the club and certainly too young to be with him.

"And to what do I owe the honor of your presence, *Crusader*?" Pythious mouthed the word like it was a foul taste.

Elidad wanted to punch him in his smug face. And what a pretty face it was. His lips were thin, perfectly shaped, almost feminine. His nose was small sharply chiseled and, above that, his high forehead was topped with flawless chestnut hair. The only thing masculine about him was his chin, which dimpled in the center. His features were young, but his eyes ancient.

If Elidad was lucky enough to take a swing at him, maybe she'd break his nose, and the blood would ruin his five-thousand-dollar suit. She'd settle for ruining his face instead.

Elidad heard the clicking of stiletto heels behind her. A girl walked into the room, nervously eyeing Elidad as she passed. She must be a regular; the bouncers didn't look twice at her. She plopped down on a cushion in front of Pythious, pulling out a stack of cash from a clutch and handing it to him. She unsnapped her bracelet, revealing two puncture wounds on her wrist. She held up her arm.

"Sasha," his words slithered, "Such a good girl."

Elidad couldn't believe he'd do business right in front of her.

Pythious took her arm, stroking it. He kissed the top of her hand. She giggled as he turned her wrist. His tongue darted out of his mouth, a black Y-shape. He looked through heavily lashed, lime green eyes; the pupils were vertical black slits lined with red. His eyes made him look more dangerous than he was. He was evil, but Elidad doubted he'd attacked many people. He wouldn't want to get his manicured hands dirty. He employed the idiots at the door for that kind of work.

Opening his mouth, two fangs stretched forward from Pythious' mouth. Like a snake, they were long and thin, mostly protected by gums. The dangerous tips glinted in his ravenous smile. He bit into the puncture wounds on Sasha's wrist.

She inhaled sharply at the apparent pain before sighing with ecstasy.

"You know the rules. You're not supposed to do business here," Elidad said, staring at Sasha as her eyes rolled up in their sockets. Sasha's body drooped like a cut flower without water in a heated room.

"I don't have a business," Pythious replaced Sasha's bracelet. "I can't help it if beautiful women throw their money at me. It would be rude of me to refuse." His face became serious. "And Sasha... she has a bad back. The use of my venom is strictly medicinal." Releasing Sasha, he sat back in his chair and snapped his fingers.

One of the bouncers picked Sasha up, her body slack, lifeless, in his arms. He placed her in the corner with three other girls that looked as high as she was.

"Medicinal, *right*. Does anyone believe that bullshit?" Elidad demanded.

Pythious' lips parted in a sneer. "What do you want, Elidad?"

"Elise. Where is she?"

His eyes narrowed. "Did her father send you?"

Elidad raised an eyebrow. "*Should* he have sent me? Is there something wrong with her?"

"Of course not," Pythious said dismissively. "Elise is fine. All parents have a hard time when their children move out and move on. Especially single fathers with their daughters."

Elidad clenched her fists until her fingernails cut into her palm. It's all she could do to keep from lunging at him.

"I'd imagine you've seen that a lot... Fathers, having a hard time with their daughters moving out. I'm sure it has nothing to do with *you* being in their lives."

"I have no idea what you're talking about. I take care of my girls," he said snapping his fingers, again.

In response to his action, one of the bouncers ducked behind a curtain.

"Why don't we go for a walk, have a conversation in private?" Elidad offered. "You can tell me how great Elise is doing."

"I have no intention of going anywhere with you, Elidad." Pythious' eyes were stone as his lips curled up. "Are you sure you didn't come for *Venom*, yourself?"

Elidad's look turned condescending. "You'd like that, wouldn't you?"

"It would help you relax," his eyes creased with amusement. "You'd be much prettier, if you weren't so uptight."

"You'd probably be prettier, too," Elidad considered. "But I'm not stupid enough to use anything you're selling."

His eyebrows pulled together. "Pity."

Elidad could hear the heavy steps of the returning bouncer from behind the curtain. A delicate clacking followed him. When he came around the curtain, Elise was following him. Her dark hair was streaked with blonde highlights. Her face looked like it'd been airbrushed, flawless skin made her eyes stand out, but no sparkle escaped them. Even with the perfect makeup and expensive dress, Elidad could see how malnourished, and anorexic looking, she was. Elidad doubted it was an eating disorder that had wreaked havoc on her body.

"Elidad?" Elise's voice was distant, hollow. "What are you doing here?"

"I came to see you. I need to talk to you," Elidad said.

Elise looked at Pythious.

"What? Do you need his permission to talk to your friends?" Elidad spat.

Pythious laughed. "Of course not. She can talk to whoever she pleases, she can *go* wherever she pleases."

Elise's lips quivered in a tentative smile. "Come on Elidad, we can talk in another room."

Elidad squared her shoulders. "I'll meet you out back in fifteen minutes, Pythious, if you're not too scared to talk to me by yourself."

Elidad flung the door to the Chapel open. As she'd suspected, there was no one inside. Elise hesitated at the threshold.

"What's wrong?" Elidad's brows tightened. "You used to hang out in here with me all the time. Now you can't even walk in the door?"

"No," Elise assured. "I just haven't been back here for a while, that's all."

Elidad dipped her fingers into a gold dish hanging on the wall. Cool water clung to the tips of her fingers. She made the sign of the cross before sitting in the back pew. Elise followed, but didn't touch the Holy Water.

"Elidad, what do you want?" Elise demanded before sitting.

"Can't I check in on an old friend without wanting anything?"

"We haven't hung out in a long time, Elidad. You don't call anymore. It can't be a coincidence that when my dad has a problem with the way I'm living my life, you show up. I know you and him. You both want something."

"I'm sorry I haven't been around…" Elidad looked at the floor, "I should've been around more, maybe I could've kept you out of this. When you and Sophia started hanging out with Pythious, I thought it was a phase." Elidad swallowed. "It was a phase for Sophia, you got stuck."

"You've been living your life, and I've been living mine," Elise said. "I don't need a babysitter."

"Do you call this living?" Elidad hedged.

Elise's face flushed. "It's none of your damn business. I'm not doing anything wrong. Pythious makes me happy. And this isn't Sophia's fault. *She* wasn't good enough to be his girl. When he fell in love with me, Sophia got jealous and left. She stopped being my friend."

"*He* makes you happy? Or the Venom makes you happy?" Elidad demanded. There were marks on Elise's neck and in the crease in her elbow. The purple puncture wounds looked old. New skin closed the holes, pink against the purple, blue.

Elise saw Elidad's inventory of her marks, she folded her arms to hide them from Elidad's scrutiny.

"I don't do it all the time. I can stop whenever I want. I'm not like those girls, I don't do the hard stuff." Elise protested.

"Are you listening to yourself? You sound like an addict. It's all the hard stuff, look at yourself in the mirror, Elise, you look like shit."

"I'm not an addict," Elise persisted.

"Then why do you have to hide your arms like one?"

"It's medicinal," Elise argued.

Elidad's laugh rang across the empty sanctuary. "What the hell is wrong with you… other than your stupid boyfriend?"

"I have anxiety," Elise said.

"You could probably fix that by losing your boyfriend. Think about it. You wouldn't be in competition for Pythious' attention, you wouldn't have to hide your V marks, you'd have a relationship with your father."

"Pythious loves me and he takes good care of me. I've thought of a way to hide the V marks for the other girls so no one has to know they need medicine. But me? He loves me. He wants everyone to know I'm his girl."

Elidad's eyes narrowed. She could feel the blood drain from her face.

"He loves you so much? That's why he scars you? He wants to show he owns you. He wants everyone to know you belong to him, *Congratulations*," Elidad sneered. Elise wore the same bracelet as, Sasha, the girl who'd given Pythious a stack of cash. Fury pulsed through Elidad's body. "He treats you like a dog treats his property…" Anger sent Elidad to her feet. "You let him mark your body, like a dog pisses on a tree. If *that's* not love… I don't know what is," Elidad's sarcasm got thicker with her breath.

"You don't have any control over my life, and neither does my Father," Elise snapped.

"Why is this scumbag so important? He's a loser. I can't believe that you'd leave your dad for someone like him." Elidad wanted to slap her. "The Elise I *knew* would never leave her dad after everything he's done. He raised you."

Elise's face hardened. "It's *his* fault. I'm sick of him judging Pythious and me. I'm an adult. He can't tell me what to do. This is my life."

"Listen to yourself, you sound like a spoiled brat," Elidad observed.

Elise sprang to her feet. "I don't have to sit here and listen to this."

Elidad reached forward and ripped the bracelet off Elise's wrist. In an instant, her face changed from shock to horror. Her skin was covered in dozens of holes, not like Sasha's two puncture wounds.

One late night, Elidad had watched a documentary about heroin addiction. They'd said that after too much abuse in the same injection sight, the veins would collapse, and the user would have to use a different vein. Sasha's wrist was clean, Pythious' teeth punctured the same holes. Elidad had guessed that Sasha wasn't a new user; perhaps V didn't collapse the vein like heroin.

However, that didn't explain why Elise's wrist was covered in purple and black marks. There were so many, it made the ones on her neck and arm seem trivial. Not all these holes punctured her veins; there was no skin left unscathed. This was something more, like a self-harmer who cut the same area, over and over. The holes weren't for the transmission of V. It was for something else. Did she like the pain? Did she like to be bitten? Maybe it was some erotic exchange between her and Pythious? Elidad didn't want to know.

"Looks like you're running out of room, you're going to need another bracelet," Elidad suggested.

Elise stripped the bracelet from Elidad's fingers and stormed toward the door.

"Elise," Elidad called after her, a hint of desperation in her voice.

Elise paused, not turning toward Elidad.

"Look at what he's doing to you," Elidad's voice was a whisper. "He's doing the same thing to your relationship with your dad. It's mangled, bruised and dying. How much more can you take? How long until your body gives up? And if you die, your dad will die, too."

Wordlessly, Elise pushed through the door and she was gone.

CHAPTER THIRTY-EIGHT

"How's the new phone?" Sophia asked.

"It's good. I can see the screen."

"How was work?" She wasn't good at small talk.

Aiden frowned into the phone. "It was fine. Why? What are you up to?"

Sophia giggled. "How do you know?"

"I just do. What is it?" He pressed.

"I want to give you something. Can I meet you?" Her voice elevated.

"Sure."

"Good. Can you meet in an hour, in our wine bar?" Her voice remained awkwardly high.

"One hour," Aiden agreed, ignoring that she called it *our wine bar.*

Sophia was sitting in their usual spot when Aiden walked in. He weaved around all the red faces, clinking glasses and laughter to make it to the back.

"Hello, love, how was your day?" Sophia cooed.

"Very funny." Aiden waived at the bar keep. "What's up, Sophia?"

Her pale eyebrows pulled together. "What's wrong with you?"

The waitress placed a glass of wine in front of Aiden.

"Thank you," he said, smiling up at her.

"You're welcome," she answered.

When his eyes were locked with hers, Sophia slipped her hand across the table and placed it on Aiden's arm. Aiden's exchange with the waitress left his lips as she turned and walked away. Realizing what Sophia was doing, he shook her hand away, violently.

"Oh!" Sophia breathed.

"What?" He demanded.

She cocked an eyebrow. "That's what happened to your phone."

"Nothing happened to my phone," he growled, picking up his glass.

"Elidad happened to your phone. Or shall I say, Lucian happened to your phone?" She corrected.

"It's nothing," Aiden said, not sure how much she saw with a three second touch.

"He's a jerk. But there could be a perfectly logical explanation for Elidad to be in the shower at Isaac's house."

Apparently, she saw everything.

Sophia took a sip of wine, as if to contemplate a reason. "You know, like, maybe she spilt paint on herself, or some chemical, and had to wash it off."

"Paint?" Aiden was astounded that Sophia was making excuses for Elidad.

"You know she's a virgin, right?" Sophia blurted out.

Aiden threw up his hands. "Wow… how would I know? No, I didn't know that. And, how would you?"

"We were friends, at one time," Sophia spun the stem of her glass in her fingers.

"What happened?" Aiden inquired.

Sophia took in a deep breath. "I let her down."

"Elidad's not the type to be so scornful after someone letting her down," Aiden pointed out.

"Do you remember a girl named Elise?" Sophia's eyes held on her glass.

Aiden thought. "No, I don't think so."

"You probably wouldn't. She moved to your school after you graduated. She was friends with Elidad; Elidad introduced us. Abraham brought Elidad to *Genus* all the time during the day. He did a lot of work in the sanctuary and he was close friends with my mother."

"Elidad said Abraham and your mother were friends. I just can't picture it," Aiden confessed.

"That's because you loved Abraham, and you don't trust my mother," Sophia observed.

"That's not—" Aiden decided it wasn't even worth trying to lie. She knew the truth.

"Elise and Elidad were close friends. Elise might've been Elidad's only friend in school. When they turned twenty-two, we started going to *Genus* all the time. Well, Elise and I did. We were just having fun." Sophia's eyes looked up, almost pleading. "I introduced Elise to some people that I'd known for a long time. You have to remember, I've been alive a lot longer and they weren't always bad. We were just having fun. I forgot that *people* get addicted to things, easier than *we* do."

"Sophia, what happened?" Aiden couldn't follow her babbling.

"Elise got hooked on Venom," Sophia cringed.

Aiden shook his head. "I don't know what that is."

Sophia swallowed hard. "There's a race of immortals; they're snake people. When they want to, they can extract their venom. Have you ever seen someone extract a cobra's venom?"

"Yes," Aiden agreed.

"These snake people can do the same thing. Venom is poison. But, in small doses, it can be a hallucinogen, it's— it's hard to describe. The closest thing I could compare it to would be heroin, just better."

Aiden's brows creased together. "You've done heroin?"

"Gross, that's a dirty human drug. I've never touched the stuff. That's the *real* poison. People have just told me it's close, I don't know from experience."

"So, Elise got hooked on Venom?" Aiden guessed.

Sophia bit her bottom lip, shaking her head. "It ruined her life and Elidad's."

"How did it ruin Elidad's life?"

"Elidad tried to protect Elise. She really didn't do anything wrong, but it led to Elidad being excommunicated. Elidad never forgave me."

"I can see why," Aiden agreed.

Sophia's eyes shot up to meet his.

"Elidad didn't handle losing her job well. It *did* ruin her life. In case you've missed it, Elidad isn't quick to forgive. It would do her soul some good to learn *how* to forgive, but she's loyal to the death."

Sophia's eyes threatened to overflow with moisture. "Great. So, she'll hate me till the day I die."

Aiden held up his glass. "Welcome to the club."

Sophia laughed, clinking her glass with his.

Aiden thoughtfully took a sip from his cup. "Why did they excommunicate her? What did she do?"

Sophia's look became empty, for the first time since Aiden had met her, she seemed at a loss for words.

"I don't think I should be the one to tell you that story," Sophia finally said.

"Fair enough," Aiden agreed. "You didn't ask me here so I could drag you through the mud," Aiden tried to change the subject.

"You're not dragging me through the mud. I did that to myself." She pressed a finger to the inside of each eye to dab away the tears. "But, you're right. I came to give you a gift." She reached into her purse and set something heavy, wrapped in a black cloth, onto the table.

Aiden picked it up, throwing back the corner of the fabric. He stared at the item.

"Do you know what that is?" Sophia asked.

"Yes," his voice was low. "Elidad is supposed to have this."

"She didn't want it, anymore." Sophia informed him.

"Why?" He demanded.

She shrugged. "I don't know. Mother said she wanted you to have it."

"She, as in Elidad? Or your mother wanted me to have it?"

"Mother. Elidad didn't want it and Mother thought you should have it," Sophia clarified.

"Why wouldn't Elidad want the Sword of Justice?" Aiden asked.

"I don't know. Who knows why Elidad does anything. Maybe she's having a hard time dealing with her father's death. If you beheaded your father, would you want to keep the weapon hanging around your house?"

"Leucosia brought this to you?" Aiden assumed.

"She did. Does that matter?"

"Everything she does is on purpose. Everything matters," Aiden stated.

"That's true. If I were you, I'd carry it with me, all the time."

Aiden closed the fabric back around it, sticking it into his pocket. "Why do I get the feeling, you know more than you're telling me?"

Taking a sip from her glass, Sophia simply shrugged her response.

CHAPTER THIRTY-NINE

The images of Elise's wrist and hollow face made Elidad nauseous enough that she needed fresh air. Elidad followed a hall to a service door that lead to the kitchen. She walked past servers, expeditors, and sous chefs barking orders to line cooks. All of them were too busy to pay her any attention. Past the walk-in and beer coolers was an exit door next to the loading dock. Elidad compressed the bar on the man door, pushing it open. She was greeted by cool night air. During the week, in the daytime, trucks would line the parking lot with deliveries. This time of night, it was empty. The employee parking lot was closed off, to ensure employees' safety and to keep patrons out.

Elidad looked at her phone—two a.m.—the employees wouldn't be leaving for a couple more hours. She slid the phone back in her pocket. It'd been twenty minutes. Pythious wasn't here. He wouldn't have the guts to confront her, not if he was smart.

The metal door made a clanking noise as it pushed open. Elidad turned back to the opening. The bodyguard who'd refused to take his hand off her exited through the door. He was short and unnaturally thick, like he'd spent too much time in the gym. He was the type of guy who'd spent his life angry, and fighting, to make up for being picked on in school. He definitely had something to prove.

"Evening," he strode out of the door, pulling a pack of cigarettes from his pocket.

"Those things will kill you," Elidad said.

"I've heard that," he responded, lighting one.

"With some luck, it'll happen quickly," Elidad smiled.

He didn't look amused, exhaling a puff of smoke. The plume hid his face in the single street light that towered over the cars in the parking lot, fifty yards away. The other bodyguard stepped out of the doorway behind him. This man was taller with black hair and olive skin. He could pass for mafia, but this life he was living was darker, more bloodthirsty. That's why they were here, blood lust. Pythious had sent them, instead of coming himself. Typical.

Elidad began calculating their sizes and guesstimating their abilities. The darker one that took his hands off her first knew something of her abilities; he wouldn't underestimate her. He'd have to go first.

"Is Pythious too scared to come get me himself?" Elidad assumed.

"I'm not sure what you mean. We came out for a smoke," the short one said.

The dark-haired man kept his mouth shut as he rolled back his sleeves, keeping Elidad in front of him as she paced the open space. The shorter one got closer to Elidad. Apparently, he didn't think she was a threat, at all. He might have to go first, just because it was easy.

"Do you have a problem with my boss?" He taunted. "Because he's got a problem with you harassing his girls."

"Is Pythious scared?" The amusement was apparent in Elidad's tone. "He should be. The only way he can keep ladies around is to keep them high. Imagine if I ripped those fangs out of his skull... he'd have nothing left. Not even *you* idiots would do his dirty work."

The short man rushed Elidad like a lineman rushing a quarterback. Elidad dropped to her knees, out of his grasp. Her hand went to the top of her boot and she pulled a knife as she sprang away. Expecting to tackle Elidad, the bodyguard stumbled forward, struggling to stay on his feet.

Elidad turned. He was already advancing again. Stepping out of the way, like a matador, Elidad thrust her knife forward as he blazed by. The blade thudded into bone, remaining there, turning his smiling face, grim. Speckles of blood led his steps across the ground.

"You stabbed me, bitch," he accused, pulling the knife from his wound.

"Oh, good. You noticed." Elidad's tone was condescending. "I was worried you'd had too much V to notice."

"I'm not too high to kill you," he promised.

"If you're going to kill me, you'll have to try harder than that," Elidad suggested.

He advanced again, this time like a fighter. He was on his guard, not careless in underestimating her. His thick arms thrust downward with the knife. Elidad blocked it with her arm, the point three inches from her shoulder. The force of the blow knocked her to the ground. She quickly rolled, kicking his legs from under him, the knife flying from his hands as he barrel-rolled before hitting the concrete.

Elidad launched herself to her feet, lunging with the knife; she threw it with precision into his chest as he found his feet. All five inches of the steel hit his chest with a thud. Only the handle remained in view. His mouth opened, as if to say a word, but only blood poured out. Elidad turned to keep the darker man in sight. He circled her, mimicking the way she circled him. His assurance felt like experience. This would be a tougher fight.

Before Elidad could make a move, a sharp pain cut into her back. Elidad inhaled sharply, staggering forward. Slowly turning, she saw Pythious walking into the dim light.

He made a tisk-tisk noise through his fangs.

"You should really be aware of your surroundings while in combat, Elidad. It's just sloppy," his eyebrows rose in a condescending gesture, "not watching your back."

Elidad crossed her arm over her shoulder to feel where he bit her. She tried to speak, but the Venom was already working. Their images grew blurry, his voice beginning to hiss in her mind.

"I expected more from the *great* Elidad," Pythious sneered. "How are you feeling? The Venom should be taking over your senses. This might be the first time in your life you've calmed the hell down," he chortled. "You're welcome for the freebee. I chose the perfect dose for you. Something that moves sss-low. We wouldn't want you to miss out, now would we? If you're going to die, let this be your last memory."

Pythious laughed. "You should have taken me up on my offer. You should've calmed the hell down. This is what you were missing... The *good* stuff. I don't waste it on those whores," he was referring to his other girls. "This is different. This takes concentration."

His long fingers cut into Elidad's chin as he held her face aggressively. "Only the best for you... and Elise," He added.

Vivid colors began to consume Elidad's peripheral vision. Her body was heavy, like she was tied down with rocks in the bottom of the ocean. She fought the weight, but it was useless. *Soon*, she thought, she'd look like Sasha, with eyes rolled back in her head.

Elidad mustered all of the clarity she had left, reaching into the inside of her jacket. Her hand found the cold, hard steel that was hidden there. Pulling the gun, she fired a shot into Pythious' chest. The blood that sprayed across him refracted in her sight. She could smell the iron in the air. Elidad shot the last bodyguard before her arms went numb.

Pythious spit a laugh. "I'm immortal, stupid girl. The only thing you've done is ruin an expensive shirt. Is that the thanks I get, for the best time of your life?"

"You're stupid," Elidad slurred. Not the insult she'd hoped for. The drugs were too much. "Shhhh... you feel that?" She whispered. "Venom... *You're* welcome for the freebee."

Elidad was too stoned to see his face, so she imagined it.

He would understand.

The bullet had been a special one, designed to disintegrate on impact and deliver the same lethal dose that he had undoubtedly injected her with. It was the only thing that would kill his type of immortal, that and severing his head. Elidad wished they'd had a fair fight so she could have enjoyed the latter.

She would die tonight, but at least she'd take Pythious with her.

Pythious held his chest, dropping to his knees, blood dripping from his hands, a morbid fountain spewing from his body.

Laughter filled Elidad's mind; she realized it was hers.

"Elidad," the voice was cool. Even in her stupor, she recognized Dedrick's tone.

"I didn't call for you," Elidad was apologetic.

"I smelled the blood. I came as soon as I could."

Of course, the perfect security supervisor. A vampire. He could smell blood on the other side of the building, even though it took up more than a city block.

"You can't be here, Dedrick, you need to leave. He's untouchable. Go. They'll execute you."

"I'll take my chances," his voice was calm in her frantic mind. "Elidad, I have to get the Venom out before it kills you," he explained. "I can smell it in your blood. It's getting close to your heart."

Elidad couldn't answer, collapsing to her knees.

"It's going to be painful. Please understand, I'm doing this to save you... It's the only way." Dedrick's face was spinning like there was fifteen of him.

If Elidad weren't out of her mind, his warning would've been ominous.

Searing pain ripped Elidad from her prismatic hallucinations. Dedrick's piercing fangs cut into the holes in her back. Elidad's scream rang across the concrete as her veins protested against the pull. It felt like the Venom, once smooth and warm, now clung to the insides of her arteries with talons as Dedrick pulled it in the opposite direction.

Dedrick placed his frail hand, that was as strong as a bear trap, over Elidad's mouth to silence her cries. Ripping and tearing ravaged through Elidad's body until the severity silenced her mind and she slipped into nothingness.

"Elidad, are you alright?" Lucian placed his hand on top of hers, resting on the gun.

"Yeah, I'm fine."

"You don't look fine. What aren't you telling me?" Lucian asserted.

"I was just thinking about the last time I saw this," she was talking about the gun.

"You want to tell me about it?" Lucian asked.

"It was made for me, for my line of work," Elidad explained.

"That's why I wanted to give it to you. I was hoping it would protect you from the demon, if he comes back," Lucian suggested.

"I don't know if I can carry it," she was honest.

Lucian frowned. "Why not? It could save your life."

Elidad took a labored breath. "Because, the last time I had it, I shot someone I shouldn't have." Elidad's eye connected with Lucian's. "I was protecting myself," Elidad defended.

"I believe you," Lucian assured.

"Afterwards… I brought the gun to Isaac, I asked him to get rid of it for me. I wanted him to destroy it. Take it far away, so no one could find it. If the Church finds it, they might use it to prosecute me."

"If you were protecting yourself, I doubt they'd do that."

Elidad shook her head. "They hate me. They'd use anything they could against me. I don't know if I can carry it again."

Lucian's look turned serious. "Elidad, it could save your life."

"I don't know if I can, Lucian. I'm afraid to… I killed those men. I provoked them. I could've avoided that fight, but I made a choice and people ended up dead. *I* almost died, and I didn't care. Maybe I deserve to face the consequences…"

Lucian stepped around the counter, closer to Elidad, placing his hand at the small of her back.

"You always make the right decisions. I'm sure you did the right thing." He shook his head in dismay. "I'm sorry I found it. I'm sorry I gave it back to you."

Elidad buried her face in his chest. "Don't be sorry. You're trying to protect me. I appreciate it." Emotion riddled her body as she tried to hold back the tears.

"I feel like a jerk," Lucian confessed.

"Don't, you're trying to help. You couldn't have known," Elidad didn't want him to feel guilty. "I'm exhausted. I need to go take a nap." It was true, but it was also a good way to get out of having to discuss the gun further.

"I'm going back upstairs."

"You need help?" Lucian offered.

"No, I'll be okay."

"Before you go, I need to tell you: Aiden called, again."

Elidad froze.

"I answered, like you suggested."

"I did, didn't I?" Elidad remembered.

"I hope that's okay? I thought he must be getting worried; you haven't talked to him for a long time," Lucian said quickly.

"You're right," Elidad agreed. "He'd be getting suspicious. It was a good idea to answer. I'm just not ready to lie to him."

"I told him that you were still angry with him, for leaving, and you're busy with Isaac. I told him you'd call when you were ready."

"Well, that will be an easy story to stick to and easy for him to believe."

"I should've talked to you about it a little more before I answered," Lucian looked worried. "Every time he called, I imagined what it would feel like, to call you with no answer. Not knowing would be hard. I'd rather know you're angry, than know nothing."

"No, you're right. You did the right thing," Elidad agreed.

CHAPTER FORTY

Aiden's heart always picked up speed as his hands touched the black glass and his eyes were scanned in the retinal reader. The Bishop's warning was always in the back of his mind as he looked up at the vent that could distribute a lethal dose of gas.

"Good morning, Aiden," Vici welcomed.

Aiden continued staring up at the vent in the ceiling. Hopefully, Vici wouldn't glitch and poison him instead of opening the door.

Click.

Apparently, Vici was operating correctly. He'd made it to work on time today. No calling in dead.

"Good morning, Aiden." Daniel said from the other side of his clear-rimmed glasses, his eyes pressed into a line from the pressure of his smile.

"Good morning, Daniel. You're here early," Aiden noted.

"Yes, I received a call that we would be accepting a drop early," Daniel rubbed his hands together.

"Do we need to be here when there's a drop?" Aiden didn't remember that being a rule.

"Oh, no. That's not necessary," Daniel assured.

"Then, why are you here to receive it?" Curiosity brought Aiden's brow together.

Daniel looked over his shoulder, as if to check for someone listening. "Well, I've been waiting to find this out for a long time. I couldn't wait. I couldn't sleep. I had to get here as soon as I could."

"Find what out?" Aiden asked. Daniel's body language had Aiden feeling anxious, even though he didn't have a reason to.

"To be honest, Aiden, I'd like to see what's in the drop before I discuss it further with you. If you don't mind?" Suddenly Daniel's excitement passed, morphing into something different.

Aiden couldn't read this new emotion.

"Okay, no pressure." Aiden walked to the desk with the mainframe, placing his hand on the screen.

"Hello, Aiden," Vici said as Daniel went to the wall and pressed the unlock button on the door.

Aiden watched Daniel remove the tray and shut the door. When he turned back to the work station, he was chewing on his lower lip. Daniel moved across the open space with grace but placed the tray on the desk with unnecessary force.

"Good heavens, I'm so clumsy," Daniel muttered under his breath.

Aiden gave him space, allowing him to work.

Daniels fingers moved items around the tray until he found something. He withdrew a satin pouch from the pile of mismatched items and carefully opened it. Protected inside was a glass beaker. At the bottom of the beaker was a misshapen clump of metal. Aiden knew what it was from years of watching crime solving shows on TV.

A spent bullet.

The color drained from Daniel's face.

"Are you okay, Daniel?" Aiden asked as if he didn't know the answer.

"I… have to scan this," Daniel's response was robotic as he picked up the handheld Vici. Pressing a button on the side, a green light beamed from his hand. Vici processed the information with a low hum before answering.

"Hollow point Venom bullet." Vici's voice looked like a shock wave across Daniel's face. "Designer unknown. Construction indicates this bullet was shot from a crusader 10-millimeter handgun. Would you like to run ballistics?" Vici offered.

"No, Vici, that's not necessary. Thank you, Vici." Daniel's voice was a whisper.

"Would you like to discuss it with me now, Daniel?" The suspense was killing Aiden.

"Not really," Daniel admitted. For the first time since Aiden met him, Daniel's eyes were wide open.

"*Daniel*," Aiden pressed as lightly as he could.

"I— I— I don't know where to start. Or what to do," Daniel began. Setting the scanner down on the desk, he plopped into a chair. "Do you know why Elidad was excommunicated from the church, Aiden?"

The question took Aiden off guard. "No." Aiden's eyes snapped back to the spent bullet.

"Elidad had a confrontation with Pythious," Daniel said his name slowly.

"Pythious Delphi?" Aiden clarified.

"Your uncle," Daniel confirmed, locking eyes with Aiden.

"You know he's my uncle?" Aiden suddenly felt like he didn't want to be here for this conversation.

"I do," Daniel agreed.

"He's been missing for over a year," Aiden's chest tightened as the words left his mouth.

"I would assume, Aiden, he'll be missing forever," Daniel's face was grim. "And I hope, for Elidad's sake, he stays that way."

Anger seared through Aiden's veins.

"Why?" He demanded. "Why would you want him to stay missing? It's killed my family, not knowing."

"It will kill Elidad, to find him," Daniel kept his tone even.

"What's that supposed to mean?"

"Aiden, there's so much you didn't know about your uncle."

"How the hell do you know what I did and didn't know about him?" Aiden roared.

"Because, I have all the information," Daniel gestured to the shelves behind him. "A watcher was assigned to you when you were young, Aiden."

"What?" The shock took away Aiden's anger. "I'm human."

"You are," Daniel agreed. "But your father is associated with the Delphi."

"They're a prominent family, why would they have watchers?" Aiden began pacing the floor.

"In Greek mythology, *Python* was a snake. Some would call him a dragon."

"Pythious is a descendant of Python?" Aiden's pacing stopped.

"Yes, the Delphi family is of Python. Snake people." Daniel clarified.

"What do you mean?"

"Did you ever see Pythious with slit eyes? Like a snake's?" Daniel asked.

"He liked to weird people out," Aiden explained. "He'd wear strange contacts for fun."

"Or were those his normal eyes and, when they *looked* normal, that was when he wore contacts?" Daniel suggested. "Did you ever see his tongue?"

"No."

"Or his fangs?"

Aiden frowned. "He didn't have fangs. I've known him my whole life. I would've seen fangs."

"Not unless he wanted you to see them," Daniel disagreed. "They're like a snake's. They lay against the roof of his mouth. He can extend them if he wishes and keep them hidden the rest of the time. There's nothing wrong with them, though. The Delphi family, I mean." Daniel added.

Aiden's right eyebrow pressed downward. "But there was something wrong with Pythious?"

"Aiden, I'm sure he was a wonderful uncle."

"I'm sure he was a nice guy," Aiden mocked Daniel. "Sorry Elidad killed him."

Daniel's lips pressed together into their usual thin line.

"Is that it?" Aiden's voice boomed in the vast space. "My friend killed him, my uncle, and never bothered to tell me? She apparently didn't regret any of it." The truth pounded in Aiden's chest. "The Church knew about my family's pain and they all hid it from me, from my family?" Aiden was pacing again. If there was a close wall, he'd consider punching it.

"Aiden," Daniel's tone was even again. "She was defending herself."

Aiden turned to assess Daniel's face. "From what?"

"Pythious."

Aiden shook his head. "He wouldn't."

"He would. He did. She only killed him after he killed her."

Aiden's hands pressed over his face. "What are you saying? She's not dead."

"I wasn't there. All I have heard is rumor. Elidad confronted Pythious about dealing drugs in *Genus*. Pythious had young girls running Venom for him for years. A lot of young girls." Daniel took a breath. "One of his favorites was Elise, Elidad's friend. After a confrontation, somehow, they ended up out back, Pythious and his two bodyguards attacked Elidad. She was bitten, twice."

By the look on Daniel's face, Aiden felt like that should mean something to him.

"He delivered a lethal dose of Venom to Elidad."

"But she's alive and Pythious is missing," Aiden pointed out.

"She is," Daniel agreed. "No one knows how. There's no way she could've disposed of their bodies with the dose of Venom she'd endured, though. She was found in the parking lot behind *Genus*, blood on the ground, enough to prove murder but there were no bodies. No other evidence was found on the scene. The three men vanished, if you'd like to call them men.

Elidad was picked up and treated as an overdose. Her gun had been discharged, but no casings or bullets were found... until now." Daniel stared at the bullet in the glass beaker.

Aiden's eyes followed.

Daniel continued "The Church leaders always suspected her. They were looking for a reason to get rid of her; she broke their rules, preforming exorcisms. She's a woman; they didn't like the fact that she was so good at her job. She broke all their rules. So, between the incident and everything else, she was excommunicated."

Daniel took a labored breath. "With this find, it proves Elidad went there, intending to kill Pythious. There'd be no other reason to carry a Venom bullet." Daniel's eyes found Aiden's. "Premeditation of an untouchable is punishable by death."

"They chose me. They sent me… to tell her, to excommunicate her." Aiden realized. "They thought I knew, or that I would know, eventually."

"They didn't know your parents kept you in the dark about your father's family."

"Did my mother know?" Aiden couldn't imagine.

Daniel shrugged. "Maybe not in the beginning. But she knew what Pythious was."

"How can you be sure?" Aiden was skeptical.

"Because of how she died," Daniel looked like another person when he wasn't smiling.

"She died of an overdose, on pills, that's got nothing to do with Pythious."

"She died of an overdose, that's true. But it wasn't pills, Aiden. It was Venom." Daniel's eyes reluctantly left his hands to glimpse at Aiden.

"Pythious." The name hissed across Aiden's lips as moisture stung his vision.

"He was her supplier," Daniel confirmed.

Aiden leaned on a small rolling cart that held a couple books, some paperwork and various office supplies. His knuckles lightened under the strain of his grip. Betrayal spilled out from his eyes and streaked down his face.

"Rhaaaaaaaa!" He growled, lifting the cart into the air, hurling it across the marble floor where it came crashing down. The noise shattered the silence, echoing through the shelves of information.

Daniel stood from his chair and began to pick up the scattered mess.

Aiden rubbed the sadness from his face with vigorous hands. He took in a breath before kneeling to pick up the debris.

"I'll get it, Daniel."

"I will help you." Daniel already had a stack of papers in his arms. "It must be hard, to learn these things now. I'm sorry, Aiden. I don't want to hide anything from you. You can learn anything you want, yourself. All you have to do is ask." Daniel's eyes drifted to Vici.

With that insinuation, Aiden knew instantly why Elidad hadn't gone to see Leucosia. Not knowing was easier. Daniel, giving him this tidbit of his past, ripped open a wound. This little secret was nothing like the burden Elidad carried and yet, it was enough. He didn't want to know the rest.

Aiden stood, straightening himself. He walked over to the black screen. He placed his hand on the cold, hard glass.

"Hello, Aiden." Vici's voice was so pleasant, it made the tension in the room unbearable.

"Vici, I need Aiden Tabor's file."

CHAPTER FORTY-ONE

Elidad couldn't see anything. She was surrounded by an oblivion of absent space. Reaching her hands forward, there was nothing. Taking a step forward, she stumbled upon the inability to distinguish up from down. The ground beneath her was firm under her feet; when her shoes made contact, the sound echoed around her.

In the distance, whispered voices drifted toward her. She stopped moving, straining to hear. More whispers drifted through the thick nothingness. Then another, closer this time. Elidad turned her body toward each voice. The whispers moved all around, she could feel the hair on the back of her neck rise, demanding attention. The hissing voices around her, moving in and out, weren't speaking words she understood.

Her breath came fast through her lips. There was no way to defend herself. Elidad turned from side to side. With nothing on the horizon to reference her movement, she couldn't tell if she was making a full circle.

In the unclear surroundings, a black figure began to emerge. There were no footsteps to announce the figure's apparition; it was eerily silent. The hazy vapor that clouded her vision began to pull away, opening the distance between her and the shadowed figure.

Coming into focus, Elidad swallowed a scream.

She'd know the grim outline of the Shadow Man anywhere. He moved forward, toward her. She tried to turn to run, but her feet were bound by something. Glancing down at her body, she wore a fitted white gown that hugged her legs and torso. Beaded and intricately designed, the dress flowed out behind her. With the lifting of the fog, she realized her eyes were still inhibited.

A veil covered her face. A veil to accompany the wedding dress she now wore.

She threw it back. The movement drew her attention to her arm. Black veins spiraled from her shoulder, down her arm, reaching all the way to her fingertips. Turning her arm over, she could see the black web had continued to weave across her skin.

The Shadow Man lifted his hand, palm up. Expectant, like a gentleman. Elidad's heart thundered in her ears. Without a thought, her dark hand reached forward in response. Every time he'd touched her, her skin caught on fire, flesh boiled away.

This time, Elidad couldn't stop herself.

The need to touch him burned in her shoulder, raced through her skin and outstretched her hand. Almost as if in response to her thought, the Shadow Man glided toward her, closing the space that separated them. Two arm lengths away, he presented no defining features. Elidad couldn't explain how she knew he was a man. She just knew, the way she knew things in her dreams. Elidad had been terrified of him, in person and in sleep. Now, her heart raced with anticipation. She could feel energy and heat from his palm pressing into her fingertips, even though it was inches away.

The pressure was unbearable, the draw to touch him was beckoning. She wanted to know what he felt like.

When her skin touched his, an explosion shocked her awake.

Elidad stood in the foyer of Abraham's house. Leaning against the casing of the study, she examined the fireplace. Her mind flickered back to her first dream of the Shadow Man: the searing pain in her hands when she'd clawed at his face, trying to free herself before he choked her to death. Elidad pulled a worn piece of paper from her pocket and unfolded Emily's drawing of the Shadow Man, remembering the little girl's words.

"The one who wouldn't go away, the one inside me, that isn't him." Emily pointed at the drawing of the Shadow Man. "The one inside me was afraid of him."

"Then who is this?" Elidad looked down at the dark figure with burning green eyes.

"I don't know. The one who wouldn't go away thought about him. He was afraid of him. He never said his name."

The crayon drawing in Elidad's hand stared back at her. His green eyes reminded her of Abraham's when he'd tried to give her a clue in this office. Without that clue, she never would've found the only key they had. Where would they find the other three?

Elidad stuffed the drawing back into her pocket and walked into the entry. Standing in front of the floor length mirror, she took off her shirt. Under her black, lace bra, her wounds were looking better, closed over and healing. However, the gray skin around them was growing. The black veins, once small webs, now reached out to her shoulder in thick lines. Why was it spreading? She was getting better. She felt well enough to come back to Abraham's house to get her things. Elidad finally had energy again. She could almost make it through an entire day without needing a nap. Elidad had continued staying at Isaac's house with Lucian. If something happened, he could've helped her. But, the poison wasn't gone, and she wasn't sure what that meant.

Maybe this is why Leucosia couldn't see her future. Maybe there wasn't a lot left to see. Elidad reached up to touch the dead skin on her chest. There was no feeling in the tissue. That fact alone made her mouth salivate with a sick churn in her stomach.

It was dead.

Elidad threw her shirt back on. Only one being could give her answers before she died. She was going to get those answers, one way or another.

CHAPTER FORTY-TWO

There were boxes on the tabletops and papers strewn across the floor. Aiden sat on a ladder, stacks of information on the steps above and around him.

Daniel quietly approached. "Aiden, do you need anything from me?" His eyes took inventory of the mess.

"My whole life is in here," Aiden held up the papers in his hands.

Daniel nodded. "Because of your relationship to your father and uncle, you were watched from time to time. Most of your life, you didn't need a watcher because you attended St. Augustine's. Abraham and a couple others kept an eye on you."

"Pythious…" the thought escaped Aiden.

"Aiden, people, or *creatures* can be many things. Just because he was a monster to some, doesn't mean he couldn't be loving and kind, to you." Daniel picked up a stack of pictures.

"He was kind to me. He was my uncle, but if this is true," Aiden shook his head, "he deserved his fate."

"He did deserve it," Daniel agreed.

"What happened to his body?" Aiden asked.

"There's only one person who can answer that."

"Elidad," her name slipped across Aiden's lips. He couldn't imagine how that conversation would go.

"There might be another," Daniel suggested.

Aiden looked up at Daniel, hopeful, "Who?"

"Not exactly human, but she could know. Her name is Sophia. She was friends with Elidad and Elise. She introduced Elise to Pythious. She's the one who put this whole thing into motion."

"Sophia… as in Leucosia's daughter?" Aiden clarified.

"Yes, that's right. You've met her, before," Daniel remembered.

"Yes, once or twice," Aiden agreed. He didn't want to tell Daniel that Sophia was in Rome. He needed to keep as much distance from Elidad—and her life in New York—as he could.

"Then you know how her power works?" Daniel assumed.

"Yes."

"She's had to have touched Elidad since that night. She probably knows."

"She probably does," Aiden choked down that truth. He couldn't let Daniel see the anger that was building in his chest. A volcano of rage. "I found these in Pythious' things." Aiden held up two coins, changing the subject. "Do you know what they are?"

"They are Delphi coins," Daniel said. "There's supposedly four of them. We've only collected the two. They're just relics, significant to the Delphi family. They date back to the ruins of Delphi and are believed to have been owned by Pythia, before she was destroyed by Apollo."

"At the navel of the Earth," Aiden's voice sounded foreign, to himself.

Daniel's smile returned at Aiden's understanding. "Yes. You know the story?"

"Pythious used to tell me that story when I was a boy."

Daniel's face fell at Aiden's memory. "I'm sorry. It's unimaginable, what you must be going through."

"Can I hold on to these?" Aiden asked.

"I told you, you're able to carry any and all restricted items, as long as you are using them for work. As far as I'm concerned, they belong to your father's family, anyway. No matter how undesirable a family is, they're still family. I don't see why you can't take them. Just bring them back."

"Thank you, Daniel. That's kind of you to say." Aiden stared at the coins in his palm. "Daniel, what will you do with the bullet you collected?"

"I give it to my supervisor, of course." Daniel's lips timidly pulled upward when Aiden's eyes darted up to his.

"You'll give it to *me*," Aiden understood.

"You *are* my supervisor," Daniel agreed.

"Who else knows what it is and that it's here?" Aiden frowned.

"No one."

"How did you know it was coming? You knew before it came down." Aiden replayed it in his mind.

"It was found in the parking lot, supposedly buried in a wall." Daniel leaned toward Aiden, lowering his voice. "Aiden, they searched the area after the incident for weeks. They would've found it before now. Someone wanted it to be found *now*. Elidad will be in trouble if they link that bullet to her gun."

"How? They have no bodies? Pythious is still missing, they can't prove he's dead."

"Remember, I told you, there was enough blood to prove murder, they just didn't have a murder weapon. The ballistics for Elidad's gun are on file. They'll have enough to nail her to the wall."

"Since when does Elidad have a gun?" Aiden stood, rubbing his tired eyes.

Daniel sat at the base of the shelf. "Abraham found a designer: a Crusader, with the skills he desired, to customize the weapon. When Elidad's training was complete, Abraham gave her the gun for protection. She's capable with a sword, and proficient with hand to hand combat, but the gun allowed for more distance between her and her attackers. Abraham hoped it would keep her safer.

The gun was blessed by the Holy Fathers; all guns carried by Crusaders are. A Crusader's gun is able to shoot all kinds of bullets crafted here at the Vatican. They are specifically customized for their targets: silver for werewolves, light for vampires, holy water for demons, that sort of thing. You get the idea."

"So, they have bullets to kill snake people?"

"No, as you said, the Delphi family is a prominent family. There'd be no reason to commission a bullet like that. It would never be allowed. She must have had it made, but I don't know anyone who would take part in its production. Making it would be a death sentence. Having possession of it would be a death sentence."

"They don't know if Elidad ever had it," Aiden thought aloud.

"When a Crusader is commissioned a firearm, a spent bullet is analyzed and the record stored with Vici. If you run ballistics on that bullet, Vici will know if it's been shot from Elidad's gun."

Aiden stared at Daniel. "That's why you didn't run the ballistics?"

"I don't want to sentence Elidad to death, do you?" Daniel's eyes searched Aiden's face.

"No. Of course not."

"Well, it's in your hands now," Daniel's words were heavy with meaning.

"I don't know what's the right thing to do here," Aiden admitted.

"Maybe you should spend a day or two praying about it," Daniel suggested. "I'm sure you'll come to the right decision."

The phone rang, Aiden looked down at the name: Elidad. His heartbeat immediately sped up. How would he talk to her now? Would he ask her about his uncle? Would she be there with Lucian? What would he tell her about the coins?

"Hey, stranger?" Aiden tried to sound casual.

"Hey, sorry I haven't gotten back to you sooner. It's been crazy with Isaac and everything." *Like almost being killed by a demon.*

"It's been a long time, Elidad. I was starting to worry about you."

"Yeah, sorry. I'm a jerk."

"What's really going on?" Aiden demanded.

"Nothing," she lied. "Really." Elidad pulled the collar of her T-shirt down to reveal the black veins crawling across her chest. Her fingers felt the scabs covering the holes in her chest.

"If you change your mind, and want to tell me, I'm always here," Aiden gave her a reminder.

She decided to ignore it, entirely. "How's the new job?"

Aiden looked for the right word. *"Interesting."*

"Oh? What do they have you doing?"

"I'm in charge of records."

Elidad's laugh echoed through the receiver. "Did you find mine, yet?"

"I saw the file, but I didn't read it."

"I told you it would be big," she reminded him.

"Bigger," he corrected.

"Why haven't you read it?" She asked.

"Doesn't seem right," he admitted. "If you wanted me to know something about your past, I'd expect you to tell me yourself."

Tension buzzed through the line.

Pythious' smug face flashed in Elidad's mind. How could such an evil man be related to the person on the other end of this phone? What would Aiden do if he found out? Suddenly, she was thankful Aiden hadn't pried into her past. Who knows what the Church leaders placed there, certainly all their assumptions about what happened that night.

Aiden allowed the quiet to sink in.

Did Elidad know Pythious was his uncle? She might not. She didn't know who his parents were. She only knew about his life at school and in the church.

"I might have found something," Aiden broke the silence.

"What's that?" Elidad was relieved for the change.

"They're called Delphi coins. They've been in records."

Elidad cringed at the name *Delphi.* "What makes them so interesting?"

"There's a story about them. The coins are supposed to open the Navel of the World, in Delphi."

"What's the Navel of the Earth?" Elidad asked.

"Supposedly, the Navel of the *World* holds a key."

"A key, like *our* key?" Elidad assumed.

"I don't know. Maybe. It's the best thing I've got. We haven't had any other leads. It's worth trying."

"How do they open this *Navel of the Earth*?"

"I'm not sure," Aiden admitted. "Maybe my father will know."

Elidad's mouth felt like the desert. "Your father?"

"Yeah, he has a coin. I'm going to need it, if I go to Delphi."

"You're going to talk to him?"

"If I have to. If it's to save the world from utter destruction, do I have a choice?"

"Do you want me to go?" Elidad offered. "So you don't have to see him."

"I'm an adult. I can handle seeing my father. I'm not sure I want you to meet him," Aiden admitted.

Guilt raced through Elidad. "I'm not a *meet the parents* kind of friend," she forced a laugh.

"He's not the *meet your friends* kind of parent," Aiden countered. "I don't want you to think differently about me because of who I'm related to."

Elidad's mind flashed to Pythious again.

"I wouldn't." *She meant it.* "I know who you are."

"That's funny. I thought you forgot I existed, all together." Aiden tried to sound like he was teasing.

"Aiden, I said I was sorry. I've been busy. Isaac is still on the verge of crazy. He won't come home, he still thinks there are demons here. You'd know… if you were here." She hated laying it on thick, but he didn't need to know about the attack.

"Here? As in, you're at Isaac's house?" Aiden tried to sound casual.

Elidad cringed. "Yeah. Lucian needed some… help."

"*Help*," Aiden repeated.

"Are you going to come see your dad, then?" The thought sparked into Elidad's mind.

"Yeah, I'll have to go see Donald," Aiden agreed. "I just have to figure out how to swing it. They're going to wonder why I'm back in New York, so soon."

"Tell them you're coming to check on me," Elidad offered.

"I don't think that will help."

"What's that supposed to mean?" Elidad's anger flared.

"They made it pretty clear, I'm not supposed to hang out with you," Aiden said carefully.

Elidad's laugh was fake this time. "Oh, finally!"

Aiden frowned. "What do you mean, finally? I thought you'd be mad."

She snorted. "Are you kidding? They hate how I think outside the box and break all their rules. They're worried I might be a good influence on you. Think about it, Jesus was executed for breaking all the rules and going against what the priests thought... I take it as a compliment."

"Are you comparing yourself to Jesus, now?" Aiden joked.

"Not even close, but I try to live like him when I can."

CHAPTER FORTY-THREE

The man at the door eyed Elidad. "Are you on the list?"

"No, I'm not. I'm a friend of Lucian De Luscious. You know him. He drives the Audi R8. I need to speak with Donald Tabor. I'll only be a minute."

The doorman remained stoic. He lifted his hand to an ear piece that was barely peeking out of his left ear.

"There's a woman who would like to speak with Mr. Tabor. She says her name is Elidad." He waited for a response. "Yes, sir," he looked Elidad up and down, again. "Go on up. Someone will meet you in the entryway to escort you."

"Thanks." Elidad waved her hand over her shoulder as she passed.

In the foyer, the same two guards stood on either side of the creepy doors. The snake handles made Elidad just as uncomfortable as they had the last time she was here.

"How long until my escort gets here?" Elidad demanded.

The guards didn't respond.

"I've been waiting here for ten minutes. This is ridiculous." Elidad crossed her arms. Still no response.

"Fine. Screw this," Elidad stormed toward the doors, reaching her hand forward to open them.

The cobra handles lunged at Elidad when she got too close. She jumped back to avoid being bitten. The black metal had morphed into smooth, black-scaled skin, fluidly rocking as the snake drifted back and forth, preparing to strike.

One of the guards smiled. "Go ahead. Go on in," he mocked.

The serpent's red eyes were pinned on Elidad as she paced the floor. One of the billowed heads lashed out. Nowhere close to Elidad, but her heart thudded in response anyway.

Elidad stepped backward when the doors pushed open from the inside. The same demon that'd escorted her to Donald the first time came strolling through the doors. The heads spun toward him with their fangs extended, considering him only for a breath before turning back to Elidad.

"What are those damn things?" Elidad spat.

The guard smiled. "Delphi guardians. Ancient magic." He turned to the snakes, speaking a word with a slithered tongue. The snakes moved back into their original position, hardening into lifeless handles.

"Follow me," he commanded.

The snakes didn't move, but once again, Elidad felt like their beady eyes followed her. "No wonder why I didn't like those damn things," Elidad muttered.

"They don't like you either," one of the door guards called after her as she walked into the casino.

People laughed and shouted from every corner of the room. The sound of chips clacking together was distinct over the sound of music coming from a band on stage. The music was different than when she and Lucian had been here. It was some kind of pop-funk blend. It was catchy; the kind of music that would put you in a good mood, if an oversized cobra hadn't just tried to kill you.

As they approached the elevator tucked away in the back, the doors drew open. Elidad followed her escort into the confined space.

"What's your name?" Elidad asked her guide as the doors drew shut.

"Does it matter?" His voice was low and abrasive, like gravel.

Elidad shrugged. "Not to me, *demon boy*. I can make it up as I go."

His shoulders barely moved, a silent cringe. "Acoose. They call me Acoose."

The elevator opened. Acoose stepped into the office, Elidad following. Donald was sitting behind his desk; three demon guards were staggered around the room. Elidad guessed they were stationed here because of her spontaneous visit.

Elidad strode across the floor, slipping a bag from her shoulder and depositing it onto a coffee table. She slid her hand inside of it. Simultaneously, the three guards pulled guns, pointing them at her.

She held up her free hand, palm facing them.

"Easy. I have a gift for Donald. That's all." She continued to slide her hand into her bag, removing a bottle. She placed the glass, filled with honey colored liquid, on the table.

"Balvenie?" Donald waved a finger; the guards holstered their weapons.

Elidad shrugged. "I heard you like whiskey."

"Most would interpret that as Crown, or Jack, not a forty-thousand-dollar bottle."

"You bought it," Elidad confessed.

Donald looked like he wasn't following.

"The chips you gave me," Elidad explained. "I won. So, it's your money, I didn't need it."

"What do you want, Elidad?" Donald demanded.

"Right, down to business. I like it." Elidad sat on the stiff sofa, her body turned toward Donald at his desk. "I want your Delphi coin."

Donald's eyes narrowed. He moved away from his desk and sat on the couch across from Elidad.

"It's not enough for you to take my brother from me, you want to take a family heirloom from me, too? There's no limit to your reign of terror, is there?"

"I didn't take anyone from you and he wasn't your brother," Elidad glared back. "Unless, I missed your split tongue?"

"I wasn't born a Delphi, but they are my family and Pythious *was* my brother, until you killed him."

His anger waivered Elidad's confidence.

"Did you know, Elidad, his mother is still alive, and will go to her grave, not knowing what happened to her son?"

Elidad shrugged to hide the remorse rising in the back of her throat. "I guess she should've kept a better handle on him. When you submerge yourself into the life of a drug dealer, terrible things can happen. It's a dangerous world."

"The most dangerous part of that life was you," Donald said pointedly.

"You want to make him the victim, but he wasn't."

"That's hard to believe, considering he's been missing for over a year, and you're the one sitting here. You *were* the last one to see him alive."

"No, I wasn't," Elidad disagreed. "I have no idea what happened to him. If I was the last one to see him alive, how did I get rid of his body when I was overdosing in the parking lot? Did you forget that part of the story? Pythious bit me. *I* should've died; he'd pumped me full of enough V to kill an elephant."

"Pity," Donald answered.

Elidad ignored him. "I couldn't even move my own body, let alone three others. Since you know everything, explain that. How did I do it? Because if you *could* explain it, I *wouldn't* be sitting here with you."

"That is a great question, isn't it?" Donald spoke his thoughts aloud. "How did you live through that much V? You should've been dead by the time they found you. One can only assume you had help to dispose of the bodies and the evidence… But that doesn't explain how you lived."

"Maybe I'm immune."

Donald's cold eyes locked with hers. "I doubt that. Maybe Pythious didn't bite you at all. After you killed three men, you had the sense to kill *yourself*, using Pythious' Venom. A poetic death, inspired by guilt. Another option is… you're an addict. Sometimes, addicts hurt people when their desperate for drugs."

"I'm not an addict," Elidad assured.

Donald eyed her arms. "*Something* happened that night and, eventually, it will come to light and you'll pay for what you did." Recognition flashed in his eyes. "Tell me, Elidad, does Aiden know that you're responsible for Pythious' disappearance?"

Elidad couldn't control the tension in her brow.

Donald's lips curled. "I didn't think so. Aiden may have walked away from his father, but he's not heartless. Pythious was his favorite uncle. I'd imagine he won't take the news well when he finds out." Donald's fingertips rapped the leather of the sofa. "Does Aiden know you're here, now?"

"He knows you have the Delphi coin and he's coming to get it from you," she answered.

Donald's face turned condescending, "So… no, he doesn't know you're here. Does he know we've met before?"

Elidad shrugged, "Does it matter?"

"I thought you were friends? You didn't tell your friend that you met his father?" Donald sat back into the black leather, crossing one leg over the other. "You were here with Lucian De Luscious, is that the reason you don't want Aiden to know about our meeting?"

"I don't have anything to hide from Aiden."

"Except for the fact that you met me and you killed his uncle?"

Elidad shifted her weight. "The only reason I didn't tell Aiden that we met is because I know he'd prefer to leave you in the past."

"The same way you'd like to leave Pythious' murder in the past."

"I came here for the coin so Aiden wouldn't have to face you. That's what friends do."

"You came here so he wouldn't have to face me, or to hide the fact that we've met?" Donald suggested. "Secrets between friends find a way of coming to light, Elidad."

"We don't have secrets between us."

Donald's eyes moved to the bottle of whiskey on the coffee table. "I can see… you knew it was my favorite."

"I thought it was a good trade for the Delphi coin," Elidad explained.

His eyes came back to her. "If Aiden wants the scarab, he can come get it himself. I won't relinquish it to the likes of you. It belongs to our family."

"It belongs to the Delphi family," Elidad corrected, "and you don't claim Aiden."

A smug look settled across his face. "Aiden considers himself *part* of that family."

"He doesn't know what he considers himself. He doesn't know what being a Delphi means. Until he met me, he thought sirens were myth and possessions were legend. He probably doesn't know snake people exist."

"With a small child, it was easier to keep the family's secret by hiding it. When he was old enough to know, he'd already made up his mind… he'd chosen the *Church*." Donald's eyes radiated anger. "Over his family, he chose *your* God and his measly, meaningless life."

"It must be hard, for someone like you," Elidad observed. "How could you understand? You must feel betrayed."

"Betrayed doesn't quite encompass the feeling," he asserted.

"His life isn't meaningless."

Donald snorted.

"Does it make you wonder?" Elidad asked.

"What?" He spat.

"Do you wonder why your wife killed herself and your son left you? I'm sure you're the type of person who blames everyone else, instead of looking in the mirror," Elidad suggested.

Donald's eyes burned with emotion.

"Get her out of here," he demanded.

Elidad stood. "I want that coin."

The two closest guards moved in, Elidad looked over her shoulder and saw that Acoose remained by the door.

"I told you, if Aiden wants the coin, he can come get it himself. Until then, you can get out of my sight."

The demons pressed in, one reached forward and placed his hand on Elidad's shoulder. "Let's go."

"Take your hand off me," Elidad demanded.

"Move it," he tugged on her arm.

Elidad curled into his body; using his weight, she hurled him to the floor, pulling her knife from her boot, she thrust it into his chest. His skin turned black as his mouth gaped.

The other demon rushed at her, his arms meant to close around her shoulders. Elidad dropped low; using his momentum, she pushed hard into his legs, sending him into the air over her back. She turned to stomp on his chest but he'd rolled away. Popping back to his feet, the demon paused long enough for Elidad to see Acoose, still holding his position by the door. Elidad's grip tightened around the handle of her knife when the demon charged her again.

Elidad dodged the first blow meant for her chest. She kicked his legs, but he was ready for it; distributing his weight, he remained standing. The next blow caught her in the gut, her breath heaving out of her lungs, folding her body over his arm. Elidad threw a knee into his groin, expelling a painful hiss from his lips.

Sinking to the ground the demon pulled a gun from his sports coat. Urgency ran through Elidad's veins as she slipped her hand inside her shirt and withdrew her gun. She expertly placed a bullet between his eyes. Ash sprayed from the back of his scalp as his eyes rolled into the back of his head. His grey skin turned black as he dissolved into a pile of dust at her feet.

Finger on the trigger, Elidad spun her extended arm toward Donald, the muzzle pointed at his forehead.

"Stay there, Acoose. He'll be dead by the time you get to me, and you'll be right behind him."

Donald's face was smooth. "Go ahead, Elidad. Leave Aiden to another tragedy."

"I don't think he'll consider your death a tragedy," Elidad analyzed.

"Good, then another disappearance won't affect him." Donald's lips pursed together to form a straight line. He didn't have Aiden's full lips.

"I didn't come here to kill you," Elidad said, allowing her gun to fall forward on her finger. "I said, I could show myself out. I asked him to take his hands off me…" Spinning the pistol back into her palm, she redirected it at Acoose, "I don't have to send you back to Hell, too, do I?"

Amusement flashed in his face, though he remained stoic, "I'll keep my hands to myself."

Elidad re-holstered her gun.

CHAPTER FORTY-FOUR

Elidad was leaning over a box of random antiques when the bell chimed. She and Lucian turned to see the customer entering the shop.

Blonde hair and radiant blue eyes moved in her direction.

"Aiden?" Elidad whispered.

"Hey," he timidly smiled back.

Elidad's stomach felt like it was on the floor. "Wha— What are you doing here?"

"I told you, I needed to come to the city," he reminded, his eyes flashed to Lucian.

"I wasn't expecting you so soon. You didn't call," She protested, embracing him. If felt strange, hugging him in front of Lucian.

"You wouldn't have answered, if I did," Aiden joked. In reality, he didn't want anyone to connect his visit to New York with Elidad. "Lucian," Aiden nodded.

"Hello, Aiden."

"Elidad, I'm only going to be here for one night. My flight leaves in the morning."

"Oh."

"I'm going to see my father, tonight."

Elidad nodded, "Okay."

"I want you to go with me," Aiden suggested.

"Okay." Elidad's mind was screaming *no*. "When?"

"Now."

"Alright," she agreed. She turned to Lucian. "I'll call you, later."

He smiled. "Sounds good," he turned to Aiden. "Too bad you're not staying longer."

Aiden doubted his sincerity.

Lucian offered a hand to shake. "I'm sure it won't be that long until we see you again."

Aiden shook it, glancing at Elidad. "I hope not."

Elidad bit her lip, unable to decide whether to tell Aiden she met Donald. The internal struggle kept her occupied until their cab stopped in front of the building.

"They probably won't let me in," Elidad suggested.

"Why?" Aiden's brow creased.

"You know my reputation with demons."

"We're going to see my father. He owns a casino," Aiden said.

"A casino guarded by demons," Elidad added.

"How do you know?" Aiden asked.

Panic flared. Elidad gestured to the guard at the door.

"You see the big guy, with the ashy skin? See how he looks a little different?"

"Yeah," Aiden agreed.

"Demon." When Elidad spoke the word, the guard's eyes landed on Elidad, his hand went right to his ear and he started speaking into his sleeve.

Acoose stepped out of the front door with three angry looking men behind him.

"Elidad," his loud voice boomed. "What can I help you with?"

Aiden stepped forward. "I'm Aiden Tabor, I want to see Donald."

The guards shot glances to one another, Acoose held his stoic position.

"You may enter, Aiden, she stays outside." Acoose said.

"She goes with me. It's not a question," Aiden was firm.

Acoose's eyes searched Aiden's. "What about her weapons?"

"What about them?" Aiden's voice was condescending.

"She needs to leave the gun," Acoose said.

The word *gun* changed Aiden in a way Elidad couldn't describe. Even with his back to her, she could see it.

"She's my guest. No demands will be made of my guest."

"You can't insure our safety," Acoose growled.

"As long as you don't pick a fight, I'll be on my best behavior," Elidad assured.

Acoose looked from Elidad to Aiden.

"Very, well. Follow me." He turned toward the door, the other demons in tow. "No one place a hand on the woman," he ordered.

Elidad smirked to herself.

The elevator doors opened to Donald's office. The entourage exited the elevator. Four demons were stationed in the corners of the room, making for a total of eight, counting Acoose.

"Well, doth mine eyes deceive me?" Donald sneered. "My wayward offspring."

"Hello, Donald," Aiden's cool voice painted disdain through the room.

"I see your choice of acquaintances hasn't improved over time," Donald assessed.

"I could say the same for you," Aiden looked around the room. "Is the army really necessary?"

"One can't be too careful, when you bring someone as dangerous as the *Great Elidad* to my place," he glanced at Elidad.

She was surprised Donald wasn't throwing her under the bus. Maybe he'd thought she would've come clean to Aiden before now.

"You have my word, she won't harm anyone, not even you," Aiden assured.

Donald sat silently. His hands came up to fold in front of him, his elbows resting on the desk. He flicked his finger and all the guards, but for Acoose, filed out of the room.

"What do you want, Aiden?" Donald demanded.

"I want the Delphi scarab," Aiden answered.

Donald's eyes flickered to Elidad. "You want it, or *she* does?"

"It's not your concern."

Donald's eyes narrowed. "Not my concern? You want to take one of the last things Pythious gave me and it's none of my concern?"

Elidad cringed at Pythious' name. It wasn't just a Delphi coin; it was *Pythious'* Delphi coin. *She wished she hadn't agreed to come.*

"You owe me," Aiden's voice was smooth.

Elidad recognized this. *He was angry.*

"I don't owe you anything." Donald's words were as dangerously fluid as Aiden's. "I brought you into this life, you owe me... and how do you repay me? By throwing away your life for a ridiculous cause. And now you ask me to give up one of the few things I have left of my brother? For what? To give to *her*?" His hate for Elidad was obvious. "Do you know who she is? Do you know what she did?"

Elidad wished she could crawl in a hole. This wasn't how she wanted Aiden to find out.

"I know exactly who she is," Aiden assured.

"Do you know what she did to Pythious?" Donald hissed.

Elidad stared at the back of Aiden's head, waiting for him to turn around and demand an answer.

"I know what she's been accused of," Aiden's words were firm.

Donald dramatically stood out of his chair.

"You know! And you still associate with her? I guess it shouldn't surprise me. You left your family for the Church; you don't care about anyone you left behind. You're just proving how deep their brainwashing goes."

"What about *your* brainwashing, Don? Would you be happier if I stayed out of the Church, got married and bullied my wife into killing herself?"

Donald put his hand into his pocket and threw the contents at Aiden. Aiden caught it in his hand. Opening his palm, he revealed the Delphi coin.

"Take it." Donald said. "May it be a reminder of the family you left behind and the criminal you're harboring."

Aiden turned, his eyes catching Elidad's for the first time. Pain radiated from them.

"Let's go."

Acoose stood at the back of the office. He'd already pushed the button to summon the elevator. As the doors drew open, Elidad and Aiden stepped inside.

CHAPTER FORTY-FIVE

"**W**hy did you book a hotel? You know you could've stayed at Abraham's house, if you needed to." Elidad broke the silence as Aiden used his key card to open the door. *Maybe he intended to confront her about Pythious and didn't expect to stay with her long.*

"I didn't know if you'd be… busy," Aiden's thought trailed off.

Elidad searched his eyes. His thoughts indicated Lucian.

He pushed the door open, flicking on the lights.

Elidad followed. "Nice place."

"I had a nicer one, but I canceled it an hour ago."

Elidad smirked.

"What?" Aiden frowned.

"You're getting good at the cloak and dagger game. That's also why you didn't stay with me. You're not *allowed.*"

Aiden stepped toward her, his hand moved to clasp the back of her neck.

Chills swam through her veins in response. Aiden's clear blue eyes glimmered with emotion. She wished she knew the complexity of his thoughts.

"Aiden, I—" how could she explain?

He pulled her to his chest. Her fingers dug into his shirt, gripping him like a life preserver. She forgot how good it felt to be this close to him. Heat swelled in her, remorse pushed away by the desire to be close to him. She pulled away to look in his eyes; she needed to say something. Her words were lost in his eyes. She remembered how close she came to kissing him before he left, and how much she regretted not doing so. He was here now, though. She stared at his lips.

Aiden's hand slipped inside the back of her shirt, the motion sending sparks shooting through her.

With one brisk movement, he gripped her gun and removed it from its holster. All the emotion she felt fell, like the blood in her face. He held it up, the rose gold glistening in the room's light.

"Is this it?" He demanded.

"Is this what?" She whispered.

"Is this the gun you used to kill Pythious?"

"Aiden…"

"Answer the question!"

Remorse turned to anger in one frantic heartbeat.

"I shot him," she blurted. The wound in her shoulder burned with rage. She could feel the black veins tear down her arm. "And he deserved it."

Aiden's brow creased. "He was my uncle."

"I didn't know that, and even if I did, it wouldn't have changed anything. He was a terrible person, just like your father."

"Thanks for the honesty," Aiden turned, walking to a desk on the adjacent wall. He placed the gun on the surface with a heavy sound, sinking into the chair next to it.

"He killed me."

Aiden glanced up at her. "You're still alive."

"He bit me with a lethal dose of Venom. As I was dying, I knew I needed to take that son-of-a-bitch with me."

Aiden picked up the weapon, releasing the clip. He numbly laid the gun back on the desk. "Why didn't you tell me?"

"I just found out he was your uncle. What was I supposed to do? Call you up and say: Hey friend, by the way, I just found out that someone I shot a year ago was your uncle. Sorry about his disappearance, he's probably dead, and if anyone finds out, I'll be dead too."

"*Probably?*" Aiden's eyes left the gun to meet hers.

"I was overdosing. I don't know what happened to him. I never lied about that. I don't know where their bodies are."

Aiden's eyes moved back to the gun. "Who made the bullet for you?"

Elidad didn't respond.

"Who?" He demanded.

"I'm not going to tell you that."

"Why? I have a right to know. Don't you *owe* me that?"

"I might," she agreed. "But the person who helped me doesn't need to lose their life, too."

Aiden shook his head. "You think I'm going to turn you in?" He rubbed his face with his hands. "Is that what you think of me?"

The anger pulsing in her chest began to fall away at his response. "Why wouldn't you?"

"Because, you're right. He *did* deserve it. He *was* a terrible *person*—snake—thing. And… I believe you, Elidad. I believe in you."

His words cut through her, more effectively than any demon's talons could. She blinked away the sting that welled behind her eyelashes. "I'm sorry… I'm sorry it was me."

"I'm glad you lived through it."

"I'm not sure I am," she admitted.

"You never would've gotten to know me, if you'd died that night," he reminded her.

"Maybe that would've been better for you…" *And me.*

"And never meet the *Great Elidad?*" He mocked.

"Shut up."

He smiled back.

"Seriously, if you turn me in, I'll understand."

"I don't have any proof. Besides, why would I? Think of what a great slave you'll make."

"Seriously?"

"This blackmail is too good to let go of. Think of all the things you can do for me." He sat back in the chair to ponder.

"I think I'd rather die."

"If you die, who will help me find the next key?"

"Did you really find the next one?"

"Someone had to work while you were here, hanging out with Lucian."

"Come on," Elidad rolled her eyes. "I've been busy." *Almost dying.*

"Yeah, yeah, I've heard it all before."

"You think you've got a lead, though? For real?" Elidad pressed.

Aiden flipped the scarab in the air catching it in his hand. "Only one way to find out."

"What are you going to do?"

"We," he corrected.

"We?"

Aiden's eyes lit up. "We leave for Greece in the morning."

CHAPTER FORTY-SIX

Elidad and Aiden's plane landed in Greece late. Flying coach, their seats were separate; Elidad was towards the front and Aiden, the back. Aiden said it was because he bought the tickets last minute, but she knew better. To help ensure Aiden wouldn't be seen with her, Elidad wore a baseball cap and large sunglasses.

Pushing through the crowded airport, a driver stood in the vestibule with a sign that read: *Aiden Tabor*. Elidad went around the outside of the SUV and slipped inside without the driver noticing.

Eventually, the driver opened the door for Aiden allowing him to climb in.

Aiden smiled. "I was wondering what had happened to you."

"We wouldn't want you to get in trouble," she beamed.

"I assume that's inevitable," he shrugged. "I've never been fired from a job before."

"I missed having you around," the words escaped Elidad before her mind could hold them back.

The stunned look on his face didn't keep his lips from forming a sly smile. "I'm surprised you noticed I was gone… with Lucian to distract you. You never did say how your date went."

The memory of Lucian's kiss glowed with warmth in her cheeks. "We just went out, it was fine."

"Where did he take you?" Aiden over acted his interest.

Elidad swallowed as she considered how to answer. "We went *out*, we drove around, mostly."

"What does he drive?" Now his interest was piqued. Aiden was a car guy. It was better to talk about what Lucian drove than where they went.

"An Audi."

"Audi, *what*," Aiden pushed. He apparently knew she was being vague.

"A nice one."

"You don't know what kind of Audi or you don't want to tell me?"

Elidad looked out the window as their driver began to weave around the airport traffic. "It's an R8."

Aiden broke into laughter. "Of course. Seriously? You're not kidding?"

"I'm not kidding," Elidad grinned. "It's expensive, isn't it?"

Aiden snorted. "Yeah, expensive."

Elidad pushed the hotel room door open. There was a lamp left on in the room, casting a golden light on the grey wallpaper. The modern décor was dry, but comfortable.

"One bed?" Elidad observed.

"They think I'm traveling alone," Aiden glanced at the bed before turning away. "I figured we'd manage. It's a king, I won't tell Lucian, if you don't."

Elidad picked up a pillow from the sofa and hurled it at him. It landed on its mark: the back of his head.

"What?" He acted hurt. "Your secret's safe with me. I wouldn't want to end up in Lucian's fronk."

"Fronk?" Elidad's right eyebrow rose.

"There can't be a trunk in his fancy car, the engine's in the back. There has to be a trunk in the front. Fronk."

Elidad rolled her eyes. "Can we get back on track? What is our *actual* plan?"

"I don't have a plan," he confessed.

"No plan?"

"I learned from the best," he flashed her his stunning smile.

She expected it to be harder than this, to fade back into their friendship, especially after Aiden had found out about Pythious.

She'd told herself a million times, on the way to Greece, she wouldn't ask, but she couldn't help it. Her eyes dipped to study the sofa.

"Did you read about me and Pythious in his file?"

"No, Daniel told me. There wasn't much in Pythious' file about you. I think they like to have concrete evidence before it goes into your file."

"Is there anything in my file about him or my parents?"

"I told you, I didn't look in your file."

"What if there's stuff in there about my parents?" Elidad hoped.

"It doesn't feel right, going through a box of what other people think about you. And if you wanted to know more about your parents, you should've gone to see Leucosia."

Elidad nodded her head. "I was going to. I just got… busy."

"Busy," Aiden repeated, a ring of doubt in his voice.

Busy trying not to die. But he didn't need to know that.

"I'm surprised Daniel threw me under the bus like that."

"He didn't really have a choice," Aiden defended him.

"Why?"

Aiden took a labored breath. "We received something in a drop."

"Oh?" Elidad's curiosity was spiked.

"The casing from your bullet."

"What bullet?" Elidad's chest tightened with dread.

"The bullet you used to shoot Pythious." Aiden's eyes searched hers.

"How?" Elidad's head shook as her fingers moved to her lips. The weight of this truth squeezed the breath from her lungs.

She was in trouble.

But before she dealt with the proof against her, there was a key that needed to be found.

Athens was beautiful. Elidad had been here before. One of the perks of growing up with Abraham was all the travel.

Aiden rented a car that morning. Elidad met him a few blocks from the hotel at a bakery. He pulled up out front where she was waiting with two paper cups, steaming with caramel-colored liquid, and a bag containing two flaky croissants.

"Cute," Elidad observed when she sat inside. "New Fiat?"

"It's not a R8, that's for sure," Aiden put the car in gear, pulling into traffic.

Elidad ignored him. "We're going to the Temple of Apollo?"

"Yes, Delphi," Aiden agreed.

Elidad looked out the window as the city zipped by. Sipping some of her tea, Elidad lost herself in a memory as the buildings grew scarce and the mountains began to lift them higher in the sky.

The road grew narrower, winding through the terrain. The Fiat's engine buzzed as Aiden expertly tore up and down the gears, making quick time of their trip.

"The parking lot isn't that busy," Elidad observed.

"I don't think this is the peak season," Aiden said.

"It's not," she agreed.

"Hopefully, it'll help us find what we're looking for. Less crowds means more freedom to look around. Less people to see what we're up to." Aiden fit the car between two others in a row and turned off the ignition.

Walking down the dirt trails, set memories free in Elidad's mind. Hiking thought these ruins with Abraham, they hadn't needed a tour guide. His love of history had led them all around the grounds, from one beautiful mosaic to the next.

"Do you see this?" Abraham pointed to the column.

"Yes," Elidad said.

"You know, when the city was in its prime, the columns looked like one solid piece of rock?"

"Yes," Elidad agreed.

"They aren't, actually. They were cut into sections, so they would be easily erected, by placing one stone one on top of the other. Here," he pointed, "the pillars have been eroded away and you can see where the pillars are joined together. Where they are protected from the weather, they are so well preserved, it's almost impossible to see the seams."

"That was a lot of work for someone," Elidad thought aloud.

"And expensive," Abraham added. "All the mosaic and the stone work. These temples," his eyes scanned their surroundings, "are in pristine condition, considering how old they are."

"Why are the buildings in better shape here? We've been to places that's almost impossible to tell any city was there, at all." Elidad's eyes traced the stones. "What makes this place different?"

Abraham beamed at her question.

"When the city was built, this was an important temple, built in honor of Apollo. Apollo was a deity, recognized as a god of healing, the sun, plague, and prophecy. This city, Delphi, was famous for its oracles. At some point, and for some reason, the city lost its importance. In the other places we've been, cities had often been conquered or natural disasters had destroyed them. In those instances, people stayed in the area, reusing the stones from the ruins to rebuild their new cities and homes. For some reason, the people in Delphi just left. They didn't stay to reuse their resources. They left it, untouched, abandoned."

"Are you ok?" Aiden's question broke Elidad out of her memory.

"Yeah, sorry. I— uh—" she wiped a tear from her cheek.

"Elidad, what's wrong?" Aiden pressed.

"Remember, I told you I'd been here before?"

Aiden nodded his head.

"Abraham and I were here when I was seventeen."

Aiden's eyebrows pressed together. "Abraham brought you here?"

"Is that bad?" Elidad couldn't decipher the look in his eyes.

"He brought you here… where we're looking for a key. Just like he took you to Trinity, where we found a hidden room under a hundred-year-old church?"

"Doesn't seem like much of a coincidence, does it?" Elidad realized.

"I thought you didn't believe in coincidences."

CHAPTER FORTY-SEVEN

They arrived earlier in the day, when Mt. Pangaeus was wrapped in a thick layer of fog. As Elidad and Aiden climbed the pathways, the wind ushered the layer upward, revealing the mountains below, one tree at a time. It felt like the mountain was slowly creeping higher, one foot at a time. The view was as magical, just as she remembered.

Elidad watched as Aiden stood at the base of the Theatre, looking over the countryside. As she approached him, he turned to face her, his blue eyes catching the light of the sun that was fighting its way through the clouds.

"It's just, majestic, isn't it?" He turned back to the view.

"It is." She agreed, her eyes taking inventory of his blond, sweeping hair and dark lashes. Even from the side, he was handsome.

The view was better with him in it. Thoughts of reaching out and touching his face gave her chills. If she reached forward and stroked his cheek with her hand, would he look at her the same way he looked out over the view? Would the view cease to matter, if she touched him?

You'd never know he was a priest in his hiking shoes, day pack and shorts. She and Aiden looked like a normal, American, tourist couple exploring Greece.

For some reason, when she was with Aiden, it was hard to find room for Lucian in her thoughts. She constantly struggled with what that said about her. If Aiden stayed in New York, would she have agreed to go on a date with Lucian? Did she go out with Lucian for the right reasons or just to fill a void?

"What are you looking for?" Elidad asked Aiden, trying to think of something else.

Aiden shrugged. "I was hoping that when we got here, it'd be a little easier to figure out."

The Theatre looked over the fissure, a volcanic opening in the earth. In mythology, this was where the Delphi seers were lowered into the ground to inhale the toxic fumes, allowing them to see the future.

Elidad eyed the hillside, taking in the sights around them. Staring down at the Temple, Elidad imagined the procession of thousands of people making their way up the steep incline. Her heart replicated the march that would've pounded throughout the valley. She could see them moving forward.

Her shoulder itched. Elidad pressed her fingertips gingerly into her cotton T-shirt, rubbing the grey skin hidden underneath. Her eyes moved to Aiden, currently captivated with the view. She pulled up the sleeve of her shirt toward her armpit. Reaching out across her pink skin were the black veins. Once confined to the wound in her chest, they now spiraled down her arm. She abruptly pulled her sleeve down to her elbow. Her eyes snapped to Aiden. He hadn't noticed.

"I don't know if we're going to find anything here," Aiden confessed.

Elidad stepped forward, closer to the edge. She rubbed her bicep; it tingled under her vigorous movement. She could see them again: the procession moving up the hill, the Delphi in the temple, line of cloaked women performing some ritualistic dance up the path.

Elidad's shoulder throbbed to her heartbeat. Hearing murmurs behind her, she turned.

The Theatre was filled with hooded figures, reminding her of the Shadow Man and the children that had tried to kill her in her dream. It was the middle of the day, but they were sitting in total darkness. The only lights were torches on tall stands at the end of the Theatre's aisles.

The ruins weren't ruins; they were intact. Turning again, she found Aiden gone and the hills masked in darkness.

Elidad's attention was drawn once more to the Delphi women who continued their dance to the main temple. As they moved, altars began to light up around the Temple, one by one, under their own power. Elidad could smell olive oil and grain burning. Slurred chants hissed from the crowd behind Elidad as the women's dance began to concentrate around the center of the Temple.

Five women formed a circle around the hole in the ground, the fissure that led deep into the earth. Circling it once, their cloaks and gowns—the only white colored clothing in the ocean of dark—billowed as they spun. Three men, who could double as executioners, heaved a thick rope that connected to a pulley. The rope coiled around a large wheel as they walked in circles, slowly bringing upward a carved, wooden platform from the pit.

When the platform came level with the earth, the rope was secured into place. A horn sounded on the mountainside and the women's dance ceased at the reverberant tone. One lady stepped forward, unfastening her cloak, dropping it to the ground. Her white chiton fluttered in the breeze that was snaking up the mountainside, from the valley floor. The same wind wafted black altar smoke toward Elidad. The uncloaked woman moved her sandaled foot onto the platform that shimmied under the weight of her body.

The Theatre's attendees rose to their feet. Elidad looked from side to side. She wasn't sure what was going on, but she wasn't afraid. No one seemed to notice her; if they did, they didn't care.

Elidad noticed the people standing around her had gold and red eyes, slit diamond-shaped irises. Venomous. These were Python, descendants of Delphi.

The woman on the wooden platform outstretched her hand. The other women began circling her anew. One by one, they each placed something in her hand as they passed by. When the last one had deposited her token, the circle of women fell to their knees, pressing their faces into the marble floor. The woman on the platform held up four coins over her head.

As if a sign, the crowd cheered and the men controlling the platform began to lower her into the pit.

"Elidad?" Aiden's hand firmly on her elbow snapped her back into reality.

She squinted at the bright light of day.

"Sorry. What did you say? I wasn't paying attention." Elidad blinked herself back into reality. Whatever she just saw, she wasn't about to tell Aiden about it.

"No kidding," he didn't release her arm. "Are you okay? It was like you weren't even here."

She looked over her shoulder, expecting to see thousands of cloaked figures. "I'm fine... I was just... thinking."

"About what?" He sounded doubtful.

"The fissure," she pointed to the hole in the center of the temple floor.

"What about it?"

"We need to go down there," the thought set her lips in a crooked line. *It was insane.*

Aiden looked at the hole and back to Elidad. "I feel like I should be surprised, and yet... somehow..."

She grinned at him. "You're not?"

CHAPTER FORTY-EIGHT

"How are we going to get in?" Aiden demanded. It had been a few days since Elidad had told him what they'd have to do.

Elidad shrugged. "We'll figure it out. It can't be that hard. It's a park."

Aiden rubbed his palms over his thighs under the steering wheel of their rental car. "I don't know Elidad. What if we get caught?"

"Then we get caught trespassing. It's not a big deal. We'll act like stupid tourists and they'll let us go. Besides, there can't be too much security. Once it's cleared out and the gate is closed, I'd imagine the guards stay at the guard shack in the parking lot."

"If we get caught, I won't be able to explain what I'm doing here to the Bishop," Aiden's hands moved from his pant legs to grip the steering wheel.

Elidad could see his hands tighten into a white-knuckled grip.

"It'll be fine," she assured. "We won't be caught. I'm a professional."

"This is heavy." Aiden said in a low voice, pulling a backpack from the back seat of the rental car.

Elidad shrugged on another backpack that was sitting in the back seat on the other side. Strapping it to her back in the dark, the clasps around her waist and chest clanged like a wind chime until she fastened them together. She pulled rope out of the seat, throwing a spool over her shoulders. Closing her door, she moved around the back of the car to throw another spool of rope over Aiden's shoulders.

"Are we going to be gone a week?" Aiden joked.

Locking the car, Elidad started up the hill.

"Come on," she said in a low voice, "this climb is going to suck."

"We're going to have to slip over the edge here," Elidad's feet moved off the road.

Aiden followed her in silence. His senses were on edge as the glow of the parking lot began to come into view. They moved slowly, stumbling over rocks in the dark. Every now and again, Elidad would stop, either to listen or to catch her breath, Aiden wasn't sure.

Sneaking past the guard station was as easy as Elidad had promised. They could hear two guards laughing in the distance as they chose their footing around a rock formation, continuing up the hill.

Eventually, Elidad led them back to the path they'd walked up a few days ago. At night, with the tourists gone, it felt different. It hummed with viability, like the impression of life never left; a hidden buzz under the marble, radiating from their surroundings.

The Temple was eerily silent as their feet kicked gravel up the pathway.

Elidad hesitated when they reached the rope line at the fissure. In the center of the Temple, the white rope was only a foot high, keeping visitors in designated areas and away from the hole that could swallow ten people at a time.

"How are we going to do this?" Aiden sounded overwhelmed.

"Just like we planned," she assured, stepping behind him, unzipping the bottom of his pack. A harness fell out. She turned him around. Grabbing through his legs, she pulled the harness up, strapping it to the waist of his backpack. In the low-lit moonlight, Elidad could see the surprise on Aiden's face. Whether the surprise was due to the fast movements through his legs or the synchronizing of the straps around his groin, she didn't know.

"Unzip the bottom pocket on my pack," Elidad's words were hard to hear above the chatter of the metal clasps dangling from Aiden's pack.

Aiden did as he was directed. Elidad felt the straps knock her in the back of the legs. She bent forward, pulling them up. Elidad strapped them firmly to her waist belt.

Pulling the rope from her shoulders, she whispered, "Grab the gloves in the top."

She felt Aiden tug at the zipper.

Taking the rope from his chest, he held it in one arm. She nodded to him; he nodded back. They stepped over the short barrier, crossing the distance to the opening of the fissure, and threw their ropes down in separate piles. Grating lay across the hole. Elidad knelt close to the metal barrier to inspect how it was fastened. She lifted a padlock.

Aiden kneeled next to her. "It's locked, how are we going to get in?"

"I didn't expect it to be open," Elidad admitted.

"You didn't?"

"No, did you?" His features were easy to see, even in this lighting. Inches away from her, she felt the urge to reach up and smooth out his hair.

"I didn't think about it," he answered.

"Think of how many visitors come here. They can't leave a big hole in the ground open with the public around. Some kid would end up in there, maybe even an adult," Elidad said. "It'd end up being Americans," she chuckled. "People are stupid."

"Very funny."

Elidad's lips curved into a big smile. "We're the only stupid Americans going in there tonight, though."

"I guess you have a point," Aiden couldn't help but smile.

Elidad pulled a small, leather case out of her pocket. Aiden could see metal tools catch what little light the night had to offer. After picking out the right sized instruments, Elidad made quick work of the lock that fastened the grating into place.

Together, they tugged the grate open. It whined as they laid it back, setting it in place as quietly as they could.

Elidad moved into place, securing the ropes to the grate with pulleys, tying knots and fastening carabiners to the bottom of the grating. When she was done, she motioned to Aiden to come closer. Aiden chose his footing carefully as he approached the opening.

Elidad smiled, grabbing the carabiners hanging from his waist.

"The grating really made this easier for us. I was worried we wouldn't have anything to secure our ropes to. Anyone passing by will never notice the grating is open. Probably even during the day time."

"Day time?" Aiden stared at her. "How long are you expecting to stay down there?"

"Not long. I'm just saying no one will notice, that's all."

Aiden knew better than to believe her. If they took too long, and the morning came, they wouldn't be able to come back out until the park closed again. There'd be no way around that. But he couldn't imagine it taking that long. It was just a hole in the ground. A cave. They'd be lucky to find the key there at all.

Elidad was digging in Aiden's backpack, again. She pressed a pair of gloves into his shoulder until he grabbed them.

"Just like we practiced," she reminded him.

"This is a little different than the gym," Aiden's heart fluttered with the realization of what was going to happen.

"You know how to do this. It's not hard," she assured. "I'll go first and turn on a light when I get down there so you can see. Just go slow and steady."

"Slow and steady," Aiden repeated.

Elidad stood taut, the way she'd taught Aiden to do, in order to lower herself down into the chasm. With a buzz to the rope, Elidad disappeared into the void below.

Aiden looked up. "Be with me, Lord. This woman is going to get me killed, someday."

Elidad's light sparked to life from below. He leaned backward, keeping his feet on the grating. Aiden's body stayed stiff to keep his head from hitting the metal as he descended. His fingers loosened around the rope and his body sunk under the grating.

"Oh shit!" Aiden's muffled despair echoed off the walls of the cave. His body plummeted down toward the ground.

"Aiden!" Elidad shrieked in horror as his body whizzed by.

CHAPTER FORTY-NINE

Falling. He was falling.

Elidad felt like her heart was on that rope, racing to the ground, with him.

Aiden's descent abruptly stopped, just below the beams of the light that dangled from Elidad's waist belt.

"Aiden?" She breathed, lowering herself to his level.

Laughing. He was laughing.

"Were you worried?" His mischievous eyes caught the light.

Elidad tried to hit him, but he dangled just out of reach. "That's not funny!"

"Come on, it kinda is," he protested.

"No, it wasn't. What if someone heard me yell your name?"

"Well, they aren't going to stop us now. They'll have to wait till we get back up to turn us in."

"You're seriously a jerk," she said.

"You've called me worse," he smiled up at her as he began his descent, again.

The cave walls weren't tight around them, like Elidad had imagined they'd be. It wasn't like a well but a cavern. As they continued down, the chasm spread farther and wider.

Elidad spoke over the hum of their decent. "When the seers were lowered into this fissure, the volcanic gasses made them hallucinate, so when they came back up to the surface, they were so intoxicated, they spoke in tongues. The Delphi people thought their gods were speaking through the women, leaving the high priests to interpret what was being said. That's how they made all their important decisions, where to build, who to go to war with, everything."

Aiden laughed out loud.

"What? Is that funny?" Elidad asked.

"Well, yes," he admitted. "People making life decisions off interpretations of hallucinations from women out of their minds on volcanic fumes—it's hilarious. But that's not why I was laughing."

"What were you laughing about?" She was afraid to ask.

"It's ironic, isn't it?"

"What's ironic?"

"We're lowering you, a woman, into this pit, and I'm a priest. Should I start interpreting your jargon?" Aiden flashed a smile.

"Maybe we should put our masks on, you're already getting delusional," Elidad sneered.

"I thought you said there weren't any gasses, anymore. The masks are just a precaution, aren't they?"

"Apparently, I was mistaken…"

"Ha… ha…" Aiden mocked. "I'm not the one who's supposed to come out of this delusional, you are. I'm just the one trying to interpret your crazy."

"I can see the bottom," Elidad announced.

Aiden looked down. "I can too," he said in a hushed voice.

They repelled the rest of the way without a word between them.

Elidad and Aiden stopped ten feet above the stone floor. A circle of white mosaic marble, intricately designed with serpent figures, was cluttered with ages of fallen rubble. The marble itself was damaged from years of falling stones. Elidad's heartbeat pounded in her chest, behind the wounds in her shoulder. Shrugging, she tried to loosen the tension in her arm. Repelling lower, she allowed her feet to lightly touch the firm surface. Elidad felt compelled to hold her breath as she stood in the center of the circle.

"Come down lower, Aiden," Elidad said. "Remember, you have to get lower to take the weight off your pulleys or you won't be able to open them."

"I remember. I just wasn't sure I wanted off the rope, yet," he admitted.

"What do you think will happen?" She smirked.

"I was kinda worried that the poisonous gasses would fill the chamber when your feet touched the ground," he said.

"I told you," she reminded him sharply, "the poisonous gasses are gone. They haven't been around for centuries. We aren't the only ones to have come down here; there've been other explorers, actual archeologists. It's fine."

"Famous last words," Aiden muttered, reluctantly lowering himself.

Unhitching herself from the ropes, Elidad stepped out of her harness before helping Aiden with his. As they moved, dust swirled through the lantern light.

"It's cold down here," Aiden observed.

"I told you it would be. Caves stay the same temperature—never freezing, never warming— keeping in the forties. That's why people used to dig root cellars. It was like a refrigerator, a consistent temperature."

"You're like a wealth of useless information, you know," Aiden joked.

Aiden was in a strange mood. He'd been teasing her a lot more than normal. Now that he'd come to terms with the reality of the supernatural, was this the new way he dealt with stressful situations? Or was this how he was coping with the complexity of their relationship?

Aiden stepped out of his harness as Elidad pulled a water bottle out of her pack. She took a swig and handed it to him. Their stealthy hike up the mountain hadn't left any time for hydration. He had to be as parched as she was.

"Thanks," he said, before taking a drink. "We made it. Now, what are we looking for?"

"I'm not sure," she admitted. "You were the one who wanted to come to Delphi.

"You seemed so sure we needed to come down here. Sure enough, you spent half a week training me to repel. So, now what?"

"Now we look around." Elidad dug in her pack again, pulling out a Clif Bar and a flashlight. Handing the bar to Aiden, she shined the light on the cave walls.

"Wow, that thing is bright," he said through bites, handing back the other half to Elidad.

"That's why I brought it."

The light moved across rock that made up the cave walls, reaching to the entrance above them. She directed the light around the circumference of the cave before she found a carved arch in the stone.

"Stay here," she instructed.

"I don't know if you should go over there alone," Aiden warned.

"It's an empty cave. I'm not sure what could happen."

"Don't jinx it," Aiden's voice carried after her.

Elidad moved nimbly over the boulders. Her fingers pressed into the crevices of the rocks to pull her body weight up and over the massive formations. She closed the distance to the arch in a few minutes. Marble was inlayed into the wall of primitive stone. The Delphi people would've had to lower massive amounts of the heavy stone into the cave to build it. It was over forty feet tall and polished to a perfect shine. The cave had done an amazing job of protecting the detail from the elements. Carved serpents lined the arch, undamaged by time.

"You see anything?" The concern was apparent in Aiden's voice.

"I see a lot. But nothing that we're looking for," Elidad answered. *No key laying around.* "What about in the circle? Is there anything there?"

A dull ache pulled at Elidad's shoulder. Her left hand crossed her body to touch the gray holes that lay hidden under her shirt. Pain throbbed down her arm. Looking over her shoulder, she made sure Aiden couldn't see her from the other side of the boulder. Pulling her sleeve to her elbow, she inspected the black veins that peeked out. A few weeks back, after Leucosia had given her the serum, there'd been no black veins on her body. They'd spread so quickly and the pain that accompanied them was concerning.

"You've let this sickness go too far. The poison in your body is growing stronger. You should've come to see me before now…" Leucosia's words resonated in her mind. *"I cannot see your future…"*

Maybe this was her dying, the serum not working. That's probably why Leucosia couldn't see her future. She was destined to die a slow death.

They needed to find this key. One more key would get Aiden one step closer. Who knew how much longer she had to help him.

"Did you find something?" Aiden's voice echoed off the walls.

"No, just looking at these carvings."

"What are they?"

She climbed back over the rock. Standing on the top she surveyed where Aiden stood. "The carvings are serpents."

"More snakes."

"Well, the Delphi worshiped Python, the serpent god," she crawled over rocks to make her way back to Aiden.

"Yeah, Pythious' ancestors," Aiden's voice trailed off, striking a vein of regret in Elidad.

Elidad's eyes faltered, drifting to the ground. She turned to avoid him, her bright light catching the detail in the marble. She knelt to the ground. Placing her hand on the cool surface, she swept away the debris, forming a plume of dust in her light. When her fingers were in contact with the ground, her shoulder burned. It wasn't painful, just a riveting longing, like a thirst that couldn't be quenched.

"What did you find?" Aiden was standing over her shoulder.

"Aiden," Elidad's voice was a whisper, "Give me one of your coins."

He handed one over without question.

Elidad held the coin in the light. In the marble, amidst the carvings, a round piece of stone was missing. It was so minute. In fact, it looked as though it had been knocked out by a falling rock.

The memory of the women and the ritual in the Temple played in Elidad's mind. Before being sent down into the fissure, the seer had held up the coins for the crowd to see. In response, they'd cheered like she'd just made the last touchdown in the Super Bowl. These coins were essential, not just tokens.

Elidad pressed the coin into the marble. It fit like a key to its accompanied lock.

Looking over her shoulder, Elidad saw Aiden's surprise. His face began to morph when a ring of light began to glow. Turning back, Elidad saw the coin glowing in the marble. The light moved across the serpent design, alighting the next hole. Aiden handed Elidad the rest of the coins.

Elidad's hands shook as she placed the next coin into its slot. The light inched around the circle. Where there was debris on the marble, the light removed it from its path. Rocks floated upward, as if gravity were being reversed.

Each of the remaining two holes revealed themselves, one after the other, in a beacon of light. It was hypnotic, the way the light moved around the circle. It reminded Elidad of the way the light glowed in the mortar of the bricks lining the hidden wall under Isaac's shop. Was it the same kind of magic? This had to be different. Delphi were followers of Python, a demonic deity.

The circle glowed. Elidad and Aiden stood motionless, waiting for whatever came next.

Nothing happened.

Elidad slowed her breaths, afraid to remove her eyes from the circle. Still nothing.

"What now?" Aiden whispered.

"I don't know. Something has to happen." Elidad said, looking at the hole.

Her eyes caught a remnant of the past. The seer, standing alone on the wooden platform, having been lowered into the circle. Stepping off the platform, she placed the coins into the stone, light leading her path to the archway.

Urged by her vision, Elidad stepped forward. Aiden caught her arm. She looked back at him, "Stay here, just in case."

"No," he protested.

"It's fine," she lied. Would the light lead to the poisonous gas? With no one to lift them out, there was no way of telling whether she and Aiden would make it out alive. They did have their masks, but this was magical, not geological.

Aiden reluctantly released her arm.

Elidad's heartbeat muffled the movement of her feet. Crossing the illuminated line, she stood in the middle of the pathway. She could feel its power surge through the soles of her feet. The light glowed brighter around her, like a beacon beckoning her forward.

Slithering, like a snake in the grass, the light moved across the ground, away from the circle, toward the arch on the wall. As it crawled forward, rocks and boulders moved aside, floating out of the way. Elidad felt the light run through her body, move up her arm and into her shoulder, removing the pain that lingered from the demon's attack.

Aiden stepped toward her.

Elidad held out her hand. "Don't."

He stopped.

"Don't come close. Just follow me," she directed.

Elidad followed the pull of the light to the opening as it came alive. In a lightning-like crack, a doorway revealed itself. The doors were as tall as the arch and appeared to be made of marble. Dark veins in the stone twisted and turned under the surface, reminding Elidad of what lay beneath her shirt. The cleared path looked like the yellow brick road, leading her home. Moving forward, the illuminated doors drew open to welcome her in.

The handles of the doors pulled at Elidad's interest the most. Two snakes, cobras, carved from a black stone, stood proud as guardians. Their eyes were a deep red, tracking her movement. Elidad's stomach churned. They were identical to the ones in Donald Tabor's casino; the same ones that had tried to kill her.

Elidad pressed forward.

Who enters?

"Did you say something, Aiden?" Elidad looked over her shoulder.

He shook his head no.

The snakeheads began to move. *Who enters?* She heard again. It wasn't in her mind and it wasn't in English, either. She looked back at Aiden. "Did you hear someone say something?"

The look on his face was enough of an answer.

"Elidad, the only one talking, is us. Maybe we need to put our masks on and get out of here."

"I'm fine. It's not gas. I promise. I think it's the light."

Who enters? The voices asked in unison.

"It is I, Elidad," she announced.

Aiden's expression changed to concern.

The snakes moved off the doors as they continued to open. *Demon slayer.* One hissed, moving toward her.

Aiden lunged forward to defend her from their advance.

One of the snakes coiled, hissing, it's fangs dripping with venom.

"Aiden, don't!" Elidad warned. She turned to the snakes. "He's from the family of Delphi and he is my escort. Don't touch him."

The coiled snake bobbed its head, considering Elidad's words before loosening its stance to slither against the cool marble at Elidad's feet. They appeared to keep an eye on Aiden but allowed him to follow at Elidad's request.

It's been ages since we've seen a prophetess. Many ages have passed since the future has been shared with human kind. She will be pleased.

"Who is she?" Elidad asked.

Pythia. They hissed.

"Elidad, what's going on?" Aiden tried to approach her.

The snakes moved between them, in a protective stance, keeping Aiden at bay.

A loud thud drew all their attention to the doors, standing open.

Black lay behind them.

Sliding down a marble path, the light drifted fluidly into the emptiness.

CHAPTER FIFTY

Aiden didn't have a good feeling about this. Following these snakes deeper into the cave didn't seem like their best plan. Stranger still, Elidad followed them confidently, like she knew something he didn't.

She was talking to them, like she expected them to talk back. There was something odd about the way she moved down the pathway and how they escorted her through the black surroundings. Did something happen to her when she stood in the marble circle?

Aiden kept a safe distance as he followed the trio into the depths of the cave.

Stand in the center. You are the key. One of the snakes moved over a circle as it came alight, like the rest of Elidad's path. Elidad's feet found the inner circle. The slow-moving light shot out from her, bursting like fireworks. Looking down at her hands, she was a radiant white. The cave sprang to life. Gold and jewels lay in heaps, pillars reached for the sky in their flawless architecture. Many plants decorated spots here and there. On the far side of the room, a harem of men gathered on sofas, laughing and talking. Servants walked around with pitchers pouring wine.

A hush moved over them, their red eyes flashed to where Elidad stood. Even from this distance, Elidad recognized the mark of the Delphi people.

From around a pillar, a woman glided toward Elidad as the light around her began to diminish. The woman looked Greek. High cheekbones accentuated by dark eyebrows and a long slender nose. Like the men watching them, her eyes burned red. This close, Elidad could see the narrow slit of her irises rimmed in yellow, identical to Pythious'.

"El...i...dad..." The name slowly rolled off her tongue.

"Pythia," Elidad inclined her head.

"What riddle has knocked on my door, after centuries of no visitors?" Pythia slowly strode the circumference of the marble around Elidad.

"Riddle?" Elidad echoed.

Pythia's lips twitched. "How does a demon slayer become an oracle of Delphi? Does not one contrast the other?

"How are you alive after being killed by Apollo?" Elidad countered. "Is that not in contrast to the other?"

Pythia made her way to Aiden. Pressing her hand into his chest, she laughed, "His heart moves at a quick speed. Is it because I am so beautiful?" Her wide smile revealed her fangs as she circled behind Aiden.

"*Lyra autem ambulaverit nocte in Delphis theough venas sanguis,*" Aiden still posture gave the illusion that Latin was his common language and not a dead one.

Pythia's mouth closed into a crooked smile.

"He *thinks* he's Delphi," Pythia spoke to Elidad.

He lies. The snakes hissed in unison. *Look at his eyes, he bears no resemblance.*

"The ages have moved forward without you," Elidad reminded. "His family *is* Delphi, and human. The family entrusted the coins to him, he's the only reason I'm here."

"Delphi people would not *mate* with humans." Pythia protested.

"As I said, the ages have moved forward. Many things have changed," Elidad argued.

Pythia's fingers touched the short fade at the base of Aiden's neck and worked upward to the long sweeps of hair at the top of his head. "He *is* lovely. No sense in wasting a beautiful thing. Come with me," she commanded.

Her dress, floor-length, looked like it was made of chainmail. The low neckline dipped to her belly button, revealing a chiseled physic. A slit up the front came to her thighs, allowing her to move across the room with ease, despite the train that drug behind her.

"Come Oracle," she said, addressing Elidad. "I will show you what you need to know."

Elidad could hear the snakes speaking to each other. *She will let him live? Delphi blood is not in his veins, I only smell human.*

Elidad grabbed Aiden by the elbow to slow his pace. "Aiden, stay close."

"You stay close," his eyes narrowed. "What's going on with you?"

His attitude drew her attention. "Nothing. Just playing along."

"You're talking to those snakes like they're your pets," he accused. "Like you expect them to talk back."

Elidad's eyes shifted to the massive reptiles twisting in Pythia's path, now thirty yards ahead of them.

Aiden couldn't hear them speak. Why could she?

"I'm trying to figure out what is going on, Aiden. I'm trying to find the key."

The look passing Aiden's eyes was doubt. "Something's wrong with you."

Pythia led them to a new chamber. Like the rest of the Temple, the room was constructed out of marble slabs, pieced together in a seamless architectural wonder. The ceilings were held aloft by pillars so wide, Elidad and Aiden together wouldn't be able to touch hands around them.

The floor was lined with trenches that held a glowing orange substance, bubbling and hissing from within the stone. The smell of sulfur engulfed the vast space; Elidad could taste it on her tongue. There were no plants in this room, just an open marble court with the flowing orange sludge weaving in and around the space. Walking past, Elidad could feel the heat on her legs. *Lava*, she realized. The moats were filled with molten lava.

In the center of the lava flow was a raised marble stone, the right size for a person to lie on top of, simulating an altar. Pythia stood near it, looking at Elidad, expectantly.

Elidad shifted. "As you said, this ritual hasn't been practiced in centuries. I'm not prepared," Elidad explained. "Do I lie here and breathe in the fumes?"

Pythia's face hardly changed, yet exhumed disgust. "I don't understand what you're asking, Oracle."

"The fumes, from the lava, that's what causes me to see the future?" Elidad said.

"I don't know of these *fumes*." She stepped closer to Elidad, grabbing her hand, she led her to the table.

Elidad sat on it.

"You lie here."

Elidad obeyed.

Aiden's whole body protested. He inched closer, trying not to draw attention to himself.

Pythia's fingers went to the base of Elidad's neck, her bone chilling touch seemed out of place for the warmth of the room. Sliding down to the base of Elidad's neck, Pythia's pupils began to expand, her head cocked to the side. "You've already tasted Venom," she assessed.

"Already?" Elidad's mind flashed to Pythious.

"A lethal dose, you received, and yet, here you are," Pythia's tone was thoughtful. "Perhaps that is how you can be both, a slayer and an oracle." Pythia's fingers continued down Elidad's shoulder resting over the wounds that the demon in the alley left. Pythia's lips twisted, "Or, perhaps, it is *something…* else?"

Elidad's eyes flashed to Aiden. He was looking agitated, but he didn't understand what Pythia was speaking about.

"There are no *fumes*, as you call them," Pythia continued, "Venom is what brings you the sight."

"Venom?" Hesitation was apparent in Elidad's voice.

Understanding seemed to light Pythia's eyes, "Not venom like you experienced, before. I am the Original. I am the only one who holds the power of the Oracles." She lifted Elidad's hand expectantly, as if waiting for permission. Pythia's hand rested over Elidad's chest over the healing wounds. Where there was throbbing pain an hour ago, now a tingling, joyous sensation radiated in its place.

Elidad's brain was revolting at the thought of being bitten, again. Tears threatened to spill down her cheeks. Reluctantly, Elidad wordlessly nodded approval.

"No!" Aiden shouted as Pythia bit into Elidad's wrist.

Elidad's cry echoed across the cavernous space.

Aiden jumped over a few motes, trying to get to her. The snakes weaved between them, their fangs and hoods fully extended.

"Aiden, don't," Elidad pleaded, sitting upright on the stone. "I'll be fine." She didn't feel different. Pythia was right, it wasn't like when Pythious bit her. She could keep her balance; the room wasn't spinning, she didn't feel out of control.

As Elidad considered her feelings, and her heart rate, she began to hear voices, from all around the room. Elidad turned her head from side to side, no one was there.

More voices. The whispers grew louder. Elidad couldn't see them.

"What do you *see*?" Pythia purred.

"Nothing," Elidad said, "I only hear."

"What are you looking for, *Oracle*?"

"I'm not an Oracle," Elidad shouted over the whispers.

"What is the Slayer looking for?" She hissed.

The voices floating around the room came in and out around Elidad, like they were floating about her body. Her eyes darted to the far side of the room, behind Aiden. Green eyes glowed from the distance. Elidad stopped moving, she tried to hold her breath.

"He can't be here," Elidad whispered.

"He's everywhere," Pythia said. "He's with you, often."

Elidad shook her head, closing her eyes. "This isn't real." Opening them again, the eyes were gone.

"What are you looking for, Oracle? What is your question."

Elidad imagined the keys. She could feel one. It was close. Whispers filled Elidad's mind. *It's here. It is in her.* Opening her eyes Elidad saw a scar in Pythia's chest. It couldn't be.

"Find your prophecy, Elidad," Pythia commanded.

Elidad's eyes snapped to Pythia's. "What did you say?"

"You want to know the prophecy about yourself, don't you? The one Leucosia wouldn't tell you? Prophecy for yourself."

"No, Elidad. Don't," Aiden pleaded.

Pythia turned over her shoulder to Aiden. "Silence!" She turned back to Elidad. "He doesn't want you to know. Just like Leucosia. He wants you divided from your destiny, the same way Abraham did. You don't need them, Elidad... prophecy."

Elidad squeezed her eyes together to avoid Aiden's look of judgment. Leucosia had kept the prophecy from her, like Abraham. It was her right. She had a right to know. Warmth shot through her arm and shoulder. The wound felt healed, alive, as blood rushed through those veins. The whispers around the room became concentrated, as though she *controlled* them. Together, they became one. She *could* control them, they were her, they became part of her, she could feel the past through them, they shared their knowledge with her. Elidad felt the words coming from within her. She expelled them into the world, the way they were meant to be:

> *"In duel, her fate is sealed, in dark and light combined;*
> *Whose future remains a tragedy, for the age, undefined.*
> *Light extinguished by evil, find a way to burn again,*
> *A life of purity made blemished by the touch of evil sin.*
> *When slain, the anger in the dragon heart,*
> *Released fury, a soul torn apart.*
> *With the rise of the fallen, a broken one brings forth an age,*
> *Temptation confines her, an ever-damning cage.*
> *Take heed, oh Babylon your keys are set asunder,*
> *Let them not be reunited in man's heedless blunder.*
> *Armies covet, the four divided, separated by divinity,*
> *The only true assembler, the Holy Trinity.*
> *Destruction shall cometh, to all inhibitors of the earth,*
> *Nothing shall remain standing, in the expanse of its girth.*
> *Beloved by God, the only way to resolution,*
> *Take arms, seek peace, there shall be none, only retribution.*
> *A bosom, riveted with justice and purity,*
> *May save the world from destruction, with sovereign authority.*
> *The Shadow reigns dominion over all misguided.*
> *Seek the light, turn from he who lives a life divided.*

The dragon covets what is not his to claim,
Woe to she… indulged by evil's burning flame.

Elidad could see flashes of her life and even prior to it. She saw Abraham finding the scrolls foretelling of her birth, her parents, their deaths, the barn in the desert where she freed Abraham from his imprisonment, the green eyes, *he* was there, during Abraham's exorcism. The Shadow Man was there. Pythia was right, he's always with her. Elidad's mind flashed to her dream when she wore a wedding dress, her hand outstretched to his, she threw back her veil to meet him. He reached for her. He wanted her. It was an invitation to be with him.

The voices, in her mind frantically uproared at the thought of them being together. She could see an ocean of cloaked minions bowing before her and the Shadow Man. Elidad, holding his hand, gazed on him with affection. His hands went to his hood, his fingers pulling back the mask. She would finally know who he was, who'd been with her this whole time… She was about to see who she was fated to be with…

CHAPTER FIFTY-ONE

A ripping pain cut through Elidad's chest as a shrill screech broke through her vision. It was difficult to decipher reality from visions. Standing an arm's length away, Pythia was screaming in pain, grasping at *her* chest. A sword had been driven through it. Aiden stood at Pythia's back, his eyes wild with worry and determination. There was no doubt in Elidad's mind how the sword got there.

Elidad felt betrayed.

Looking down at her own chest, she expected the sword to have pierced her too, but there was nothing. No wound. She *felt* what Pythia felt. They all did, the screams in her mind confirming it. Aiden threw Pythia off the blade, her body crumpling onto the marble. Half of her body fell into the lava trimming the side of the stone he was standing on.

"No!" Elidad cried, grasping for Pythia's hand. The smell of burning flesh caught in the back of her throat. She wasn't sure if it was the smoke or her emotions that caused her eyes to sting.

The snakes lunged at Aiden. He swung the sword missing one, but he caught the flesh of the other. As they circled around, Aiden grabbed Elidad's hand, pulling her upright. "We have to go."

"Why did you do that!" Elidad demanded. "I was about to know… everything," tears streamed down her face. "I could've known, everything. You ruined it."

Aiden yanked on her arm. "Let's go." He pushed her away from the mangled body partially dissolving into the mote.

The look in Aiden's eyes was one Elidad had never seen before. As his fingers firmly grasped her arm, she knew there would be no more discussion. They were leaving.

"Look out!" Elidad cried as a snake lunged for Aiden.

Aiden spun, swinging the sword. The snake lunged backward out of its way.

"Come on," Aiden pulled Elidad, again.

"Wait." Elidad ran back to Pythia, kneeling next to her.

"Elidad, leave her."

Elidad took a breath. The wound Aiden inflicted sliced through the scar on Pythia's chest. Elidad drove her hand into the open flesh, past her ribcage.

"What are you doing?" Aiden's voice was elevated.

Elidad didn't look up she continued plunging her hand. "Behind you, Aiden."

Aiden slashed the sword, severing a snake's head before it could devour him.

Elidad's fingers touched something different than bone. Something foreign. Elidad caught it between her fingertips and withdrew it. The key. Standing, Elidad kicked the snake's head into the lava. It hissed and snapped its fangs until it was dissolved completely.

"We have to go," Elidad's voice was commanding.

Aiden followed Elidad over the trenches. The remaining snake lunged at them as they moved across the room.

Traitor. She's coming for you… Slayer.

The cave began to shake, rocks fell from the ceiling. Elidad and Aiden dodged the falling debris, although a large stone caught Elidad in the shoulder knocking her to the ground. Aiden grabbed her hand, pulling her to her feet giving the snake time to move in front of them, coiling in their path.

She's not finished with you.

Elidad looked over her shoulder. Pythia was dragging herself out of the moat, the flesh on half of her body eaten away by lava. Her skeleton glistened like metal, clinking when the bare bones of her fingers pressed into the marble.

"Aiden, she's coming for you," Elidad whispered. She wanted to help Aiden, but she had an urge to help Pythia, too.

Looking down at Aiden's hands, this was the first time she saw the weapon he was holding. Elidad recognized the inscription on the shaft. He had the Sword of Justice.

"Where did you get that?" Elidad demanded.

"It's a long story, and by the look of it, we don't have a lot of time," Aiden observed. The snake was still behind them, and Pythia, now on her feet, began to close the distance between them.

"Give it to me," Elidad held out her hand.

Aiden's fingers tightened around the hilt.

"Give it to me, I have way more experience with a sword."

Aiden reluctantly gave it over.

The blade sparked with blue light in Elidad's palm, she squinted at the flare as the sword began to withdraw. It was vanishing from existence, shrinking until Elidad only held a small piece of metal in her hand.

Elidad's eyes shot to Aiden. "What happened? What did you do?"

The surprise on Aiden's face said enough. "I didn't do anything. What did *you* do?" Aiden took the hilt back from her. The blade began to appear, again, taking shape into the sword.

Elidad and Aiden exchanged glances.

"What's going on Aiden?"

"We don't have time to figure it out," Aiden said, grabbing Elidad's hand, "We need to get out of here. Run!" Aiden tugged Elidad toward the snake. It wasn't the best option, but it was the better one. The exit lay behind him, and they needed to head away from Pythia.

Anger seared though Elidad. The fury burned through her arm and tingled in her palm. Hate for the snake and their circumstances raced through her veins. Elidad slid her hand inside her shirt as the snake lunged at them, fangs agape. Elidad pulled her gun and unloaded her clip into him.

The snake's body crumpled to the ground.

Aiden scowled mid step. "Why didn't you do that earlier?"

"I didn't think it'd actually work," She huffed as their footsteps picked up pace past the snake's lifeless body. They pushed hard toward the dark, leading them to the foyer.

Get up. Elidad heard Pythia's voice in her mind as if she were standing right next Elidad.

Glancing over her shoulder, Elidad saw Pythia move past the snake with a flair of her hand, the snake spasmed to life.

"See, I didn't think it was going to be that easy," Elidad huffed.

"Shit," Aiden must have seen what she did.

Elidad slowed to a walk, pulling a clip from her pocket. She dropped the empty one on the ground, inserting the other. Pointing the matte black muzzle at the snake, she fired every round into him.

Pythia held up her hand. Each bullet stopped a foot from him, levitating for a drawn out second before plunking to the ground.

"Run!" Elidad shouted.

"Don't let them leave," Pythia commanded.

The men from the other room surged forward forming a line, a military blockade, in their path. At a quick glance, Elidad counted over a dozen of them. There was no way for Elidad and Aiden to fight them all, especially with Pythia descending on them; she wouldn't need their help.

Elidad's mind swirled with whispers, pain screamed through her brain. Elidad cried out, stumbling her steps, she stopped running, pressing her fingers into her temples.

"Elidad, what's wrong?" Aiden reached for her hand, again.

"Don't touch me, Aiden," Elidad pulled her hand from his grip.

The Shadow Man flared in her mind. She could see him… she could see herself, hand in hand with him, standing above their followers. Thousands knelt before them… before *her*. She felt them, chanting her name.

The tremors in the cave floor brought Elidad back into reality as chunks of marble began to fall from the ceiling. In Elidad's hatred, she'd imagined the rocks crushing Pythia. Elidad wanted something to stop her. A large piece of stone fell, causing Pythia to jump backward in order to avoid being smashed.

Pythia's eyes narrowed. She looked at the ceiling above Elidad and curtly nodded her head downward. Stones began falling like rain on Elidad and Aiden. Elidad held her hands up to protect them; the stones held away from their bodies at Elidad's command. The strain was daunting. Elidad wasn't sure how long she could protect them.

Protect us. Elidad pleaded in her mind. *She's trying to kill me.* The line of men moved between Elidad and Pythia, their backs to Elidad.

They heard her. They responded to her pleas for help.

"Protect the Oracle!" Elidad shouted.

The men surged toward Pythia who exhaled a scream full of a ravenous rage that bounced off the walls of the cave and echoed in Elidad's mind. The force weighing down the rocks lifted. Elidad was able to cast them away with little effort.

Pythia no longer had power to attack, she needed it to defend herself. Raising her hands, the moats of Lava began to rise into a wall of angry heat.

"Come on," Aiden tugged at Elidad.

"Wait," Elidad panted, "I'm more powerful than she is."

"Who cares, run!"

The wave of lava surged forward from Pythia advancing on the men. Their offensive line looked like cards cast into a fire, their bodies consumed by flame as soon as they touched the wall.

Aiden and Elidad ran toward the marble opening as the doors began to drag closed.

Aiden burst through them first, looking back he saw Elidad, stopped on the other side of the threshold.

"Elidad what are you doing? Come on! Get out of there!"

Pythia walked out of the wall of lava, a smirk on the half of her mouth that still had skin, "You *want* to stay, Slayer, you want to know," Pythia hissed. "If you leave this place, you will never know. You'll no longer have the sight. You'll have nothing."

"Elidad, don't listen to her, come on." Aiden held his hand forward, expectantly. "You'll have me."

Aiden's voice pulled at something inside Elidad. She wanted to be with him, but she needed to know… she couldn't have both.

Elidad opened her mind to the voices while keeping a shield from Pythia's rage. Elidad pushed against Pythia, her lava wall began to recede, dissolving back into its moats .

The half beauty, half skeleton moved in closer to Elidad.

She didn't want Elidad dead, Elidad could feel it. She wanted her to stay. *She needed her.* For what, Elidad didn't know. It took more concentration than Elidad had.

"Come, Elidad, stay with me, you can have all the knowledge you wish. Nothing shall be hidden from you. I'll tell you everything." Pythia offered.

Elidad *wanted* to stay. The desire to know burned on the tip of her tongue. She was so close, she just had to stay…

Steps came so fast behind Elidad, she didn't have time to turn. Out of the corner of her eye, Aiden came around the side of Elidad, wielding the sword. He slashed it through the air, severing Pythia's head from her body.

With no power from her lungs, Pythia's mouth opened in a silent cry. Her dislodged head rolled across the marble.

Screams filled Elidad's brain. She pressed her finger into her temples. "No!"

Lava shot up like fireworks from the moats , the ground split as stones cascaded from the ceiling.

Aiden pushed Elidad toward the exit.

"I can't go!" Elidad protested. "I have to know."

"We have to go. We're going to die!" Aiden drug her through the falling debris. The doors were almost closed, now.

Elidad frantically pulled in the opposite direction.

Aiden scooped her up and sprinted the last few yards through the opening. The pair barely squeezed through, steps in front of a new wave of lava rushing to the doors. The lava didn't pass over the threshold. Other than Elidad and Aiden, nothing from the other side passed the threshold.

Aiden ran, still holding Elidad. He was determined not to stop until they were under the opening where their ropes still hung. In his last few yards, Aiden tripped on a stone, tumbling to the ground. He protected Elidad in the fall as best he could.

They lay there, both breathing heavy.

Finally, Elidad broke the silence. "Aiden, what's wrong with me?"

Peering over at her, he could see a clarity in her eyes that wasn't there inside the cave. "Remember when I told you I didn't think you should stand in the circle?" He joked.

"I wanted to stay there."

He rolled to his side to lock eyes with her. "You almost did."

"My visions, they were real… I had so many thoughts in my mind. I wasn't thinking for myself, it was a collective thought. I believed what they showed me, I wanted what they wanted." Elidad reached for his face. "I almost got you killed," her voice quivered. She laid her head against the stone.

"You almost got *you* killed," he reminded.

Elidad's fingers went to his blonde locks as emotion swelled in her chest. She couldn't stand to be so far from him. She could've died, not knowing what it would be like to kiss him. It couldn't end that way. She couldn't die that way.

"The only thing I want more than my past… is you." She pulled him toward herself.

He didn't resist. His breath caressed her face as his blue eyes radiated a deep emotion she'd never seen before.

Moving forward, he pressed his lips against hers.

Aiden's arms wrapped around her body, pulling her tight against him.

Her lips hungrily scathed his. Everything else disappeared. Nothing mattered. For one second, their kiss was the only thing that mattered; everything else fell away.

None of the complications on the surface could reach them down here.

CHAPTER FIFTY-TWO

Elidad woke in a strange room with sunlight bursting through the sheer curtains that lined the far wall. Sitting up, she was surrounded by plush bedding and soft pillows.

Aiden peeked around a corner. "Elidad?" he sounded relieved.

"Aiden, what's going on? Where are we?"

"We're in a hotel in Greece, not too far from Delphi."

She looked around, trying to pull any memory. Nothing came. "Why don't I remember leaving the ruins?" Elidad pressed her hand to her forehead, tying to silence the throbbing.

"What *do* you remember?" His eyes were pressing.

A kiss. His kiss. How could she forget? Her body tingled at the memory. "I remember… wanting to stay in the cave," she recalled. This was true, both before the doors had closed, and after—for very different reasons, but she was afraid to share that.

Aiden's eyes lost some light. "You… don't remember *anything* else?"

"Not really…" she half-lied.

How could she say it aloud? What good would it do? He'd chosen his life and his job, none of it could include her, not the way she wanted. Nothing changed. When this was over, he'd go back to his life and leave her, like he had before. But… he'd kissed her *back*. Why did he do that?

"I remember the key," Elidad said slowly. "We got the key. Where is it?"

"It's in the safe."

"What safe?" Elidad's arm tingled at the thought of it being close. "I need it."

"We're in a hotel, there's a safe in here. It's fine. We'll figure out what to do with it after you get some rest."

Elidad rubbed her forehead with her fingertips, the pounding refusing to relinquish.

"Did everything happen the way I remember?"

"What *do* you remember?"

"Pythia, she was real, right? And the snakes, there were snakes trying to attack us?"

"Yes, that all happened," Aiden confirmed.

"Could you hear them talking?"

"Who?" Aiden's look was puzzled.

"The snakes, and the *others*…" she wasn't sure how to describe them. *The others*. What were they?

"I didn't hear the snakes talking, but you spoke to them like you could." Aiden said. "There wasn't anyone else."

"What about… the Shadow Man?" Elidad was reluctant.

"Did you see him? Was he there?" Aiden's eyes widened.

"No…" She trailed off in thought. "He wasn't there, but he *was*… in spirit, maybe."

"Did he try to hurt you?" Aiden crossed his arms.

"No. It's different now," Elidad stared out the window.

"What do you mean *different?*"

Elidad hesitated. "He doesn't want to hurt me. Something's changed."

"How do you know? He's tried to kill you, and *now* it's different? What changed? Stockholm Syndrome maybe?"

"Don't be ridiculous. I don't know anything about him, there's nothing for me to get attached to.

"I don't know how to explain it. After Pythia bit me, I heard things, I *felt* them. I just knew, *everything*. I know the Shadow Man doesn't want to hurt me, like I knew that the key was in Pythia's chest. That's all I can say, there's no way to describe it."

Elidad's eyes stared through the wallpaper.

"I could control them, the voices. They helped me find my prophecy and the key. That's how all the Oracles see the future, connecting with the past and present like it was alive, an organism. If I'd had longer, I could've seen *everything*."

"That's why Pythia wanted you to prophesy," Aiden thought aloud. "She needed you to. After you did, you *changed*. You weren't the same person until we passed over the threshold. When I got you out of there, you started to be yourself… for a little while."

The hurt in Aiden's voice made Elidad consider telling him the truth. *She remembered*.

"You really don't remember anything that happened after the doors closed?" Pain radiated from Aiden's blue eyes.

Typically, she loved how he conveyed emotion through his brow line, but not today, not this emotion.

Elidad looked at her hands. "No."

"I told you not to look for the prophecy. I didn't have a good feeling about it."

"We never would've found the key if I hadn't," she reminded him. "I needed to."

"Why was the Shadow Man there? What does he want?"

"He wants…" *Me,* she thought. "I don't know what he wants." Elidad lied, steeling a glance at Aiden.

"How do you know so much, but still don't know *that?*"

Elidad's mind replayed the vision of herself in a wedding gown as the Shadow Man reached for her hand… and saw herself reaching back.

"When I looked for the prophecy, I wasn't looking for *him*, my thoughts just took me to him. Our connection was stronger than my desire to know my past. I don't know if it was his thoughts that drew me in, or my desire to know who he is and to know why he's hunting me."

"The dragon covets what is not his to claim…" Aiden recited the words.

Elidad inwardly cringed. "You remember the prophecy?"

"Of course, don't *you?*"

Elidad shook her head. "I remember."

They marinated in the memory.

Realization passed over Aiden. "He wants *you*. That's what the prophecy is talking about," Aiden's jaw tightened.

Elidad swallowed, looking at the comforter between her fingers.

"Is that why you wanted to stay? You *wanted* to stay with him?" The betrayal was thick in Aiden's voice.

Elidad locked eyes with Aiden. "You think I want this? Any of it? I wanted to stay so I could find out what happened to my parents. I want to know why I was chosen for this. I want to know what I did to deserve this."

"You chose to stay out of your own free will. You could've gotten answers from Leucosia before now, but you were too stubborn to go. In the cave, it was about getting what you want. You didn't care what the cost was. That's why everything happened the way it did. You're being a narcissist. You want it your way, on your terms, and it almost got us killed. You're still trying to rebel against Abraham, because you're angry with him. That's why you didn't go to Leucosia, you refuse to give him his dying wish."

Elidad couldn't lift her eyes. It *was* Abraham's dying wish. He wanted Elidad to go to Leucosia for answers. Why didn't she go?

"You almost got us killed," Aiden sighed. "Apparently you don't care about your life as much as you used to, but you almost got me killed, too. Doesn't that matter to you?"

The thought of Aiden perishing because of her selfishness made her eyes sting. "It's not that easy, Aiden. You don't know what it was like. It wasn't just me, *they* were pushing me."

"In the end, it was your choice. You wanted to know and, in the end, you wanted to stay. Think about it. I was in the cave too. Why didn't it affect me? Why didn't I hear the voices? Why couldn't I hear the snakes talking?"

"You weren't bitten," Elidad defenses sprang forward.

"You heard things *before* you were bitten. You were talking to those snakes before we met Pythia."

"You're a man," Elidad justified.

"Is it that? Or was it something else?"

"What?" Elidad demanded. "Say what you want to say."

Aiden took in a deep breath. "You haven't been the same since we got back from Mexico. You've gotten worse since I left. You've done nothing but push me away. You're angry. I understand you've lost your father, but you need to let it go. You're letting your anger eat you alive. How far will you let it consume you?"

"I didn't want this curse. I didn't want my parents to die... any of them."

"But they did and there's no way to change that," Aiden felt guilty for being so blunt. "They died, and you have to deal with the obstacles in your path, whether it's a prophecy or whatever. You can't blame God for what you're going through. Take responsibility for the choices you've made."

"Are you blaming me for my parents' deaths and for being hunted by the Shadow Man?" Heat radiated through Elidad's arm, she could feel it searing through the black veins into the puncture wounds in her chest.

"I'm blaming you for living in the past. You're so busy mourning over what can't be changed, you can't even see what's standing in front of you."

Was he speaking metaphorically or was he literally talking about himself?

"Woe to she indulged by evil's burning flame," Aiden threw the words at her like an insult.

Elidad wanted to scream.

The sound of a door shutting silenced them both. Through his agitation, Aiden didn't look surprised that someone had entered the room. Footsteps moved toward them.

Sophia blew through the door.

"Oh good, she's up," Sophia's angelic voice was like shards of glass in Elidad mind.

"What the *hell* is she doing here?" Elidad demanded.

Sophia crossed her arms. "Saving your ass. You're welcome."

Elidad scowled at Aiden.

"We're lucky she showed up. When we started coming out of the fissure, you were acting strange. Like you were on drugs."

"She was," Sophia reminded. "A heavy dose of Venom," one of her eyebrows arched in judgment.

"I was bitten hours before," Elidad shook her head. "there's no way it could've taken that long."

"No way?" Sophia's question hummed. "Think about it. It was the same way for every Oracle, Elidad. Oracle goes down, spends time in the hole, she comes up speaking tongues. You're no different."

"No," Elidad disagreed. "It was the volcanic fumes."

Sophia rolled her eyes. "That's the human explanation. It was the only way scientists could make sense of the Oracles. There were never any gases, just Venom. And a susceptible subject…"

Elidad's eyes shifted to Aiden. They were in cahoots.

"What's that supposed to mean?" Elidad spat.

"You were susceptible. That's why you heard things *before* you were bitten. Apparently, you were in the right place, emotionally, to receive something evil. Pythia's venom was only a catalyst. It helped you to the other side. Her Venom has a magical element in it; it is a connection to the body of evil. When you were with her, she could control it, keep it from overdosing you. Once you left, you were on your own and the Venom could take its normal course. The same way it did with all the Oracles."

"No," Elidad disagreed. "this was different. It wasn't like doing V."

"Pythia's Venom is nothing like what you would find in shithole nightclubs," Sophia argued. "Certainly not what you'd get from diluted bloodlines. Pythia is the Origin. Refined. Top of the line. There will never be another like her on the earth. Think of how much her Venom would cost on the street."

"I wouldn't know. I'm not a drug dealer," Elidad glared.

Sophia shrugged.

"How did you know where to find us?" Elidad changed the subject. "Your visions don't work like that. How did you get here?"

Sophia's lips pursed together before she answered. "Mother sent me."

"She didn't send you to save me from the experience, just to help Aiden get me out, after?"

"You chose to go. You chose to stand in the circle and offer to be bitten. If you'd gone to see Mother before now, you would've known the prophecy. If you already knew the prophecy, maybe you wouldn't have been won over so quickly."

"Won over so quickly?" Elidad couldn't believe what she was hearing. "What the hell does that mean?"

"It means, you almost got Aiden killed because you're so damn stubborn. You should try thinking of someone other than yourself."

They'd conspired against her.

"Think of someone else?" Elidad's heart was a freight train. "Like Elise? Because I think of her every day. What about you?"

"That's not fair, Elidad."

"No? Don't talk to me about selfishness. You never looked out for her." Elidad sprung out of bed, pointing a finger at Aiden. "Did she tell you about Elise? Did she tell you how she introduced Elise to your uncle… that *filthy* snake?"

"Elidad," Aiden looked affronted, "Maybe you should calm down."

"Don't tell me to calm down. She took Elise to *Genus*. Elise tried V for the first time with Pythious and Sophia. She got hooked on both, the Venom and that looser. After his disappearance, Elise stuck a needle in her arm with that monster's Venom in it… enough to kill herself with." Fury heaved Elidad's chest up and down. "I don't know how you live with yourself," the disdain was thick on Elidad's tongue as she spoke to Sophia.

Sophia's eyes glistened with Elidad's words. She stormed out of the room without another word.

"Elidad." Aiden's brow creased in the center. "I think that's enough. She came here to help you. You don't need to rake her over the coals."

"Rake her over the coals? How about we nail her to a cross?"

"Elidad, stop."

Madness burned through Elidad's shoulder and raced down her arm.

"Stop? It was your precious uncle that did it all. He's the reason I lost my job. He's the reason Elise killed herself. He didn't deserve to live. He's done as much damage in death as he'd done in life."

"If you wouldn't have killed Pythious, perhaps Elise would still be alive." Aiden's words were clear and calm.

"Don't put this on me. It wasn't my fault."

She wanted to hurt Aiden for suggesting it was.

Elidad's eyes narrowed. "Why are you so protective of Sophia? What does it matter to you? Are you *friends*? You only met once, at *Genus*, when I took you to meet Leucosia. How is she here, in this hotel with you? When did she get here?"

"I met her— after that— after Genus." Aiden stumbled on his words.

Elidad had him. She could see it. Anger riveted through her bones.

"You just happened to meet again and never told me about it?"

"I tried to tell you. You never answered your damn phone," Aiden blurted. "You wouldn't even call me after your message boy answered."

Elidad vigorously itched her arm trying to stifle the fire under her skin. "How long has she been here?"

"She's been here a while."

"That's pretty vague, Aiden."

"I don't owe you any explanations."

Elidad wanted to punch him.

"How did you get the Sword of Justice? I gave it to Leucosia. Did that just happen, too?"

Aiden's lips formed a defiant line.

Elidad burst into a fake laugh. "Sophia gave it to you. Of course."

Aiden didn't deny it.

"Why the hell did it work for you, and not me?"

"Maybe you're too broken," Aiden's glare was as painful as his words.

Elidad closed the distance between them. Swinging her hand, the crack against Aiden's cheek stung her palm and burned up her forearm. Rage swimming though her, she lifted her hand to strike him again.

This time, Aiden caught her hand.

"I may have deserved the first one, but that's all you get." Aiden held her wrist tight as she struggled against his grip. "What's on your neck?"

"Nothing. Let me go," she demanded.

"There's something. Hold still."

She struggled like a cat in a cage.

"Elidad, seriously, there's something under your skin." Looking at her arm, he saw more dark lines. He pulled up the sleeve of her shirt, revealing skin contaminated with dark veins. Was it a *disease?*

Elidad's eyes flashed yellow. Aiden recognized Elidad's labored breath, not as her own, but like Emily's, the little girl who'd been possessed in an apartment, months ago.

Elidad's voice dropped a few decibels in a fierce growl that was nothing like her own, "I told you to let me go, Priest."

AFFLICTION
SWORD OF JUSTICE: BOOK 3

CHAPTER ONE

E lidad opened her eyes.

Darkness.

She couldn't remember where she was. Where was she last? Greece—Delphi. A hotel room with Aiden. *Sophia.* The thought of her name was revolting.

Elidad tried to sit up. There was something restraining her.

"Hello?" Elidad called out, pulling harder against whatever was tight around her chest and arms.

The light clicked on.

"Hello, love," Sophia's features were flawless in the unnatural light cast across her face from the tableside lamp.

With the light on, Elidad could see they were in the same hotel room. Elidad could also see she'd been tied to the bed.

"Sophia," Elidad's voice was harsh, "Untie me."

"Sorry, doll. I can't do that."

Anger heaved Elidad's chest. "Let me out, right now!"

"That's not going to happen any time soon. You better get comfortable."

"Why? What did you do?" Elidad demanded, fear creeping past her anger. "What did you do with Aiden?" Elidad's eyes cast around the room.

Sophia's laugh rang through the room. "You mean what did *you* do to him?"

"I didn't do anything."

"Of course you did," Sophia crossed her arms. "Don't you remember?"

"I can't remember anything." When Elidad tried to pull the memory of how she'd become restrained, her head felt like it was going to split in two. "Untie me. Right. Now!" Elidad demanded.

Sophia's eyes were . "Can't you feel it? I don't know how you don't know."

Elidad stared at her. "Feel what?"

"You've let this go on for a long time, Elidad. I don't know how you don't know."

"Just tell me what the hell is going on." Elidad pulled against her restraints until her skin protested.

"I can't believe you waited so long," Sophia said, a sly smile across her lips.

"Waited for what?" Anger kept Elidad from processing Sophia's riddle.

"Waited to kiss Aiden."

Elidad stopped struggling, sweeping the room with her eyes to assure Aiden wasn't there.

"He… didn't tell you?" Elidad whispered.

Sophia held up her fingertips, waggling them. "He didn't have to."

"You're a bitch." Elidad laid her head on the soft pillow, the feeling a stark contradiction to the emotions raging in her chest.

Sophia's giggle was dainty. "You've called me worse."

"You *are* worse. I just don't have the energy to be creative."

"Do you want to know how he feels about it?" Sophia offered. "It'll be like high school."

"Stop trying. I'm not going to be your friend again."

There was a long pause as Elidad stared up at the ceiling.

Sophia broke the silence. "He thought it was like kissing his sister."

"He doesn't have a sister."

"You know what I mean." Sophia said. "Aiden is right where he's supposed to be, Elidad. He belongs at the Vatican. He knows it and so do you."

Elidad's eyes stung at the thought. She didn't want to know it. What if he belonged with her?

"Why am I tied to this bed?" Elidad lifted her head to lock eyes with Sophia. "What the hell is going on? Are you *that* desperate for a friend that you have to keep me tied up for a conversation?"

The arch in Sophia's brow was condescending, at best. "I don't know how you don't know, Elidad. Think about the alley, and the Houdoch demon. Think about your wound that never really healed. What about the anger you've been experiencing… anger you can't control."

Elidad wanted to race across the room and hurt Sophia. "You touched me? That's the only way you could know all of that. You had no right to pry into my life! My memories are none of your damn business."

"It wasn't my fault. You made me. Someone had to save Aiden."

"Save Aiden from what?" Elidad demanded.

"From you." Sophia took a breath. "Elidad, think back, think about the demon and your dreams. Think about your dreams of the Shadow Man… think about Delphi and Pythia."

"What about them?" Elidad snapped.

"Close your eyes, Elidad."

Elidad begrudgingly obeyed… whatever it would take to get Sophia to untie her.

"Listen," Sophia prompted. "Can you hear them?"

"I don't hear anything," Elidad said.

"Shhhh… they're there. You've kept them quiet. I don't know how, but you have."

Elidad tried hard to focus on what Sophia was saying.

Suddenly, Elidad heard them… just like in the Delphi cave, she heard the voices. Whispers. Like the chant of the hooded crowd in Delphi or the children in the park. Whispers…

Elidad's eyes sprang open. "What did you do?"

"I didn't do anything."

"What's going on?" Elidad demanded.

"You need to see for yourself, Elidad. *Look* for the answer, you'll never believe me."

Elidad laid her head back on the bed, trying to focus. She concentrated on slowing her breathing. She thought of the Houdoch demon and the wound in her shoulder. It led her to thoughts of the veins across her chest that eventually trailed down her arm. Visions of dead flesh made her mouth water.

The whispers came again… louder.

They were the same whispers that connected her to the past and the present… the whispers that could tell her everything.

She saw him. The Shadow Man. His green eyes burning under a dark cloak. She felt her shoulder encourage her to reach forward for him. She wanted him.

In her mind, Elidad looked down at her arm; she wasn't controlling it, the pulse in her veins had instigated the movement.

Elidad pushed for answers. Why? What was Sophia talking about? What did Sophia know that she didn't?

Emily, the little girl that was possessed in the apartment in New York, her voice came forward… *I remember— I remember he wouldn't let me go—*

Elidad's breath began to intensify.

He was there. The Shadow Man was always there. In her mind, in her dreams, following her on the streets… everywhere.

Elidad's heart led the pace of her breathing.

Why could she hear them? She pushed again for answers. Elidad centered her mind. Why was the Shadow Man reaching out for her? Why was it so easy for her to connect with Pythia?

Elidad's mind moved backwards to the demon in the alley. What did the demon have to do with it? Elidad's fingers tingled in response to her inner investigation. What did he do? Her puncture wounds in her shoulder burned. His poison had almost killed her.

Leucosia wasn't confident she'd had a cure: *"This will be the most likely option to heal you."* Leucosia had said when she gave Elidad a potion to keep the poison from killing her. *"I cannot see your future, Elidad,"* was her following warning. *"Not seeing your future doesn't mean you don't have one, it just means it is undecided."*

What was undecided? Elidad thought of the Sword of Justice. It had worked for her, every time she needed it, until after Abraham's exorcism.

What changed?

She'd stopped praying. She was angry. That's what Leucosia told her the Houdoch demon's venom fed on: hate and anger.

Whispers clouded her thoughts… she'd heard them calling to her. The Shadow Man was in them. It was his voice. Like the Holy Spirit of the Divine Trinity, these voices were *his* voice, his power, in everything, influencing everything. The Houdoch demon had infused her —already angry system—with his venom: a catalyst for her burning rage. It had slowly crept into her heart and influenced her thoughts and feelings.

Keeping her eyes closed, Elidad remembered Emily had told her that when she was possessed, she could hear *them*. She heard their thoughts and feelings, she could hear specific conversations.

Elidad focused on another pressing question. What did the triangle mean? The triangle that surrounded Abraham, the same one Emily drew on her wall in her own blood. In a moment of clarity, the whispers hushed and Isaac's voice spoke, *"When Abraham was taken, where he died, were there markings on the wall, or the floor?"*

The triangle flashed in Elidad's mind, "Yes."

Isaac nodded his head, as if he could see it, himself. "There was no way you could have saved him. He fought a greater battle than you were prepared for."

"What battle?"

"The rise of the Inferno…"

The Inferno… What was the Inferno? An ocean of voices filled Elidad's mind as she pressed into that question. What was it?

Elidad saw the Shadow Man… standing on a balcony of a castle, a crowd of millions surrounded him… them… She was standing next to him. She wore a white gown, her face covered by a veil. Elidad threw the veil over her head.

The faceless figure next to her reached forward, with his palm up. Elidad reached back, her heart racing with anticipation. She wanted to touch him, desire stirring in her belly, exploding through her limbs.

When her finger met the palm of his hand, electricity surged between them. The energy looked like a shockwave between their bodies, sparking into the atmosphere, shooting upward before returning to the ground.

Elidad's white gown began to turn black as the wave fell across it. The fabric grew darker and darker until the detail was difficult to distinguish.

The crowd below them began to chant. She could hear them in her mind as well as her ears. The voices echoed.

She knew what they wanted.

Elidad followed the Shadow Man to a pedestal where a large book rested. Under a metal trim sealing the edges, was worn leather. In the center of the cover, there was a skeleton key hole.

Elidad knew this book.

The crowd chanted louder as she stepped closer to it. They wanted her to open it. She felt compelled to open it.

Looking down at her hands, she held two keys in each hand, they glowed from the energy of being so close. She needed only to place them together.

Elidad opened her eyes. Her breath was so fast across her lips, she was afraid she'd never catch it.

Sophia was still in a chair in the corner, the lamp next to her was still the only light.

"I'm…" Elidad's words failed her.

"What?" Sophia coaxed.

"I'm possessed?"

"You are," Sophia confirmed.

"How?"

"You know how it happens."

"It doesn't happen to *me*," Elidad argued.

"Think about it," Sophia suggested. "It started in your heart. You were angry with the Church, which made you angry with God," Sophia snorted, "As if they're the same thing.

Then you lost your father, then Aiden and, as you thought for some time, Isaac. The Houdoch demon infused you with his poison. It was enough, even for you."

"Is that why I open the book?" Elidad asked.

"What book?" Sophia leaned forward.

Elidad pressed her lips together.

"*The* book? You saw yourself open it?" Sophia demanded.

"I don't know what I saw," Elidad tried to backtrack.

"If you're seeing things, you're seeing what the demon inside you sees. They are connected through the spirit. If you saw yourself opening the book, that's their plan for you."

"I don't want to open it."

"Did you see any reason, in your vision, for you to open it?" Sophia asked.

Elidad imagined the Shadow Man's hand reaching for hers. "No," she lied.

"Just because they have a plan for you, doesn't mean it will become reality, Elidad. You can impact your future."

The door opened.

Aiden walked into the room with a bag under his arm. His face was swollen, black and blue marks starting at his forehead and ending at his chin.

"Aiden, what happened to you?" Elidad couldn't help but ask, though she already knew the answer.

He looked at Sophia. "Is it really her?"

"It is now." Sophia agreed. "It won't be for long."

Aiden looked back at Elidad. "You happened."

"I'm so sorry, Aiden," Elidad cut her apology short to avoid the emotion stinging her eyes.

Aiden began pulling items from his bag: Holy water, a Bible, and a black vestment that he unfolded. He kissed the cross embroidered on the vestment and placed it over his neck. He did the same for his crucifix.

Elidad's blood began to boil at the sight of his ritual. "Put that away, Aiden. What are you doing?"

"I'm going to save you, Elidad," his response was mater-of-fact.

"I don't need your help," Elidad could hear her voice change in her ears. It wasn't her speaking.

Aiden stepped closer sprinkling Holy water on the ground around the bed.

Elidad's fury escaped her, screams echoing in the room. Aiden's face was the last thing she saw as her mind faded to black.

ABOUT THE AUTHOR

Novelist Eva Hulett has always been enchanted by the great outdoors in the state of Oregon where she was born and raised and currently lives with her two dogs. When she's not enjoying hiking, camping, and hunting, she spends time running her business in Sunriver Resort. Eva was included in the Central Oregon Writer's Guild Harvest Writing Winners Collection and was a judge in the 2017 Top Of The Mountain Book Awards.

Made in the USA
Monee, IL
21 January 2020